*Praise for*

# Heidi Swain

'Brimming with warmth and Christmas
cheer' **Sarah Morgan**

'Sweet and lovely. I guarantee you will fall in love
with Heidi's wonderful world' **Milly Johnson**

'A little slice of joy' *Heat*

'Grab a hot chocolate and lose yourself in this heart-
warming story of romance, community and secrets.
The perfect story to read by the fire!' **Phillipa Ashley**

'Sparkling and romantic' *My Weekly*

'The queen of feel-good' *Woman & Home*

'The most delicious slice of festive fiction:
a true comfort read and the perfect treat to
alleviate all the stress!' **Veronica Henry**

'Sprinkled with Christmas sparkle' **Trisha Ashley**

'Grab a glass of mulled wine and enjoy this
sparkling, snow-filled romance' *Culturefly*

# Heidi Swain

# That Festive Feeling

SIMON &
SCHUSTER

London · New York · Sydney · Toronto · New Delhi

First published in Great Britain by Simon & Schuster UK Ltd, 2023

Copyright © Heidi-Jo Swain, 2023

The right of Heidi-Jo Swain to be identified as author
of this work has been asserted in accordance with the
Copyright, Designs and Patents Act, 1988.

1 3 5 7 9 10 8 6 4 2

Simon & Schuster UK Ltd
1st Floor
222 Gray's Inn Road
London WC1X 8HB

Simon & Schuster Australia, Sydney
Simon & Schuster India, New Delhi

www.simonandschuster.co.uk
www.simonandschuster.com.au
www.simonandschuster.co.in

A CIP catalogue record for this book
is available from the British Library

Paperback ISBN: 978-1-3985-1954-1
eBook ISBN: 978-1-3985-1955-8
Audio ISBN: 978-1-3985-1956-5

Typeset in Bembo by M Rules
Printed and Bound in the UK using 100% Renewable
Electricity at CPI Group (UK) Ltd

MIX
Paper | Supporting
responsible forestry
FSC® C171272

# That Festive Feeling

*To Claire Howard,*
*my friend through it all*

# Chapter 1

I was sitting cross-legged on the floor in front of the sofa, surrounded by a plethora of packing boxes when my mobile rang out, making me jump and pulling me out of the reverie I hadn't realised I'd fallen into.

'Dad,' I answered, my tone an octave higher than I would have liked and definitely far too bright. 'Hey. Is everything okay?'

It said a lot about our relationship that I had assumed there must be something wrong for him to be calling just a few days after our last interaction. And yes, I know interaction might seem an odd choice of word to describe a conversation with my parents, but no one who knew them would think that. My parents and I didn't go in for idle chit-chat. I doubt they would even know what the word meant.

'Yes,' Dad briskly said. 'Everything's fine.'

He didn't say anything further and I checked my phone to make sure the call hadn't been cut off.

'So,' I prompted, dragging the word out. 'You're ringing because ...'

'Your mother asked me to,' he eventually said. 'She would

have rung herself but she's been called in to attend an unscheduled departmental meeting.'

'I bet she was thrilled about that,' I commented, knowing how much she abhorred anything unplanned.

Both my parents were university lecturers. Mum was physics and Dad was maths. Their entire lives, their very essence, was ground in logic and fact and they didn't allow an iota of space for imagination or adventure. I supposed that was why they had always found me, their only child, such a conundrum. I was almost thirty now and they still hadn't worked out the formula which would explain how between them they'd managed to create someone ... well, creative.

'Far from it,' said Dad, stating the obvious. 'I'm not disturbing your work, am I?'

That was something else they didn't understand. My work. I had ditched their preferred university course, the one they had goaded me into applying for and gone to art college instead. After graduating, I had then embarked upon what they saw as a precarious and insecure career path as a children's book illustrator. Thank goodness I'd met and started dating Piers before leaving uni. Marrying him had made me less of a disappointment in their eyes, only now I didn't have Piers ... or a marriage ...

'No, no,' I quickly said, before my mind took a darker turn. 'I'm packing today, not working.'

Dad didn't miss a beat.

'You are putting everything into storage, Holly, aren't you?' he asked, sounding panicked. 'Because we really haven't got room for you and all of your ...'

'Yes, Dad,' I cut in, thinking of the empty rooms in my childhood home and trying not to feel too affronted that there was no space in any of them for my few worldly goods. 'It'll just be me, a suitcase and a couple of bags and for the shortest time possible. You won't even know I'm there.'

'Right,' he said, sounding mollified as he let out a breath. 'That's great. Good.'

I knew neither of them wanted me moving back in. *I* didn't want me moving back in. Had I been able to find an alternative that wouldn't have meant rinsing through my divorce settlement money, money I was supposed to be using as a down payment if I could decide where I wanted to move to, then I would have grasped it with both hands. But I hadn't, so here we were. All set to face the most miserable Christmas we'd ever spent together and that was saying a lot.

'So why was Mum going to phone me then?' I asked, trying to get to the cause behind the call.

'Oh, well, we just wanted to double-check that you were definitely still coming, really.'

He did have the grace to sound at least a little shamefaced to be asking again. But that could have been more by accident than design.

'Yes, Dad,' I said, sounding every bit as miserable about it as he obviously was. 'I'm really sorry, but as I told you both just a few days ago, I'm definitely still coming.'

We said our slightly strained goodbyes and I resumed my staring into space, mulling over the events which had led me to this wretched point.

'*And you're sure you definitely don't want kids?*' I heard my voice from the past echo in my head.

'*I'm definitely sure I don't want kids,*' Piers answered with a smile in his tone and sounding completely certain.

That had been the question I had asked before I accepted his proposal of marriage. I wanted to be absolutely convinced of that before I said yes. I didn't want there to be any danger of him changing his mind a few years down the line because I knew I wouldn't.

I'd lost count of the number of times since then that I'd wondered what might have happened if his brother hadn't fathered twin boys and then a daughter. Would Piers have been happy with it being just him and me forever had his brother not subsequently been perched on the most fertile family member pedestal after doing his bit to increase the world's population?

I don't suppose it mattered now because it wasn't just me and Piers anymore. When I hadn't succumbed to the pressure to change my mind about making babies and starting to think about the viability of my dwindling eggs, which was aimed at me from both his family and mine, it had soon become Piers and Tamara. And then, swiftly after our separation, Piers and Tamara and their bump. I'd been ruthlessly cast aside by his previously doting mum and dad, my brother-in-law and his wife after the happy announcement and of course, I'd further disappointed my own parents into the bargain.

'Poor me,' I huffed as I felt the sharp sting of abandonment again, then reached for the jumper I'd previously pulled off because packing boxes had been warm work.

The house felt cold now, but then it was the end of October. I'd left the heating off to economise as it was just me living there and paying the final bills. Piers and Tamara were cosily installed in a family friendly out of town newbuild awaiting the arrival of their precious firstborn and I was only staying in the house a few more days, until it was time to hand in the keys to the estate agent who would then pass them on to the ecstatic newlyweds who were moving in. I hoped they'd be happier here than I'd been.

I wondered if it was too early to open a bottle of wine, and was poised to fully wallow in a few hours of indulgent self-pity when my phone started to ring again.

'Hello,' I answered, not bothering to check the caller ID.

'Hey, Holly,' came the enthusiastic response. 'You've answered at last! How's tricks, my darling girl?'

I leant back against the sofa again. I wasn't someone who had a wide circle of friends but I was grateful that there were two stalwarts in my life who I could rely on. For me, friendships had always been about quality over quantity. Not that I really deserved the quality or the devotion this pair offered, because recently I'd been rubbish at keeping in touch with them. The unanswered messages stacked up on my phone were proof enough of that.

'Neil.' I smiled, turning my gaze away from the packing carnage which was currently threatening to swallow me whole. 'I'm great. Very nearly out of here now and eager to—'

'I'm assuming you've found somewhere to go then?' he cut in. 'Even if you haven't messaged us a forwarding address or talked to either of us in weeks.'

I'd been introduced to Neil by Piers soon after we'd got together during Freshers week at university and Neil, and later his husband, Mark, had become close friends who had properly stuck. Friends I felt terrible for not keeping in the loop because they'd faithfully been Team Holly during the last year and a half.

'Sort of,' I gloomily said. 'All of my stuff is going into storage at the end of the week ...'

'And you're heading where, exactly, after that?' Neil interrogated, his voice full of concern that tugged at my heartstrings.

'I'm going to my parents',' I said, biting my lip.

He burst out laughing, his concern momentarily forgotten.

'No, I am,' I told him. 'Just until I . . .'

'But you can't,' he screeched, when he realised I wasn't joking. 'You know you can't. You'll drive each other mad.'

'All I know,' I said, 'is that I haven't got any other choice. Not unless I want to start eating into my savings and I really can't afford to do that. At least I can stay with Mum and Dad rent-free.' I took a moment to consider that. 'At least, I'm assuming I can stay there rent free. We haven't actually spoken about it . . .'

'Is this why you've not been in touch?' Neil asked. 'Because you couldn't bear to tell us you were moving home?'

'No,' I said, 'it's not that. Well, not just that.'

'What else then?'

'Oh,' I said, trying to sound jolly and failing. 'I've just been so busy, you know. Work's been flat out and I've still got all this packing to do. I haven't been talking to anyone, really.'

Not that there was anyone else for me to talk to and I hadn't been working flat out either. But I couldn't think about that right now. If I added that to the equation, then it really would be wine o'clock.

'Well,' said Neil, sounding soothed. 'That's some consolation, I suppose, and it's just as well you picked up when you did,' he added, sounding smug.

'Is it?'

'It is,' he confirmed. 'Because I'm about to save your bacon.'

'You are?'

'For the next couple of months, anyway.'

'How so?'

'By inviting you to stay here and in the process save you from your ghastly parents,' he proclaimed, with a shudder.

'You mean you're inviting me to stay in your house?'

'Yes,' he said. 'In our house. You know, the one in Nightingale Square that you haven't visited for ages.'

It was a beautiful house, located in a stunning part of Norwich, but it would be a squeeze for three adults for longer than a few days and to be honest, I wasn't sure I could cope with Neil watching my every move or Mark trying to set me up with the single, straight men he seemed to have a knack for spotting when they came to buy pastries from the bakery he worked in.

'But—'

'But nothing,' Neil carried on. 'Before you say no, let me tell you that I'm not only asking you to come here out of the goodness of my heart, I'm asking you because we *need* you to come.'

'You *need* me to come?' I frowned.

'Desperately,' he insisted. 'And you won't have to worry about overcrowding, because Mark and I won't be here. Not for a couple of months, anyway.'

'Oh.' I frowned. That put rather a different complexion on the situation. 'Why? Where are you going?'

'I've designed a house for a client on the outskirts of Barcelona,' Neil, who like Piers was an architect, explained, 'and I'm heading out there, all expenses paid, ahead of the build to iron out a few wrinkles and Mark is coming with me. We're going traveling for a bit after, so our place is going to be empty between this weekend and right into the new year.'

'Oh, wow,' I gasped, dreaming of their winter, or part of it at least, spent in sunny Spain. 'How exciting is that?'

I was quite envious of their plan, especially as Christmas was creeping ever closer. The last one had been hellish but it was going to be even worse this year, stuck with Mum and Dad. Since I'd left home, I'd turned into a big fan of the winter celebration and didn't want it to be tainted forever, even if I wasn't quite in the mood for feasting and fairy lights just yet. The gauge on my festive feeling barometer was still firmly fixed on gloomy, but I wouldn't let it be stuck there for the rest of time.

'It is,' Neil carried on, sounding less buoyant. 'Or at least it was.'

'Why, what's happened?'

'Well, we hadn't planned on leaving the house empty,' he sighed. 'We'd booked a sitter, but she's had to pull out at the last minute on account of her mother having had a fall and we can't get anyone else at such short notice.'

'Oh,' I said, 'I see.'

'So, Mark's now saying he should stay behind.'

Neil sounded so disappointed. I closed my eyes for a moment and thought it through. I'd always enjoyed the many trips Piers and I had made to Nightingale Square in the past. There was a strong sense of community surrounding the place, which tightly bound together the neighbours, who lived in houses around a communal green.

They all looked out for each other, and it seemed like an idyllic way to live in a city, but that in itself could be an issue. If I took up Neil's offer, was I going to want the neighbours potentially watching out for me at a time when I would much rather keep my head down and waffle along unnoticed? If I ran into them, they were bound to question where Piers was, given that we'd spent some time with a few of them during previous visits and I wasn't sure I had the stamina yet to dole out endless explanations. At least with my parents the questions had all been asked and addressed.

And then of course there was the community garden, The Grow-Well, which was situated across the road from the square in the grounds of the magnificent mansion house, Prosperous Place. Everyone got stuck in there, but I barely knew the difference between a dahlia and a dandelion. I'd be more of a hindrance than a help. A horticultural liability.

'So, what do you reckon?' Neil asked, his tone full of hope.

'Can I think about it for a bit?' I hedged.

'Seriously?' he gasped. 'You really need to consider if what we're offering trumps moving back into the box room at your parents' place?'

'Just a day or so,' I said, knowing it was madness not to immediately snatch his hand off, but feeling cautious nonetheless.

'There really is no time to dither,' said Neil, sounding flummoxed.

'But the Grow-Well . . .' I pointed out.

'Is all tucked up for the winter,' he immediately countered. 'You won't have to do a thing there. This is literally a "sit in the house and keep the heating on so the pipes don't freeze" kind of commitment. I daresay you won't see a soul.'

His desperation was palpable and, to be honest, given the alternative, it was a Christmas gift come early, especially if I really did end up not seeing a soul. I'd just have to keep my head down and fly under the radar. And the act of kindness my stay would be for them would go some way to making up for the fact that I hadn't kept in touch when they'd both been so determined to keep looking out for me.

'Go on then,' I therefore agreed. 'I'll ditch the parents and come, but on one condition.'

'What's that?'

'Mark has to lay in a decent stock of cake.'

'He'll be delighted to,' Neil confirmed, still laughing. 'We leave on Friday afternoon. Can you be here for then?'

'I have to drop the keys for this place with the agent that morning,' I explained, 'so I can be with you by lunchtime.' My worries about the neighbourly neighbours aside, I knew it was going to be a real luxury to have the peace and solitude in which to consider my next steps and my new life. And I could quietly celebrate the season, too, should I feel inclined.

I would use my time alone in the square to properly decide where I wanted to move to next, a decision I had found impossible to make while still living in my former marital home and I'd get my work head in gear, too. And reconcile myself to my marriage ending. I knew it was a lot to cram in, but suddenly, freed from the prospect of seeing out the year with my parents, anything felt possible!

'You're a doll!' Neil cheered. 'We'll see you then!'

# Chapter 2

I tried not to feel too hurt that Mum and Dad were so obviously elated that I wasn't going to be arriving on their doorstep because to be honest, I was more than chuffed about the situation, too.

'I'll text you the full address when I've checked the postcode,' I told Mum.

'Do you think we'll need it?' she asked.

'Well,' I said, 'you might want to send me a Christmas card, mightn't you?'

'Oh, yes,' she said. 'Of course.'

I ended the call feeling a palpable sense of relief on both sides and turned my attention back to a more pressing matter. What was I going to do about the illustration requests still sitting in my inbox?

With my most recent commission completed and returned I decided, after much soul searching, to turn the two new projects down. I had found it hard to accept that I hadn't enjoyed creating the images for the last book in the Baby Bee collection. I had worked on the series for some years, right from its inception in fact, but the final illustrations hadn't sparked any of the joy that the previous ones had.

I knew that some days at my desk I had just been going through the motions, whereas usually my head would be full of the stories and the antics the insects, who Baby Bee was friends with, got up to. The time would fly by as I would first draw and then paint, but this time around I'd felt like I'd been wading through treacle to complete them and I hoped my lack of connection wasn't noticeable in the end results.

I put my inability to immerse myself in the narrative down to the emotional tumult and life changes I had endured during the last few months and privately cited both as my reason for rejecting the new offers. It wouldn't be fair either to myself or the authors to say I'd go ahead when I wasn't really feeling it and couldn't produce my best work. Even though turning the projects down felt risky because I worked freelance and really could have done with the money, I believed, in this instance, it was necessary.

A proper break, during which I would be able to completely empty my head, would doubtless restore my equilibrium and reignite my creative mojo and that would put the fire back in my belly. At least, that was the hopeful thought I carried with me during the next couple of days and on the journey to Nightingale Square on Friday.

'Oh, thank god you're here!' Mark fussed before I'd even rung the bell, grabbing my hand and pulling me over the threshold into the house. 'Neil's in a right old tizz.'

'And is it any wonder?' Neil tutted, stepping around Mark and pulling me in for a hug. 'When we're leaving in less than an hour and you still haven't finished packing because you're faffing about with toffee apples!'

Mark rolled his eyes and I couldn't help but laugh. There was always some domestic drama occurring with these two and I was particularly grateful for it that day because it made my arrival all the easier.

'Toffee apples?' I then frowned, shrugging off my coat as the subject of the theatrics sank in and Neil led me along the hall and into the kitchen. 'That's hardly a regular in-flight snack. Wouldn't you be better off with a bag of peanuts or a tub of Pringles?'

The lingering sweet scent of melted toffee made my tummy rumble and I hoped Mark had followed through on Neil's promise of cake.

'They're not for the flight,' said Mark, with a tut. 'They're for the bonfire party at the Grow-Well on Sunday night. I've wrapped them up tight and I'm putting them on a shelf in the larder, which should be the right temperature. You can take them with you when you go over. Everyone loved them last year, so I had to make them again . . .'

'But at the cost of buggering up our schedule,' said Neil, impatiently tapping his watch.

'All right, all right,' said Mark, depositing the tray and backing out of the kitchen. 'I'll be five minutes. Ten, tops. Are you all right, Holly?' he then asked, stopping to properly take me in.

'I'm fine,' I said, waving him away for fear of incurring more of Neil's wrath. 'Absolutely fine.'

'I did wonder if you might turn up having had a disastrous hair cut or something, in an attempt to reinvent yourself,' he said, looking me up and down. 'Like the sister in *Fleabag*. You know the episode where she ends up looking like a pencil. I love that—'

'Oh, for pity's sake!' shouted Neil as he finally ran out of patience.

'I'm going,' said Mark with a grin, as he turned tail and finally headed up the stairs. 'I'm gone.'

'What party at the Grow-Well is this?' I demanded the second Mark was out of sight. 'You told me the garden was all tucked up for the winter.'

'It is,' Neil shrugged, looking shifty. 'But the fun doesn't stop just because it's November. There's always a party on November the fifth, but no fireworks. It's all braziers, sparklers, a bite to eat and then a film projected on to sheets strung up on the walls.'

I was tempted to string him up. So much for not seeing a soul! Perhaps I'd be able to drop off the toffee apples earlier in the day and leave before everyone else congregated ...

'It's a much quieter affair than Hallowe'en,' he then said in a failed attempt to reassure me. 'And it will be handy for you to reacquaint yourself with the neighbours, just in case you need them for anything while we're away.'

'I'm sure I'll be able to manage here just fine on my own,' I told him, shuddering at the thought of any sympathetic head tilts and shoulder rubs that might be destined to head my way if he'd taken the time to fill them in on my recent change of circumstances. 'I'm planning to hibernate—'

'Come and see your room,' he said, cutting me off. 'We've made it really cosy.'

Piers and I had never stayed at the house when we were visiting because there wasn't quite enough room for two in the second bedroom, but now I was single, it was more than adequate and certainly bigger than the room I'd begrudgingly been assigned at Mum and Dad's.

The bedroom, situated at the back of the house, was prettily decorated with ditsy floral print curtains and bedding and had a tiny original cast-iron fireplace with a small collection of glossy leaved houseplants next to it and a Jo Malone candle on the mantelpiece.

'It's perfect.' I smiled, giving Neil a squeeze. 'Thank you.'

He had also packed up the tools of his architectural trade in the office room next door and had arranged the space so I would be able to work in there without disturbing any of his plans and drawings.

'Will this be okay?' he asked, looking around. 'It's by far the best room for catching the light, especially at this time of year.'

'It's perfect,' I repeated, only this time, I had to force the words out. 'Thank you.'

I found myself unwilling to tell him that I wasn't going to be working while he was away. I knew he would be worried and it was too much to try to unpack in such a short amount of time. And besides, I felt sure that once I'd had a decent rest, I'd be raring to go again, quite possibly even before he and Mark got back.

'Good.' Neil smiled. 'Great. Move anything you need to but please, don't change the settings on the desk. It took me forever to get . . .'

'Neil!' Mark shouted up from the hall below. 'John's here. Are you ready or not?'

Neil shook his head.

'Can you believe him?' He tutted, making for the stairs.

It only took a minute for neighbour John, who was driving my friends to the airport, to pack their cases into his car and then they were finally ready for the off.

'Are you sure you're going to be all right?' Neil frowned, before climbing into the back, while Mark sat shotgun. 'I'm not

sure we should be leaving you when you're in such an emotionally vulnerable state.'

'I'm not in an emotionally vulnerable state,' I told him force-
fully, giving John a fleeting glance. 'And I don't want either of
you to give me or the house another thought.'

'I won't.' Mark grinned.

'I'm looking forward to some proper me-time,' I carried on,
addressing Neil's concern. 'It's just what I need.'

'Maybe you could book a haircut while we're gone?' Mark
suggested and Neil swatted the back of his head.

'Well,' Neil said, 'as long as you're really sure . . .'

John looked at me and shook his head. 'She'll be fine, Neil,'
he said kindly, his sympathetic tone suggesting he was privy to
at least some of the changes in my life. 'You know my Lisa will
want to be popping in and out every five minutes to make sure
she's okay.'

I baulked at that and Mark laughed. I'd met Lisa a few times
before. She was the archetypal matronly mother hen type. I
suddenly had the feeling that I was going to be plagued by
offers of tea and sympathy in spite of the fact that all I wanted
to do was stay hunkered down in this beautiful house in
Nightingale Square.

The assumption I'd made when I waved Neil and Mark off
turned out to be unfounded as I was left in complete and blissful
isolation for the rest of that day and much of the weekend. Neil
had left lengthy 'how to' lists covering everything from how to
adjust the heating to the best takeaways in the area and, given
how full the fridge and cupboards were, I hadn't had to venture
out at all.

Everything seemed to be working out exactly as I had hoped it would and as Neil had promised. Or it was until Sunday afternoon when the square became a hive of activity and I remembered the tray of toffee apples sitting on the shelf in the larder.

In an attempt to block out the sight of my neighbours rushing backwards and forwards across the road to the grounds of Prosperous Place, where the Grow-Well community garden and the party were located, I'd closed the curtains and snuggled down into the depths of the sofa. However, just before five, a hammering on the front door roused me.

I opened the door, fully expecting and braced to find Lisa on the doorstep, but was instead faced with a girl in her early teens who looked very much like her.

'Hi,' she said, walking in as if she owned the place. 'Do you mind if I come in for a minute? It's freezing out there.'

'No,' I said, closing the door behind her. 'Not at all. Be my guest.'

She wandered down to the kitchen, pulling off her hat and gloves as she went.

'I'm Tamsin,' she said, looking over her shoulder at me. 'Mum has sent me round to get you.'

'You're Lisa's daughter?' I asked, just to be sure.

I knew she had to be, but she'd grown so much since the last time I'd seen her that I wanted to be certain. Not that I was going to say so. There was nothing worse at her age than an adult telling you you'd got so tall. Or even worse, that you looked like your mother!

'That's right,' she said, lifting the glass lid on the cake dome and helping herself to a slice of the carrot cake Mark had left as part payment for my house-sitting duties. 'I reckon this is my favourite,' she then said, taking an enormous and appreciative bite. 'But then, Mark makes a mean coffee and walnut too, doesn't he?'

The girl certainly had some swagger.

'He does, but the carrot is my favourite,' I said pointedly as she chewed, but she didn't look in the slightest bit abashed about having helped herself to the biggest slice. 'That's why he made it for me.'

'Just as well I came around now before you polished it all off then, isn't it?' she said, grinning, and licking her fingers as she made short work of devouring the lot. 'How are you settling in?'

'Good,' I said. 'Thanks.'

'Great.' She nodded. 'You're here for a couple of months, aren't you?'

'That's right,' I replied. She sounded much older than her age. 'Would you like a drink to wash that down?' I offered.

'Best not,' she said, checking the time on her phone and not picking up on my sardonic tone. 'Mum will be wondering where we've got to.'

I went to the larder and carried out the tray of toffee apples. They looked to have survived the weekend without melting and Tamsin's eyes lit up at the sight.

'Well,' I said, putting them down on the counter. 'Here you go. One tray of toffee apples. To be honest, Tamsin, I'm not really in the mood for a party. As you're here, you might as well take them and, if you don't mind, maybe you could make my excuses . . .'

Tamsin looked at me as if I was completely mad or had spoken another language. Or both.

'You're kidding, aren't you?' she laughed. 'Mum would go nuts if I went back without you and then she'd be over here like a shot. I can't tell you the lengths my dad has gone to this weekend to get her to leave you in peace.'

'Oh,' I said, taken aback. 'I see.'

'She's not wanting to be nosey,' Tamsin then said defensively. 'She just wants everyone who lives here to be happy and have a good time. And she likes them to be joining in too, of course.'

'Even if they don't want to join in?' I asked meaningfully. 'And are only staying here for a few weeks?'

'You'd be surprised how many people don't want to get stuck in when they first arrive here,' Tamsin laughed, pulling her hat back on, 'but Mum always gets them in the end.'

Well, she wasn't going to get me, but I didn't much like the thought of Tamsin getting in trouble, or Lisa arriving on the doorstep and frogmarching me across the square.

'In that case,' I said resignedly, 'I'd better get my coat.'

'And a hat and gloves,' Tamsin insisted. 'Because it really is cold enough to freeze your—'

'I get the idea,' I said, cutting her off.

Tamsin carried the tray from the house to the Grow-Well and I tagged along next to her. As we crossed the road, I felt a rush of nerves and found myself wishing that I was about to face a group of strangers as opposed to people who had first met me when I was a happily married woman.

'Holly!' said Kate, the very second we walked through the gate which was set in the old brick wall. 'You came!'

Kate lived at Prosperous Place with her partner Luke and their children. From what I could remember, the house had been built by one of Luke's philanthropic ancestors and when Luke had moved in, he'd taken up the mantle by opening the grounds and sharing them with the local community almost before he'd finished unpacking.

'Hi, Kate,' I said, swallowing as Tamsin disappeared around a bend in the path with the toffee apples. 'Of course. How are you?'

'I'm good, thanks,' she said, closing the gate behind me.

'And don't look so worried,' she then added, linking her arm through mine and guiding me along the path in the direction Tamsin had taken. 'No one's going to come at you with a barrage of questions. We were very sorry when Neil and Mark told us that you're now divorced, but no one's going to mention it.'

'Not even Lisa?' I half-joked.

'Well,' said Kate, giving my arm a squeeze. 'Almost no one's going to mention it.'

As it turned out, no one said a word about it. Luke greeted us at the entrance to the Grow-Well with a mug of warming mulled cider, which soon knocked the edge off my nerves, and then re-introduced me to everyone in such a way that I felt like it actually was my first time there and I was grateful for that. Though I already had a passing relationship with many of the residents, it really did feel like a fresh start.

Everyone insisted that should I need anything I only had to knock on any of their doors and someone would be able to help. In spite of my desire and determination to keep my own company for the duration of my stay, there was something reassuring about knowing I had people to call on should an emergency arise.

'Come and grab a sparkler,' offered a neighbour called Carole, once Kate and I had done the rounds. 'They always make me feel about five years old again!'

It had been years since I'd held one. I was initially a little wary as the sparks began to fly, but seeing even the youngest children writing their names in the air, or attempting to, I knew I had nothing to fear and soon got into the swing of it, holding the stick out at full stretch and drawing patterns and stars.

'Champion, aren't they?' laughed Harold, a former resident of the square who now lived in a nearby care home.

'Absolutely,' I agreed, taking a discreet step to the side as he was a little on the wild side when flourishing his.

He was there with a young couple, Sarah and Pete, who didn't live in the square, but I didn't have time to find out what their connection to the place was before Lisa came to find me, clearly intent on saying more than our earlier brief 'hello' had allowed.

'Hello again,' she said, while at the same time corralling her brood, and everyone else's, into settling down ready to watch the film. 'How are you getting on in the house?'

'Really well,' I told her with emphasis. 'And I'm looking forward to a few peaceful weeks on my own now.'

I didn't think there was any point in beating about the bush. Far better to let her know what my intentions were right from the off, especially given what Tamsin had said back at the house about her enthusiasm for getting people to join in.

'Well, that's great.' Lisa nodded, a smile lighting up her face. 'But don't get lonely over there.'

'Oh, I won't,' I said, mindful of my every word.

Having had Lisa's genuinely kind motives explained by her daughter, I did feel a bit bad for wanting to cut her off, but then that could have been part of her cunning plan, couldn't it? She might have been relying on using my feelings of guilt to coerce me into somehow getting involved. I could see John lingering nearby, no doubt keeping an eye and an ear on the situation and poised, if necessary, to stage another intervention, which made me smile.

'I've got plenty of work lined up to keep me occupied right up until Neil and Mark get back,' I added, just to make sure she really got the message. I hoped the universe wouldn't begrudge me that one tiny white lie, especially as it was told with the best of intentions to secure my privacy.

'In that case,' she said, 'you must make sure you properly factor some downtime into your schedule to enjoy the festive season.'

'Of course.' I nodded.

'We've got the Christmas tree decorating and switch-on happening in the square soon, if you fancy that. Just an informal gathering in the evening so it won't eat into your—'

'Lisa,' John interrupted. 'Hadn't we better get this film started?'

'In a sec,' she said. 'I'm just telling Holly about the switch-on and that there's no need for her to spend the whole of her time here on her own.'

Even if I wanted to, apparently.

'That's great,' said John, reaching for her hand, 'but we really need to get on, otherwise this lot will still be up at midnight.'

'That's a good point,' she said, casting an eye over them all. 'And most of them are still on a sugar high from trick or treating.'

'Are you talking about the kids or the adults?' I quipped.

'Both!' she laughed.

She strode away again and I felt happy to have put a smile on her face. Knowing I'd got off lightly, I took a final look around the happy gathering and slipped stealthily away.

# Chapter 3

My conversation with Lisa about having lots of work on and that I was more than happy in the house on my own must have hit home, and been circulated because the only person who ventured down the garden path was the guy delivering the post.

Unfortunately, however, the longed-for peace and solitude didn't pan out in my favour because rather than emptying my head and relaxing before trying to decide what to do with my life next, all I could think about was work – or, more worryingly, my continued desire to not work. And rather than not stress over my potential next home for a while, there was also the preoccupation with where in the country I might want to move to, ceaselessly buzzing about in my mind, too.

My fuzzy head and muddled thoughts were a timely reminder that I needed to be careful what I wished for because that little white lie I'd told Lisa had jumped up and bitten me squarely on the bum. I kept trying to remind myself that I was entitled to chill out first and make decisions later but it wasn't working and it all continued to spin around my head in a dizzying whirl with no beginning or end.

I knew the financial settlement Piers and I agreed on had

been decent because we'd had a good chunk of equity in the house; however, the money sitting in my bank was in no way enough for me to buy another property outright, so what was I going to do in order to pay a mortgage once I'd decided where I wanted to buy?

My reputation as a children's book illustrator had been hard worked for, carefully grown and was now financially well rewarded. My work had been in demand for a while, but what if, at the end of my stay in Norwich, I decided I didn't want to go back to it at all? Being a creative in today's world was tricky enough but no work equalled no income and that ultimately added up to no home.

Having spent another night tossing and turning, I knew that fretting over my future was not conducive to re-lighting my passion and it was turning my time house-sitting into a nightmare rather than a perfect opportunity to rest, refresh and recuperate. As far as blissful solitude went, apparently, I could have too much of a good thing. But thankfully there was a solution: I would go for a walk. Freeing myself from the confines of the house would doubtless loosen the knot of inner turmoil.

It was only just light and bitterly cold when I set off, and I hadn't walked far from the square before I was craving some carbs and caffeine.

'Morning, my love,' beamed the cheery woman serving behind the counter in Blossoms, which was the bakery where Mark worked. 'What can I get you?'

I rubbed my gloved hands together and looked at the extensive array of tempting fresh treats already on offer.

'You're early enough for a breakfast bap,' said Blossom herself as she walked out of the baking area. 'Hey, it's Holly, isn't it?'

I was amazed she recognised me, but then recalled that Mark had told me that his boss had a gift for remembering faces as well as pastry preferences. Being able to offer that extra personal touch must have been a blessing in her line of work.

'Mark said I should be on the lookout for you,' she carried on, 'but what are you doing up at this hour? I thought you were here on holiday as well as house-sitting for that pair of buffoons. Is everything all right with the house?'

'Everything's fine,' I reassured her. 'I just fancied a bit of a walk this morning and something to sustain me while I pounded the pavements.'

She bagged up a huge flour-topped roll which was packed full of lean grilled bacon and slow-roasted tomatoes and insisted it was on the house.

'But you don't want to be pounding the pavements,' she tutted as she handed me the bag. 'Not when you've got that beautiful garden to explore just across the road.'

I might have wanted to leave the solitude behind for a little while, but not at the cost of potentially running into Lisa and getting roped into doing something. That was why I'd ducked out of the square even though it was early. I was looking to get some balance, not be bowled over, but I didn't tell Blossom that.

'Or perhaps you could take a walk around Whitlingham,' she carried on thoughtfully. 'A trot around the lake will soon blow the cobwebs away.'

I'd previously visited the lake with Mark and Neil and knew going there would mean getting the car out, but I didn't mind that because having stood idle since I arrived, it needed a run.

'That's an excellent suggestion, Blossom.' I smiled. 'Thanks.'

'You'll need to wrap up extra warm though,' she warned me. 'The wind cuts across that water something wicked.'

She was right and after a successful first trip, I'd added even more layers under my coat and headed there every morning since. I felt far happier for getting some fresh air and accompanying rosy cheeks and the trip gave my day some structure and variety too. I guessed it would be a different story at the weekend, but there weren't many people around when I ventured out. That said, there was one person I saw every day and we'd gone from exchanging head nods to a brief 'hello', to commenting on the weather in just a few days.

I wasn't looking to make a friend, but I did look forward to passing the time with my fellow early-bird walker because I was intrigued by her appearance. Whereas my outfits were exclusively either navy or black, this woman, who I guessed was in her early sixties, wore every colour of the rainbow, and mostly all at the same time. She confidently barged her way across and around the colour wheel. Even her ankle wellies were wildly patterned. It was a look I'd tentatively tried myself as a teenager, but had abandoned when my mother said I was beginning to look like a clown. Admiring this vibrant and elegant woman now, I rather wished I hadn't paid any heed to my mum's cutting words, but like a lot of teens, I hadn't wanted to stand out for the wrong reasons.

Thrillingly, my fellow walker's love of colour wasn't confined only to her outfits; her diminutive dachshund companion had a diverse wardrobe of its own too. So far, I'd seen the little dog sporting tweed, a yellow sou'wester and tartan, and all with aplomb. The pair of them were a treat for the eyes and I kept a constant lookout for them, but when we reached the weekend, the daily walk went belly up for them both.

'Oh, my dear!' cried the woman, as she rushed towards me on one of the narrowest paths around the lake early on the Saturday morning, which was, as I had predicted, already busier than during the week. 'Have you seen my Monty?'

Given that she was holding a bejewelled lead with no dachshund on the end, I guessed she meant her dog.

'My little dog,' she continued when I didn't say anything. 'Have you seen him?'

'No,' I said. 'I'm sorry, I haven't.'

'Oh, dear,' she sniffed, wringing her hands and looking around.

'Does he usually disappear when you let him off?'

I hadn't meant to cause offence but she drew herself up to her full height and pushed back her shoulders, letting me know I had.

'I didn't let him off,' she snapped. 'I never let him off here.'

'Oh,' I said, swallowing. 'Sorry. I didn't mean—'

'We were set upon,' she cut in, her shoulders dropping again and the words coming out in a sort of hiccup as her eyes continued to scan around. 'There were two other dogs, both off their leads, and they took exception to Monty's yellow coat.' I guessed she was describing the sou'wester hat and coat combo. 'One of them made a grab for the hat.'

'Oh no!' I said, horrified to think of the assault on the little hound and indeed, the woman herself. 'That's terrible.'

'I tried to pick him up,' she sobbed, 'but got nipped in the process.' I noticed then that her left hand was bleeding a little. 'And Monty somehow broke free of his lead and ran off with the other dogs giving chase.'

'You really should get that bite looked at,' I said.

'I'm not worried about my hand,' she shot back impatiently, giving it a cursory glance. 'I need to find Monty.'

'Of course, you do,' I said, realising that he was her priority. 'Come on. I'll help you. Which way were they headed?'

'Oh, will you help?' she cried. 'Will you really?'

'Absolutely.' I nodded. 'Come on. Those little legs of his can't have taken him far.'

'That's what I'm afraid of,' she said shudderingly. 'What if those two menaces caught up with him when he ran out of steam . . .'

'Let's not think the worst,' I told her, even though the thought had already crossed my mind. 'I'm sure he'll be fine.'

Our search took us much further than I would have imagined Monty could possibly run in his rainwear, but eventually I caught sight of a flash of yellow right down at the edge of the lake that was furthest from the car park. The coat and hat combo might have made him an easy target for rogue dogs but I was grateful for its garishness as we might never have spotted him had he not been wearing it. I was also grateful that there was no sign of his tormentors.

'There!' I said, pointing at the spot that wasn't far from where we stood, but was well off the path, down by the edge of the water. 'That's him, isn't it?'

'Oh, Monty,' the woman stammered when she saw him, her hands flying to her face. 'It is. How on earth are we going to reach him?'

She called his name and he looked in her direction, but didn't move.

'I'll have to risk a dunking,' she said, stepping closer to the lake.

'No,' I said, putting a hand out to stop her. 'I'll get him.'

I hoped I wasn't about to get nipped too. I knew it would only be because he was scared, but that didn't make the prospect any more appealing.

'Hey, Monty,' I said, trying to sound soothing.

As I inched carefully closer, I became aware that a couple of passers-by had stopped to see what I was doing.

'Fancy a dip, do you, love?' one man shouted, which made Monty flinch.

'Be quiet, you stupid man,' Monty's owner said tersely, which instantly silenced him and made me smile, in spite of my precarious position.

I soon realised that it was the muddy bank which was stopping Monty from moving. His short legs had all but disappeared and he couldn't have run back to his owner for all the treats in the world. He was shaking, too, and looked utterly miserable. His hat was nowhere to be seen and his coat had been ripped and roughed up. Thankfully he didn't appear to have suffered any physical harm, although he would obviously need carefully checking over.

'Can you reach him?' his owner called and at the sound of her voice he stopped cowering and strained to move.

'Yes,' I said. 'I can get him.'

I unwound my scarf and laid it out next to me along the bank, then stretched as far as I could without falling forward into the water. My fingers caught the back of the coat and with a squelchy tug, I plucked Monty free, then bundled him into the scarf and wrapped him up tightly so he couldn't make a bid for freedom. He didn't object at all and lay limp and heavy while I staggered back up the bank to the path.

'Oh, my darling boy,' sobbed the woman as I transferred the wrapped up and forlorn pooch from my arms to hers. 'Are you hurt?'

Monty didn't answer, but I did think he looked relieved.

'How can I ever thank you?' said the woman, turning her attention back to me.

'There's no need,' I said, looking at my boots and wondering how I was ever going to get them clean. Not that it mattered. Monty was back in safe hands, hands that clearly worshipped him and that was the most important thing.

The two onlookers carried on with their walk now the excitement was over and I went to make my excuses, too.

'Will you be all right now?' I asked. 'Can you get home?'

'Yes.' The woman nodded. 'I'm about a half hour walk from here. We can manage.'

There was no way she was going to be able to walk that far with Monty in her arms. He might have only been a small dog, but he would weigh heavy at that distance, especially after the drama of what had occurred. The woman looked suddenly pale, although the effect could have been intensified because the woollen zigzag patterned cape she was wearing was so dazzlingly colourful and bright.

'You don't drive to the lake then?' I asked, even though the answer was obvious. Had she come in a car, she would have said so.

'No,' she said, 'I'm off driving at the moment and the extra walk does us both good. Well,' she sighed, 'it usually does us good. I'm not sure I'll want to come here again.'

She was beginning to look tearful.

'My car is in the car park,' I told her. 'I can easily drive you both home.'

Had you seen the look on her face, you could have been forgiven for assuming that I'd offered her the world.

'Are you really sure it's no trouble?' she asked, shifting Monty in her arms.

'No trouble at all,' I insisted. 'Let's go this way. I think it's quicker.'

Once we were safely inside the car, she looked Monty over as much as was possible in the confined space and, feeling satisfied that he didn't need a vet, she then gave me her postcode and house number, which I keyed into my satnav. I set off, a little more sedately than I might usually drive, to an area not all that far from Nightingale Square but which I hadn't visited before.

'I'm May, by the way,' she said, once I'd negotiated my way back to the ring road and she'd finished kissing the top of Monty's head, which seemed to be the only part of him that wasn't encrusted in mud.

'And I'm Holly,' I said back, adjusting the heater to warm us up faster and feeling relieved to see she now had a little colour in her cheeks.

'I'm extremely pleased to have properly met you, Holly,' she said shakily. 'Although I wish it had been in less dramatic circumstances.'

'Likewise,' I agreed. 'This has been a far cry from our usual relaxed early stroll, hasn't it?'

'That it has,' she tutted, kissing Monty again. 'Do you live in the city, my love?'

'No,' I told her. 'I'm just visiting for a couple of months. House-sitting for friends.'

'So, you'll be in Norwich for Christmas then?' she enquired.
'Yes.'

'And are you here on your own?' she asked. 'If you don't mind me asking.'

'I don't mind,' I told her. 'And yes, I'm on my own.'

'I'm on my own, too,' she said, stroking Monty's silky

looking ears. 'Apart from having Monty who, of course, is a fine companion.'

'I can well believe that.'

'And my son is heading to Norfolk for a few months over winter too, so I'm going to be seeing lots of him over Christmas.' She sounded thrilled at the thought.

'That will be nice.'

'More than nice.' She beamed and when I glanced at her, I saw her face was transformed. 'I haven't seen him for months so it will be a total treat. I'm a widow now,' she added, her smile faltering again, 'and I miss my darling husband terribly. We'd both been looking forward to the next twenty, maybe even thirty, years together.' She sighed heavily, before finishing, 'I moved to Norfolk a few months ago, looking to make a fresh start. To tell you the truth, I've been on a bit of a journey.'

'Me too,' I said unguardedly, then quickly got in another question of my own before she requested details. 'And do you like living here?'

'I do,' she said, though she didn't sound completely convinced, 'but I'm still finding my feet, you know, and getting used to life on my own after being one half of such a happy duo. The city is wonderful, but I can't seem to find the oomph to go out and search for my tribe, as folk say these days. What about you?'

I wasn't sure if she was asking about my marital status, if I liked the city or if I'd found my tribe. Whichever it was, I decided I'd shared enough personal details for one day.

'Is this it?' I alternatively asked, as the satnav announced that I'd reached my destination and I flicked down the indicator to turn left.

'No,' she said, looking out of the window, 'mine is the next one. I've downsized and what with it being a bungalow, I've future-proofed too.'

She sounded appalled by the term and I couldn't suppress a smile. I pulled off the road and onto the gravelled drive. A sprawling bungalow filled the width of the plot and I couldn't help thinking that if this was May's idea of downsizing, I would have loved to have seen where she had lived before.

'If you could unlock the door?' she requested once I'd helped her out of the passenger seat with Monty still in her arms. 'That way I won't have to put him down until we're inside.'

'What about the alarm?' I asked, noticing a box on the wall just below the line of the roof as I pushed the key that she had managed to pull out of a pocket and hand to me into the lock.

'Oh, I don't bother with it,' she said dismissively. 'I'm no good with that sort of thing. Keypads and codes are completely beyond me. You will stay for a cup of something, won't you, Holly?'

I had planned to head straight off, but it was kind of her to ask and I didn't want to come across as churlish by turning her down. I might have still been looking to carry on protecting my privacy and not get drawn into sharing more about myself, but not at the cost of being rude.

'That would be lovely,' I said, feeling resolved to see the escapade through. 'Thank you, May.'

I pushed the door open and May stepped in ahead of me while I wobbled about on the mat, trying not to dislodge too much of the thickly encrusted, but quickly drying, mud that was clinging to my boots. The footwell in my car was already caked in it and I didn't want to give May more clearing up to do. It wasn't until my feet stepped off the mat and touched the wooden floor and

I closed the door behind me that I realised how cold the place was. And also, how spectacularly colourful.

'Oh, my goodness,' I gasped, taking the large hallway in.

The walls, the little I could see of them anyway, were a dazzling shade of tangerine and the canvases and framed paintings which practically covered every square inch of them, were all the colours of the rainbow. May's home was clearly every bit as colourful as she was and I wondered what it had been like for her son, growing up in such a stimulatingly decorated environment. Assuming the look was something May had nurtured in the past.

It was just the sort of aesthetic I had dreamed of as a child and I rather envied May's son if this had been a look he'd always been familiar with. My own parents' home was completely bland. Perhaps that was why I had embraced such a colourful palette to embellish my work? Although not my wardrobe and remembering mine and Piers's home, not that either. It was all elegantly understated and completely devoid of personality, I now realised.

'Here,' I then said, when I realised May was still holding Monty. 'Let me take him and you can get your wellies off.'

Assuming she wanted to, given the glacial temperature.

She transferred the little dog, who didn't object at all, from her arms to mine and then she pulled off her boots, leaning against a slightly chipped six-foot tall statue of a faun, complete with hooves and horns. I couldn't take my eyes off the figure and when I looked down, found he was accompanied by a couple of rabbits who were looking adoringly up at his impish expression.

My eyes scanned back up again as May lifted off her cape and draped it over one of the faun's outstretched arms. Had I not been holding Monty, I would have pinched myself, just to make sure

I wasn't really in bed in Nightingale Square and having some sort of surreal dream.

'I think I'd better get this young man into the bath straightaway, don't you?' May sighed, not spotting my dazed expression or taking any notice of her unusual coat stand.

It was all I could do to simply nod in agreement.

'And today of all days,' she tutted, walking further in. 'It would have to be so cold.'

'Is your boiler out of action?' I asked, finally coming to as we moved further away from the friend of Mr Tumnus.

'No,' she told me. 'It's the thermostat I can't fathom. The engineer fitted a new one, which he assured me he had programmed but I can't suss it and even though I've rung him a dozen times he hasn't come back to help me with it. I'm leaving it now for my son to look at. The hot water is working, so that's something.'

'I'll see if I can sort it, if you like?' I offered.

I couldn't leave her and Monty to freeze in this igloo. The walls might have been decorated in colours hotter than the sun, but they didn't have the power to lift the temperature and I was certain I could see my breath when I spoke.

'Oh yes, please.' She smiled warmly. 'If you can do that, Holly, then we'll be even more indebted to you!'

My toes recoiled when we reached the kitchen and the flooring changed from chilly wood to frozen tiles, but I wasn't so frozen through that I didn't notice how stylish the space was. The whole back wall in the kitchen was made up of bi-fold doors which offered an uninterrupted view of the beautiful gravel garden beyond. It was a stunning feature, even if it did do nothing to warm the place up.

'If you could get the heating to work,' said May, 'then I'm sure Monty would enjoy his bath all the more.'

'And I'm sure you would too, May,' I said with a shiver, and she laughed.

It turned out there was nothing wrong with the thermostat, which had been programmed according to the preferred times and temperatures which May told me she had instructed the engineer to key in, it was the boiler setting which was amiss.

'It's set to just heat the water,' I told her, turning the dial one notch to the right so it was pointing at a tap and a radiator as opposed to just the tap.

Right on cue, the boiler fired up and May rolled her eyes.

'You think I would have spotted that,' she said exasperatedly. 'Or that wretched engineer would have suggested it on one of the many times I've called him.'

I crossed the room and touched the radiator. It was starting to warm up at the bottom.

'It's working now,' I told her. 'Would you like me to run you through the settings on the thermostat?'

'No, I would not,' said May, backing away as if the wireless box was something which could inflict actual physical harm. 'Thank you, but no,' she then said more reasonably. 'I'm sure it will be fine now. Why don't you fill the kettle and make us some tea, Holly, and I'll go and run Monty's bath.'

'And check your hand, too,' I reminded her.

By the time I'd found mugs, made the tea and further admired the view of the garden, May and Monty had returned, both looking far happier and less dishevelled, and the bungalow had started to warm up.

'There now,' May sighed, sounding blissful as she wafted in

wearing a full-length brightly coloured kaftan and matching turban. 'How wonderful is this? I haven't been warm enough to wear one of these since the summer!' There was a plaster on her hand which suggested the nip she'd incurred was more of a scratch than a bite.

'Has Monty got one too?' I smiled and May laughed.

On hearing his name, the little dog came over and jumped up at my legs. I bent to scratch his head, but he wasn't satisfied with that so I picked him up and he licked my chin, wriggling ecstatically.

'I know you probably think his wardrobe is ridiculous,' May said with a grin.

'Actually,' I said, putting Monty down again, because it was impossible to keep hold of him and he was still a bit damp, 'I think it's very stylish.'

'Not your cup of tea though?' asked May, looking me up and down and taking in my head-to-toe navy outfit, socks included.

I stood out like a sore thumb in her colourful home. A dull one.

'I wouldn't say that,' I said, then changed the subject. 'And talking of tea, we'd better drink ours before it stews.'

Once we'd emptied the pot and Monty was quietly snoring in his thickly padded bed, I realised just how late it was and decided I should go.

'You could stay for lunch if you like,' May offered.

'Thank you, May,' I said, 'but I really should be getting back. I haven't left the heating on and I did promise my friends I wouldn't let the pipes freeze. I daresay I'll bump into you at the lake tomorrow though.'

'Oh,' she said, looking over at Monty with a deep frown etched across her forehead. 'I'm not sure I'll be going back.'

'Oh, May,' I insisted. 'You must.'

'I don't think I dare.' She swallowed.

'Would you go back if I came and picked you both up and we walked around together?' I asked her. As I was going to be heading there anyway, it wouldn't make any difference to me, but it might to her and Monty.

She looked at me and her eyes widened in surprise. She appeared to be as taken aback by my offer to accompany her as she had been when I suggested I could drive her home.

'I would,' she said, her eyes bright. 'I would go back then. Thank you.'

'How does half eight suit you?'

'That would be perfect.' She smiled. 'I like a bit of a lie in on a Sunday.'

'That's settled then,' I said, standing up.

'Wait a sec,' she then said, dashing out ahead of me. 'I've got something I want to give you.'

I had pulled my muddy boots back on by the time she reappeared carrying what I thought was a length of brightly patterned fabric, but it turned out to be a silk scarf.

'There now,' she said, draping and tying it around my neck before I could object. 'This'll make up for the one you wrapped Monty up in and which is now no doubt ruined.'

'I'm sure mine will be fine once I've given it a wash.'

May ignored me and carried on. 'Perfect.' She nodded when she finally stepped back, looking delighted. 'I had a feeling this one would suit you and it does. It really brings out the colour of your eyes.'

I put a hand up to touch the fabric, which was incredibly soft to the touch. The scarf pattern was a riotous jumble of orange, lilac and blue.

'The orange, you mean?' I smiled. 'Or the lilac?'

'No, the blue, you loon.' May laughed. 'You can keep that,' she carried on. 'And don't say no,' she added, pre-empting my refusal. 'I've got a whole trunk full and it's my way of saying thank you for coming to our rescue today.'

'In that case,' I said, before turning to open the door, 'thank you, May.'

'It would be lovely if you wore it tomorrow,' she called from the bungalow as I climbed into my car.

I waved in response, thinking there was no way I could, but then I caught sight of myself in the rear-view mirror and I realised May was right, the colour did bring out my eyes and I didn't look like a clown at all.

# Chapter 4

I was unexpectedly buzzing for the whole of the rest of the day and my mind wasn't preoccupied with new home or work worries at all. My act of kindness seemed to have released an entire host of happy hormones and chemicals and as a result, I rinsed off my boots with gusto under the outside tap, but I took more care with my soiled scarf.

I picked off as much of the mud as I could, then decided I'd have to let it air dry for longer and after that give it a good shake before either machine or hand washing it. I didn't really mind the state of it though, not when it had been used for such an important purpose.

It wasn't until I went to get changed into my PJs early that evening to cosy up in, that I remembered I was still wearing the scarf May had gifted me. I looked at my reflection in the hall mirror and marvelled at how the colours enhanced the look of my entire outfit and apparently my mood, too, because I couldn't seem to stop smiling. I carefully lifted the scarf over my head, managing to keep in place the knot May had expertly tied, and set it down ready to wear again the next day, should the fancy take me.

While I waited for my supper to warm – a defrosted portion

of Neil's chilli con carne – I picked up the pen he kept next to the noticeboard for list-making purposes and began doodling on the back of a piece of scrap paper.

It was a habit I'd developed in childhood and it had driven my neat and tidy parents to distraction. It annoyed them to such an extent, in fact, that I, having got so tired of their tutting, had given it up. However, one day when Piers gathered up an entire pile of abandoned scraps and handed them to me, I realised I'd started again.

Subsequently, I had since discovered that I did it mostly when I was talking on the phone in our office, and after Piers flagging it up, it became commonplace to find my scribbles left anywhere I'd had access to paper, pencil or pen. Some of my best illustration ideas had landed during those moments of absent-minded sketching, but my doodles after my time with Monty and May were created purely for fun.

After I'd eaten and washed up, feeling inspired, I carried on with the pictures, which mostly featured a comical little dachshund who looked remarkably like Monty. I sketched him wearing the variety of outfits I had seen him in and then made a final one of him elegantly, and slightly jauntily, wearing a scarf decorated in the same pattern as the one his mistress had so kindly gifted me.

'Wait up!' called Lisa, just as I set off in my car for May's the next morning.

I opened the passenger window as she rushed down her path, waving, and then leant right inside.

'Hello, stranger.' She smiled. 'I haven't seen hide nor hair of you since the bonfire party. How are you getting on?'

'I'm good, thanks,' I told her. 'Keeping busy, you know.'

'Are you busy today?' she asked, then carried on before I could answer. 'Only we're all heading over to the Grow-Well later to harvest some of the winter veg and have a bit of a tidy up. I know Neil said you weren't a knowledgeable gardener, but you can't go wrong with what we have planned for today.'

I remembered what Tamsin had said about her mum always getting people involved in the end and had to admire her determination to get me gardening. I also remembered what Neil had said about the garden being 'all tucked up' for the winter and felt rather less charitable towards him than I did towards Lisa.

'I am busy, I'm afraid,' I told her, relieved that I had a genuine reason for not joining in. 'I'm now off to meet a friend.' I knew it was a bit soon to consider May a friend, but telling Lisa I was off to meet a stranger I had only started properly talking to the day before didn't have quite the same ring to it. 'I'm sorry about that.' I shrugged.

'No, no.' Lisa smiled, looking thrilled. 'Don't apologise. I was just worried that you were all on your lonesome, but clearly, you're not.'

'No,' I said. 'Definitely not and I do appreciate you checking in, but like I said at the party, I really do have plenty to keep me occupied until the guys get back.'

I knew from my experience at the bonfire party, that I no longer needed to feel awkward around any of the Nightingale Square gang, but that still didn't mean that I was going to get involved with the garden. My time in Norwich was going to run on my terms, no one else's. I was determined to do what I wanted, when I wanted to do it. It might have sounded selfish, had I said it out loud, but that was how I needed the next few weeks to be.

'Right.' I smiled. 'I better be off.'

'Okay,' said Lisa, who suddenly looked very much as if she was about to say something else. 'I'll catch you later, then. Lovely scarf, by the way. Is it Hermès?'

'Thanks,' I said, my hand going to touch it. 'I don't think so.'

She was still standing on the pavement watching me as I left the square and I realised I'd just dodged a bullet. She might have admired my scarf, but that wasn't what she'd really wanted to say and, knowing Lisa wasn't the sort of woman who would run out of ammunition, it would only be a matter of time before she deployed another tactic to get me involved.

'Well, now.' May beamed as she threw open the door the moment I knocked on it. 'Don't you look wonderful, Holly!'

I was in my usual dark attire but the inclusion of her scarf – now my scarf – and the fact that I was wearing my blonde hair loose, rather than pulled back in a ponytail, clearly met with her approval. I touched the scarf again and her smile grew all the wider. There was no label on it and I hadn't studied the pattern closely enough to spot a name, but now wondered if Lisa had been right about the brand.

'Thank you.' I smiled back. 'I do love it, but it isn't Hermès, is it, May? Because I couldn't possibly accept—'

'No,' she cut in. 'Definitely not. Now, shall we have a cuppa or get straight off?'

'As appealing as a cuppa sounds,' I said, dropping the provenance of the scarf because I didn't want to upset her, 'I think we'd better get straight off. I've heard talk of rain for later this morning.'

I left her to collect Monty and lock up, and climbed back into the car.

'Oh now, Monty,' I said admiringly when they joined me. 'I can see I'm not the only one looking dapper today.'

He wriggled about on May's lap while I fussed him and he ecstatically licked my hands.

'He's incognito,' May told me, tapping the side of her nose as she explained the reason behind the camouflage gear. 'So, if those two hellions are on the prowl again, they hopefully won't spot him.'

'He looks like a little soldier,' I laughed, then checked myself.

I didn't want to dent his confidence. I'd heard cats didn't like being laughed at so it might well be the same for dogs.

'They won't have any trouble finding you though, May, will they?' I said as I turned over the engine. 'That's quite a poncho.'

'Thank you,' she said with dignity as she pulled on her seatbelt and untangled it from the elaborate fringe. 'It's not waterproof, but it is Gucci.'

That made me think that Lisa had probably been right. My scarf most likely was Hermès.

'Crikey, May.' I smiled. 'Are you sure you want to wear it for a walk around the lake?'

'Absolutely,' she insisted. 'I have lots of lovely clothes and I don't save any of them for best or special occasions. Every day is a special occasion as far as I'm concerned. I might still be adjusting to my status as a widow and coming to terms with how short life can be, but I don't need to dress in black to prove the point. No offence,' she quickly added.

'None taken,' I reassured her, mulling over what she had said.

The threat of rain made for fewer visitors and subsequently a quiet walk and there was no sign of any dogs running about without their owners. We were all relieved about that.

'After you left yesterday, I found a phone number and reported what had happened,' May told me as we walked around. 'I gave a description of the dogs and sadly, it doesn't appear to be their first offence. The site manager said the staff and volunteers would be even more on the lookout for them now.'

She was on the lookout too, glancing over her shoulder every few paces. Monty, on the other hand, didn't seem fazed at all. What a resilient chap he was. Perhaps it was the outfit which gave him the confidence to trot so merrily along.

'Well, that's something, I suppose,' I said. 'And how's the bungalow? Is it still feeling warmer.'

'It's like a completely different place,' May told me. 'I enjoyed living there in the summer, with those bi-fold windows always wide open, but when autumn arrived and the days started to get shorter and darker, I began to brood and wonder if I'd made a mistake . . .'

Her words trailed off and she looked a little sad.

'Had you lived in your other house long?' I asked.

'Oh yes,' she said. 'Almost forty years and throughout the whole of my marriage. It was quite a wrench to leave it, but deep down I knew it was the right thing to do. The place was far too big for just Monty and me. That said, I do sometimes wonder now if moving quite so far away from everyone I knew, and the life I had there, was the most sensible idea I've ever had.'

At least, my not having a wide circle of friends meant the worry of moving away from them wouldn't be something I'd have to take into account when I finally set my sights on deciding where I wanted to live. I could probably get away with sticking a pin in a map and popping back to see Neil and Mark a few times a year!

'It's a shame you don't drive, May,' I said, bending to give Monty a fuss, 'then the pair of you could travel a bit further afield and get out more.'

'I do drive,' she told me.

'Oh,' I said, stopping to look at her. 'I got the impression yesterday that you didn't.'

I tried to remember exactly what it was that she had said.

'No, I do,' she repeated. 'Have done since I was a teen. I'm just not allowed to at the moment, so my car is in a rather special garage for safekeeping and being looked after by a friend who will keep it ticking over and in good repair.'

'You're not allowed?' I frowned.

'Banned,' she shocked me by saying. 'For speeding.'

'Oh dear.' I grimaced.

'Again.'

That didn't sound good.

'A longer ban this time, too.' She sighed heavily. 'And a much heftier fine to go along with it.'

I tried to imagine her flying along, far faster than she should have been and found it wasn't difficult to picture.

'You obviously didn't learn your lesson the first time you got caught then, did you?' I said forthrightly. 'Sorry,' I then apologised. 'I didn't mean to sound so harsh. It's just that I once dated someone who passed their test and immediately thought they could drive at any speed they liked. Needless to say, the relationship didn't last after he hit another car at a junction with me in the passenger seat.'

My parents had never liked the lad, which ensured my fascination with him but his stupid driving completely put me off him too.

'Oh, Holly,' May gasped. 'How dreadful. After an experience like that you have every right to sound harsh. I'm ashamed to say I used to love driving with my foot to the floor,' she then admitted. 'As long as I was in control, I couldn't see what the problem was, but then one day I suddenly realised I wasn't in control and almost caused a crash. Thankfully I avoided it at the last gasp, but my speed had been clocked just before it.' She shook her head. 'I never would have forgiven myself had someone got hurt and I'll certainly never speed again when I get my licence back.'

'Well,' I said, feeling relieved she had changed her ways and without injuring herself or anyone else, 'I'm very pleased to hear it. Now come on. I think I felt a spot of rain.'

May linked her arm through mine and we had just made it to the car park before the heavens opened.

'How lucky were we?' I laughed as I turned on the wipers.

'And how brave was Monty?' she praised. 'He was fine, wasn't he?'

'He was,' I agreed, giving him a fuss.

'He didn't seem bothered about coming back at all,' May carried on. 'Not even when that overenthusiastic spaniel bounded up to say hello.'

'He was completely unfazed,' I said, as I pulled out of the car park. 'So, you won't worry about going back again on your own now, will you?'

'Not at all,' she said, fondly stroking Monty's silky ears. 'Although, if there are times that suit us both before the winter weather really kicks in, it would be lovely if we could take a few walks together. We could do that, couldn't we, Holly?'

'Absolutely,' I immediately and enthusiastically agreed, surprising myself. 'I would love to do that.'

I knew I quite possibly wasn't someone who May would have included in her usual tribe, because in many ways we were chalk and cheese, but I was fascinated by her and her love of colour and darling Monty and felt that only good could come from us getting to know each other better.

It was quite a turnaround given that I had arrived in Norwich resolved to enjoy only my own company. I never would have believed it was possible to feel such an affinity for someone I'd only just met, and accidentally at that, but there was something very special about May and I was keen for our friendship to continue.

'That's settled then.' May grinned. 'But, if the forecast is correct, we might have to miss the next day or two. Now,' she added as the bungalow came into view, 'I don't know about you, but I could really do with that cuppa and a biscuit.'

'Oh, me too,' I happily agreed again. 'Me too.'

# Chapter 5

As the rain continued to fall hard and fast for the next couple of days and I stayed hunkered down alone in the house, I thought more about my surprise fledgling friendship with May, as well as how both my work and marriage might have impacted on my life in more ways than I had previously understood.

The nature of my work and the fact that I worked from home meant that I didn't have that opportunity for the water cooler chat lots of other people indulged in. There was no Christmas office party, no dress down Friday or end of the working week drinks. However, in spite of the fact that I didn't have those opportunities, I hadn't felt either alone or lonely, because I had Piers.

Our mutual agreement not to have children had, I began to realise, led me to assume that I would *always* have him and that he would be enough. Me and Piers, Piers and me. It was going to just be the two of us. For always. Forever. And consequently, I hadn't felt the desire to include anyone else. Metaphorically – and ironically – speaking, I had put all of my eggs in one basket.

As it turned out, of course, the exclusive egg club I had been a member of wasn't exclusive for Piers because, along with changing his mind about wanting a baby, he'd also had the water cooler banter and annual office parties, courtesy of the family's architectural firm he worked for.

I thought I had come to terms with the end of our marriage but clearly, I was going to be picking apart, processing and accepting certain aspects of it for a while to come. I knew this latest thread I had unexpectedly unravelled and released was down to meeting May and her four-legged companion. I had drawn lots more sketches of Monty during my rainy-day periods of reflection. There was even one of him floating about in a shiny, silver spacesuit, which I was fairly certain he didn't have, but he did look mighty fine in.

In spite of the continuing rain, I heard someone run up the path and knock on the door on Wednesday afternoon. I hastily shoved the growing collection of sketches of Monty out of sight, and rushed to see who it was.

'Lisa,' I said, feeling immediately on guard. I imagined her wearing a Stetson and being locked and loaded with more ammunition and, even though I knew I was the one in the firing line, I was unable to stop a smile from spreading across my face. 'Come on in out of the rain.'

'Thanks,' she said, stepping inside and pulling off her boots.

It wasn't going to be a fleeting visit then.

'Coffee?' I offered.

'Oh, yes please.' She nodded. 'I've just done five hours straight at the keyboard and I'm in need of caffeine. And a recommendation for un-numbing my bum, if you have one.'

I had to laugh at that.

'The words are flowing, I take it?' I asked as I filled the kettle.

I knew from my previous visits to Nightingale Square that Lisa was a prolific author and even though I was finding her a pain in my own backside, I had to admire her ability to juggle deadlines, a family and all of the community things she was involved in. Her lifestyle wasn't one I craved for myself, but I could appreciate that on her terms, she really was living her best possible life.

'They are now,' she said, puffing out her cheeks, 'but it's taken a while with this one. Anyway,' she carried on, taking a seat and getting down to the real purpose of her visit, 'I'm not here to brag about my word count.'

'Oh?' I said, bracing myself for impact.

'I just wanted to remind you that the festive decorating and switch-on in the square is happening on Saturday the twenty-fifth.'

'I hadn't forgotten,' I said, pointing at the calendar where it was already highlighted.

'Excellent.' She nodded. 'And there's also—'

'Please don't say something else to do in the garden,' I groaned, rushing to cut her off at the pass.

She shook her head and laughed. 'No,' she said. 'It's nothing to do with the garden.'

'Thank goodness for that,' I said, feeling relieved and foolishly allowing myself to relax.

'It's The Chapel,' she carried on. 'We could really do with you there. Mark said you'd be happy to pick up his role, but that I wasn't to mention it until you were properly settled in. And you are now, aren't you?' she added, firing my own words back at me. 'You've told me so yourself on more than one occasion.'

I bit my lip, unwilling to comment until I had more of an idea as to what she was talking about. Mark had never mentioned a chapel to me and I knew neither he nor Neil had ever been religious. I also knew this was the bullet I'd dodged on Sunday.

'Here's your coffee,' I said, purposefully avoiding either confirmation or denial of the depths of my settled status. 'Sugar?'

'One, please.' She smiled. 'John's always saying I'm already sweet enough, but I can't seem to break the habit.'

I thought it best not to comment on that.

'So,' she said, after taking a sip. 'How about it?'

'I honestly can't answer that, Lisa,' I told her, 'because I have no idea what The Chapel is. Unless it's a functioning chapel, in which case I'd be no help at all because I'm an atheist.'

Lisa laughed but when I didn't join in, she stopped.

'You're being serious?' she asked.

'Deadly,' I confirmed.

'Has Mark not mentioned the place at all?'

I shook my head.

'Oh, for pity's sake,' she said. 'What's he like?'

'Do you really want me to answer that?'

'No,' she said. 'Best not. I can't believe he hasn't told you about it, because he's been volunteering there for ages.'

I wasn't going to tell her we hadn't really talked for ages. Not about anything other than Piers's defection to Team Parent anyway.

'So,' she said, finally getting down to it, 'The Chapel is a community space where we run drama, art, music and creative writing workshops, mostly, but not exclusively, for eleven- to eighteen-year-olds. There's little provision for this sort of thing on the school curriculum, so we're carrying on the work of Moira Myers, who set up and ran a similar establishment, called

The Arches, here in Norwich, years ago. She sadly died a while back, but we were determined to pick up her legacy in a new venue after The Arches was lost.'

'It sounds amazing,' I said, before I could check myself. I hoped she wouldn't take my approval for more than was intended.

'It is,' she responded, sounding proud, 'and it's almost entirely run on volunteer hours, mine included.'

'Oh Lisa,' I praised. 'I don't know how you manage to squeeze so much in every day.'

'Neither do I.' She grimaced. 'But I wouldn't have it any other way. There's a huge wealth of up and coming creative talent in this city and we need to do what we can to support it.'

'I can tell you feel passionate about it,' I said, nodding. 'What exactly is it that Mark does there? Not singing, I hope.'

'God, no!' she guffawed. 'Can you imagine?'

She'd obviously heard his caterwauling too.

'Sadly, yes.' I snickered.

'He does all sorts of general stuff that would eat into the time of the session leaders,' she explained. 'He sets out chairs, arranges rooms, makes drinks, clears up and occasionally helps out with some of the workshops if they're down on volunteer numbers.'

I couldn't really imagine Mark just bustling about in the background because he always liked to be centre stage but, fair play to him, he was obviously doing whatever was needed. I then hastily reminded myself that he had told Lisa that I would take on the *whatever was needed* in his absence. Between him and Neil getting me in the garden for the party and pinning me on the neighbour's radar as a result, they'd really stitched me up. I was of half a mind to let the pipes freeze, just to get my own back.

'But given the age of the attendees,' I then said cleverly, raising what I thought was a valid point and therefore a legitimate excuse, before I said a very firm thanks but no, 'I'd have to have had some sort of check before I could help out, wouldn't I?'

'A DBS,' said Lisa, but she didn't sound concerned by my pointing it out. 'They're taking a couple of weeks to go through at the moment, but you can get started straightaway as long as you're not left unsupervised with any of the kids. That said, quite often what Mark does is completed before the kids even arrive.'

That wasn't the response I had been hoping for. I could feel the foundations of my 'I do what I want, when I want' mantra being given a hefty shove, but I wasn't going to give in without a fight.

'The thing is—' I started to say, but it was impossible to stop my neighbour now she'd fired the bullet.

'I probably wouldn't have even asked you if we hadn't got in such a pickle with the Christmas production,' she informed me sadly.

'The Christmas production,' I echoed.

'It's supposed to be happening a month from today but we're way behind with it. We need more hands on deck. And your hands, Holly, would be a huge help.'

'I can't honestly see how my presence could make any possible difference to the outcome,' I told her, feeling a bit mean.

'But it will,' she pleaded. 'Even if you just made the drinks and washed up, it would free someone else up to do something else.'

I supposed I could see the sense in that.

'And I know Mark shouldn't have spoken on your behalf,' Lisa continued, hammering the point home. 'I do feel bad about asking when you've already said you've got so much work on.' My cheeks reddened when she said that. 'But we really are desperate.'

It was my turn to feel bad then because, the sketches of Monty aside, I had absolutely no work on at all. My only regular commitment was going for a morning walk when the weather allowed and I could hardly turn her down on the basis of that, could I?

That said, even though I believed The Chapel was a worthy cause and everyone involved was bound to be wonderful, I still wanted to make the most of the freedom I was currently enjoying. I had only gifted myself the start of my stay in Nightingale Square to do exactly as I pleased and sticking to that plan felt important to me because I knew I wouldn't get the opportunity to do it again.

I took a deep breath.

'I'll think about it,' I then said firmly. 'I promise I'll give it some thought.'

'Oh,' she said, looking floored as her eyes widened in surprise. 'Right. Okay.' She shrugged, slipping off the stool. Clearly, she wasn't used to not immediately getting her own way and she sounded as put out as she looked while she pulled her boots back on in the hall. 'I'll leave you to it then.'

As she finished wrapping up before heading back out, she fired one last shot. 'We're having a quiz in the pub on Friday night to raise funds,' she said tersely. 'Maybe you could say yes to that?'

'Of course.' I swallowed.

'I'll put you down for the Nightingale Square team.'

'Yay,' I cheered. 'Count me in.'

I felt awkward knowing I'd upset her but I wasn't going to give in. This situation was Mark's doing, not mine, and I was well within my rights to give it some proper thought before deciding what to do about it.

'Right then,' said Lisa, still sounding disgruntled. 'We're all meeting on the green at seven and walking to The Dragon together, so I guess we'll see you then.'

I really didn't want to go out on a freezing Friday in November, especially as I still hadn't made up my mind about whether to help at The Chapel or not, but I kept my word and joined some of my Nightingale Square neighbours on the path next to the green at seven on the dot.

'Hi, Holly,' said Kate, who was there with Luke. 'I'm so pleased you're joining us.'

'I'm probably going to be useless at the quiz,' I told her, 'but I wanted to do what I could to support the fundraising.'

Lisa gave me a look. It was obvious that she'd far rather I supported The Chapel in person as opposed to via a feeble intellectual contribution.

'I know it's little consolation, Lisa,' I told her, 'but I promise, I am still thinking about helping out.'

'I appreciate that,' she said, sidling closer. 'And actually, I think I owe you an apology.'

'You do?'

'I do.' She sighed, her former expression changing. 'It was hardly fair of me to barge in, lay this on you and then try to guilt you into saying yes when you'd no idea what you'd be saying yes to.'

'Well,' I said, feeling my shoulders relax a little, 'I appreciate you acknowledging that, unless . . .'

'Don't worry.' She laughed. 'I'm not trying to get you to lower your defences and give in. I appreciate that your time here is already accounted for, what with your work commitments and the fact that you have a friend in the city who you no doubt want to spend more time with, so please don't give it another thought. We'll manage.'

I resisted the sudden urge to capitulate, prompted by her heartfelt apology, as she started to usher everyone together. Her passion for both The Chapel and the closer community was obvious and I wondered if I might benefit from it in the same way as I was profiting from my friendship with May. My time with her had already greatly enriched my life, so maybe volunteering at The Chapel would have a similar impact. It might do me good, while I was doing good . . .

'Did my wife just apologise to you?' John asked, sounding awed.

'She did.' I smiled. 'But don't tell her I told you so, otherwise she'll have my guts for garters.'

'Come on then, folks,' Lisa said firmly, rounding everyone up in her trademark mother hen style. 'If we don't get a move on, we'll never get a seat.'

Assuming the event was going to be popular, I set off first with Kate and Luke, leading the way. It didn't take us long to arrive at The Dragon and I soon realised, as we all squeezed through the door, that Lisa wasn't only referring to the quiz's popularity, but also the fact that the pub was so small. I must have walked by the place on my way to Blossoms, but with its inset door and dark exterior, I'd never noticed it.

The inside was dark, too, and very beautiful. It felt like I'd actually stepped back in time when I crossed the threshold. The thickly beamed ceiling was low, the subtle lighting dimmed, and the whole bar smelt of woodsmoke, courtesy of a fire which was merrily glowing in the grate on the opposite side of the room to the door. The place felt like something from a tale Tolkien would have told and I wouldn't have batted an eye had a few hobbits arrived, or even a rider from Rohan.

'What are you drinking, Holly?' asked Luke, as he pulled out his wallet.

I looked along the bar and didn't recognise the names of any of the ales on offer. Clearly The Dragon supported every micro-brewery in the area.

'Um,' I said, aware that a queue was forming as Lisa was cor-ralling everyone together and handing out sheets and pencils for the quiz. 'A pint of something light would be great, but I'm not sure which of these . . .'

'Leave it with me,' Luke laughed. 'Why don't you and Kate go and find us a seat, if you can?'

I was happy to leave the decision up to him. Kate and I squeezed in next to Heather and Glen and Freya and Finn, four other residents from the square, who I'd met on earlier visits.

Lisa was reminding everyone to put their phones away as Luke came back with a tray of drinks.

'Is it always as busy as this?' I asked.

'It is,' our table chorused, as the lights were then adjusted to burn a little brighter.

'It's actually as popular with tourists as it is with locals,' Heather elaborated.

'Norwich is famous for its dragons,' Freya added, as I turned to admire a cleverly lit sculpture on the wall which appeared to be made from scrap metal and was a joy to behold. 'So, the name gives the place even more appeal.'

'Finn made that,' said Kate, giving me a nudge.

'Did you?' I gasped, turning to Finn who, with his long, braided hair, looked every inch a Viking and completely befitted the place.

'Yeah,' he said, ducking his head. 'It's one of mine.'

'It's stunning,' I told him, making him blush beneath his beard.

There was no time for further chat. Lisa banged her glass on the table, which quietened the entire bar, thanked them for coming and gave us all a quick run-down as to what and where the evening's funds were being raised for. I felt further inclined to step in for Mark as she said her impressive piece, and then the quiz began.

I was able to offer a few right answers, but the competition was stiff and the winners were eventually announced as Sara and Pete, who I still didn't know but recognised from the bonfire party. Their team included Beth and Eli, also from the square.

'Eli manages The Chapel,' Kate told me. 'And Pete plays a big part in the music workshops there too. They're in a band with Beth. They're really good.'

'I'm beginning to realise just how many people are involved with the place,' I told her, before gathering up the empty glasses to take back to the bar for another round.

The lights had been dimmed again and there were even more people packing the place out. I had to literally breathe in as I squeezed my way through the crowd. I noticed there was one customer, wearing a battered wax coat, who seemed to take up far more space than most and having deposited the empty glasses on the bar I had to take a step away again as he went to turn around, oblivious to the fact that I had squeezed in behind him.

Unfortunately, I hadn't realised there was a dog laying at his feet and, as I moved, I put my foot down heavily straight on the poor thing's paw. It let out a yelp which silenced everyone around me and I felt my face flush because I knew I was the cause.

'Oh, you poor love,' I said, awkwardly bobbing down in the

confined space and giving the dog, which had got to its feet, a hug. 'I'm so sorry.'

It was a beautiful white English bull terrier, a small one, with a comical dark patch over one eye. It accepted my apology with good grace as I rubbed the paw I had trodden on and stroked its head.

'There,' I soothed. 'Does that feel better?'

'Good girl, Queenie,' I heard a gruff voice say above me as the owner of the voice reached for my elbow and rather unceremoniously pulled me back up to my feet.

I was taken aback to be manhandled and snatched my arm out of the guy's grasp, before glaring up at his face. I was further surprised to find he was glaring straight back at me. At least, I assumed the set of his forbidding brows suggested he was glaring.

It was impossible to be sure as the rest of his face was practically hidden by what could only be described as a tangle of hair and an almost out of control beard. Both the hair on his head and his beard were dark, but the latter was streaked with silver and grey. I guessed he was older than me, but not by much. His unkempt aesthetic had me thinking of Hagrid, but on a bad day.

'You shouldn't have done that,' he said bluntly, his dark eyes fixed on mine.

I swallowed, but my throat had turned completely dry.

'I didn't mean to,' I eventually managed to say. 'It's such a squeeze in here, and I didn't realise she was there until I stood on her—'

'I meant you shouldn't have fussed her like that,' he cut in, sounding marginally less gruff.

'I was only apologising for standing on her,' I stammered, reaching to stroke her head again.

'Come on, Queenie,' he muttered, ignoring my explanation as he stepped away from the bar. The dog followed obediently, thankfully without a limp. 'It's time we moved.'

He left me standing there, feeling a total fool, like a child who had been chastised for something they hadn't done. The gap he left was soon filled and I ordered the next round of drinks as well as I could remember it, minus another pint for myself and then carefully carried the heavy tray back to the table.

'I'm going to head off,' I said to Kate, as she inched along to make space for me to sit down again. 'I've got a bit of a headache.'

'Will you be all right walking back on your own?' Luke asked.

'Yes,' I said, pulling on my coat. 'I'll be fine.'

'You can come with us, if you like,' offered Heather. She and Glen were now standing up. 'We need to make a move because our sitter can't stay as late as usual tonight.'

I accepted her offer, said a quick goodnight to everyone else, then tagged along with the pair back to the square. My face flushed as I played over what had happened with the dog and her owner but, in spite of my continued annoyance and mortification, I couldn't seem to stop wondering what the bloke would look like with less of a beard.

# Chapter 6

The weekend dawned, frosty and bright, but the arrival of the blue sky didn't do much to help my head. After a restless night spent mostly getting tangled up in the duvet, it still ached when I climbed out of bed and I knew it wasn't a hangover because I hadn't had anywhere near enough to drink.

While I waited for the kettle to boil, my mind returned to the guy who had told me off, and his dog, Queenie. By the time my first coffee of the day was made, a doodle of her had joined a new one of Monty. The mismatched pair looked good together, in spite of their obvious physical differences.

As I finished my drink, I set the drawing aside and glanced at the clock on the kitchen wall. It had just turned half past eight. There was every possibility that I might bump into the two Ms if I made an immediate decision to take a walk and, thinking how much I'd missed them during the previously wet days and wishing we'd swapped telephone numbers, I rushed back upstairs to get dressed.

I was in luck when I arrived at the lake.

'Well, hello stranger!' called May when she realised it was me walking towards her.

Monty, very flatteringly, started skittering about and pulling on his lead to get to me.

'How wonderful is this upturn in the weather?' May beamed when I reached them and made a fuss of her ecstatic dog. 'I've only been out far enough to whizz Monty around the block since our last trip here.'

I hadn't given a moment's thought to the fact that May would still have to give Monty some exercise.

'I don't blame you,' I told her. 'Had I been in your shoes, May, I would have just ushered him out into the garden.'

'Um,' she said, eyeing him critically, 'unfortunately and in spite of his age, he has too much about him to be satisfied with that.'

Watching him skip about, I could see she was right.

'We really should have swapped telephone numbers, shouldn't we?' I suggested. 'That way we could have kept up with each other's walking plans.'

'Well,' May said, shrugging, 'no harm done, but we wouldn't have minded if you'd just turned up at the bungalow. We would have been delighted to see you.'

'Next time I will.' I smiled, feeling thrilled that she and Monty felt that way. 'Let's make the most of the sunshine now though, shall we?'

'Absolutely,' she agreed, linking her arm through mine in a way that felt both familiar and comfortable. 'So, what have you been up to? You look a bit tired.'

'Not much really,' I began, but no sooner had I started telling her than she cut me off.

'Actually,' she said, 'don't tell me now. Let's finish our walk and you can come back to the bungalow for a post-stride coffee and fill me in then.'

'Sounds good to me,' I told her. 'I happened to pick up a bag of breakfast pastries on my way here which would go down a treat with a shot of caffeine.'

'Perfect.' She beamed. 'My son is coming to see me this afternoon, so this is going to be the busiest Saturday I've had in ages.'

'In that case, are you sure you've got time to play host to me?'

'Of course, I have,' she insisted. 'Plenty of time, but where's your scarf, Holly?' she then tutted. 'You're looking very navy again today.'

The bungalow was wonderfully warm and while May got changed and Monty had a drink and settled himself down for a nap, I looked about the hall and kitchen, marvelling again at the riot of clashing colours which, in her own inimitable style, May had made work. When I finally found my new home, I would strive to make it every bit as interesting and exciting.

'That's my newest addition,' she said, when she stepped out of her bedroom wearing another of her kaftan and turban combos and found me looking at a huge canvas covered in thick textured splashes of yellow, pink and green paint. 'A treat to celebrate turning sixty-eight earlier this year.' She was a few years older than I had guessed then. 'Do you like it?'

I cocked my head to one side and bit my lip.

'I do,' I told her. 'I really do.'

The combination of colours reminded me of one of the spring Baby Bee stories I had illustrated early on in the series. It was wonderful to see them transferred to something so much bolder than the pages of a children's book.

'I'd love to see a spring outfit in those colours,' I said wistfully, as my imagination ran away with me.

'Oh yes,' said May, giving me a nudge and also getting carried away. 'You'd look wonderful in a pink and yellow patterned tea dress with a green cardigan and pumps.'

'Would I?' I laughed.

'You would,' May said seriously. 'But in the meantime, I'll find out the artist's details for you. She lives near a town called Wynbridge, not all that far from here,' she elaborated. 'She's a young woman with a wonderful eye and bags of style. She turned up to deliver this in her bright yellow vintage Citroen 2CV. She calls it her banana-mobile!'

'How on earth did she get it to fit?' I laughed, recalling the unusual shape of the car.

'She had the roof down,' May laughed back. 'She only delivers canvases of this size on dry days.'

I hoped she hadn't delivered it recently because she would have frozen to the steering wheel even if Wynbridge wasn't all that far off.

'Now,' said May, drifting into the kitchen with a rustling waft of fabric, 'where are those pastries you promised?'

While May made the coffee and I plated up the treats from Blossoms, I told her a bit about my week and how I was still feeling torn about helping out at The Chapel, in spite of the fact that I knew it was a wonderful cause.

Her eyes lit up as I explained why the place had been taken on and what it was now being used for. I had also planned to tell her about the embarrassing ticking off I'd received in the pub from the Hagrid lookalike, but I didn't get the chance because she had latched on to the subject of The Chapel and grilled me relentlessly about it, eventually going to get her laptop to google it, when I couldn't furnish her with all the details she wanted.

'So, tell me again,' she said, impatiently jabbing at random keys rather than simply waiting for the machine to start up. 'Why are you not sure about going to help out?'

I could sense that she thought my indecision about getting stuck in was a bit mean-spirited. I was beginning to feel that way too, in spite of my desire to protect the free time I had gifted myself ahead of getting down to some serious thinking.

'Because it doesn't fit in with my plans for my time here,' I told her. That sounded feeble now, even to my ears.

'I thought you were just house-sitting for friends.' She frowned. 'I didn't realise you had anything more specific lined up to do.'

'I haven't got a list of places to visit or people to see or anything like that,' I carried on, not wanting to trot out the lie about having lots of work to do as I realised how little I'd actually told her about my current circumstances. 'But I'm taking some time to clear my head ahead of figuring a few things out. There are some decisions I need to make as well as things I need to come to better terms with.'

'What sort of things?' she asked, abandoning the laptop and looking keenly at me.

'Well.' I swallowed, deciding to be candid. 'Since my recent divorce, I've been feeling increasingly unhappy about my work and I need to fathom out if it's simply a result of the upheaval or something which runs deeper. If it turns out to be more than a hiatus connected to my personal circumstances, then I need to decide whether I'm going to soldier on regardless or try something new that's still related to my profession.'

'I daresay you know me well enough already to know what my reaction to the words *soldier on* would be.' May shuddered.

'Life's too short, my darling. There's no joy working away at something that no longer lights you up.'

I knew she was right, of course, but that idealistic ethos wasn't going to pay a mortgage, was it?

'I'm sorry to hear about your divorce,' she then said kindly. 'Unless, of course, he was a total rotter and you're well shot of him.'

I laughed at that and Monty's ears twitched.

'Not a total rotter,' I said generously, then decided to explain more of the details. 'He changed his mind about wanting children and I didn't. By which I mean, he wants them and I don't,' I added, just to clarify the situation.

'It's magnanimous of you not to consign him to the rotten barrel for that,' May said softy.

'Yes, well,' I carried on, 'I knew he couldn't help it, not really. Although,' I admitted, 'I haven't always been quite so noble about it. The day he told me his new partner was pregnant before our divorce was finalised, I was as far from high-minded as it's humanly possible to get.'

'Goodness me!' May gasped, sounding horrified. 'That really was a bit much.'

'It was rather, wasn't it?' I agreed.

'What did the rest of his family make of his change of heart?' May asked. 'Did *they* think he was a rotter?'

'Far from it,' I sighed. 'In fact, I was the one who came off worse because with a new and pregnant partner on the scene, they all dropped me like a hot potato.'

May didn't say anything and when I looked at her, I could see her eyes were filled with tears.

'I know how much the sting of abandonment hurts.' She

swallowed. 'Thirty years I'd been best friends with someone who dropped me the day her daughter's relationship with my son ended. I know I don't need to tell you how keenly I felt her loss. And it wasn't even my son who ended things.'

'Oh, May,' I sympathised.

I hadn't known Piers's family anywhere near that amount of time, so could only imagine a little of the pain May felt, but it was enough to get the gist.

'Trying to cope with Jonny's loss,' she said, handing me a photograph of her and her handsome husband on their wedding day, 'without my friend's support, was heartbreaking. As if my heart wasn't already broken enough.'

'Have you had no contact with her at all?'

'No,' she said briskly, taking back the photo. 'Nothing, and I wouldn't want to now, either. And I'll certainly never set myself up for that sort of painful parting again. Now,' she carried on, neatly drawing a line under the subject, 'we were talking about you, weren't we? I can appreciate why you're wondering if the discontent you're feeling about your work is the result of the emotional tumult you've been through.'

I took a moment to gather my thoughts before carrying on.

'Thank you, May.' I smiled. 'I'm pleased you can see it from my point of view. Although,' I added, 'I'm not supposed to be trying to puzzle it out yet. For the time being at least, I'm supposed to be emptying my head before going back to it with a fresh perspective. And that's why,' I finished up, circling right back to where we had started, 'I need the free time, peace and tranquillity to clear the mental decks.'

'I see.' May smiled wryly back. 'And that's why you're so happy to spend time with me and Monty, is it?'

The mention of his name made Monty's ears twitch again.

'Well,' I laughed, 'I admit I discovered early on that there's such a thing as too much free time.'

'In which case,' May said cleverly, running with the opportunity I'd just inadvertently gifted her, 'why not fill a bit of it by helping out at this chapel place? In my recent experience, which conveniently backs up your own, peace and tranquillity can actually be perversely hard to come by when you have a surfeit of empty hours.'

She spun the laptop around before I could praise her wisdom and I could see she'd found the right webpage for The Chapel.

'I'm guessing this is it?' she asked.

'Yes,' I said, looking at various photos which featured Lisa, Pete and Eli. 'That's the place. Crikey, it's impressive, isn't it?'

She didn't seem to hear me, but turned the laptop around again and clicked on various pages while reading snippets aloud as she went along. I turned my attention to the pastries. So much for her not being good with tech. She seemed more than capable of finding her way around a website.

'You better stop reading and eat some of these, May,' I eventually said, 'otherwise I'm going to polish off the lot.' I'd already made short work of a pain au chocolat and was tearing into an apple turnover. 'May?'

It took a moment for her to respond and I began to worry that something was wrong.

'No, no,' she finally said, sounding fey and faraway, 'you carry on. I'm not sure I fancy them now.'

'Are you all right?' I frowned.

'Yes.' She nodded, her eyes tracking back to the screen. 'Just reminiscing, that's all.'

'Reminiscing,' I repeated. 'About what?'

She stopped staring at the laptop and looked at me properly instead. Her eyes were shining and there was a glow about her that was different to the one she usually had when we were warmed up from walking. She was radiant.

'My time on the stage and screen,' she announced theatrically, elegantly inclining her head.

'Your time on what?' I spluttered, choking on my coffee.

'My time on the stage and screen,' she repeated, only this time with a puckish grin.

'Were you an actress, May?' I goggled.

Her expression changed to a thoughtful frown.

'I am an actress,' she then said, with emphasis. 'If it's in your blood, you never retire.'

'Well, I never.' I beamed, realising I had as much to learn about her as she had to discover about me. 'Tell me all about it. I want to know everything.'

The two of us moved from the kitchen to the sitting room. It was a space I hadn't seen before, and I walked around, admiring framed posters, photographs and theatre bills. They all featured May from when she was a very young woman until when I guessed was far less than a decade ago.

'My stint in *The Crescent* was what I was best known for,' she said, naming a soap opera which had faded from popularity but the name of which I was familiar with. In fact, I was sure some of the parents of kids I was at school with used to watch it. 'My dear Jonny and I actually played a couple in it,' May carried on, 'but it was Constance Confectionary that made my fortune. I was the voice of the brand for a few years and it was extremely lucrative.'

'Oh, May.' I smiled. 'I had no idea I was in such famous company!'

'Not that famous if you didn't recognise me,' she pointed out with a laugh and I began to blush. 'I'm only teasing.' She smiled. 'My days of being recognised are, for the most part, behind me, but I do wonder . . .'

'What?' I asked, picking through the box of memorabilia she had handed me.

'No,' she said, sitting down next to me. 'It's silly.'

Monty wandered in looking miffed to have opened his eyes and found an empty kitchen. May picked him up and I noticed some pastry flakes around his chops, so clearly, he had capitalised on being temporarily abandoned. An idea for a sketch of him snaffling forbidden food popped into my head.

'What's silly?' I asked, zoning in again.

May kissed the top of Monty's head, then put him down and stood up.

'Well,' she said, drifting across the room and standing in front of the fireplace where she looked effortlessly chic and artistic, 'I was wondering if you might take me to The Chapel. I know you're not all that keen to help out, but with my experience, I might turn out to be of some use.'

I looked at her and blinked.

'Like I said' – she blushed, sounding heartbreakingly vulnerable as she misinterpreted my reaction – 'it's a silly idea. They wouldn't want me.'

'No,' I said, jumping up. 'It's not. It's not silly at all. I'm certain everyone there would be thrilled to welcome you aboard.'

'Do you really mean that?' May exclaimed, her excitement immediately restored.

'I really do.' I nodded vehemently and then took a breath. 'And if you're so willing to pitch in, then I suppose I could give it a go, too, couldn't I?' The thought of helping out with May in residence felt like a far less daunting prospect than turning up on my own for some reason. 'As long as I really do only have to set out chairs and fill jugs with squash,' I breathlessly added. 'Oh, I could kiss you, May!'

'Do you think we've found my tribe?' she giggled, as she clapped her hands and Monty yapped.

'You know what?' I laughed back. 'I think we have.'

# Chapter 7

May was still on cloud nine when I eventually left her bungalow. so she could prepare for her son's arrival. I was thrilled to think that he was going to find her in such high spirits.

She had admitted to me that she'd been trying her best to convince him that she was happy and settled, but had been worried that, as good an actress as she was, she hadn't quite succeeded. I felt certain that the light in her eyes and the smile on her face, now she had the prospect of volunteering at The Chapel ahead of her, would soon allay any fears the guy might have had.

We swapped phone numbers before I headed back to the square and I promised that I would talk to Lisa, who could then chat with Eli, the manager, about what we had in mind. Providing they were happy with the idea, I would then arrange a convenient time for us to rock up, as May had put it, and get stuck in. I had to admit that the prospect of rocking up and getting stuck in felt much more appealing knowing that my new friend was going to be doing it with me.

Frustratingly, there was no one answering at Lisa's house on the Saturday so I headed back first thing the next morning, after yet another night of broken sleep, but for far more exciting reasons than thinking about gruff giants.

'Is your mum about?' I asked Tamsin when she answered the door after I'd been knocking for ages.

She gave a theatrical yawn and pulled her Disney patterned dressing gown tighter around her, keen to let me know the inconvenience I had caused by turning up so early.

'She's at the Grow-Well,' she mumbled, then added with emphasis, 'And I was asleep.'

'Thanks,' I said. 'Sorry to have got you up . . .'

The door closed with a thump even before I'd got the last word out. I decided that as I had such good news to share, I would risk going over to the garden and potentially getting roped in to help with something. With any luck, the really mucky winter work would have been finished the previous weekend.

Carole's husband, Graham, was just opening the gate when I crossed the road to Prosperous Place, which was a blessing as I had completely forgotten that I would need the key code to get in.

'Are you coming to help out, Holly?' he asked, sounding hopeful.

'Not really,' I admitted, following him inside and along the path through the grounds. 'I just need a quick word with Lisa.'

'Righto,' he responded, with no guilt trip attached, even though he had obviously hoped for a different answer. 'As you're here, you might as well take some of the carrots and a squash away with you – if you like them, that is. We happily have a bit of a glut of both at the moment.'

'Thanks,' I said, thinking I could have a go at making soup. I knew that was what Mark and Neil often did so they were bound to have the right pans and utensils. 'I do like both.'

'Visitor for you!' Graham called to Lisa, who was bent over one of the beds.

She stood up and frowned, stretching out her back. I hoped the frown wasn't in response to my arrival and that what I was about to tell her would soon turn her expression into a smile.

'Morning, Holly,' she said, pulling off her soil-encrusted gloves. 'What can I do for you?'

'It's more what I can do for you, actually,' I took great pleasure in telling her. 'Have you got a minute?'

'Always,' she said, sounding interested. 'How about I put the kettle on?'

We sat in a snug but practical bothy, which had been made comfortable with a mismatched assortment of chairs set around a slightly rickety table. The place smelt earthy and slightly damp. It wasn't unpleasant, but not really my cup of tea. Probably because it was so unfamiliar.

While waiting for the kettle to boil, Lisa filled a few modular trays with compost and rifled through a box stuffed to the top with packets of seeds.

'We might as well work while we talk,' she said craftily, handing me a packet of parsley seeds. 'You do those,' she said, nodding. 'They're bigger than the chive seeds and easier to handle.'

I was grateful to not be working outside and wondered if Tamsin was right. Had her mum got me in the end? Given my current situation, especially when coupled with what I was about to say, I supposed that, in a roundabout sort of way, she had.

'You'll have to show me what to do,' I told Lisa. 'I've never sown seeds before.'

She gave me a demonstration and, seeing it was so easy, I

quickly set to with the parsley while she made short work of the chives.

'Will these really grow in the winter?' I asked her as she lightly covered the seeds she'd already expertly distributed with a substance she told me was called vermiculite. It let the light through better than compost did, apparently.

'In the greenhouse, which has a bit of heat, they'll soon germinate,' she explained. 'Now, what is it that's got you over here so early on a Sunday morning. Have you changed your mind about helping out at The Chapel?'

I put the seed packet down and brushed my hands together. 'I have actually.' I beamed at her and then laughed when she jumped up and down.

'You absolute bloody star!' she screeched, reaching over and pulling me into a hug. 'Eli will be as thrilled as I am.'

'But you do promise that I'm only going to be a gopher, don't you?' I insisted.

'I do,' she said, releasing me and holding up three fingers in the Scout Salute. 'Unless you feel inclined to do more, but that will be entirely up to you. Like I said, you're a star for agreeing to come along.'

'Talking of stars,' I couldn't then resist carrying on, 'would it be okay if I came along with someone else?'

'Someone else who wants to volunteer, you mean?'

'Someone who is itching to volunteer.' I laughed again, thinking of May's excitement.

'The more the merrier!' said Lisa. 'Who do you have in mind?'

'A new friend,' I said proudly. 'Her name is May and she's an actress. She's recently moved to Norwich and would very much like to offer her expertise and experience.'

'Oh wow,' said Lisa. 'A professional then. Do you know if she might have worked on anything I've heard of?'

'Not so much recently,' I said, building up to the big moment. 'But in the past, she was the voice of Constance Confectionery and had quite a big role in ...'

'*The Crescent?*' Lisa gasped, banging down the coffee mug she'd only just picked up.

'Yes.' I glowed, basking in the warmth of May's success. 'She starred in it with her late husband.'

'Oh my god,' said Lisa, jumping up again and reaching for her phone. 'You're talking about May Madison, aren't you?'

'I am,' I confirmed. I had noticed May's surname on the flyers and programs back in the bungalow.

Lisa quickly scrolled on her phone before thrusting it in my face. 'This is her, isn't it?'

'Yes,' I said, pushing it away a little so I could focus on the images of May looking like the goddess she was at various soap award ceremonies and on the cover of a plethora of TV guides. 'That's the May I'm talking about.'

Lisa looked back at her phone. She was speechless and I congratulated myself on the miracle I'd performed of stemming her conversational flow, even if it was only temporary.

'And she's *really* said she wants to help out at The Chapel?' she eventually asked, having found her voice again.

'She *really* has,' I told her, feeling like I'd just gifted her the best present ever. 'Can I take it from your reaction that she's going to be welcome to come along and have a chat with you there? Do you need to run it by Eli first?'

'She's more than welcome.' Lisa nodded, sounding awed. 'And I know Eli will be onboard, so don't worry about that. When you say she wants to help, do you know in what capacity?'

'You'd have to ask her that.' I shrugged.

'She'd be wasted making squash,' Lisa muttered. 'No offence.'

'None taken.' I smiled, thinking that was the second time someone had said that to me since I'd arrived in the city. 'And I'm pretty certain she'd like to be more involved than that. I haven't known her for long, but she strikes me as a very hands-on type of person.'

I was about to say that she'd been lonely since moving to the city, but bit the words back, because they weren't mine to share.

Lisa shook her head. 'I can't get my head around this,' she said, beaming. 'You couldn't have come over here with better news. Everyone will be so thrilled.'

'Assuming they know who she is,' I pointed out.

'Of course, they'll know who she is,' Lisa shot back, sounding shocked. 'Everyone knows May Madison. She's soap opera royalty! Or she was, back in the day.'

I felt a bit bad that I hadn't recognised her but then the television in the house I grew up in was never tuned into soap operas because Mum and Dad only ever turned it on to watch documentaries. I preferred to stay in my room to sketch and paint. They had both vociferously considered the skills a complete waste of time that wouldn't go any way to getting me qualifications to do a proper job. I pushed the memory of our many arguments about that away.

'So, when can she come?' Lisa asked. 'We've got a meeting scheduled for tomorrow evening and if you could both make that, it would be great. It's listed as the Christmas Crisis meeting, but with May onboard, I think I should rename it. Perhaps the

Christmas Crisis Averted meeting would now be more appropriate. Actually ... I won't do that ... and I'm not going to tell anyone about May, either. That way, when they walk in, I can enjoy the look on their faces. What do you think?'

Most of what she'd said didn't require a response as the words had fallen out of her in a sort of rhetorical monologue, no participation from me needed at all.

'Well,' I said, answering the bit I could, 'I know I can make the meeting but I'll check in with May and let you know if she has other plans.'

I was fairly certain she wouldn't be otherwise engaged, but with her son now back, I couldn't be sure and didn't think it would be appropriate to answer on her behalf.

'Excellent,' said Lisa, looking happier than I'd ever seen her. 'We'll be starting at six, but come along a few minutes before, if you can.'

She wasn't so starstruck that she'd forgotten about our seed sowing and didn't let me go until we'd filled a few more trays. Then she was happy to send me off with a very cheery wave and a jute bag full of carrots and squash, with a huge cabbage perched on top. If the soup was a success, I'd have to give some to May and fill Neil and Mark's freezer because I'd never get through it all on my own.

By the time I had left the Grow-Well and set off along the path through the grounds to the gate back to the square, I was ready to swap hands because the bag was so heavy.

Just as I stopped, I heard someone calling, 'Holly!' I turned to find Luke walking towards me.

He wasn't alone.

'Hey, Luke,' I said, my face aflame as I realised his companion bore a striking resemblance to the guy I had upset in The Dragon on quiz night.

In fact, on closer inspection I realised it was him, but he'd had a makeover since our run in. His legs were now clad in dark jeans and his moss green hand-knitted jumper had a couple of holes in the cuffs. His thick tangle of hair had been cut and almost, but not quite, tamed and his beard had been cropped into submission. The tidy – but not too tidy – version of him made my insides unexpectedly fizz. I had been wondering what he would look like tamed and now I knew.

'I'm guessing that Lisa has roped you in to helping in the Grow-Well after all?' Luke beamed, pointing at the bag by my side.

'Sort of,' I said, as I pulled my eyes away from his companion. 'I thought I might make some soup.'

'Cabbage soup?' Luke grimaced.

'No,' I laughed. 'I thought I'd go for carrot and squash. They're under the cabbage.'

'That sounds more like it.' He nodded. 'Sorry,' he then said. 'Let me introduce you to my friend here.'

'Oh, we've met,' I said, thrusting my hands into my jacket pockets, more to stave off the cold than come across as defensive.

'Oh?' said Luke.

'Briefly,' his friend said succinctly. 'In the pub.'

He had the deepest voice and, in the light of day I noticed, the darkest brown eyes and longest thick lashes. In that moment his eyes met mine and I bent down ostensibly to rearrange the cabbage sitting on top of my bag. I hadn't really expected him to remember our encounter, but then, as I'd almost injured his dog, I supposed I shouldn't have been surprised.

'Oh right,' said Luke, when neither of us gave up more information. 'Well, I'm feeling over the moon because Bear is now working with Freya to reinstate a long lost part of the Prosperous Place garden.'

Had I misheard, or had Luke just called the man Bear? It was fitting if he had, but certainly unusual.

'You're a gardener?' I asked, which I knew was stating the obvious, but I felt as though I had to say something because he hadn't.

'Sort of,' he said. 'I do more garden restorations than hands-on gardening now.'

'He's being modest,' said Luke, slapping him squarely on the back. 'He's actually one of the country's top garden restoration experts, but he'd never tell you that himself *and* according to Freya, he's still pretty handy with a spade.'

I eyed the giant with renewed interest as he shook his head.

'And I'm extremely lucky to have him working here,' Luke carried on, 'because he was planning to take a few months off. Our running into each other, which also happened in the pub, was a total fluke, because it turned out—'

'I was looking for somewhere to park my home,' Bear said, picking up the thread and finally joining in, 'and we were able to settle on the perfect arrangement to benefit us both.'

'A parking spot traded for your years of experience and knowledge and consultancy skills,' Luke laughed. 'I definitely think I've got the better half of the deal, mate.'

'I think we're both going to do all right out of it,' Bear said, returning Luke's former gesture by slapping him on the back but inadvertently knocking him halfway across the path.

I bit my lip to stop myself from laughing.

'Anyway,' said Bear once he'd set Luke back on his feet. 'I'd better get on. Queenie!' he then loudly called, scaring me half to death.

There was a scrabbling noise on the gravel path and Queenie, the bull terrier, appeared around the corner behind him. She came to a stop at Bear's feet for a mere moment, then spotted me and rushed over. I didn't bend to fuss her, given what had occurred the first time but that didn't stop her somehow wedging herself between the bag and my legs. She sat heavily on my feet and looked questioningly up at me.

'You seem to have got yourself a fan, Holly,' said Luke, who still had no idea of what had previously occurred.

'Yes,' I said, 'I do rather, don't I? She's an absolute sweetie.' I still didn't stroke her though. 'Anyway,' I said, 'I better go. This soup won't make itself . . .'

I shifted a bit and Queenie got up and walked back to Bear. I hoped she wasn't offended that I'd ignored her.

'We'll see you Saturday then, Holly, if not before,' said Luke as I picked the bag up again.

'Saturday?'

'The switch-on in the square,' he reminded me.

'Of course.' I nodded. 'I'll see you there.'

'Bye,' said Bear.

'Bye,' I said back.

I had just reached the gate in the garden wall when I heard someone quickly walking up behind me again.

'Holly! Wait up.'

It was Bear, with Queenie right on his heels. I set the bag down for a second time and put my skittering heart down to the fact that he'd just made me jump.

'I just wanted to say I'm sorry,' he said, as Queenie once again perched on my feet. Bear rubbed a hand around the back of his neck while I waited for him to elaborate. 'For snapping at you in the pub.'

'It's fine,' I said. 'I get it. You don't like people petting your dog.'

'No,' he said, shaking his head. 'It's not that. Well, it's sort of that . . .'

I looked down at Queenie just as she looked up at me. 'Is he always like this?' I asked her and she wagged her tail, which made her whole back end move because she was sitting on it. 'Or can he usually string a sentence together?'

She barked at that and I laughed, then looked back up at Bear who had turned bright red. Given how my body had responded to him, I was relieved to be able to tease him a bit and hopefully disguise my own surprising feelings.

'I'm usually perfectly eloquent.' He swallowed, shifting from one foot to another before folding his arms and curling in on himself.

'So,' I said, helping him out, because I then felt bad about taking such blatant advantage of his discomfiture, 'have you had Queenie since she was a pup?'

'No,' he said, squatting down and she shuffled close enough for him to stroke her. 'And that's why I didn't want you fussing her. She's only been with me a few months and we're just now working our way through some different social situations. The evening in the pub was a real test for her. Her busiest outing so far.'

'Ah, right,' I said. 'I see.'

'It's usually just the two of us at home,' Bear carried on. 'And a small team of gardeners during the day, all working outside in a large area and she can get away from us there if she wants to.'

'Did she have a rough start in life?' I asked, guessing that's what he was getting at.

'You could say that,' Bear said, looking up at me.

He looked very lovely from that angle.

'Do you see these scars?' he then said, looking back at Queenie and pointing out some marks on her back and around her muzzle that I hadn't noticed before.

'I do now you've pointed them out.' I nodded.

'They're most likely the result of her fighting with other dogs,' Bear said sadly. 'Although the centre I got her from couldn't be sure as they didn't know her whole history. She was found by a farmer in a ditch. She was in quite a state, but the wounds weren't all that recent so it was hard to tell precisely how she came by them.'

'Oh, poor Queenie,' I gasped and her tail thumped harder.

'The rescue centre vet thought she'd probably had a few litters of pups in quick succession, too.'

'The poor love,' I sighed, watching the dog who clearly adored her new owner and vice versa. 'So, that's why you didn't want me getting in her face after I'd hurt her.'

'Exactly,' said Bear. 'I had no idea how she was going to react.'

'I see,' I said, realising that mine hadn't been the most sensible of actions. I had just wanted to show her that I was sorry.

'But, as it turned out, my reaction was far unfriendlier than hers,' Bear carried on with a wry smile, 'and I apologise for that.'

He stood back up and Queenie shifted again and put a paw on my leg, clearly expecting some attention now explanations had been made.

'Would it be all right if I fussed her now?' I asked him.

'I'm sure that would make her very happy indeed.' Bear nodded, his smile growing wider.

Queenie was thrilled with the attention and would have lapped it up all day.

'I'm so pleased I've had the opportunity to explain,' Bear said, blushing again. 'It's been on my mind all weekend and I thought there was no chance I'd ever bump into you again. Just to explain my reaction, I mean.'

He was getting tongue-tied again. It was endearing in a man of his size who you might have assumed would be all bluster and swagger.

'Well,' I said, deciding not to tell him that it had been on my mind too, 'what with unpredictably running into Luke in the pub and me here now, it sounds very much like serendipity in action.'

'Perhaps it is.' He smiled, fixing me with a look of such intensity it quite took my breath away. 'Luke just told me that you're only staying across the road for a couple of months. Not that we were gossiping ... that is ... I mean ...'

He was off again.

'That's right,' I said, picking my bag back up and rescuing him for the third time. 'I'm just house-sitting for a couple of friends over Christmas.'

'I'm not going to be here for all that long either,' he told me. 'I've got a job starting in the south west in the early spring, so I'll be heading down there then.'

I was intrigued to know more about his work as well as the home that he'd parked up at Prosperous Place. I wondered if it was a caravan or perhaps a motorhome. I wasn't sure he'd be able to stand up straight in a caravan and with the wind getting up it was really too cold to hang about and keep the conversation going long enough to find out.

'Perhaps I'll see you around.' He tentatively smiled and I thought he sounded hopeful, but that could have been my imagination.

'Maybe you will,' I said, finally taking a step away.

'I'll be at the switch-on next weekend,' he carried on. 'So, if I don't see you before, I might see you then.'

'You're bound to.' I smiled back. 'I'll definitely be there.'

'It's a date then,' he said, then panicked. 'Not a date, date! I mean I'll be there and you'll be there . . .'

'Bye, Bear,' I laughed, walking away before he tied himself up into an even tighter knot.

# Chapter 8

As hard as I tried not to, all I could think about was Bear as I unloaded my bag of heavy veg, filled the kettle and reached for my phone to call May and give her the good news about The Chapel. He was an entirely unforeseen preoccupation and a surprising one too. With his scruffy jumper and endearing jumble of words he had somehow managed to jumpstart feelings in me which had long been dormant. Having not looked at a man other than my ex in years it was an interesting sensation, not that I planned to act on it.

We were both only going to be in Norfolk for a short while and I wasn't looking for a casual hook-up. I daresay he wasn't either. I'd watched enough romcoms to know that casual equalled complicated and I needed to keep my life as simple as possible, with no impulsive rebound reactions, as I tried to fathom where my new life was going to take me as well as the work I was going to take on to pay for it.

I stopped dead in my tracks as I realised the turn my thoughts had taken. In the space of literally minutes, I'd leapt from talking pleasantly to someone to telling myself I mustn't leap into bed with them! I really was out of practice if I thought that was how relationships worked.

Poor Bear. For all I knew he could be gay, happily married, have a life partner or be contentedly single. I shook my head as both my traitorous head and heart wished that none of the above would turn out to be the case.

'Hello?'

I was still in a dream world when May answered her phone and I had to give myself a mental shake to get my act together and start speaking.

'Hello?' came her voice again, this time with a frown attached.

'Hi, May,' I said, clearing my throat. 'It's only me, Holly. Sorry, I don't quite know what happened there.'

I did, of course, but I could hardly tell her I'd been imagining . . .

'Holly,' she said smilingly. 'I was hoping to hear from you. Have you had a chance to talk to your friend yet?'

'I have,' I told her. 'And it's good news.'

'Go on,' she urged.

'Lisa was absolutely over the moon when I told her that you'd like to visit The Chapel and be involved,' I said, with no desire to play my neighbour's enthusiastic reaction down.

'She was?' May gasped.

'Of course, she was,' I laughed. 'It's not every day that some-one of May Madison's calibre moves into the neighbourhood and offers you her expertise.'

I supposed she was a bit like Bear really. He was doing Luke a favour with his knowledge in exchange for free parking, and May was offering her know-how in exchange for feeling more settled in her new life. Not that I should still have been thinking about Bear or comparing him to May.

'So,' she said excitedly, 'when can we go?'

'There's a meeting early tomorrow evening,' I told her. 'A crisis meeting to try to get a grip on the Christmas performance which, according to Lisa, needs more than a little fine tuning before it's ready to be presented to a live audience in less than a month.'

'That sounds like a challenge,' said May, clearly thrilled by the prospect. 'I'll be there! I'll book a taxi now. What time?'

'No need for that,' I insisted. 'As I'm going to be helping out too, although in a very different capacity, I can easily pick you up and take you home after.'

'Are you sure?'

'Completely sure.'

'Thank you so much,' she said emotionally. 'I can't tell you what a relief it is to have something so special, and genuine, to tell my son about. I was still bluffing a bit when I saw him yesterday because nothing had been confirmed and I think he knew it.'

'Oh, May.'

'But it doesn't matter now,' she carried on happily. 'Do you know, you've arrived in my life at just the right time, Holly.'

Her words made me well up a bit.

'And you in mine,' I said, thinking of her friendship and Monty's affection and the fact that she'd got me out of an awkward situation with Lisa.

'It's serendipity,' May laughed.

'There's a lot of it about.' I smiled, thinking again of my chance encounter with Bear and how I'd described his meeting both Luke and me in exactly the same way. 'Are you going to have a walk at the lake this morning, May?'

'No,' she said, as if I was mad to even suggest it. 'I don't have time for that. I've got to decide on what I'm going to wear tomorrow and my son is taking me out for lunch later. What about you?'

'No,' I said, 'I'm not going to make it either. Lisa has given me a whole bag full of veg so I'm going to have a go at making soup. What about tomorrow?'

She pondered on the question for a moment.

'No,' she finally said. 'I think I'll give it a miss then, too. I'd like a clear, full day to mentally prepare for the meeting.'

I wondered what that would involve.

'Unless you'd like to?' she then asked.

'No,' I said, even though I could still just as easily go on my own. 'I won't mind giving it a miss again. It is cold, after all.'

'Perhaps you could start your Christmas shopping instead,' she suggested. 'You did say you haven't been to the city yet and the big day is only a few weeks away now, you know.'

'I'll think about it,' I said, rather than telling her that I only had two nephews and a niece to buy for and that I was thinking of sending them either money or a voucher. The nephews seemed to enjoy choosing things for themselves now and the niece would be old enough to do the same soon, too. 'I'll see you tomorrow around half five, okay?'

'Very okay,' she said, 'thank you, Holly.'

Having sent Mum a quick text telling her my current address because I'd forgotten all about it until May mentioned Christmas shopping, I plugged my phone into its charger and then re-boiled the kettle ready to make myself more tea and litres of vegetable stock from the organic cubes I had seen in one of the kitchen cupboards.

I found an easy recipe for soup to follow courtesy of Google and within a few minutes of settling to my task, I was up to my elbows in vegetable peelings. By the time I had haphazardly cut everything into almost similar size chunks, my arms were aching and my hands were sore. The squash had been harder to handle than I had given its inoffensive appearance credit for and I wished I'd started with that.

I set a huge and very heavy cast iron pot on the stove, added the veg along with the stock, seasoning and a pinch of turmeric and set it on a low heat to simmer away. The delicious aroma soon filling the kitchen made up for the peeling and chopping marathon.

'And now I wait,' I sighed contentedly, feeling like a domestic goddess as I gave the pot an occasional stir and set up the hand blender ready to give it all a blitz once it was cooked through.

While I waited for the veg to soften, I sat at the kitchen counter and began to doodle again. I already had almost enough sketches of Monty to fill a book, so I focused on adding more of his new accomplice, Queenie. The mismatched couple made for a fascinating pairing and as I drew, I thought about the rough start the beautiful bull terrier had had in life. It made my blood boil to think that anyone could treat a dog, or indeed any creature, like that, and I dreaded to think how Bear would react if he came face to face with her tormentor.

And there was that man, slipping into my thoughts yet again . . .

'I hope you like carrot and squash soup, May?' I asked, when she opened the door the next day, rather earlier than she was expecting me.

I'd passed on even thinking about a trip into the city because the return of the wet and windy weather hadn't been conducive to going out anywhere. As a result, I'd started to go stir crazy in the house, constantly thinking about Bear and pondering on his relationship status, and consequently I'd turned up at May's ahead of our formerly agreed time.

'That depends,' she said, opening the door wide enough to let me and the bags of filled plastic containers I was carrying in. 'Has it got bits in?'

'Nope,' I said, handing the bags over so I could pull off my boots. Or try to, while Monty skittered around my feet. 'It's been blended to silky smooth perfection.'

'In that case,' she said as I abandoned my footwear and fussed her four-legged friend, 'I love it. And forgive me for asking,' she then said, 'but are you early, Holly, or am I running late?'

'I'm early,' I said, still standing on the mat. 'Is that all right? I was going a bit bonkers back at the house.'

She laughed at that.

'What?' I pouted.

'Nothing.' She grinned, no doubt thinking of my former insistence that I wanted to be left alone. I was pleased that on this occasion she didn't know what I had been thinking about. 'I'm delighted to see your scarf has made a reappearance.'

'It doesn't look as good as when you tied it though, May,' I admitted as I fondled the inexpertly tied knot. 'You're going to have to teach me how to do it properly.'

'I will,' she promised, 'but not right now. Why don't you go and see if you can find space for the soup in the freezer and then let Monty out, while I get changed.'

'I was rather hoping you were going to wear that,' I said, nodding at the glamorous satin vintage dressing robe she was currently wearing.

'Can you imagine?' she giggled. 'No, I've found something far more appropriate.'

While May carried on with her lengthy preparations to leave the house, I sorted the freezer, let Monty into the garden and pottered about. I was sure I could feel my vitamin D levels being topped up as I walked along the sunny hall and into the sitting room.

Having so far only allowed colour to creep into my life as far as my work, I began to wonder if, while I waited to settle on a new home and fill it with pattern and print, I could give my dark wardrobe a rainbow inspired overhaul.

Just like my parents, Piers had always favoured a neutral palette when it came to interior design and, on further reflection, his own wardrobe was rather bland too. No wonder Mum and Dad had taken to him so enthusiastically, but Piers wasn't a determining factor in anything anymore and it was about time I shrugged off the last of his influence.

'Was your son pleased about your association with The Chapel?' I called along the hall as May flitted between rooms.

'He was,' she happily confirmed. 'I tried to play it cool though. I didn't want to big up my involvement too much, just in case things don't work out tonight.'

She sounded a little apprehensive, but I knew she had no need to be feeling any sort of negative emotion or nerves about what was to come.

'You don't need to worry about that, May,' I therefore reassured her. 'When I told Lisa your name, and what you wanted to do, I honestly thought she was going to fall into a dead faint.'

'Well,' said May, sounding somewhat mollified. 'That's good to know. Maybe I have still got it, after all.'

With perfect timing, she chose that moment to reappear and she was a vision. Someone who most definitely had still got it.

'Will I do?' she asked, turning on the spot so I could take in the full ensemble which was made up of a rich jewel coloured layered dress with a handkerchief hem, leggings and knee-high dark aubergine leather boots. Her hair was loosely tied up in a scarf that coordinated perfectly with the dress. 'I've got a lovely lambswool wrap to keep me warm if the place is a bit lacking in heating,' she added, giving a little shimmy. 'These sorts of venues often are.'

'Oh, May,' I exclaimed, taking in her effortless ability to pull off bohemian and arty. 'You look stunning.'

She was quite the chameleon and I wondered what the inside of her wardrobe looked like. A rainbow explosion of indefinable style, I would imagine. One day, when I knew her better, I might ask for a tour.

'Thank you.' She beamed, giving me a little bob.

'Right,' I then said, 'are we all set? We really should get going.'

She handed me her bag while she quickly retied my scarf. The bag was a leather tote, one, she told me, she'd picked up in Italy and had forever. It matched her boots perfectly and was as soft as butter.

'There,' she said, 'that's better. I'll have time to teach you that knot properly another day. Now, what shall we do about Monty?'

'Do you want to bring him with us?' I asked.

I hadn't thought to ask Lisa if he would be allowed.

'On the one hand I do, because he'll steady my nerves,' May told me and I felt further amazed that she still had any. 'But on the other, he does have a tendency to steal focus.'

'From you?' I laughed. 'Never.'

'I'll leave him,' she laughed back, heading to the kitchen to refresh his water bowl.

'I'll do that,' I insisted, when she bent down to pick it up. 'We don't want you to arrive all wrinkled.'

'Um,' she said thoughtfully as she ran a hand over her forehead, 'I have enough of those already, don't I?'

'May Madison,' I sternly responded, 'you don't look a day over forty-five.'

'You minx,' she said, grinning. 'But that's no bad thing because I can't bear the thought of Botox.'

'Me neither.' I shuddered in agreement. 'Or fillers.'

'Come on,' she then said, 'or we really will be late and I don't want anyone thinking I'm a diva.'

The Chapel was easy to find and there was on-site parking right outside the door so May was in no danger of getting ruffled or windswept between the car and the door.

As we walked in, Lisa rushed forwards. 'Oh, my goodness,' she said. 'It really is you.'

Her cheeks were flushed, her eyes bright and for a moment, I thought she was going to curtsy.

'I'm Lisa.' She beamed at May.

'And as you've guessed, I'm May.' May smiled back, holding out her hand and making the many bangles she was wearing jangle.

'Of course, you are.' Lisa giggled, grinning like a loon as she shook it.

'And I'm Holly,' I added, which made us all laugh harder and seemed to settle Lisa's jitteriness.

'Everyone else will be here in a few minutes,' she carried on, ushering us further in.

The inside of The Chapel looked much as it did in the photos May and I had looked at online, but it felt larger and it was wonderfully warm, too. I imagined it was the ideal space for a creative arts centre. I could see there were more rooms leading off the main hall, which had a roomy stage at the back and high windows.

'The other people who are coming . . .' May frowned, sounding all business, as Lisa gave us a quick tour. 'They're not late, are they?'

'Not at all,' Lisa explained, turning pink again. 'I just happened to ask Holly to bring you a few minutes before everyone else was scheduled to arrive so I could have you to myself for a little while.'

May looked thrilled.

'Well now,' she said, squeezing Lisa's arm. 'Aren't you the sweetest? I'm not sure I deserve all this attention.'

'Oh, you do,' Lisa insisted. 'And I'm secretly hoping you're going to save our Christmas production, May. If that's not too big an ask.'

'That would rather depend on the state it's in,' May chuckled.

'Well,' said Lisa, 'you'll soon find out, because everyone will be here to tell you, any minute now.'

'Is there anything I can do?' I offered.

'You could get the kettle on, hon, if you don't mind?'

'Not at all,' I said, eager to blend into the background. 'One brew, coming up.'

I was still selecting mugs when I heard everyone arrive and the cheer that went up echoed through the building and left me in no doubt that May's presence had been well received.

'Can we have three coffees, please?' Lisa said, bustling in

and checking the contents of the biscuit jar. 'As well as the pot of tea.'

'Three coffees coming right up.' I nodded. 'How's it going out there?'

'May's a total hit, of course,' said Lisa, shaking her head. 'I still can't really believe that she's here. Did you say you hadn't known her long?'

'About a week,' I admitted and she burst out laughing.

'Really?'

'Really,' I said, amazed that it had only been that long and wondering if Lisa would work out that I had been going to see May the morning she tried to rope me into harvesting the winter veg. 'Although, it feels like much longer,' I then added. 'May is one of those people you just find yourself falling in love with.'

'I totally get that,' Lisa said, nodding. 'Now, what can I carry?'

When we went back in, everyone had congregated around a table which had been moved into the middle of the room and was already covered in notebooks and files.

'You can take the seat next to May,' Lisa told me. 'And Freddie, if he ever gets here, can sit at the end, as usual.'

I handed out the drinks and took my assigned seat.

'Do you know who everyone is?' Lisa asked me as I'd missed the round of introductions made for May's benefit.

'I think so,' I said, looking around the group. 'We were all at the pub together, although there wasn't much opportunity to chat.'

Sara gave me a little wave from her end of the table.

'We're delighted to have you onboard, Holly,' her partner, Pete, said kindly.

'Not as delighted as you are to see May, though, I'd bet,' I joked.

'Oh, I don't know,' said Eli. 'You can never have too many mugs of tea.'

'As long as you're all aware that's as far as my skills extend,' I told them. 'You won't be getting me up on that stage.'

'Duly noted,' said Lisa, pretending to write that down. 'Now, let's get started. Freddie will have to catch up on his own time.'

I ducked in and out with trays of drinks and more biscuits and caught snatches of the conversation as I came and went. May was writing copious amounts of notes and asking plenty of pertinent questions which had Eli, the official Chapel manager, scratching his head on more than one occasion. I got the impression that she was going to keep everyone on their toes.

'Any chance of another mug of tea?' she quietly asked me, when the meeting was about an hour in and I was discreetly collecting used crockery. 'I think we might be here a good while yet.'

'Of course,' I said. 'Will Monty be all right? I could go and check on him, if you like.'

'No, he'll be fine,' she said, jumping as the door to The Chapel was thrown open with a bang and a suave-looking gentleman in his eighties sauntered in. 'Now,' she said, narrowing her eyes and not sounding at all impressed, 'I wonder who this could be?'

'Don't get up,' the man said with a smile, even though no one had moved. 'Have no fear, the cavalry is here.'

'The cavalry is already here, Freddie,' Lisa loudly responded. 'And you are *very* late.'

'I hope you told someone at the Cavell that you were heading out,' Sara added.

The man, identified as latecomer Freddie, scanned the table as he unwound a long scarf from around his neck and his eyes widened when they reached May. She looked back at him without blinking but I noticed her eyebrows were raised and she looked rather cross to have had the flow of the meeting so loudly interrupted and disrupted.

'Are my eyes deceiving me,' Freddie gasped, as he clutched Pete's shoulder, 'or am I looking into the angelic face of May Madison?'

'Your eyes are not deceiving you, you old fool,' tutted Lisa. 'Though at your age, you probably should be wearing glasses.'

Freddie, who was very dapper and sprightlier than most men of his advanced years, didn't look impressed that Lisa had referred to his age.

'Well, well, well,' he said, releasing Pete and moving around the table. 'May I say what an honour this is?'

'You may,' said May, offering her hand, which he took in his own and kissed rather than shook.

'I'm guessing this seat is for me?' he said, sitting on the empty chair next to her.

'It is not,' said Lisa, shooing him away. 'You always sit at the end, Freddie. That chair's for Holly.'

Freddie only then seemed to notice me.

'Another new maiden gracing us with her presence.' He beamed, turning the full wattage of his smile on me.

Was I really going to blush in response? Apparently, I was. What a charmer!

Lisa rolled her eyes, then diverted him to his chair and told him to be quiet while she quickly brought him up to speed.

'I think I'll go and make that tea,' I said to May, making a hasty exit with the packed tray as Freddie gave her a cheeky wink.

By the time the meeting had drawn to a close, the Christmas

performance was, everyone agreed, in far better shape than it had been just a few hours before. From what I'd been able to gather, the performance was going to be some sort of creative mash up featuring best bits and favourite characters from a few classic pantomimes. Having never been to a pantomime it was all a bit beyond me, but what I did know was that May's fortuitously timed arrival and offer of help meant that no one had to spread themselves or their skills too thinly from then on, and that had already taken some of the stress and pressure off.

May was going to take over the role of director as no one else really felt they were up to the task. Once the title had been reassigned, everyone was willing to admit that they had been blundering along and hoping for the best. I could tell the role was a huge undertaking but I didn't waste my breath asking if May was sure she wanted to take it on, because she was already quite transformed.

'I'll look over the lines,' she said, waving the sheets of script Lisa and her creative writing students had come up with, 'and then start putting the actors through their paces and pulling it all together.'

I had no doubt she would.

'And feel free to tweak it if needs be, May,' said Lisa, which drew gasps from the rest of the team. 'What?' she tutted. 'I don't mind a bit of constructive criticism.'

Cue more gasps followed by laughter.

'We'll carry on with the music rehearsals,' said Beth, pointing between her, Freddie and Pete.

She and Pete had collaboratively written the music and lyrics with the musically gifted attendees and Freddie, who was a whizz on the piano – his words, not mine – had played a part in that, too.

Sara was working on the costumes with Lisa and they were being kept as simple and inexpensive as possible. There was no mention of a set being built, but Eli was sourcing, begging and borrowing props.

'From tomorrow onwards,' May announced, 'I can be here for a couple of hours every day, as well as for rehearsals, just to make sure we're on top of everything.'

'That's so generous,' said Beth.

'And much appreciated,' added Sara.

'It's the least I can do,' she graciously said. 'This performance is going to be a triumph.'

'You've got us all fired up again, May,' Beth said tearfully. 'We'd begun to feel that we'd taken on too much, but I just know you're going to pull us through.'

'You can certainly count on me.' May beamed.

'And me,' twinkled Freddie. 'I won't be able to stay away knowing there's such wonderful company waiting for me here.'

'You're an old flirt, Freddie Fanshawe,' May said bluntly, making everyone laugh, except him. 'If you turn up, I'll put you to work. Make no mistake about that.'

Freddie looked rather taken aback, but not put off.

As everyone else said their goodbyes, I carried the last of the mugs back to the kitchen and set to with the washing up.

'I'll just do these before I run May home,' I told Lisa, who had followed me and proceeded to dry up.

'I'm going to get May's DBS forms filled in tomorrow,' she said as she put everything away. 'There's no way we're letting her go after the Christmas performance.'

'It sounds like it's going to be a lot of work for just two performances.'

'It is,' she agreed, 'but it'll be totally worth it. And I wonder if you might consider carrying on here too, even after Mark gets back. Don't tell him I said this, but your tea is far superior to his.'

'I won't say a word,' I laughed. 'And I'll let you know about carrying on, when I've decided where I'm going to end up living.'

'Of course,' she said. 'He did mention that you were . . .'

'Homeless?'

I said it flippantly, but the word made my stomach lurch.

'I didn't want to say that,' she tutted. 'But thank you so much for filling in here, while you can.'

'I'm only here because you—'

'Nagged?' she suggested. 'What is it my Tamsin says? Mum always gets them in the end.'

'Um.' I smiled. 'Something like that.'

I helped Lisa lift the boxes of Christmas decorations out of a cupboard ready for putting up the next weekend while Freddie, who was seated at the piano on the stage, belted out the Jerry Lee Lewis classic, 'Great Balls of Fire', enthusiastically accompanied by May singing the lyrics.

'It's his signature tune,' Lisa told me, rolling her eyes. 'I don't know how Beth and Sara cope with him.'

'What do you mean?'

'He's a resident at the care home they work in.'

'Rather them, than me,' I laughed, realising that was the place Sara must have been referring to when he arrived.

'They both have side hustles, as well as working there,' Lisa carried on as she plunged her hands into a box of tinsel and pulled out a huge tangled mass. 'As you know, Beth sings in the band with Eli and Pete, and Sara writes fairy stories for children, inspired by the garden at Prosperous Place, which Pete illustrates.'

'Oh,' I gasped, 'I had no idea. How wonderful is that?'

'They're gathering quite a following,' she said. 'And they work really well as a team.'

You only had to see the couple together for five minutes to know that they were a match made in heaven.

'I'll have to look out for their books.' I nodded, wondering if Pete's style of illustrating was anything like mine.

'You should,' Lisa said. 'They're stocked in the indie bookshop in the city and there's a toyshop which takes them now, too, I think. My kids love them, even though they make out they're too old to read them now.'

I wondered if the books might make more thoughtful Christmas gifts for my nephews and niece than the vouchers I had been considering.

'Holly!' Freddie then called. 'Come and join us.'

I shook my head. 'No way,' I told him. 'I can't hold a tune and besides, I need to get May home. She's got someone special waiting for her.'

'Oh yes,' said May. 'I really should go, Freddie, before my young man misses me.'

She hopped down off the stage, leaving Freddie looking crestfallen.

'Always leave them wanting more.' She winked as she sauntered past me and right out of the building.

# Chapter 9

May was in such high spirits that she chatted without drawing breath all the way back to the bungalow and Monty's ecstatic welcome home only added to her upbeat mood. I, on the other hand, although happy with the part I had played at The Chapel, (hot drinks and an endless supply of biscuits were considered a vital component in keeping the creative cogs turning), was in a quieter and more reflective mood.

I had tried to shrug the word 'homeless' off when I had used it to fill in the gap in my conversation with Lisa. Compared to those who were genuinely without a home and had no prospect of finding one, my current 'no fixed address' hiatus was nothing, but it unsettled me nonetheless and when added to my indecision about what I was going to do next on the work front, it felt like a whole lot more than a mere hiccup which would sort itself out if I left it alone for a while.

The realisation that my desire to bring the wonderful words of others to life was still lying dormant rather took me by surprise. It was beginning to feel increasingly likely that my reluctance to pick up where I'd left off meant that its continued absence was to do with much more than the emotional rollercoaster I'd been on during the last year and a half. Having promised to leave my creativity alone to recuperate when I first came to the square, I was now wondering if it might need a gentle prod to kickstart it. Something a little different to get the inspirational juices flowing again.

I downed a couple of painkillers to dull the thumping in my head. 'You've got this, Holly,' I said on an out breath. 'You've got this.'

But, as hard as I tried, after my off the cuff comment to Lisa, I couldn't quite make myself believe that I had.

With May fully immersed in looking over Lisa's script ahead of going back to The Chapel, I walked around the lake on my own the next morning. It didn't feel the same without her and Monty, but I did feel better for striding out and blowing the cobwebs away and after a quick shower and change back at the house, I set off into the city before more unsettling thoughts on any topic had the opportunity to descend. My plan was to hunt down copies of Sara and Pete's books and then treat myself to lunch somewhere in the narrow, cobbled Norwich Lanes.

The city festive switch-on had happened the week before and the shops were already dressed in their sparkling finest for Christmas, which was only to be expected given the date. I lingered longest at the Winter Wonderland scene created in the windows of Jarrolds, and remembered how I had stayed holed up at home alone the year before, brooding over Christmases past and looking at photos of the annual trips to different cities Piers and I had always taken. I hadn't felt in a celebratory mood whilst looking through those at all.

I had fully expected the imminent advent of December this year to feel equally as dismal, but as I explored the city, I soon discovered that I didn't much mind the carolling and the trees, the smell of chestnuts roasting on the market and the extra shoppers flocking to stock up on gifts and indulgent treats.

My desire to re-embrace some festive feeling, even if only in a small way, along with the joys of the season, gave me hope that the other aspects of my life which were still in hibernation might, in time, come back to me too.

'Are these all of the titles in the series?' I asked the assistant, as I pointed at the shelf in the beautiful independent bookshop where I had found the books Sara and Pete had written and illustrated together.

As I had made my way along the shelves, I had found some books featuring my own illustrations too, but I hadn't picked any of those up. Forcing the issue by initiating some sort of book-based exposure therapy might have turned out to be a prod too far in such a public setting and therefore I focused instead on the work of the talented duo who lived just up the road.

'Yes,' the assistant told me, smiling when he saw what I was looking at. 'That's everything they've published so far. I'm hoping there'll be another one to add to the collection next spring and a box set would be wonderful. The couple who creates them lives locally. Did you know?'

'I've just read about that in the bio in the back of this one,' I said, holding a copy up.

I didn't want to get further embroiled by mentioning that I knew Sara and Pete.

'We usually have signed copies,' the assistant carried on. 'But they all sold out over the weekend. Everyone seems keen to get ahead with their Christmas shopping this year and books make such wonderful gifts.'

He didn't need to tell me that, but I admired him dropping it into the conversation.

'You're right.' I nodded.

I flicked through the exquisitely detailed pages, then picked up a copy of each and took them over to the counter. I didn't think Sara and Pete would mind if I asked them to add their signatures the next time I saw them at The Chapel and I smiled at the thought.

'I'll take all of these, please,' I said. 'My nephews and niece will love them.'

My niece, Daisy, was still a bit young to fully appreciate them, but I knew their mum, Maddie, would enjoy reading them to her and these were a huge improvement on the nondescript vouchers or cash alternative I'd previously settled on. I'd save those for when they were teenagers, when I really would have no idea what to get. Assuming it still felt appropriate to be sending them things that far in the future.

'Would you like them gift wrapped?'

'No, thank you,' I said, having a momentary panic over whether it was still okay for me to consider Daisy and her brothers my niece and nephews given that I had been replaced. Something else to think about.

It was lunchtime by the time I'd finished admiring window displays as well as looking in a couple more shops. I had found the perfect Christmas jumper for Monty in one, but couldn't decide what to pick out for May. I hadn't planned to buy gifts for either of them, but I'd always enjoyed giving every bit as much, if not more, than receiving and the vision of Monty looking jaunty in a jumper featuring others of his breed also wearing festive themed outfits, had proved impossible to resist.

One of the grottos I'd walked by even had provisions for dogs to visit Santa and I wondered if May knew about that. I had picked up an information leaflet and added it to my bag to pass on just in case she didn't.

With that done, I headed to a café in the Lanes, which Neil and Mark had taken Piers and I to on a previous visit to the city. It served the loveliest lunches as well as offering a takeaway service. However, when I arrived, I found the place was rammed with lots of other tired shoppers who all had the same idea. One of them I recognised. I could only see him from the back, but it was definitely him.

'Hey, Holly,' said Bear, when he turned around in the queue and spotted me before I could squeeze myself back outside again and find somewhere quieter. He had almost taken out those closest to him with his many bags and parcels and he apologised profusely. Once he'd checked everyone was okay, he turned back to me. 'Are you hoping for a table, too?'

His face was flushed as much with embarrassment as with the cold and I found his calamitous character – unhelpfully, given that I was trying to banish all thoughts of him – even more endearing. His bulk was taking up so much space it was impossible for anyone else to wait inside and as a result a queue had begun to form on the pavement outside.

'Hi,' I said. 'Yes, I am, but I have a feeling I'm going to be out of luck. I didn't expect it to be this busy on a Monday.'

'Me neither,' he said, looking over the heads of everyone and into the rapidly filling seating area.

'No Queenie today?'

Bear laughed at that. His booming baritone drew even more attention, but all I could notice was how his eyes crinkled at the corners when he smiled. It was my turn to colour up again then.

'Thankfully not,' he said. 'Can you imagine? No, it's just me today. Very much just me on my lonesome. Just as it always is when she isn't with me.'

I supposed that, in a roundabout sort of way, answered my question about his relationship status.

'I'm on my own too,' I told him and he nodded and smiled, catching my drift.

By the time everyone ahead of us was either served or seated there was just one table for two left available. Bear jumped at that and kindly offered me the empty seat. I hesitated for a moment and he smiled.

'It's just a space at a table, not a lunch date,' he said, referring back to the muddle he'd got into the last time we'd talked and which I could have taken as proof enough that he was single.

I couldn't help but appreciate that he could laugh at himself and I accepted his offer. The table was towards the back of the café and had just enough room for him to stow his bags and sit down without knocking anything, or anyone else, over.

'Thank goodness for that,' he said, letting out a long breath as he relaxed into his seat and picked up the menu.

'Have you been Christmas shopping?' I asked him, once our drinks had been ordered.

He looked over the top of the menu. He was still deciding what food he fancied and I swallowed in response. On the couple of occasions we'd met before, we'd been standing up. We'd never been properly eye to eye like this and I found his nearness and ability to look straight at me a bit intense.

'Yes,' he said croakily, and I couldn't help but wonder if he felt the same, 'and also stocking up on a few wardrobe essentials. I'm not a fan of shopping so tend to make it an annual event.'

I rolled my eyes at that.

'What?' he asked.

'Well, you couldn't have picked a more stressful time to head to the shops, could you?' I pointed out. 'The world and his wife are out Christmas shopping today.'

'That's true,' he agreed, with a wry smile.

'You'd be better off ordering online.'

'I've tried that,' he sighed, 'but I can never get the sizes right.'

Having been caught out trying to buy for myself online I could understand that. I was an average size twelve but ordering sight unseen could be a risky business and given Bear's generous frame I could imagine that one man's extra-large could well end up looking like a skinny fit on him.

'And in my line of work,' he carried on, 'I'm rarely in one place long enough to make delivery and returns a practical option. I'm better off putting myself through one hellish morning of stripping off and trying on, knowing there's a good lunch waiting as a reward at the end of it.'

I swallowed again, feeling rather shocked by how my body had reacted to the thought of him stripping off and trying on.

'In the spirit of that then,' I suggested, my voice huskier than I intended as I tried to ignore the heat which was building up much further south than my face, 'how do you fancy sharing a bowl of chips as an extra treat for a job well done?'

Given the amount of bags he had, I assumed it had been a morning well spent.

'Oh, good plan,' he laughed. 'You're my kind of woman, Holly.'

This admission caused us both to blush and I was grateful for the timely arrival of the waitress to deposit our drinks and take our food order. We stuck to small talk after that, mostly the weather, but after our sandwiches and extra chips arrived, I let my curiosity get the better of me.

'I hope you don't mind me asking,' I said, as I picked up and dipped a chunky salted chip into the little bowl of thick mayo I'd also requested, 'but I'm intrigued to know more about your work and where you live, Bear.'

'You are?' he asked, sounding surprised, but pleased.

'I am,' I confirmed. 'When you were with Luke you said that you had been looking for somewhere to park your home and that's not something you tend to hear in general conversation.'

'I don't suppose it is.' He nodded, also dipping into the chip bowl, but favouring the ketchup over the mayo. 'But thanks to that serendipitous introduction to Luke, I have been gifted the perfect spot to park it in for the few weeks I'm going to be here.'

'In exchange for helping Freya in the garden, as I recall?' I remembered. 'Have you always worked in garden restoration?'

'Sort of. I started my career as an apprentice gardener with the National Trust,' he told me. 'And worked my way up to head gardener a few years later. Then I worked on the most incredible project with the National Trust for Scotland, restoring a garden that had been bequeathed to the organisation, but not touched for years. It took a long time to restore it to its original glory and I loved every minute of it.'

'But you don't work there or for the Trust now?'

'No,' he said. 'I decided to move on about a year after the project was completed. The maintenance and upkeep was a huge undertaking, but it was bringing the garden back to life that I had really enjoyed. That was what had sparked my creative fire and kept it burning.'

'I see.' I nodded. 'You preferred the challenge of creation and restoration to working on the finished result.'

'That pretty much sums it up,' he agreed. 'I was beginning to feel a bit stuck knowing that I was just going to be going through the same routine year after year as I had been during the time I worked my way towards becoming head gardener. Consequently, I wanted to move on before I lost my love for the job.'

Given my current situation, I could completely relate to that.

'So, what did you do?' I asked.

'Well,' he carried on, 'as a result of the renovation making quite an impact and receiving lots of attention in the world of horticulture, I'd been approached by a couple of private estate and historical home owners who were looking for someone to bring their gardens back to life or, like Luke, restore at least part of them, and so I decided to take the plunge and go freelance to do that.'

'That was brave,' I said. 'I daresay you could have had a job for life if you'd stayed with the Trust.'

'You're right,' he confirmed, 'but at what cost?'

One that he clearly thought was too high. Settling hadn't been an option for Bear and again, I found his situation echoing my own. For the sake of buying a house, I might well end up settling and even though I wasn't convinced that would be the right thing to do, I couldn't imagine there would be an alternative. Or at least if there was, I hadn't yet discovered it.

'So, is that what you do now?' I asked. 'Move around the country from one project to another.'

'That's it,' he said. 'And on occasion I've ventured across the

Channel to work in Europe, too. I've got work lined up in the UK well into the year after next now. All exciting projects that I'm looking forward to getting stuck into, including one in Cornwall in February. I generally take the whole of December to the beginning of February or thereabouts off, because I prefer to work solidly through the spring, summer and autumn when, if I'm lucky, the conditions are better.'

'But this year, you're helping Luke and Freya, which brings us back to the question of where you live,' I said, slowly making sense of it all and feeling rather excited by the thought of it. 'I can't really see you squeezing into a caravan and besides, aren't you ever offered accommodation by the client you're working with?'

'Sometimes,' he said, 'but I prefer to be completely independent. I couldn't really have Queenie if I was staying in someone else's home or in a string of bed and breakfasts and it's much cheaper too, flying solo.'

I hadn't thought of that. He was a genuine nomad and I found the image of him traveling about rather romantic.

'But you're right, Holly.' He smiled. 'A caravan would be a bit of a squeeze for me to stretch out in.'

'So, where do you live then?'

'In a converted horsebox,' he told me. 'It was originally designed to transport six horses and it took me just over a year, on and off, to completely strip it out and design it how I wanted it but I got there in the end and it's my permanent home now. It's quite a size, so a parking spot in the generous grounds of Prosperous Place while I wanted to stay in Norwich, has been a godsend.'

'Oh, wow,' I said, trying to imagine it, 'that sounds amazing.'

'It is,' he responded proudly. 'You're welcome to come and have a look around it, if you like.'

'I might take you up on that,' I said, knowing I wouldn't be able to resist.

'And the best thing about it is,' he further said, and sounded extremely happy about, 'that I'm completely mortgage free and give or take a few of the narrowest roads, I can take my home with me everywhere that I need to go.'

'You know,' I told him, after I'd eaten more of my sandwich and mulled over the incredible work-life balance he'd achieved, 'I envy you.'

He really was all set.

'You do?'

'I do,' I confirmed. 'I'm currently facing a similar predicament about my work to the one you came up against when you worked for the Trust. I still love what I do, but I've fallen out of love with the end result and I have no idea yet what to do about it.'

He put down the half of his sandwich he was eating and looked me straight in the eye.

'You need to do exactly what I did,' he said seriously, making it sound as if it was the easiest thing in the world. 'You need to find a way to carry on doing the bit that you're still in love with, but in a way that makes you happy. Life's too short to get stuck doing the same thing over and over again for the rest of your working days if you've lost the passion for it.'

Had he uttered the word passion in any other context while looking so deeply into my eyes, I might have been tempted to respond quite inappropriately, but given the situation, my reaction was tempered. What Bear said echoed some of what May had pointed out and made total sense but I couldn't think what I could do with my illustrating that would provide a stable enough income stream to satisfy a mortgage provider.

'I know you're right,' I sighed, picking up the second half of my sandwich. 'What you're saying makes sense, but unlike you, I need a new roof over my head and the mortgage to keep it there.'

'You do?'

'I do.' I nodded, deciding to share more of my circumstances with him than I usually would, given that I barely knew him. It was another similarity to my quickly formed friendship with May. 'You see, I'm recently divorced and even though my ex and I had a decent financial settlement, there's nowhere near enough in my bank to buy a house outright.'

'Do you have any dependants?'

'No,' I said. 'No kids. It's just me.'

'And are you restricted to living in a certain area because of your work?'

'Nope,' I said. 'I'm freelance too, so assuming I stick at something related to what I already do, I can work anywhere.'

'And you definitely need a mortgage?'

'To buy a house, yes.'

'But what if you didn't buy a house?'

'If I didn't buy a house' – I frowned – 'then where would I live?'

Bear raised his eyebrows and the penny finally dropped as to which road he was leading me down. Or trying to.

'On a converted bus,' he suggested. 'In a narrowboat or a cabin in the woods—'

I put up a hand to stop him, but to no avail.

'You could own something outright, paid for by your settlement money, and that would really take the pressure off how much money you'd need to have coming in. Obviously, you'd still need an income, but—'

As appealing as the prospect of having the luxury of having to earn less was, he really was barking up the wrong tree.

'I'm not you, Bear,' I jumped in, cutting him off. 'That kind of lifestyle really wouldn't suit me at all.'

'Don't knock it till you've tried it,' he immediately shot back.

'I'm telling you,' I insisted. 'I couldn't do it. I need my space and I need—'

'Please don't say you need possessions.' He groaned.

'Well,' I said, sounding prim. 'I do. I like my things and I'm pretty sure the weight of them would sink a narrowboat.'

'And where are all your *things* right now?' he asked.

'Well,' I said, 'they're in storage.'

'I see.' He grinned. 'And you're feeling all right without them, are you? You're managing to breathe in and out?'

The truth was I hadn't given any of my bits and pieces a second thought since I'd arrived in Nightingale Square, but that didn't mean that I never wanted to set eyes on them again or was willing to give them up.

'I am,' I said. 'But only because I'm having to.'

Bear didn't look convinced.

'Look,' I said, 'I'm just not the type to live that sort of life. I like my home comforts and don't think it's fair that you're judging me for that.'

'I'm not judging you.' He shrugged.

'It feels like you are.'

'I'm sorry,' he apologised. 'That was genuinely never my intention.'

He reached into the bowl at exactly the same time as I did

and our fingers collided. He had hold of one end of the last chip and I had the other.

'If you're really apologising' – I smiled – 'then you should do the honourable thing and let me have the last chip.'

'I do feel bad.' He smiled back, then plucked the chip from my grasp, popped it in his mouth and winked. 'But not that bad.'

'I don't believe you!' I gasped, peering into the empty bowl which had just a few bits of rock salt sitting in the bottom.

'I'm a growing lad,' he chuckled. 'I need my chips.'

'You're a greedy gannet,' I countered. 'You could have gifted me that last chip, given that you've got me all stirred up.'

'I have?' he spluttered, then said again in a deep and very sexy tone, 'I have?'

'Not like that, you idiot.' I blushed, although he had a bit. 'About buying a house.'

'You don't need a house, Holly,' he insisted. 'You need a home.'

# Chapter 10

Having pinched the last chip, Bear insisted on paying for lunch and, as he still had a couple more things to find in the shops and errands to run, we parted company outside the café and I walked back to Nightingale Square alone.

My unexpected lunch date really had got me all stirred up, as I'd put it. Not only had Bear offered me something different to think about on the home front, though I didn't really believe an alternative lifestyle would turn out to be an option for me, but he'd also ignited feelings of further attraction. Feelings that I hadn't honestly expected to ever experience for anyone again, but especially not so soon after everything that had happened with Piers.

I had already had to remind myself since meeting Bear that a casual hook-up wasn't my kind of thing, and knowing that he was heading off to the faraway south-west in the spring should have made me feel even more cautionary. However, feeling certain now that he felt something for me in return made it even harder to resist the temptation to succumb to anything more than a little mild flirting and prolonged eye contact, should the opportunity present itself.

As seemed to be becoming a regular habit, that evening after a bowl of my homemade soup, I sat and sketched while the television jabbered away in the background. I drew just one image: Monty and Queenie, both sporting lifejackets, luminous pink for Monty and orange for Queenie. They were standing aboard a green narrowboat, the top of which was covered in pots full of flowers and growbags of veg. It was much more detailed than the ideas I'd previously come up with and highlighted in bright crayon, too.

As I closed my eyes and imagined what the inside of the boat might look like, I pictured a riot of colour, the vibrant space filled with crocheted blankets, books, houseplants, a tiny pot-bellied stove and of course, dog beds. It was very beautiful, but when I opened my eyes again and refocused, I also knew it was pure fantasy.

I slept right through that night but I dreamt through it, too, and I awoke with a start long before it was light. I had been aboard the narrowboat I had drawn, with Monty and Queenie for company. Piers was outside and kept handing me the boxes from storage, which he'd turned up with in the seemingly endless back of a van.

I kept telling him there were too many, far more than I really had, but he carried on handing them over and I carried on piling them up in the space next to the door. Then, when I eventually opened the door, I found the interior half filled with water and the dogs swimming about. When I turned around to look at Piers, he'd morphed into Bear who was shaking his head. That was the moment I woke in a cold sweat.

It took two very strong cups of coffee and one long, hot

shower before I felt more like myself again. It was now a more sociable hour of the morning and, in spite of the fact that I felt convinced that life inside anything other than four brick walls and under a tiled roof wasn't for me, I set off to Prosperous Place to find out what Bear's version of alternative living looked like.

Having remembered the key code, I quietly skirted around the perimeter of the Grow-Well and after being scared almost to death in the half light by a couple of cats, I found the courtyard where Bear's horsebox home was parked up. It was every inch the size I had imagined when he had described it, which was a perfect match for him and looked very well-maintained.

'Bear,' I hissed, having knocked on the door a couple of times and received no response. 'It's me, Holly. Are you there?'

There was no light inside and the windows were shuttered. With a deep sigh and heavy heart, I made my way back to the square. I was initially disappointed to have been thwarted in my visit but then relieved. Given the early hour, Bear might have answered in his PJs, or less, and I couldn't be sure how I would have reacted to the sight of him looking all sleepy, tousled and still warm from his bed . . .

I decided I would head to May's instead and tempt her out for a walk. My raging libido would be far better behaved in her presence.

'Holly,' May said, beaming, when I arrived at the bungalow and presented her with a bag from Blossoms which was becoming a customary treat. 'How wonderful to see you. Now, come in out of the cold and tell me what you've been up to. I know it's only been a day, but given all the excitement, it feels like so much longer.'

I made the usual fuss of Monty, who I was relieved to see wasn't wearing a lifejacket, then pulled off my boots and handed May my coat. Her mouth fell open, just as I had imagined it would.

'Oh, Holly,' she spluttered, 'you're a vision!'

'Am I?' I grinned, smoothing down the pocket of the bright red hoodie I was wearing.

'You really are.' May laughed. 'It's not yours though, is it?'

'No,' I admitted. 'It's my friend Mark's. But the socks are mine,' I added, wriggling my toes.

I'd spotted a pair of bright red polka dot socks while shopping the day before and found them impossible to resist. It was only a small start to adding some colour to my wardrobe, but a start nonetheless.

'I'm impressed,' said May, nodding in approval.

'Good,' I agreed, then noticed she was looking at me a bit weirdly. 'What?' I asked, checking I hadn't spilled anything down myself.

'There's something else . . .'

'Not coffee, I hope,' I said, still checking. 'Mark will skin me if I ruin this. I know it cost him a fortune because I remember him going on about it.'

'It's not the hoodie,' said May. 'It's you.'

'Me?' I frowned. 'What about me?'

'You're all sparkly,' she said.

I'd never been described as sparkly before.

'Have you met someone?' she then immediately pounced, far too astutely for my liking.

'I went into the city yesterday,' I blagged, 'and I met loads of people there.'

'That's not what I—'

'Come on,' I interrupted. 'Otherwise, these rolls will be cold.'

'All right,' she relented. 'And after you've told me what you got up to yesterday, I'll fill you in about my first day at The Chapel.'

At the mention of the place, she was off and running and her monologue ran right the way through an entire pot of tea and both the breakfast rolls. I didn't mind her lengthy explanation as it saved me from having to talk about my trip into the city. I didn't feel prepared to even mention Bear's name in front of May because I just knew she'd hone in on my feelings with dogged determination and I wasn't ready for an in-depth interrogation as to what was going on with me. In truth, I probably wouldn't be ready for that until he'd headed off to Cornwall, assuming he left before I did.

Once we'd finished eating and May had run out of steam, I suggested going for our usual walk.

'I'd not planned on going out this morning,' she told me as she put our empty plates into the dishwasher, 'because I'm due back at The Chapel later and that's a bit of a trek in itself.'

'How about I drive us to the lake,' I suggested, handing her the mugs, 'and then on to The Chapel after? I'm happy to stay on today and I'm sure someone will want a cup of something at some point.'

'Oh, that would be wonderful,' said May, clapping her hands while Monty yipped and chased his tail. 'I know that there's plenty to be getting on with, so the more the merrier.'

'That's settled then.' I smiled, feeling light-hearted as well as happy to know that I could be of some use. I also hoped that helping would stop me brooding, daydreaming, fantasising, call it what you will. 'And I can pop back to check on Monty later if you wanted to stay longer today too, May.'

'No need,' she said. 'He's coming with me from now on.'

'Oh,' I said, 'how wonderful is that? So, tell me, Monty, what are you going to wear today as you're treading the boards?'

Monty yipped again.

'I have something far better suited to the occasion than his acting outfit for today,' May trilled, rushing out of the kitchen.

Monty cocked his head and I shrugged.

'Here,' she said, whizzing back in a minute later. 'You get him in this while I get changed and then we'll be off.'

'Oh Monty,' I laughed, unfolding and holding up a red hoodie, which was a perfect match for the one I was wearing. 'It must be a twin thing!'

The walk around the frosty lake was bracing, but by then I was in such a good mood, I didn't much mind the temperature or the sting of the wind. May put me in charge of Monty's lead and, having insisted I kept part of my coat undone so Mark's hoodie was on display, we drew many an admiring glance.

I'd remembered the leaflet I'd picked up about dogs visiting Santa in his grotto and May, having not heard of it, was keen to book her beloved boy a spot to collect a present and have his photo taken with the big man.

'He could wear his hoodie,' she excitedly suggested, and although I agreed, I was already wondering if I should gift him his festive sweater before Christmas Day. 'And he's been such a good boy this year, I'm sure he's on the nice list, so there shouldn't be any awkwardness.'

We'd almost thawed out on the drive to The Chapel but the warm welcome we received when we walked in defrosted us completely.

I hadn't been expecting Lisa to be there, but once she and May had air kissed and Monty had been fussed over, she turned to me. 'Well, hello you,' she said. 'Are you staying, Holly, or just dropping our celebrity off?'

May rolled her eyes, but I could tell she was pleased with the attention. Apparently, I wasn't the only one who had been transformed recently.

'I'm staying,' I said, as May went to get Monty settled in the bed that she'd carried in with her. 'That is, if there's anything for me to do?'

'You know, there's always something to do,' Lisa laughed. 'But what about all the work you told me you had lined up?'

I waved her words away, unable to come completely clean and admit there was none.

'It's all in hand,' I told her, thinking that the dog doodles could take care of themselves while I got stuck into something else for a while.

'In that case,' she said, sounding thrilled, 'why don't you go and put the kettle on? Eli's in the kitchen.' She then lowered her voice a little. 'He used to be a barista, you know, so the coffee isn't a problem, but he's useless at making tea.'

With drinks made, I then made a beeline for Sara, who was set up on the stage and working on a couple of the costumes before she headed off for her next shift in the care home.

'I found your books in the city yesterday,' I told her as I handed her a mug and she stirred in a spoonful of sugar.

'You did?' she said, her cheeks turning prettily pink. 'How did you know about them?'

'Lisa told me.'

'Of course, she did.' She laughed.

'I bought the lot,' I elaborated, 'to send as Christmas presents. I was wondering if you and Pete would mind signing them.'

'Oh, my goodness!' she gasped. 'That's so kind.'

'I couldn't resist them,' I told her. 'They're absolutely lovely and the assistant in the bookshop told me they'd sold out of copies so you might want to go in and ask them to quickly restock while people are Christmas shopping.'

'That's fantastic,' she said, 'but I don't want to be pushy and they might have ordered already.'

'No harm in checking though,' I told her. 'You could sign the new stock if they have already filled the shelves. You have to be pushy in publishing, you know.'

'Lisa is always telling me that,' she said, putting down the dress she was hemming in favour of drinking the tea. 'But how come you know what the industry is like, Holly? Do you work in publishing, too?'

'Sort of,' I explained. 'I have a different style, but I'm in the same line of work as Pete.'

'You're an illustrator?' Sara smiled.

'Of children's books, yes.' I nodded.

'Well, I never,' she said, in wonder. 'What are the odds of that? Which books? Any big names?'

'A few,' I said modestly. 'Have you heard of the Baby Bee series? I've recently finished the last one of those, which comes out next summer.'

I didn't tell her that as much as I had loved bringing the words to life, I was now ducking out to make way for something different. *Possibly* ducking out, I mentally corrected. If I couldn't come up with a way to pay the prospective bills soon, I'd have to dive back in.

'No way,' said Sara, her eyes shining. 'We love that series. We don't have kids ourselves, but when you're in the same line of work, you're naturally drawn to read and look at every title you can lay your hands on, aren't you?'

It had been a while since I had read or looked at anything beyond the pages I was illustrating, but my own enthusiasm would have matched Sara's once. It was further proof that I had lost the passion.

'I don't know how you do it though,' Sara then said with a little shudder.

'Do what?'

'Share a project,' she said. 'I don't mean to come across like a total control freak, but the thought of anyone other than Pete drawing the pictures to accompany my words just freaks me out.'

'Hm, I've never really thought about it like that.'

'Maybe it's an author thing.' She shrugged. 'Haven't you ever created an illustration for someone and then wanted to use it to tell a different story?'

'No,' I said, 'thankfully not.'

I didn't tell her that I had once written a story to accompany some of my own illustrations and the reception it'd received had crushed all thoughts of including the keyboard in my professional toolkit. I'd secretly been quite pleased with what I'd come up with, but had kept it to myself. Unfortunately, however, Piers had found it, read it and was so scathing about it, I had been mortified.

'Best stick to the artwork,' he had laughed, handing back the pages of my first attempt at a story. 'At least you know what you're doing with a paintbrush.'

It wasn't like him to be cruel, so I knew my efforts must have been really bad and I'd told myself I'd never stray from the path of illustrating again.

That said, as my mind tracked back to my doggy doodles in light of what Sara had just asked, I felt a rush of protectiveness towards them. In the past I would have handed them over on spec, but Monty and Queenie felt very much like they were mine in a way I had never experienced before.

'Well.' Sara smiled, handing me her empty mug and picking the dress up again. 'Maybe one day you'll create an image you won't be able to resist writing about.'

'Perhaps I will.' I swallowed, feeling a little dazed as I wondered if this was the day.

As I loved my images of Monty and Queenie so much, would I be able to find the words to do them justice? Could I possibly describe their antics and adventures in a story to accompany them? Not according to my ex-husband, but perhaps it was time I stopped giving Piers's former comments the continued power to put me off trying.

'But for now,' I carried on, refocusing on the task in hand, 'I've got plenty to do here, so—'

'Oh, Holly,' Sara then gasped, putting the dress down again, 'exactly how much have you got to do here, right now?'

'Well, I'm on tea duty, at the moment,' I told her, 'but I know Lisa will soon rope me into something else. Why?'

'Is there any chance,' she said, crossing her fingers and looking hopeful, 'that you'd consider helping Pete with the posters and flyers for the show? He's really swamped at work and struggling to find the time to finish them.'

'But if he's already started them—'

Given what she'd just said about control, I wasn't sure he'd want me taking over and more to the point, I wasn't sure I wanted to. The posters and flyers needed to be spectacular to sell tickets and draw the audience in. There really was a lot riding on them and I didn't want the responsibility of creating something that had to be capable of that.

'He wouldn't mind,' Sara insisted, in spite of my hesitation. 'In fact, he'd be thrilled. It would be a weight off his mind. What with sorting the music for the show, rehearsals *and* lining up gigs for our band on top of running the shop . . .'

'What shop?'

'He runs On the Box,' she explained. 'It's a shop that sells film and TV merch and memorabilia, along with figures and clothes and stuff.'

I remembered the last time I'd seen him, Pete had been wearing a *Fellowship of the Ring* T-shirt. A well washed, vintage one.

'Of course,' I said. 'I bet it's his dream store.'

Sara laughed. 'It is,' she said. 'And he's worked there forever. He started as Saturday help and worked his way up to manager. It's Mecca for geeks and they visit from all over as well as buying from the online shop. Pete imports the craziest stuff. Apparently, it's cool to be a nerd now. Oh,' she added, 'and we're part of the local historical re-enactment group too.'

'What with all that, and your own books to work on, you really are swamped,' I said, biting my lip.

'We are,' she agreed, 'but it's great though. Life's too short to waste time doing nothing, isn't it?'

I thought about the original plan I'd had for the start of my time staying in Nightingale Square and how keen I had been to do nothing. Even though I knew the value and importance of taking a break, for me, on this occasion, it hadn't worked out. Thankfully, meeting May and now helping in The Chapel had redressed the balance, even if it hadn't so far helped me settle on my future, but there was still time to sort that.

'It is.' I nodded. 'And in the spirit of that,' I added, taking a big breath, 'and if Pete agrees, I will help with the posters and flyers.'

Just a few minutes later, I was furnished with directions and heading off on foot to the shop with Monty on his lead for company. Sara had called ahead to tell Pete what she had in mind and he was more than happy to go along with her suggestion.

He was just putting the finishing touches to a display of Manga figures in a huge glass cabinet when I arrived.

'You,' he said seriously when I walked in, 'are an absolute lifesaver. Are you sure you don't mind finishing them?' He didn't give me time to answer. 'I had no idea we were in the same line of business. Although, your work is really famous and mine—'

'Is enchanting,' I cut in. 'I have copies of the books to give to my nephews and niece for Christmas, so I know what I'm talking about.'

Pete blushed as deep as his boots and shrugged.

'Sara seems to like them,' he said, sounding smitten. 'And who is this?' he asked, bending to give Monty a fuss.

'May's dog, Monty,' I told him.

'I love your hoodie, Monty,' Pete said. 'You and Holly are a matching pair today.'

I laughed at that.

'Don't let May hear you say that.' I smiled as the realisation landed. 'Otherwise she'll be wanting to coordinate our wardrobes every day and I can't rock a sou'wester like Monty, here.'

Pete looked thoughtful for a moment. 'Matching pet cosplay . . .' he then muttered, drifting off.

Monty looked up at me and I laughed, imagining the two of us walking around the lake, dressed in the spacesuit I had drawn.

'So, about these posters,' I said, bringing both myself and Pete back to earth.

'Yes,' he said, giving himself a shake. 'I've got the lettering done, literally spelling out all of the details. Time, date, venue, ticket prices and so on, but it's the decorative flourishes which will really make the thing stand out that I haven't found the headspace for.'

He showed me what he'd completed so far. The details were all beautifully drawn up and centred but there were no embellishments to – like he had said – make them really stand out and draw the paying audience in.

'Have you had *any* thoughts about the border?' I asked him, hoping he might at least have had the tiniest kernel of an idea.

'Not a single one,' he admitted. 'Until yesterday, there was still some uncertainty as to what was definitely going to make it into the final show and in the short time since the decisions have been made, I've had no chance to come up with anything. I was going to try to find the time to ring Lisa this afternoon and ask ...'

Just then the shop bell rang out. Pete served the customer who was collecting an order and then the phone rang. Monty was starting to get fidgety as another customer came in the moment Pete ended the call.

'Sorry,' he apologised, looking a bit stressed.

'It's fine,' I told him. 'It's good that you're so busy and I can certainly see why it's a squeeze trying to fit in working on these on top of everything else. How about I take them with me now? I'll ask Lisa for a better description of the performance, then I can work on them this afternoon.'

'Are you sure you don't mind?' he asked, sounding as hopeful as Sara had when she'd first come up with the idea.

'Not at all,' I told him and I meant it.

I was invested now, especially having seen first-hand how pushed for time he was.

'You really are an angel,' he said, giving me a high five.

'Well, I don't know about that,' I told him, while pretending to polish an imaginary halo, 'but I'll see what I can do.'

Monty lifted his leg at the first available stopping point as we walked back to The Chapel and I was relieved he hadn't done it in Pete's shop.

'Come on,' I said in a singsong voice, which I hoped would encourage him to keep walking.

His little legs had already run a marathon, what with the walk around the lake and the trip to On the Box, but I didn't have enough hands to carry him and the paperwork Pete had given me. I imagined Monty with a thought bubble over his head, his plan to snooze the rest of the day away amusingly expressed.

'It's not far now,' I told him, striding out.

Back at The Chapel, I discovered Sara had filled everyone in on what my profession was, along with what I was now planning to do to help.

'You're a dark horse,' said Lisa, giving me a nudge. 'I had no idea you worked in publishing too.'

'There was no reason for it to come up.' I shrugged.

It made me sigh to think that they had all known about the more personal details of my private life, but had no idea how I made a living. Was that amusing or exasperating? I couldn't decide and didn't have time to ponder, so let it go.

'There's still so much space to fill.' Lisa frowned, as she looked at what Pete had drawn up so far. 'Are you sure you can spare the time to squeeze this in, with your other work commitments?'

'Yes.' I nodded. 'Don't worry about that. I'm sure I can manage. I might even get them finished today, if I put my mind to it.'

Now I had a plan and something I could actually do buzzing about in my head, the concern in her voice didn't make me feel quite as guilty as it would have before.

On the walk to and from the shop, I had mulled over my conversation with Sara and, having determinedly set Piers's reaction to my attempt at storytelling aside, I had decided that the dynamic duo of Monty and Queenie were going to become a proper project featuring both images and words.

I still had enough time to allow the fledgling idea to slowly take shape and without the current pressure of having to work to pay any bills, I would just . . . play. I would put the hours in, but enjoy them and see what happened. And if, at the end of the day, it was a total disaster, I would be the only person who knew about it, and at least I would have tried.

Having made the decision, I could feel my heart starting to race. This was a thrilling prospect. Not only was I brightening up my wardrobe, I was also daring to branch out profession-ally. Colourful socks and writing a story might not mean much to anyone else, but they felt like monumental strides forward to me.

'In that case' – Lisa nodded and grinned – 'I'll let you get to it.'

She gave me a script which she explained was a clever combi-nation of elements from *Cinderella* and *Robin Hood* with a dash of *Aladdin*, and then together we picked out a few prominent things which were going to either raise what she called a classic panto laugh or impress the audience and could be easily incorporated. It was time for lunch by then so after a feast of sandwiches and brownies from Blossoms, I settled down to an afternoon of filling in the gaps around the words Pete had already written.

I let my mind wander and I drifted with the creative flow. It was a complete surprise to later discover how quickly the time had flown by.

'I really love the guitar,' said May, pointing out the red Fender acoustic guitar I'd included as I gingerly stretched my neck and rolled my shoulders.

I'd been sitting in the same position for far too long, but the stiffness that had built up made me feel good – it was proof that I had been utterly absorbed. It was something I hadn't felt for a very long time while sitting at my desk in my former home studio.

'Red's your colour today, Holly,' May further said, as she patted my shoulder.

'And I love the fabulously flamboyant Dame,' chuckled Lisa. 'You've captured them perfectly, eyelashes and all.'

A local drag artist had agreed to act as compere for the evening and was supplying their own traditional panto dame costume, but with extra embellishments. I'd searched for photos of them online and then positioned them between the lamp from *Aladdin*, Cinderella's lost shoe and a couple of sprigs of holly.

'And the bells are great too,' joined in Eli, who also came to look over my shoulder.

'I had no idea you were so talented.' May beamed.

'Well.' I shrugged, feeling a bit flustered by all the attention, but also pleased that everyone seemed to like what I'd come up with. 'Everyone has something they can do well, don't they?'

'You're right,' said Lisa. 'And some of us are lucky enough to do it full-time. Now, who fancies fish and chips?'

Though I hadn't planned to, I decided I would stay for the evening and watch the rehearsal. That way, I wouldn't have to turn out again to run May and Monty home and, when Pete

arrived, I was able to talk him through the additions I'd made
to his flyers and posters.

'They're fantastic!' he gushed, when I handed them over.
'That Dame is such a triumph, Holly. Totally brilliant!'

The Dame was certainly proving popular and I could
immodestly admit, the images had all turned out rather well.

'Now they're finished, I'll get them off to the printer tomorrow,' Pete said.

'You don't want to add anything else?' I asked. 'Maybe tweak
them a bit?'

'Nope,' he said flatteringly. 'You've nailed them. Absolutely
no tweaking required.'

I was delighted about that.

There was a sudden crash and a collective chorus of groans
from the stage.

'I keep losing my mark!' screeched one of the young actors
who had collided with their neighbour. 'We really need something here to represent a tree, otherwise it looks like I'm hiding
behind thin air!'

'I know it's hard with no set and only a couple of props,' Lisa
tried to say soothingly as May rushed around, manoeuvring
everyone back to where they should be standing. 'But we will
be getting more. Props, that is . . .'

'We need a set,' tutted another young thespian. 'We're
going to look ridiculous otherwise. It's supposed to be a proper
Christmas performance, not improv!'

Lisa ran a hand through her hair while May checked everyone's correct positions. They were all nowhere near where they
had been when they'd collided.

'I'm well aware of that,' said Lisa, sounding frustrated, 'but sets cost money and now costumes and props have been sorted, we're woefully lacking in funds.'

I'd imagined what a simple set could look like when I'd read the script and knew it wouldn't necessarily take much to make a huge difference. Some sheets of MDF, a sketched backdrop, a few pots of paint and they'd soon be in business. A few basic but well-placed set pieces would give the cast something to act off and do no end of good for the overall aesthetic too.

'We really are doing the best we can, guys,' Lisa further said, sounding upset.

'And so are all of you,' said May, clapping her hands and rallying the troops. 'There's still plenty of time to polish this performance and I wouldn't put my name to anything that wasn't shined to a bright finish, so come along. Where were we?'

I felt my feet move towards the stage without my really meaning them to and then the words were out of my mouth before I'd even started to think them through.

'I could try to come up with some sort of set, if you like,' I offered, my legs wobbling beneath me. 'I don't think it would take too much to create an impact and give these guys something other than each other to bounce off.'

The actors gasped and looked thrilled by my suggestion, but May and Lisa were understandably more cautious.

'We really would be operating on a shoestring,' Lisa said quietly.

'And having been through the books with Eli' – May backed her up – 'I can confirm that.'

'Let me know how much there is in the pot,' I told the pair, feeling that I couldn't back out now, even if there was only enough money available to create and paint one spindly tree.

'And I'll see what I can do. I've never worked on a set before, but how hard can *trompe l'oeil* really be?'

Really, really hard probably especially given that I would be upscaling from working on picture book size images to metres and metres of fabric, and that was just for the backdrop. I chewed my bottom lip and glanced around. Well, I'd offered now and, looking at the excitement and hopeful expectation on the young actors' faces, I would just have to give it my best shot.

'Well,' said Lisa. 'Perhaps . . .'

'I'm sure we could beg and borrow some tools and other kit to work with from someone you know,' I recklessly carried on. 'And if I paint a few generic pieces, like some trees for example, you could use them again. Or maybe hire them out to local schools.'

That was perhaps taking faith in my ability to pull it all off a little too far.

'The only real sticking point—' I further mused.

'Apart from the money,' said May.

'Apart from the money,' I repeated, 'is people power. I know you guys are pushed to the limit right now but it would be really good to have another pair of hands to help me if this comes off. Preferably ones who know their way around power tools . . .'

As I said that, my offer to further pitch in sounded rather less doable to my ears. It was highly unlikely that, this close to Christmas *and* the performance, we'd find someone with spare time on their hands. However, the sudden smile lighting up May's face suggested she might have an idea.

'Leave the people power to me,' she said mysteriously. 'I happen to know just the person.'

# Chapter 11

I was tired out by the time I arrived back in the square, but contentedly so. After dropping May and Monty off, I had stopped at a supermarket and picked up a few essentials: a bottle of wine, a lined notebook, a large glue stick and a cheap but cheerful sketchbook being the four most important items in the trolley.

After a quick shower, I poured a chilled glass of the wine, which I felt I thoroughly deserved. Then, after jotting down a few ideas for the potential Christmas performance set, I settled down to pasting the doodles and more detailed drawings I'd made of Monty and Queenie into the sketchbook. I left room around each of them to add a few words and make a few notes.

Buoyed up by my earlier conversation with Sara, and determinedly not worrying about whether or not I could do it, I added explanations and key words to each, starting with the sketch of Monty in his sou'wester. If this was how it felt to play with an idea, as opposed to immediately turning it into something with a specific purpose, outcome and conclusion such as my parents and even Piers to a certain extent, had always encouraged me to aim for because it was the way they worked, then I liked it. I liked it very much.

The themes of acceptance and understanding came to the fore around the first sketch and respect and kindness wove their way around the image of Queenie with some of her scars more prominently displayed. I wasn't sure if it was the wine that freed up my creativity and quietened the internal chatter, but by the end of the evening, I had a whole story mapped out featuring the two intrepid adventurers, who I imagined had been thrown together after being singled out and mistreated by their peers. Having then joined forces, they travelled about, overcoming prejudice and fear and righting wrongs wherever their paws landed.

I pictured the story and sketches in a beautiful finished book that would appeal to both children and adults alike, and wondered if my dreaming could result in a real-life manifestation, preferably one that wasn't ushered in via an impending deadline or in a stifling time specific way. The books could even end up forming an entire series rather than just one title. I then realised I'd probably had one glass of wine too many and decided to go to bed.

I wasn't quite up with the lark the next morning. Over a virtuous breakfast of porridge sweetened with Grow-Well honey, I decided it was most likely too late to catch Bear in his horsebox home, but I might find him working in the garden. I knew he, and the feelings I held for him, were a complication I didn't really need but for some reason that morning I felt as compelled to seek him out as the bees were to go in search of the summer flowers from which they made the honey I was currently enjoying.

As I walked around the vast lawn and along the gravel path to find him, he saw me. 'Holly!' He beamed.

I had been right about him working in the garden, but as I wasn't familiar with the layout of the grounds it had taken me a while to spot him. It was the sound of a spade hitting the earth that eventually led me to him in a tucked away corner. Freya was there too and Queenie was curled up on Bear's coat, which he had abandoned on the path having obviously worked up a sweat. It was a look that suited him and did nothing to temper my enthusiasm for him.

'Hey,' I said, feeling a bit awkward as I realised I didn't actually have a specific or well thought out purpose for my impromptu visit. I had just wanted to see him.

'I don't suppose you've got a flask of coffee hidden anywhere about your person, have you?' Bear grinned as he checked the height of a line which was attached to a wooden peg and marked out a pattern I couldn't decipher. 'I'm parched.'

He seemed completely relaxed and at ease. There was no hint of his tongue being tied and I wondered if that was because he was in his happy natural habitat. My thoughts drifted off for a moment as I imagined including him in the sketches I'd made of the dogs.

'Afraid not,' I said, when I realised that I hadn't answered. 'But I could probably rustle some up in the bothy.'

'You don't have to do that. I can make some in my office,' offered Freya. She checked the time and scraped mud off her boots on the top of the spade she was holding. 'I've got an order I need to chase and there's bound to be someone available who I can phone and nag about it now. I won't be long.'

I felt my face redden as I wondered if she was making herself scarce on purpose. She had cast a curious glance between the two of us before heading off to her office.

'So,' I said before a silence had a chance to settle, 'how are you getting on?'

'Great,' said Bear, running a hand through his hair which, because he was hot, made it stand up in a sort of softly curled crest. 'We've traced the outline now and marked out most of the design, so it won't be long before we can start reinstating it.'

He sounded absolutely thrilled and I marvelled at his ability to get so excited about bare soil, wooden pegs and string.

'And what exactly is it that you're reinstating?' I asked.

'Sorry,' he laughed, shaking his head which made some of the crest collapse. 'Luke found some archive photos of the garden and discovered that there was once a knot garden here. That's what we're recreating. Or I should say, what Freya will be recreating,' he corrected. 'I won't be here long enough to see it planted up, which is a shame because it's going to be fabulous. Here, look.'

He pulled his phone out of his back pocket. After scrolling for a few seconds, he showed me the black and white photos Luke had found that illustrated how the part of the garden we were standing in used to look.

'So, that's a knot garden.' I nodded.

'It is. They're an enclosed formal design feature, laid out with an intricate internal pattern,' Bear further explained. 'Their history can be tracked right back to the sixteenth century.'

'Wow,' I said, suitably impressed. 'This one isn't that old though, is it?'

'No,' said Bear, 'nowhere near.'

'It looks quite complicated.'

'They all take some thinking about.' He smiled, staring at the image on the screen. 'The low hedges which form the shape of the design will be kept closely trimmed and the internal beds all filled with herbs and aromatics, like lavender and thyme. It's going to smell amazing.'

He smelt amazing. I tried my best not to breathe in too much of his seductive scent which had my senses tingling.

'Some people prefer to fill the beds with summer bedding and spring bulbs which can be striking too,' he further said. 'But Luke wants to replicate what we can see on these images.'

I looked back at the muddy laid out area with fresh eyes and wished we were both going to be around long enough to see it come into its own.

'It's going to be stunning,' I breathed.

'I'm glad you think so.' Bear smiled, clearly pleased with my reaction.

'But why would someone get rid of it in the first place?'

'Well, they involve quite a bit of maintenance so I daresay that could have been a deciding factor. These old places used to have teams of gardeners looking after them but as the world changed and staffing levels dwindled, some things, such as more labour-intensive features like these, were sacrificed.'

'That's a real shame,' I said, then gave him a nudge, 'but it keeps you in business putting them back for people who now want to reinstate them, doesn't it?'

'I suppose it does,' he laughed again and looked down at me. 'I've been thinking about you.'

'You have?' I squeaked.

'Yes,' he said, putting his phone away and leaving me with no choice but to move away again. 'I have.'

It would have been weird to stay standing so close to him when he didn't have anything else to show me.

'You're not going to try to talk me into parting with my possessions again, are you?' I asked, pretending to frown.

'No.' He smiled. 'I don't think you're quite ready for a complete decluttering yet, do you?'

'Definitely not,' I agreed, but was amused to note that he considered that there could be a time when I might be.

I pushed away the thought of the pretty narrowboat I'd imagined and also drawn. As beautiful as it had been in my waking mind, my dream state had presented it in a completely different light and not a good one.

'Although the offer still stands to come and have a look around my place,' he reminded me.

I didn't tell him that I'd already called around once but he hadn't been home.

'And I'm definitely going to take you up on that,' I said instead. 'So, if it wasn't reducing the things I love to the size of a couple of suitcases, what was it that you were thinking about?'

Before he had a chance to answer, Freya came back carrying a tray with two huge mugs of coffee on it. I guessed that was my cue to leave them to it. I'd have to ask him again another day.

'Don't rush off,' Freya said as I made a move to go. 'These are for you two. I'm still waiting to get through about that order.'

'Oh, thank you, Freya,' I said. I was happy to stay put. 'I could do with warming up.'

I took one of the drinks and Bear picked up the other. The mug didn't look oversized in his hand at all.

'Yeah, thanks, Freya,' he said, raising it. 'I really needed this.'

Once she'd gone again, I steered the conversation back to Bear thinking about me. It was a far from unpleasant thought and one I was happy to hear more about.

'Well,' he said, shuffling about a bit as the tongue-tied version of him popped back up for a visit, 'I suppose I was just wondering, given that I know you're here on your own, if you've been able to properly talk to anyone about this conundrum you mentioned that you're facing with your work.'

That was sweet of him but not at all what I had expected him to come out with. Truth be told, I was still feeling shocked that I had said anything about it to him at all. I didn't generally go in for sharing confidences, especially with someone who was practically a stranger, but just like my other new friend, May, Bear had somehow unlocked something in me.

'Having been there myself,' he carried on, 'I know how much headspace this sort of thing can take up. I've realised now that when you brought it up in the cafe, I railroaded you into thinking about where you should live, rather than discussing with you how you might find a new way to earn your living from the work you used to love.'

Thinking back, he had got a bit carried away.

'Alternative living is a pet subject of mine,' he clarified, in case I hadn't worked it out. 'But you needed someone to bounce ideas off and I rather missed my cue. I told you what I thought you should do, but offered no help as to how you might find a way to do it.'

He sounded cross with himself, but he was making too much of it.

'You really didn't miss anything,' I insisted.

'So have you got anyone to talk to?' he asked. 'What about your parents?'

I had to smile at that. 'Believe me,' I told him, 'they're the last people I could talk to about it.'

'Oh,' he said, sounding surprised, and I guessed he was close to his.

'We don't get on.' I swallowed. 'We're completely different in every conceivable way. They don't understand me and I certainly don't get them. All I'm capable of doing as far as they're concerned is making life choices which disappoint them.'

'I'm sorry,' said Bear, but I bowled on before he told me if he was apologising for bringing them up or sorry that we didn't get on.

'They've never understood my chosen profession. I'm an artist by the way, well, an illustrator and they're both academics with successful, carefully curated careers. I couldn't go to them with anything resembling an issue with work even if I wanted to. Which I don't. And added to that,' I said, barely drawing breath, 'they think I'm a failure as a woman too, because I don't want children and allowed my marriage to fail as a result. Even though Piers and I were in complete agreement that we didn't want a family when we got married . . .'

I was properly out of puff then and as I took a breath and looked at Bear, I found him blinking at me and looking completely dazed, which was hardly surprising.

'Oh God, I'm so sorry,' I apologised, feeling embarrassed by the depth and length of the sudden unburdening. 'I have absolutely no idea where that total overshare came from.'

'No apology necessary,' he said, kindly trying to save my blushes. 'It's the caffeine. Freya makes a potent, fully loaded coffee. You should see me working after she's kept me plied with this stuff for a few hours. I'm practically superhuman.'

I could well believe that. Even without the caffeine. He certainly had a knack for drawing things out of me that I'd usually keep private and that alone was a superhuman skill as far as I was concerned. I didn't show him my mug to make the point that I hadn't touched my coffee yet.

'You're right.' I nodded instead, latching on to the excuse. 'The coffee definitely loosened my tongue and in response to your question, thank you for asking, but you really don't need to worry about me having someone to talk to. I have very recently started to figure a few things out, but I'm not ready to share the details of them with anyone yet.'

I hoped I wasn't putting my playtime project under the unnecessary pressure I had only the evening before realised it was a joy to be without, but my sketches, along with the lists of words and story plan that now went with them, really did feel as though they were starting to mean something.

'Well,' said Bear, with a smile, 'that sounds like progress.'

'It is,' I agreed, then hastily steered the focus of the conversation on to him. 'I'm guessing your parents have always been completely behind your life choices as well as your decision to change the direction of your work, haven't they?'

He nodded at that. 'Always,' he confirmed and I can't deny I felt a little envious. 'They were both completely onboard when I decided to go freelance. Dad even helped me strip out and redesign the horsebox.'

'You're very lucky,' I said, as I spotted Freya heading back towards us again.

'It helped that they both had unconventional jobs themselves,' he explained. 'I think that probably made a difference.'

I daresay it did, but I also knew he was being kind.

'I know we've only just met, Holly,' he then said, stepping closer and putting a hand on my arm, 'but in lieu of anyone else to talk to, I really don't mind if you want to talk to me when you've thought things through further.'

I had just been going to tell him about May – we might not have gotten right into it, but I'd given her a heads up that I was unhappy with my work when we had talked about my divorce and I knew that should I need to chat, she'd listen in a heartbeat – but the feel of Bear's hand on my arm took the words right out of my mouth.

'Thank you,' I said instead, laying my chilly hand over his warm one.

'I mean it,' he said, sounding serious.

'I know you do,' I gratefully sighed, then came to my senses a bit. 'And I also know, in light of the out of character chatterbox moment I've just subjected you to, that I most likely will take you up on the offer. Whether I want to or not. You seem to have a knack for getting me to talk about things, Bear.'

We both laughed and I sensed Freya had stopped in her tracks. She must have spotted our body language and felt stuck between a rock and a hard place.

'I'm going now, Freya,' I called to her, reluctantly lifting my hand away from Bear's and quickly downing my coffee. 'Thanks for the drink.'

'You'll be buzzing all day,' she laughed, coming over properly now I'd given her the all-clear.

She wasn't wrong about that, but it most likely wouldn't be down to her potent brew.

'I'll see you later, Holly.' Bear smiled, making my heart skitter. Although that might have been the coffee. It was, I appreciated, as it hit my stomach, very strong.

I hadn't realised until I got back that I'd left my phone in the house and it was flashing where I'd set it to charge the night before on the kitchen worktop. While I had been over-sharing in the garden with Bear, May had called and left a message to say that she wouldn't be walking at the lake and would make her own way to and from The Chapel. She'd see me that evening, hopefully with some ideas for the set to show everyone.

No pressure then. The sound of her voice did make me feel guilty for not making a point of mentioning her friendship and kindness to Bear. I'd have to rectify that the next time I was showering him with too much information.

Knowing now that May, and most likely everyone else, would be expecting me to share with them some thoughts as to what I had in mind for the set, I spent the rest of the day coming up with some simple designs and ideas to add to the brief notes I'd made the evening before.

It wasn't easy, given that I hadn't been told the budget I was working to but, using the script Lisa had copied for me as a guide, I noted down a few things that I thought might work and which were also adaptable enough to be used more than once in the hour-long show, and could also be used in any future performances with a little tweaking.

I'd just finished eating an early dinner when Lisa knocked on the door. 'I'm off to The Chapel,' she said. 'Would you like a lift?'

As I didn't have May and Monty to chauffeur, I accepted. We picked up Beth on the way, too.

'Lisa's told me that you're going to design a set for us,' Beth said, leaning forwards between the seats before we headed off.

She sounded super keen.

'I'm going to try,' I said, hopefully tempering her excitement a little. 'I've come up with some preliminary ideas this afternoon, but it's proved a bit tricky because I don't know what the budget is. For the most part, I've just assumed there isn't one.'

'You'll go far,' Lisa laughed. 'That's literally about the size of it.'

Everyone except May was at The Chapel when we arrived and, given their enthusiasm, it was impossible not to talk about certain aspects of creating the set, even though I wanted to wait for her.

'My John has said we can use his tools,' said Lisa, managing to make the offer sound rude and everyone laughed. 'But I've had to promise him that I'll only let them be used by someone qualified to handle them.'

That counted me out then.

'He's power tool rich,' Lisa told us, 'but time poor. Otherwise, he'd be taking some of the construction on himself.'

'And I popped in to see Luke earlier,' said Eli, 'and he's got some leftover MDF and paint that he said we're welcome to. He said you could go and have a look at it, Holly, and if it's of any use, Finn will bring it here in his van.'

'That's great,' I said, 'although I do wonder at the wisdom of turning this place into a workshop. Painting here shouldn't be an issue, but the sawing and shaping might get a bit messy.'

'I'll talk to Finn about that too, then,' offered Eli, jotting it down. 'Maybe he could let us use his studio for a few hours to get the sawing done.'

'Or even better,' put in Lisa, 'ask Luke if someone could cut and shape it where it's currently being stored, assuming it will be any good for what Holly has in mind.'

Pete rubbed his hands together. 'So,' he said, 'what exactly do you have in mind?'

'Shouldn't we wait for May?' suggested Freddie, echoing my thoughts as he quietly played a festive tune on the piano in the background. 'She messaged me earlier to say she was coming with a surprise tonight.'

She hadn't mentioned a surprise to me and I wondered what she was up to. Mischief, most likely if I knew her as well as I thought I was beginning to. Given they'd exchanged numbers, she obviously approved of Freddie now.

'I'm here!' she then announced noisily, rushing into the room and letting the door swing wildly behind her. 'So sorry I'm late.'

We all turned to look at her.

'What's this surprise then?' Freddie asked, stepping down from the stage.

'Hold on,' she said and bustled out again.

I noticed Monty hadn't appeared yet and wondered if he was about to make a grand entrance dressed as a fairy to go on top of the Christmas tree or something equally as kitsch. That could be another sketch to add to my collection. A suitably seasonal one.

'What's going on?' Lisa frowned in my direction when we heard May talking to someone.

I shrugged in response because I was as clueless as everyone else.

'Ta da!' May then sang out, rushing back in again. 'I've got the people power I promised you, my loves.' She beamed and my mouth fell open. 'I'd like to introduce you all to my dear son, Teddy.'

# Chapter 12

To say that, in that moment, my jaw hit the floor might be considered a cliché, but it also happened to be completely accurate. I looked from May to Teddy – which was obviously where the name Bear derived from – to the rest of the group. They looked momentarily as stunned as I did, but then recovered far quicker.

'I don't believe it,' said Eli, rushing to shake Bear's hand.

'Me neither,' added Lisa, also stepping forward. 'We all know Teddy, May. We've already met.'

'You have?' May gasped.

'We have,' joined in Pete. 'In The Dragon.'

'I might have known it would be in the pub,' May chuckled.

'You're doing some work for Luke, aren't you?' Lisa asked Bear.

'That's right,' he said. 'I daresay some of you might have already spotted my horsebox parked up at Prosperous Place. Luke's letting me keep it there over winter in exchange for starting some restoration work in the garden.'

He hadn't noticed me and I wished I had been nearer the kitchen when he and his mum arrived. That way I could have ducked out and recovered from the shock in private, and then reappeared bearing tea and a smile, my composure fully intact.

'Do you have a horse?' Beth asked him, jumping to the obvious conclusion.

'No.' Bear beamed. 'The box has been converted so I can live in it.'

'Oh my,' said Freddie, his bright eyes twinkling. 'How cool is that?'

'Very cool,' said Pete, looking at Bear with something akin to admiration and I wondered if he was imagining him as some intrepid travelling warrior in one of the fantasy stories he loved.

If Bear ever did run low on funds, he could certainly offer his services as a movie extra. He'd look outstanding wielding an axe on horseback and rescuing dogs in distress . . . My imagination was getting the better of me again and I quickly put my mind back in the room to address the unforeseen complication now standing in front of me.

May presenting Teddy, Bear or whatever his name was, as her son *was* a complication and it was a tricky one too. If I was being completely honest, I couldn't help feeling that it was a complete disaster, but only for me, not anyone else.

Just at that moment, Bear's eyes met mine and widened in surprise.

'And this,' said May, reaching for his hand and dragging him over to where I stood, still dumbstruck, 'is my new friend. The one I've been telling you all about.'

Everyone else had stepped aside, like the parting of the Red Sea and their full attention was now focused on the two of us.

'You're the bright young thing?' Bear beamed down at me.

'That's how I've been describing you,' said May, for my benefit as she looked between her son and me.

'Actually, Mum hasn't stopped talking about you since I arrived back in Norwich.' Bear laughed, looking fondly at her.

He seemed far more capable of setting aside the impact of the shock than I was. But then, perhaps he wasn't feeling it quite as deeply as me. Perhaps he hadn't been imagining getting to know me better in quite the same way that I'd been thinking about him. I wasn't sure if that was a wrench or a relief.

'All good things, of course,' May rushed on.

'Apparently, you've changed her life,' Bear said, gifting me an accolade I wasn't sure was merited for the few things I'd done for May.

'And you're the prodigal son,' was all I could croakily manage to say in response.

It was all getting rather biblical.

'Your mum didn't describe you as that exactly,' I then elaborated. 'But that was the gist I got from what she said about you.'

'Well,' Bear joshed, turning the flushed crimson shade that was becoming endearingly familiar as he shrugged his broad shoulders, 'if the cap fits.'

May swatted his arm.

'Don't go getting any big ideas about yourself.' She smiled, clearly full of love for her son. 'Otherwise, you'll never fit through the door.'

'I won't.' Bear grinned, still looking at me. 'I didn't for one second expect Mum's bright young thing to be you though, Holly.'

I raised my eyebrows at that.

'I don't mean that you're not a bright, young thing,' he stuttered. 'I just meant that I had absolutely no idea that you were the person Mum had been describing because she never mentioned your name.'

May shook her head and laughed.

'I think you'd better fill me in.' She smiled. 'I want to hear how come you two already know each other, too.'

'I also met Holly the night I met everyone else in the pub,' said Bear, carrying our narrative on when I didn't say anything.

'Was it a meet cute?' May gasped, clapping her hands together.

'Sadly not,' Bear admitted, before I had the chance to respond. 'It was as far from one of those as it possibly could have been because I was rude and bullish—'

'But only because I'd clumsily stepped on Queenie,' I jumped in, cutting him off. 'And you didn't know how she was going to react.'

'That's kind of you to say,' he said softly, 'but I still could have handled the situation better.'

I didn't agree, but I didn't contradict him either. I was still reeling from the shock that the first man I had looked at and felt attracted to since the end of my marriage could only now be a sounding board and a friend. I had fancied Bear from the moment I met him but discovering he was May's son put him completely off limits.

The irony wasn't lost on me that I had told myself, more than once, since getting to know him, that Bear was a complication my life currently didn't need and now fate had played a very firm and decisive hand in making sure that I wouldn't end up ruining our time in Norwich or spoiling our efforts in helping out at The Chapel.

'I don't like the sound of this, Teddy Bear,' said May, making Bear cringe. 'You weren't raised to be rude, whatever the circumstances.'

'Please don't call me that, Mum,' he pleaded and everyone laughed.

'And he wasn't really rude,' I reiterated. 'Just protective of Queenie and making sure I didn't get on her wrong side. Not that I actually think she's got one. Where is she, by the way?'

'At the bungalow with Monty,' Bear told me. 'They'd only met briefly once before and after that hadn't seen each other at all until I arrived, so they have a lot of catching up to do.'

I had to smile at that. I imagined them stretched out together on the sofa, exchanging gossip and news and drinking tea. My imagination was off again . . .

'Are we doing this then, or what?' tutted one of the young actors who had just arrived and found us all standing around chatting.

'Yes,' said Lisa, 'we are, and that's enough of your attitude, thank you, Vincent. I hear you were acting up in class today and hope I don't need to remind you that your theatrics need to be consigned to the stage here rather than the classroom.'

'Tamsin been talking about me at home, has she?' Vincent asked cockily, as he slung his rucksack down.

'Yes,' said Tamsin, choosing that moment to step out from behind where the Christmas decoration boxes were stacked. Vincent turned bright red. 'I have and none of it has been good. You're not actually impressing anyone, Vinny Cartwright.'

'I wasn't trying to,' he shot back belligerently, jutting out his chin as his swagger instantly deflated.

'Right, come on!' said Lisa, clapping her hands and cutting the potential spat off. 'That's enough of that, you two. Let's get to it.'

I ducked into the kitchen before Bear and May could say anything further. I busied myself making an endless number of hot drinks and prepping jugs of squash. Unfortunately, Bear soon sought me out and finding myself in the confined space of the kitchen with him, my cheeks turned as red as Vinny's had when Tamsin knocked him off his pedestal.

'Here,' said Bear, stepping forward and taking the tray of mugs from me. 'Let me carry this lot, you bring the squash.'

Our fingers briefly brushed together and I cursed the Mexican wave tingle his touch set off in me. I had the feeling that my body and my heart were going to take a while to catch up with my head, which I was now striving to pack full of caution and common-sense.

'Eli said the three of us can talk in one of the side rooms,' he told me, looking back over his shoulder. 'He tells me that you're in charge of the set design and build and Mum has already stated that I'm merely here for construction purposes, so feel free to boss me around, won't you?' The cheeky smile on his face told me he was enjoying this.

I nodded, but had no chance of forming a verbal response.

'This all looks simple enough,' said Bear, once I'd taken him and Eli through the few things I so far had in mind for embellishing the stage in time for the performance.

Ideally, we would be able to get it all sorted with time to spare so the actors could get used to sharing the space, but that would depend on the amount of time everyone – Bear in particular, given his role – would be able to give the project.

Once I'd looked at the materials available and given him a more detailed brief, I hoped I would be able to leave him to it because I didn't think the sight of him wielding power tools in a too-tight T-shirt would help in my quest to keep reminding myself that he was May's son.

Not that he was likely to do the work wearing a too-tight

T-shirt. He didn't seem the type, so where had that image sprung from? My imagination, having now been unleashed, was getting far too creative for its own good.

'Are you all right, Holly?' Eli asked me. 'You look a bit flushed.'

'I'm fine.' I swallowed. 'Just a bit worried about getting this all done in time and I still don't know if we can afford any of the extras I've been thinking of.'

'That's my fault,' he said, jumping up. 'Hang on and I'll go and get the figures. I meant to bring the file in with me, but we all got so caught up in Bear's arrival, I completely forgot.'

'Don't blame me,' Bear called after him.

'I'd really like to paint some kind of backdrop,' I said quickly, so we didn't fall to talking about anything other than the performance. 'And I think I can do it cheaply enough with some dustsheets sewn together, but I'm not sure how we would hang it.'

Bear moved to sit next to me, which was no help at all.

'Can I borrow a pen and some paper?' he asked.

'Sure,' I said, sliding both over.

'How about something like this?' he suggested as he started to draw a rough diagram of what he had in mind. 'Luke would be more than thrilled for me to cut down some of the bamboo which is making its presence a bit too felt at Prosperous Place.'

He spun the paper round so I could see more clearly what it was that he'd come up with.

'Oh wow,' I said, 'that's perfect.'

'And fittings aside' – he smiled – 'practically free. You could even have two painted backdrops per performance. Simply slide one along and the next into its place at the point when the set pieces are being switched.'

'You're a genius,' I told him, completely forgetting that I

was trying to dial my feelings down, but his plan was genuinely inspired.

'Well.' He shrugged as Eli came back in. 'You know . . .'

'What's this?' Eli asked.

'Bear's come up with a brilliant idea for hanging a backdrop curtain behind the stage,' I said, showing him what Bear had sketched out.

Bear then explained how it could be fixed to the top of the wall or the ceiling, how easy it would be to take down when it wasn't in use and how simple it would be to change the backdrop when it was.

'That's a genius idea,' said Eli.

'That's exactly what I said,' I laughed. 'So don't go on about it, otherwise we'll never hear the last of it.'

'Hey,' said Bear, who hadn't gone back to his original seat, as he gave me a nudge. 'That's not fair. I'm usually very reluctant to wax lyrical about my talents.'

'I suppose I have to believe you.' I smiled as I risked a look at him. 'Especially as Luke said something similar the day we met in the garden.'

Bear held my gaze and smiled back and I found myself, in spite of my best intentions, grinning more broadly in response. Had Eli not cleared his throat and jolted me out of the moment, I'm not quite sure what would have happened next.

'So,' he said, drawing the word out, 'this is the amount we're looking at. Do you think that's a figure you're going to be able to work with, Holly?'

I looked at the number he was showing me.

'Well,' I said, 'I've never designed a set before, obviously, but knowing that we've been given so much in the way of materials, coupled with the fact that we now have Bear's brawn to help us transform what we've got, I think that's enough to make a decent show of it. No pun intended. What do you think, Bear? Are we looking at a merry Christmas performance?'

'Oh yes,' he agreed, 'we're looking at a very merry Christmas indeed.'

That sounded like an answer to a different question, but I nodded in approval nonetheless.

'How about we go and have a look at where you might be able to attach the bamboo for the backdrop, Bear?' Eli suggested.

'Sure,' he said, and drained the last of his mug of coffee. 'Are you coming, Holly?'

'I'll be along in a minute,' I told him. 'I just want to jot down a few more ideas I've had, before I forget them.'

Eli closed the door behind them and I lowered my head so that it was resting on the table and let out a long breath. Had I had a pillow to hand, I would have screamed into it.

Surely my life had been dealt enough blows now? The end of my marriage, the dissatisfaction with my regular work and the still to be decided upon next new home were all waiting in the wings for me to properly get my head around and now there was this. How was it even possible that Bear was my new best friend's son?

In just a couple of weeks May had become not only a best friend, but someone who was beginning to feel like family. Given that I didn't have any I wanted to call my own, and that I had been abandoned by those I formerly had when someone else who would give them what they wanted appeared on the scene, I wasn't going to jeopardise that for all the Bears in the wood. And of course, I knew May wouldn't have wanted to risk our relationship either, given that she was still feeling the impact of what had happened with her former best friend when Bear's relationship with her daughter went wrong.

Thank goodness I hadn't already charged in and clumsily acted on my feelings. That was the one silver lining. But then, given that Bear didn't seem at all fazed to discover that I was his mum's *bright young thing* I might only have been rebuffed if I had. Whereas before I had been convinced he had feelings for me, his initial reaction on seeing me tonight suggested otherwise, so perhaps it had been a lucky escape all round?

# Chapter 13

Lisa and Beth spent the whole of the journey back to the square – thankfully it wasn't too far – talking about Bear and what a coincidence it was that he had turned out to be May's son. The more I listened to them and thought it through, the more I realised there had been a few potential clues which, had I picked up on them, wouldn't have made the evening's revelation quite the shock it turned out to be. However, I hadn't pieced the hints together and as a result, I was still reeling.

'I reckon he's got a bit of a thing for you, Holly,' said Lisa, giving me a nudge while she waited for the traffic lights to turn green.

'Definitely,' agreed Beth, leaning forward between the seats as she was sitting in the back. 'He couldn't take his eyes off you all evening.'

'I daresay that's because he has May's best interests at heart,' I told them hastily. 'And he was keen to make sure I wasn't someone who had just befriended his mum because she's famous.'

Lisa snorted at that. 'Yeah, right,' she mockingly responded, shifting into first gear and smoothly pulling away as the lights changed. 'I'm sure that's exactly what was on his mind.'

'And even if it wasn't,' I said bluntly, hoping to shut the topic down, 'I don't want you, or you, Beth, giving another moment's thought to his staring at me. I'm fresh out of a divorce, remember, and only here for a couple of months while I house-sit for Neil and Mark. The last thing I need is a . . . romantic complication.'

'How about a fling, to see you through the festive season instead?' Lisa suggested in spite of my protestation. So much for shaming her into shutting up.

'No, Holly's right,' Beth chipped in, thankfully sounding far more understanding. 'So don't you go getting any ideas about misplacing bunches of mistletoe, Lisa.'

'My mistletoe is always placed exactly where I want it,' she immediately responded, with unsettling emphasis.

I thanked Lisa for the lift and gladly closed the front door of the house, revelling in the silence that welcomed me. An early night to put some distance between my head and the evening's events was what was needed, but as is often the way, the moment my head hit the pillow my muddled brain began playing everything over and I was wide awake again.

So awake, in fact, that I decided to get up and, armed with a mug of warming cocoa and my sketchpad, I made a comfy nest of fleecy blankets and cushions on the sofa and spent the next few hours writing the rough draft of a story, the bones of which had been rattling about in my head for a few days.

It told how Monty and Queenie had initially found themselves living on the water and traversing the canal system in their green narrowboat named Hope. They went about, kindly improving the lives of and helping solve problems for those in predicaments that they encountered on their travels.

For some reason, my head kept going back to Bear's boat idea and even though I knew it was utterly impractical, I could quite easily imagine myself in either a flowery, floaty summer dress, tending the makeshift garden outside or wearing woolly layers and snuggling up inside in a chair in front of a tiny wood burning stove.

The aesthetic was extremely appealing and surprisingly colourful and I couldn't deny that the prospect of living mortgage free was very tempting, too.

'I'll go and find Bear,' said Luke, as we walked towards one of the Prosperous Place outbuildings the following morning after I'd let May know that I wouldn't be walking around the lake.

I hadn't wanted to miss another meander, but didn't feel ready to face her and the only inevitable topic of conversation just yet. I cited sorting things for the performance as my excuse for ducking out and she was thankfully willing to accept that.

'He's working with Freya on plans for the knot garden today,' Luke further said, before I could explain that I wasn't there for Bear, 'so I know he's about here somewhere.'

I knew, given that we were working on the set construction together, that our paths would cross at some point, probably quite a lot until the curtain fell on the Christmas performance, but I had snuck stealthily into the grounds hoping to avoid him. The memory of the evening before, along with Lisa and Beth's astute observations, were still too fresh and I hadn't yet had the chance to reinforce my defences against further falling for him.

'There's really no need,' I said hastily to Luke. 'I don't need him at this point. I just wanted to have a look at what you've so kindly offered us so I can work out if I'm going to need to source and buy much more.'

'Fair enough.' Luke nodded, letting me go inside ahead of him. 'I had a bit of a sort out in here with Finn yesterday and you're welcome to all of that lot.' He pointed at some sheets of ply and MDF in all shapes and sizes which were stacked up behind a collection of pots of paint. 'And the paint is up for grabs too, if you'd like it.'

'Really?' I gasped, distracted from thoughts of Bear. 'Are you sure?'

There was far more on offer than I had been expecting.

'Yeah,' he said. 'Go for it. It's only taking up space so I was going to have to get rid of it at some point and I'm happy to lend any tools John hasn't got and for you to do the sawing and prep in here, too, if you need to.'

'And I'll ferry it all to The Chapel in my van when it's ready,' offered Finn, who had seemingly appeared out of thin air, startling me so much it made my feet almost leave the ground. 'Sorry.' He grinned. 'Did I make you jump, Holly?'

I was clearly on tenterhooks, but until that moment I hadn't realised quite how antsy I was.

'You did,' I said, covering my heart. 'That's my cardio done for the day.'

'What's up?' Luke asked Finn who had clearly come to find us with more of a purpose than scaring me half to death and offering a courier service.

'Ned from Wynter's Trees is here with your delivery,' Finn told him.

'Oh, thank goodness,' said Luke, puffing out his cheeks. 'I was beginning to think we'd be having a switch-on with no trees tomorrow night. Ned promised he'd deliver, but I was starting to wonder. Do you mind if I leave you to it, Holly?'

'Not at all,' I said. 'I can take it from here, but before you go, thank you, Luke, and you too, Finn, for all your help. The Christmas performance will really come to life now, thanks to you two.'

'It's the least we can do, but you're the one who'll be supplying the vital creative flourish, Holly,' said Luke. Finn nodded his agreement, and I hoped I would be able to pull it off. 'And besides,' he added wryly, 'Lisa would be wearing all our guts for garters if we weren't doing our bit.'

As the pair rushed off, I knew that he was right about that. Even I, a mere fleeting visitor to the square, had been somehow subtly coerced into rolling up my sleeves. I was surprised Lisa hadn't been drafted into working for the secret service or diplomatic corps. That said, there could be no denying that, Bear bother aside, I was beginning to enjoy myself.

I took my time looking through the list and sketches I'd come up with for set pieces that would work well with the performance script. Practically everything we'd need was covered courtesy of Luke's scrap and leftover pile. He'd even left a box full of paintbrushes and kettles for us to use and a box of screws and wood glue, so the outlay was going to be minimal. I wouldn't be making any rash promises to Eli or Lisa that I'd come in under budget, but the truth was, I might.

My phone pinged with a notification from Lisa just as I thought of her. Spooky. She'd asked for my number the evening before and had now added me, along with May and Bear, to the WhatsApp group chat for the performance. Bear had already responded with a bear emoji and I was just about to add a comment of my own, when I heard the gravel scrunch outside and shuffled back into the shadows, holding my breath.

'Come on, Queenie,' said Bear. 'You can't go nosing about in there.'

There was a heart-stopping pitter patter of four paws venturing inside and I just knew that Queenie had sniffed me out.

'Hey,' said Bear again. 'Come on. There's no one there.'

Given how close he sounded, I was going to look a total fool if Queenie blew my cover and I had to make my presence known. Thankfully she turned around and trundled off again.

I gave it a minute, then slipped out and headed back to the square. I was eager to hunker down and draw up the more detailed designs of exactly what it was I hoped Bear would be able to cut out and make and that I would then paint.

I spent the rest of the day productively organising everything and sourcing the dust sheets I would hopefully be adding a convincing looking backdrop to. Even though the ones I asked Lisa to order were huge, Sara said she would sew them together for me once we knew what the final dimensions needed to be, and she was also going to add a simple channel to the top so we could slide them on and off Bear's brilliant bamboo pole idea.

The morning of the Nightingale Square festive switch-on dawned sunny and bright. Even though I had wanted to wriggle out of walking with May and Monty again, I knew I couldn't let my inconvenient feelings for Bear impact on my friendship, otherwise what would have been the point in denying them? Or trying to.

'We all missed you at The Chapel last night,' said May, when she opened the bungalow door to let me in while she finished getting ready.

I was pleased she had made that a general, rather than person-specific comment.

'I meant to pop in,' I said truthfully, 'but I got carried away making plans for the set.' That part of the tale wasn't entirely true because at the very end of the day, when everyone would have been convening at The Chapel, it was one of Monty and Queenie's adventures that I had been immersed in, not the set prep, but I wasn't going to explain that. 'Luke has offered us so many materials, it's going to be amazing.'

'Lisa filled me in about that and said he had offered to help out.' May nodded. 'So, when can you and Bear get to it?'

'Sorry?' I blinked.

'Making the set,' she said. 'When can you start?'

'Oh.' I swallowed. 'Next week, I hope. Maybe even tomorrow if Bear doesn't have any objection to working on a Sunday.'

'I'm sure he doesn't,' said May as she picked Monty up and wrestled him into a tweed caped Sherlock Holmes style coat. I hoped he wasn't going to be looking for clues about my love life. 'But I do.'

'You do?' I asked. 'Are you religious, May?'

'No,' she said, 'but I already have plans for the two of you for tomorrow, so work on the set will have to wait.'

'What sort of plans?' I grimaced, my stomach filling with a thousand knots.

'I'll tell you tonight,' she said, grinning, 'when you're together. I still can't believe that the two of you had already met before I'd introduced you and that I'd been talking to you about him and to him about you. What are the odds?'

She sounded as amazed about how things had turned out as I was.

'A million to one, I would have thought,' I sighed, then frowned as what she'd previously said sunk in. 'But why do you think we're going to be together tonight?'

'Because you'll both be at the switch-on in Nightingale Square, of course,' she tutted. 'Don't tell me you'd forgotten.'

'Oh,' I said. 'No, of course not.'

The square had been a hive of activity when I set off so it was impossible to forget but I hadn't expected May to be heading there for the evening's entertainment. There was no way I'd be able to keep a low profile if she was in attendance.

'Lisa extended an invitation from Luke to everyone at The Chapel last night.' She beamed. 'Everyone's going to be there and I'm really looking forward to it. Bear is quite smitten with Prosperous Place, so I can't wait to see it and the Grow-Well for myself and the square too, of course. It all sounds rather idyllic.'

'It is,' I told her. 'A real city paradise.'

'And with so much going on,' May said approvingly. 'Although as I understand it, there's no Winterfest this year which is a shame because I would have enjoyed coming to a couple of the sessions.'

I hadn't heard of Winterfest or its associated sessions but I didn't ask for details. I had more than enough on my plate to contend with now I was a player, of sorts, in the Christmas performance.

'Come on then,' I said instead, 'we'd best get off for this walk, otherwise the car park will be heaving.'

'You're right,' said May, slipping on a caped coat which almost matched Monty's.

By the time I arrived back in the square, the central green

had been totally transformed and I couldn't resist heading over for a proper look. I had enjoyed looking at the decorations in the city more than I had expected to the day I went Christmas shopping and didn't feel any of the anguish I'd succumbed to the year before. I didn't even experience that now the seasonal embellishments had landed right on my doorstep.

In fact, I could almost feel a fizzing sense of excitement in the base of my belly, but that could also have been the result of seeing Bear in the distance, clad in one of his chunky sweaters and stringing up lights over the Prosperous Place garden gate. I turned my back on the spectacle and made a beeline for the huge potted tree in the middle of the green instead.

'This looks amazing,' I said to Poppy, who was a neighbour I so far hadn't seen that much of. 'Can I do anything to help?'

'Oh, hey Holly,' she said. 'Yes, you can actually.'

'Name it,' I said, rubbing my gloved hands together and thinking how different my time in the square was turning out to be from what I had originally planned.

'Well,' said Poppy, 'there's loads to do, but top of the list are the lights for Mark and Neil's front garden. You don't happen to have a key for their shed, do you?'

I hadn't realised they normally decorated the garden. Looking around I could see some of the neighbours were busy in their own front plots, so I shouldn't have been surprised.

'I've got a bunch of keys back in the kitchen,' I told Poppy. 'So, it's most likely there. I'll go and see what I can find.'

'It's the lights for the front that we want,' she said. 'We all decorate our hedges or gates with matching sets and the lights track right around the square, pulling us all into one big circle.'

'That sounds very community spirited.' I smiled.

'Of course, it is,' she laughed. 'It wouldn't be Nightingale Square if we weren't all pulling together, would it?'

'No.' I smiled back. 'I don't suppose it would.'

It didn't take me many minutes to track down the key. The shed was very organised, obviously Neil's domain. The box with the lights in was even labelled, so I was soon back on the path, lifting the lid and untangling the few strands which had got muddled in spite of the fact that they had been carefully packed away.

I seemed to be tangling more than untangling and I was just about to swear with frustration when a shadow crossed my path.

'Need a hand?'

'Bear.' I swallowed. 'I didn't know you were out here.'

I had no reason to lie, but the words were out of my mouth before I could check them.

'Lisa came and found me,' he said, nodding in her direction. 'Finn's off somewhere delivering one of his sculptures and she needed someone with a bit of height, apparently.'

He certainly had that in spades.

'In that case, I'd slope off now, if she's finished with you,' I suggested. 'Before you get roped in to doing something else.'

'I don't mind really,' he told me, taking one end of the strand I was getting increasingly wrapped up in. 'Besides, you look like you're making more of a mess than you started out with.'

'Hey,' I huffed, but I let him unravel me anyway.

'There,' he said, just a few seconds later. 'No more knots.'

He wouldn't have said that if his insides felt anything like mine.

'Thanks,' I said, looking around at what the rest of the neighbours had done with their lights, as well as where they might have plugged them in. 'I think I can manage now.'

'Where's the socket?' Bear frowned, not taking the hint.

'No idea.' I shrugged.

He stepped through the gate before I could stop him and began looking around the shrub which was growing up the outside of the house and over the front door.

'Found it,' he soon said. 'There's a double external socket here.'

It didn't take us long to festoon the lights over and around the hedge and tuck the cable away so it wasn't a trip hazard. I'd decided I'd tweak the lights if necessary once it was dark because it was impossible to get the full effect with the winter sun shining. Not that I was complaining, because the weather was lovely.

'By the way,' said Bear as he stepped back to admire our handiwork, 'I'm not working tomorrow, so if you're free too, I thought we could have a look at the materials Luke has offered for us to make the set from.'

'I've already seen them,' I told him, then added because I hadn't meant to sound so blunt: 'There's loads of paint too. Lisa and Eli are going to be thrilled that I'm not going to be asking for more money, which I'm fairly certain wouldn't be available . . .'

My words trailed off as I noticed Bear's expression and before I'd had a chance to warn him that May had different Sunday plans for us anyway.

'What is it?' I asked.

'You've been over already?' he said, sounding surprised and looking hurt.

'Yes,' I said, feeling guilty for making him frown. 'I called over first thing yesterday. Luke said you were with Freya working on the plans for the knot garden again, so I didn't want to disturb you.'

It was only a slight tweaking of what had occurred.

'And I was only there for a few minutes to get the measure of what there is before I came back and got on with properly planning everything out,' I added.

'Oh, right,' he said. 'Well, that's fair enough, but don't feel as though you have to take it all on single-handedly, Holly. I'm genuinely happy to be helping out and can spare the time to do it.'

'Of course.' I nodded. 'But I really was only there for the shortest time.'

'Jacket potatoes and chilli are now being served in the Grow-Well!' John shouted from across the road, making everyone jump. 'Get it while it's hot!'

'I didn't know we were going to be fed,' I said, trying to bring back Bear's smile.

'It's another tradition apparently,' he told me, sounding more like himself. 'Are you going over?'

'Yeah,' I said, thinking I might as well join in. 'I don't see why not. What about you?'

He looked at me intently for a moment and I tried to return his gaze.

'We are all right, aren't we?' he asked, rather than answering my question.

'Of course, we are.' I swallowed. 'So, are you coming to eat?'

'No,' he said. 'I can't. I promised I'd take Mum out, so I better go and get changed but I'll see you later.'

'All right,' I said. 'I'll see you tonight.'

'Unless you'd like to join us?' he offered.

'It's kind of you to ask' – I smiled – 'but I've got the taste for homemade chilli now.'

'Fair enough,' he said, rubbing his hands together. 'That'll warm you up.'

He strode off back across the green to Prosperous Place and as I watched him go, I thought I was plenty warm enough already.

# Chapter 14

The square was packed with far more people than I had been expecting and I guessed that folk from further afield, who didn't have the benefit of a beautifully maintained green in front of their own homes, came to see what my current neighbours had done with theirs.

'When you think,' said John, who was carrying around trays of mulled wine and cider, while Tamsin and Carole handed out a non-alcoholic alternative, 'just a few years ago, before Luke and Kate arrived, we didn't even have so much as a Christmas tree on the green.'

There was far more than just a festive tree to see now.

'Did you all talk to each other then?' I asked curiously.

'We did.' John nodded. 'But it was Luke's offer of the garden that really pulled us all together and got us more involved in each other's lives.'

Well,' I told him, taking a mug of the cider and warming my gloved hands around it, 'I'm not a gardener, but even I can tell that was a beautiful thing to bond over.'

'Oh, it was,' he said, moving along. 'We're blessed to have it.'

There was a brief bit of feedback from the PA system and then the familiar sound of Wizzard filled the square and people started singing along. It was gearing up to be a fun evening and the lights hadn't even gone on yet.

'Hey,' said a voice next to me. I immediately knew who it was.

'Hey,' I said back. 'Where's your mum?'

'Talking to Luke,' Bear told me. 'She's Mum times ten tonight. She's so happy to be here.'

'Me too, actually,' I said. 'I didn't expect to want to get into the festive swing at all again this year, but the Nightingale Square magic seems to be rubbing off on me.'

Bear shifted around so that he could see me properly. He was wearing a woolly hat pulled down low and a matching scarf wrapped quite high. His gorgeous dark eyes were the only thing to focus on and I couldn't decide if that was more or less seductive than looking at his whole face.

'I'm delighted to hear it,' he said, the lines around his eyes suggesting that he was smiling. 'And I'm pleased that everything between us is okay,' he added. 'Because I'm really looking forward to working with you on the set for The Chapel.'

'I'm looking forward to that too,' I agreed. 'It's going to be great to be able to contribute something so special to the performance. Not that I would have said that if you'd asked me even just a few days ago.' I laughed.

I stopped as he started to shake his head and pulled the scarf down and tucked it under his chin.

'I don't care about the set,' he then said urgently. 'Well, I do,' he hastily amended, getting tongue-tied again. 'Of course, I do. It's an important and worthwhile project, but what I really meant was that I'm looking forward to working with *you* on it because I want to spend every moment I can with you, Holly.'

I choked on the sip of cider I'd just taken and my eyes welled up as a result. Every drop of air felt as though it had been sucked out of my lungs and I gulped down another mouthful to stop myself properly coughing. It didn't really help.

'I want to be with you, Holly,' he forthrightly declared, pulling the hat off his head and twisting it around in his hands as if he was wringing it out. 'Every minute of every day.'

*I* felt wrung out. I didn't know what to say. Just a few days ago, hearing him say those words would have been my Christmas wish come true, but . . .

Suddenly both the music and the level of chatter had been turned right down in my head and all I could hear was a whooshing noise filling my ears. Had Bear's mum been anyone other than my dear new friend, May Madison, and had she not suffered such a painful loss of friendship when Bear's former relationship went belly up, I was certain I would have been embracing the romantic complication I had been trying to convince myself I could live without. But May was Bear's mum and therefore I couldn't risk embracing anything.

The longer we stood there, the harder I found it to respond and the redder Bear's complexion turned.

'How else,' he then said with a nudge and a jolly hop from one foot to the other, 'am I going to convince you to live in something other than a boring old house? If I never get to hang out with you, I'll never be able to convert you, will I?' I didn't for one second believe that was what he had really meant. The way he'd spoken and the look in his eyes was way too intense if all he was genuinely intending to do was get me to consider alternative living arrangements.

'I even know someone who made their home out a couple of shipping containers,' he rushed on, swiping a mug from the tray as someone walked by and downing the contents in one. 'And a yurt. Have you considered life under canvas, Holly?'

'No,' I said, finally finding my voice and taking the subject up rather than imagining how my time in the square would have panned out if him and May weren't related. 'I haven't, but I can't deny my mind has tracked back to the narrowboat idea you mentioned that day in the café.'

'Really?' He nodded, sounding almost manic. 'Well, that's great. I know three people who live on boats. Three! So it's not as unusual as you might think.'

Given the number of people who by comparison lived in houses, it was still pretty rare.

'One's not all that far from here,' he carried on, waving about the empty mug and going completely over the top. 'I could take you. You could have a tour.'

'A quick one,' I quipped. He didn't seem to get the joke.

'There you both are,' said May, coming to stand between us and linking arms with me. 'Didn't I tell you that I'd talk to you both when you were together, Holly?'

'Um,' I said. 'Yes, you did, didn't you?'

'You should put that hat back on, Teddy,' she then tutted. 'Otherwise, you'll catch a chill.'

He did as he was told, and I found myself smiling because it was impossible not to be amused at seeing someone of his size being bossed about by his mum.

'And what was it that you wanted to say, May?' I asked, as her gaze swung between the two of us.

'What have I missed?' she then pounced, completely taking me by surprise. I'm sure Bear must have felt the whiplash too. 'Is there something going on between you two?'

'Yes,' he said, in spite of my warning glance.

'No,' I quickly countered.

He then gave me a return look I couldn't fathom.

'I'm trying to get Holly to embrace an alternative lifestyle,' he told May, sounding completely convincing. The sincerity in his tone made me question whether I had genuinely misinterpreted the implication behind his previous words, even though they had been so emotionally expressed. 'It could save her a fortune and genuinely change her life, but so far, she's resisting.'

May rolled her eyes and laughed.

'He tried to get me into a shipping container once,' she told me, giving my arm a sympathetic pat, before I could say that I wasn't feeling quite as resistant as I had been when he'd first mentioned it. 'But I wasn't falling for it.'

'Actually,' I said, thinking more of May's current home than my next one, 'I think your art would look spectacular against a metal backdrop, May.'

'I'm not sure he was planning to get me to live in the container,' she laughed. 'I reckon what he really had in mind was craning me aboard a ship which was about to set sail for far-off seas.'

'You clad the insides,' Bear said, not keeping up with the funny turn the conversation had taken. 'And pack the space between with insulation, so Mum's art wouldn't actually have had a metal backdrop.'

'Oh, Bear,' I tutted.

'What?' He frowned, sounding puzzled.

'Never mind,' May said, smiling, before I could explain. 'He's got a one-track mind when it comes to talking about alternative accommodation, so don't waste your breath, Holly. As you might have guessed, his efforts to get me to downscale my possessions failed miserably.'

'What have I missed?' Bear asked again.

'Nothing,' I said, pointing towards Luke as he stepped up to the podium which had been erected next to the vast potted Christmas tree. 'I think the lights are about to go on.'

A hush fell over the green as the music was turned off and all eyes turned to Luke.

'So,' he said, his voice amply amplified by the microphone, 'here we are again, folks.'

A cheer went up at that.

'A warm welcome to you all, especially those of you who haven't visited before. Nightingale Square and Prosperous Place have been graced with two new, but sadly only temporary neighbours since the last time we congregated here. Welcome, Holly and Bear,' he said loudly, pointing us out and making me cringe. 'I hope you will both enjoy spending Christmas here.'

'Oh my god, oh my god, oh my god,' I whispered, as I felt so many people turn to look in our direction.

'I know,' Bear muttered, next to me. 'I was not expecting that.'

'And I can see someone else who is new to the area standing over there with them,' Luke then carried on. 'It's May Madison, everyone.'

'Or that,' Bear added, his eyebrows shooting up.

Not surprisingly, the mention of May's name caused far more of a reaction than either mine or Bear's.

'May,' said Luke, 'would you please do us the honour of turning on the Nightingale Square Christmas lights this year?'

'I'd be delighted to,' she called back and then strode off, brimming with confidence.

Thankfully everyone's attention turned back to the podium as Luke handed the microphone over to May.

'What an honour.' She beamed and everyone clapped. 'I've only just realised that Christmas Day is exactly one month today!' Cue more clapping. 'How wonderful is that?'

She said a few more suitably festive words which had me wondering if she had known in advance that she was going to be called upon. Surely no one could step up and do something so eloquently and successfully off the cuff?

'Did she know?' I whispered to Bear while she held everyone in thrall.

'If she did,' he whispered back, 'she didn't mention it to me.'

We joined in with the countdown which started at ten and had the children jumping up and down in excitement.

'Five, four, three, two, one!'

Suddenly, the square was lit with far more lights than those on just the Christmas tree. Every other tree and shrub had their own adornments and the railings which ran around the green were decorated too. It was a beautiful sight.

'Oh, my goodness,' I gasped, feeling quite choked. 'I wasn't expecting all this.'

'Neither was I,' said Bear, who also sounded touched as he looked around. 'What a wonderful place this is. I'm so happy that Mum has moved to Norwich.'

His kind words and the obvious affection he had for his mum made me feel even more emotional. I wasn't sure now if earlier he really had meant that he did just want to spend time with me to convince me to buy a different kind of home, but whatever his true meaning, I knew I really must succeed in keeping things with him on a platonic and friendly footing.

'Me too,' I told him. 'She couldn't be living anywhere better.'

It felt like ages before May made her way back to me. There had been so many people who wanted to talk to her and she more than happily had a word for them all.

Bear had long since gone off to find Freya and Finn and, rather than go with him, I had opted to mooch about, admiring the decorations, chatting with my neighbours and filling up on chestnuts and the most amazing cream and chocolate topped waffle which was as light as air. There was raclette too and candied almonds and sausages covered in mustard and pickles, served in Blossoms rolls and baguettes. The entire square smelt every bit as seasonally enticing as it looked.

'How clever of Luke to invite all these vendors,' said May, looking around as she rejoined me and tucked into the biggest sausage I'd ever seen.

'Yes,' I agreed, while she chewed. 'It's more like a festive food fair now, than your average switch-on.'

'I'm getting the impression that nothing about this place is average,' she said, daintily wiping the corners of her mouth with a serviette.

'Do you feel like you've finally found your tribe, May?'

'I certainly do,' she said, after enjoying another bite. 'And it's all down to you, Holly.'

'I'm not so sure it is,' I told her with a smile. 'I reckon Bear would have somehow got you here if I hadn't.'

'I still can't believe you'd met him before I introduced you,' she laughed. 'What a wonderful coincidence.'

'It was certainly a coincidence,' I agreed.

'And where is the boy?' she asked, looking around. 'He really shouldn't have abandoned you.'

'He hasn't,' I said firmly, 'because we weren't officially here together, were we? He came with you and we just happened to have bumped into each other while you were talking to Luke.'

I was very keen to point that out.

'There he is,' she nudged, ignoring me and having spotted him in the queue for hot chestnuts. 'Come on.'

She ushered me towards him and then pulled him out of the line.

'Finish this instead,' she said, handing him over half of the sausage she had attempted to eat. 'It's too much for me.'

'It looks too much for anyone,' he laughed, but started eating it anyway.

'Now, you two,' she then said, linking arms with me on one side and Bear on the other. 'I want you both to come to dinner at mine tomorrow.'

This was obviously the plan for us both that she'd previously mentioned. Bear went to say something but she talked right over him.

'I won't hear of you making excuses about working on a Sunday, Teddy,' she told him and I grinned. I don't think I'd ever get used to hearing the giant of a man being called that. 'In our house, Sundays have always been for family, you know that, and now you're here for a while, I expect to at least try to pick the tradition up.'

'But I'm not family,' I pointed out. 'So, I don't really have to come, do I?'

I didn't wish to cause offence, and as much as I loved that

May had included me, I didn't think I could handle being at the bungalow with Bear.

I could just about cope at The Chapel because we had a project to work on and it was busy, but I wasn't ready to face general chit-chat and a conversation which might well end up with me promising to go with him on an excursion to look at his friend's narrowboat while we passed the gravy boat between us. I didn't think it would be a good idea for me to agree to go anywhere alone with him, not until I was entirely convinced of the real meaning behind his earlier words anyway.

'I'm devastated, Holly,' May said, this time properly pouting. 'You genuinely feel like family to me now, so of course you have to come.'

'Well, all right,' I relented, with the least amount of resistance imaginable on hearing her say that, and in spite of the fact that I had already acknowledged to myself it was going to be a struggle to be there.

The thinking behind my immediate change of heart was the undeniable truth that not even my own family wanted to call me family and Piers's family had ditched me. As result I genuinely felt an irresistible urge to embrace May's affection, the strength of which I also felt for her. It was further confirmation that I needed to keep Teddy Bear in the friend zone if I didn't want to risk jeopardizing it.

'What time would you like us?' I asked.

'Sherry at one, lunch at two,' May said succinctly. 'And I have a surprise for you too, Holly.'

'A surprise?'

'What about me?' Bear piped up. 'If I'm eating one of your lunches, surely I deserve a surprise.'

What on earth had he meant by that?

'Don't be rude,' May scolded. 'I daresay, Holly's surprise will surprise you too.'

'I don't know whether to be worried or excited now,' I exclaimed.

'Go for both,' said Bear, looking around his mum at me. 'Cover all bases.'

'Fair enough.' I laughed.

'Whichever you go for,' said May, 'be at the bungalow on time tomorrow. Now.' She smiled, releasing the pair of us. 'I'm going to do the rounds just once more and then we'd better get back for the dogs, Bear. See you tomorrow, Holly.'

She air-kissed both my cheeks and then swept away, looking as elegant as an extra from *Dr Zhivago*.

'What a woman.' I smiled after her.

'You should have tried growing up with her as your mum.' Bear smiled back.

'I would much rather have had yours than mine,' I told him.

'Yes,' he said, biting his lip, 'given what you've told me, I daresay you would.'

I wished he wouldn't do that. The lip thing, I mean. It was devilishly attractive.

'I think I'll head home,' I said quickly.

'Or you could come with me to take Mum back and then have a look at my place,' he suggested keenly. 'Now you've admitted you've been thinking about potential other options, I want to give you a taste of where I live to further help you make up your mind.'

On the one hand, I was tempted because I genuinely did want to see where he lived, but on the other, I'd now drunk quite a lot of mulled cider and was already far too aware of his soft full lips. Alcohol fuelled lowered inhibitions might not a platonic friendship make …

'Let's do it another time,' I told him. 'When I've got a clearer head and can take it all in properly, but thanks for the offer.'

'Okay,' he said, wiping his fingers on the serviette the huge sausage had been wrapped in and then stuffing his hands in his jacket pockets. 'If that's what you want, but you know I'll get you in the end.'

As I crossed the road to the house, I couldn't help thinking that if he was as adept at bending folk to his will as Lisa, then I really was in trouble.

# Chapter 15

As I was feeling jittery about spending the afternoon with Bear and potentially getting drawn into a conversation of a more intimate nature, like the one we'd had at the café in the city before I knew May was his mum, I decided to take the ideas I'd had for the Christmas performance set with me.

It would give me something to switch direction towards if the chat started to flow too freely or worse, if I found myself continuing to moon over him. I had been in earnest the evening before when I had been going to tell May that I was now feeling more open to the idea of living somewhere less conventional, but I was also mindful of the danger of Bear being the person who could show me the ropes. I was playing the subject over in my head again and gathering everything together in readiness to head off when someone knocked on the front door.

'Bear.' I swallowed, ostensibly checking the time when I found him standing on the doorstep and finding it hard to accept that my plan to keep him at a safe distance had been scuppered already. 'What's up?'

Given that I hadn't been expecting to see him so soon, I was

woefully unprepared and felt my heart bounce about and temperature rise as a result. I couldn't help wondering if he was acting
out what he had formerly said and genuinely was now attempting
to spend every moment he could with me. But to what end? Was
he here to try to sell me life on four wheels or on the water? Or
was he here for *me*?

My stomach, head and heart further ramped up their response
and knowing none of them should have been quite so excited
by the prospect of him talking about anything other than my
current property search, I felt even more pleased I'd got the set
sketches together as a conversational back-up.

'Nothing's up,' he said, glancing at the sky. 'I just wondered,
as the weather is so lovely again, if you might fancy walking to
Mum's, rather than getting your car out. Assuming, that is, that
you were going to take your car ... thinking about it now, I
suppose you could actually have some detour or errand to run
before you got to the bungalow, in which case—'

'Yep,' I cut in, taking pity on him because he was getting in
one of his characteristic muddles again. 'A walk sounds good. If
only to stop you jabbering on.'

'Hey.' He pouted.

'Well, I'm sorry, Bear,' I laughed, suddenly feeling more
relaxed, 'but you really do overthink things sometimes.'

I was grateful for the muddle he'd got himself in again because
it gave me a chance to present myself as the calm and collected
one out of the two of us. If only on the outside.

'Overthink or oversay?' He frowned, stepping inside when I
opened the door wider.

'I don't suppose I know you well enough to know the difference,' I admitted.

'Yet you're more than happy to point out my discomfiture,' he said shrewdly. 'Why is that, I wonder?'

'I'll just grab my stuff,' I said, quickly heading off before he saw through me, and treating his question as rhetorical.

Bear didn't take off his boots because we needed to leave straightaway as we were walking, and waited for me on the doormat. I appreciated him taking such care to not bring mud further into the house.

'Where's Queenie?' I asked over my shoulder, only just then noticing she wasn't with him.

'Still at Mum's,' he told me. 'She was all curled up with Monty when we arrived back after the switch-on, so we decided to leave her where she was for the night.'

'She's very adaptable,' I commented. 'Especially for a rescue who'd had the sort of rough start in life she'd had. Rescue dogs generally have a bit of baggage, don't they?'

'So I've been told,' he said, 'but she's turning out to be pretty resilient and she loves Monty. It will be a wrench to part them when the time comes.'

'What a mismatched pair they are,' I said. I didn't want to think about the dogs being separated or acknowledge the fact that my time with Queenie and Bear's presence in my everyday life had an expiration date, so I quickly turned my mind to my sketches of the dogs instead.

I had started to properly weave the words around the drawings now and I wondered what Bear would think of them. And what May would think too. Not that I currently had any intention of showing either of them, but I understood now what Sara had meant that day in The Chapel when she told me about her desire to have full control over her work.

I was very much enjoying the process of creating both the words and the images, having shrugged off Piers's harsh comments about my first attempt. In fact, I would go as far as to say that it was all beginning to feel a little less playful and rather more serious.

The exercise might have started out as a passion project, but it had reignited my desire to create to such an extent that I might at some point even consider submitting it all to my favourite editor. It was quite a turnaround, and a delightful one at that given that just a few short weeks ago, I had really thought there was no way back to any of it for me.

'At the moment, they seem to be totally smitten.' Bear beamed, describing the special relationship between his four-legged friends.

My friends now, too. My parents had always refused my appeal for a pooch, but once I was eventually settled, I might consider rescuing myself a canine companion. And, if my narrowboat fantasy continued to grow and somehow magically transformed into reality, Monty was going to end up needing that lifejacket I had dreamt about and drawn him wearing, because he'd definitely be invited to visit.

'Well,' I said, refocusing as I pulled on my coat, having loosely tied May's scarf around my neck, 'they do say opposites attract. Although I'm not sure they stick together.' I then frowned. 'That said, I had thought that Piers and I being similar in lots of ways would . . .'

'Would what?' Bear asked, eyebrows raised. 'How did that work out for you?'

I knew he was getting his own back on me for highlighting his ability to get into a muddle whenever he opened his mouth and I biffed him with my bag.

'Too soon?' he said, shielding himself with the coat stand.

'I realised what I was saying as soon as I'd starting saying it,' I tutted. 'There was no need for you to make something of it.'

We both grinned then, knowing we'd levelled up the score.

'What have you got in that bag?' he then asked, rubbing his arm where I'd batted him with it. 'It weighs a tonne.'

'Plans for the Christmas set,' I told him, feeling grateful for the change in subject. 'I thought if we get a minute this afternoon, we could look through them and then hit the ground running next week.'

'Sounds good to me,' he said, still rubbing his arm.

'And the bag's not that heavy,' I said, rolling my eyes. 'It's only got my sketch book in it. And my purse, car keys, spare hairbrush, tablet, phone—'

'Practically nothing then,' he said, taking it from me while I locked up. He dramatically dropped his shoulder to show it weighed him down on one side.

'Idiot,' I said, snatching it back and setting off.

It took us a while to walk the distance between the square and May's place. En route we talked easily about nothing in particular and I began to think I didn't have anything to worry about after all. Bear gave no indication that he was in any way interested in me, in a romantic sense, that is, and as a result I forced my unruly heart not to feel disappointed and allowed myself to relax. I thought he had chilled out too, until we reached the bungalow's drive. The moment we set foot on May's front path, however, he stopped dead and cocked his head.

'What is it?' I frowned.

'Shush,' he said, putting a finger to his lovely lips. 'Listen.'

'I can't hear anything,' I whispered after a few seconds had passed.

'Me neither,' he said, letting out an exaggerated sigh of relief. 'I think we're safe. Come on.'

'What were you expecting to hear?'

'At this time on a Sunday when dinner is in the offing and Mum's responsible for it,' he said, checking the time, 'a smoke alarm.'

'What?' I laughed.

'Or the distant sound of a fire engine siren.' He grinned. 'Or both. Dad was the cook in our house. And a good one. Mum's more . . .'

'Mum's more what?'

He took another moment before settling on the word he was looking for to best describe May in the kitchen or, more precisely, at the stove.

'Experimental.'

I wasn't sure I liked the sound of that and was about to comment when the door opened. Thankfully there was no billowing smoke, only May, smiling broadly and offering us both a warm welcome.

'I didn't think I heard your car, Holly,' she said. 'You've walked here together – how lovely! Well, come in, let's not dither and let all of the heat out.'

I discreetly sniffed the air as I walked in. I couldn't smell anything burning, but I couldn't smell food cooking either. Perhaps she'd settled on winter salad. Even if Bear's description of her cooking talents was true, not even May could screw up a salad, could she?

She took my coat as the dogs skittered around our feet.

I scooped Monty up, realising that it was the first time I'd been inside May's bungalow and not been acutely aware of the vast array of colours which filled it. I kissed Monty's silky head, feeling happy that I was becoming more acclimatised to the rainbow.

Had mine and May's paths not crossed, I wondered if that would ever have happened. Without the spark she had ignited, I might have been destined to carry on, unaware of the joy of a technicolour life and lived mine in tones designed to fade into the background, rather than pop, and with colour only featuring in my work. Knowing how excited I felt about the simple tweaks I had already made to my wardrobe and the plans I had for my next home, that would have been a tragedy.

'No red hoodie today.' May nonetheless frowned when she took in what I was wearing beneath my coat.

'No,' I said, putting Monty down and turning my attention to Queenie, 'but I am wearing your scarf.'

'Your scarf,' she said, smiling, sounding mollified.

'My scarf,' I corrected.

'Is that really one of yours, Mum?' Bear asked.

'It was,' she told him, 'but I gifted it to Holly to bring a little colour into her life.'

Bear smiled at that. 'That's what you're known for.' He grinned.

'And look at my socks,' I said, pointing my toes ballerina style. 'I ordered these online.'

Both May and Bear admired the purple and orange pair I'd picked out of the pack because they went best with the scarf, and then the doorbell rang and the dogs went bananas.

'Take them into the kitchen, would you, my loves?' May

requested. 'And I'll be through in a minute. And do pour the wine,' she said as an afterthought. 'We'll have to skip the sherry because this delivery is a little earlier than expected.'

Bear and I did as instructed, shepherding the dogs into the kitchen and closing the door. The kitchen was as neat as a pin and the table beautifully set for the three of us, but there was nothing in or on the oven, or the microwave.

'I hope we're not going to be dining on fresh air,' Bear grumbled. 'I had a big breakfast, but that walk in the cold has burned it off and I'm starving.'

'You're hungry,' I corrected, 'not starving.'

'I'll be hangry if Mum doesn't feed me something substantial,' he said, picking up the bottle of red wine which was open and the only thing set out on the worktop.

The sound of May's melodious laugh reached our ears and Monty cocked his head towards the door, while Queenie licked the top of his head. She looked like she was properly mothering him and an idea for another story popped into my head. I would have to write it down, before I forgot it. I immediately reached into my bag for my phone.

'Holly,' said Bear. 'I just asked if you wanted wine?'

'Sorry,' I said. 'Just half a glass please. It's still a bit early for me.'

'I'll have the same,' he said, filling his glass to the same level as mine.

I quickly fired off an email to myself, outlining the thought Queenie had inspired and then put my phone away again.

'That wasn't Lisa, was it?' Bear asked. 'I don't know how she gets time to write her books because she seems to be posting in The Chapel WhatsApp group all day.'

'No.' I smiled, relieved that it wasn't just me who felt a

bit overwhelmed by the constant influx of notifications. 'Not Lisa.'

'Would you like this now?' Bear offered, going to hand me the wine.

'No, thank you,' I said and he put the glass next to one of the place settings instead. 'I think I'll wait to find out what's on the menu first.'

'Good plan.' He beamed.

'Bear!' May called from the hall. 'Can you give me a hand, please?'

He opened the hall door and the delicious aroma of a roast dinner wafted into the kitchen. My tummy growled in response, so goodness knows how Bear's had responded.

'On my way,' he said, rushing to help. 'What is all this, Mum?'

'Sunday dinner, of course,' she said, coming into the kitchen with a large box, which she quickly deposited into the fridge.

Bear trailed behind her, weighed down with a vast insulated bag and another couple of boxes.

'Let's serve it all up quick, while it's still hot,' said May, handing me a pile of plates which had been warming on a trolley next to the radiator.

'You've ordered in?' I smiled.

'The pub up the road cooks the most wonderful Sunday roast beef dinner,' she told me, 'and we came to a little arrangement that once a month, they'd deliver mine rather than me going to them. It was a large, last-minute order I put in for today, but they were still happy to oblige.'

I hadn't imagined May as a pub regular, but then I shouldn't have been taken aback because since the moment I'd met her, she'd been full of surprises. It was just as that thought landed that

I remembered that she had said she had something up her sleeve for me. I wondered if it was the huge Yorkshire puddings she was currently plating up.

'Meals on wheels, Mum's way.' Bear grinned.

'I'm not sure I'm quite ready for those yet,' May laughed, giving his arm a squeeze. As Bear started heaping crispy roast potatoes straight on to the plates, she continued, 'But yes, I suppose you could say this is meals on wheels, my way.'

Bear put the tray of potatoes down and gave his mum a hug. I felt a lump form in my throat and had to turn away but the next thing I knew, May was turning me back around and giving me a hug, too. I squeezed her back and she kept hold of me far longer than she had Bear, probably sensing I needed it more than he did. It had been a very long time since I'd been hugged, and I happily reciprocated.

'Come on,' Bear eventually said, 'otherwise I'm starting without you.'

Every mouthful of the dinner was delicious. From the tender slices of slightly pink beef, to the crunchy potatoes, perfectly cooked glazed carrots and thick, rich gravy. By the time my plate was empty May had added more wine to my glass and I had drunk it all.

'Why miss out on having a Sunday lie-in to get up and cook when you can order in a dinner of this quality and get up when it arrives?' May shrugged, sounding blissed out.

I was feeling rather replete myself and could get used to life lived on May's terms.

'Absolutely,' I agreed. 'Thank you so much, May.'

'And no matter what time you got out of bed, you wouldn't have been able to manage to cook up a meal of this calibre, would you, Mum?' Bear grinned cheekily.

'You're very naughty to point that out,' May pretended to scold him, 'so you can clear the dishes.' Bear rolled his eyes. 'Even though you're absolutely right,' she relented.

Once we'd decided pudding – which was a huge trifle – could wait, Bear set to, clearing the plates and filling the dishwasher. It didn't take more than a couple of minutes because there were no cooking pots or roasting dishes to contend with.

'There,' said May, while I wiped down the table. 'All done.'

'I'm not sure the dogs would agree,' said Bear, nodding to where they shared Monty's bed and were looking very eager.

The pair hadn't moved while we ate and I had to admire both their willpower and impeccable manners.

'There's an extra container with some slices of beef and gravy for them,' May told Bear. 'Can you share it out between them, please?'

Bear picked up their separate bowls and their tails began to thump. 'They've been very patient,' I said.

'Monty knows I wouldn't tolerate a fuss at the table,' May said softly.

'Same with Queenie,' added Bear.

The bowls were licked clean in a trice and we all moved from the kitchen to the sitting room. I took a few minutes to again admire the memorabilia May had decorated the room with and then slumped down on the sofa.

'Don't you go getting too comfy,' said May, who was looking a little sleepy herself. 'I've got a surprise for you, remember?'

'I haven't forgotten.' I smiled. 'But I thought it was my delicious Sunday dinner.'

'No,' she said, 'as much of a treat as that was, that wasn't it. Come with me.'

Bear reached across me before I could stand up. I felt quite giddy, not knowing what he was going to do, but then he picked up the remote and leant back on the sofa.

'Have fun.' He smiled.

'She will,' said May, 'and don't you go getting ensconced in the box. You can take the dogs for a walk.'

He looked set to object, but one look at May's face told him she meant business.

'I'll get their leads,' he said, reluctantly standing up.

I followed May down the hall and into her bedroom. No, forget that. It was more boudoir than bedroom, although it did include a sumptuous, cushion-covered bed along with an old-fashioned dressing table, velvet drapes and matching covered pouffe and chaise longue. The tented ceiling was a stunning surprise, as was the colour. Dusky pink, soft pink and the odd accent in Wedgwood blue made the space a complete contrast to the rest of the bungalow. It was still colourful, but much more restful and calming.

'I couldn't sleep in an orange bedroom,' said May, as if she had read my thoughts. She picked up an old-fashioned cut glass atomiser and gave herself a spritz.

'It's such a serene room, May,' I said admiringly, breathing in the flowery scent.

'See you in a bit!' Bear shouted from the hall.

'Bye!' we both called back.

'That room, however,' said May, nodding to the double doors opposite her bed, which were painted the same colour as the walls and blended in so well that I hadn't previously noticed them, 'is a little more colourful.'

'Oh, really?'

'Take a look,' she said.

'Oh, my goodness, May!' I laughed. 'This is incredible.'

Lights had come on when I opened the doors and discovered an entire room adapted to accommodate her clothes, coats, boots, shoes, bags, accessories, you name it.

'I haven't thrown anything away for years,' she said, coming to join me on the threshold. 'So, when I moved here, I had one of the spare rooms knocked through to create this closet.'

'It's stunning,' I said, trying to take it all in. It was miles away from being just a cupboard. 'But it's hardly a closet and I can't see a lot of navy or black.'

'There are a few pieces,' she said, stepping in. 'But only a few. Now,' she said, heading to a rail on her left. 'What do you make of this little lot?'

There were dresses, tops, a couple of jumpers and a jacket, all in perfect condition and a few displaying labels I'd heard of.

'It all looks fabulous,' I said, having worked my way along the rail. My desire to admire May's wardrobe had come true. 'I know a good thing when I see it.'

'I was hoping you'd say that,' May laughed.

'Why?' I frowned.

'Well.' She shrugged, pulling out the prettiest Prada dress, which was my favourite of the lot. 'None of these pieces fit me anymore and as you seem so keen to include some colour in your wardrobe now, I wondered if you might like to pick out your favourites.'

'Oh, May,' I gasped, taking a step back and pulling my fingers away from the dress I had been fondling.

'You're very welcome to take it all if you'd like it,' she carried on.

'I couldn't possibly,' I said, although I was tempted.

'Don't make me put it all on Vinted.' She frowned.

'You just told me you haven't thrown anything away for years,' I reminded her.

'But I didn't say anything about selling things, did I?' she countered craftily.

I looked at the rail again.

'Do you want to try any of it on?'

'No,' I said, shaking my head. 'No, thank you. I promise I will think about what you've suggested though, but only if we can come to some sort of financial arrangement.'

May didn't look as though she liked the idea of that.

'I was rather hoping this would be your big Andrea moment,' she said, sounding deflated. 'You know, from the film, *The Devil Wears Prada*.'

'I know who you meant,' I told her, with a smile. 'I've seen the film. But, would that make you Nigel or Miranda?'

'Either,' she said, hanging the dress back up and gliding out. 'They're both fabulous.'

'You're not mean enough to be Miranda,' I laughed, following her.

She spun around and fixed me with a steely glare.

'You haven't seen me when I've got my heart fixed on a role,' she said fiercely, before her lips cracked into a far more familiar smile.

'Fair enough,' I said, pretending to nervously back off.

'Come on,' she laughed. 'Let's start serving up that trifle, ready for when Bear gets back.'

I never would have believed that I could eat anything so soon after the blowout roast, but the trifle, accompanied by the pre-lunch sherry we'd missed out on, was both sweet and sublime.

'So,' said Bear, once he'd devoured the three huge scoops May had filled his dessert bowl with and topped off with more cream, 'what was the big surprise, Holly? I don't like to think I've missed out.'

May went to answer on my behalf, but I cut her off.

'I might tell you later,' I told him. 'At the moment I'm still processing. Now, before we all fall asleep, why don't we have a look at these ideas I've come up with for the Christmas performance set?'

May was keen but Bear wanted to bow out and nap instead. Given I'd brought the sketches with me to ward off topics of conversation I wanted to avoid, his going for a nap should have been perfect, but the wine followed by the sherry had softened me up and I wanted them both to see what I'd come up with, regardless of the lack of intimate chat.

'Fine,' I therefore told him in a sing-song tone, 'but if your mum agrees to something that you're then going to struggle to build, don't come crying to me, Teddy Madison. And you did say you were willing to give up your time to commit to this.'

May nodded in approval. 'You tell him, Holly.'

'Okay,' he relented, looking peeved that I'd called him Teddy. 'Fine. Let's look together, then.'

I pulled the plans from my bag and laid them out on the table. May gushed over them and wanted to say yes to everything which was a wonderful ego boost for me, but not really practical.

'There won't be room for the cast if we have all of these trees,' Bear sensibly pointed out as he looked at what I'd drawn and once he'd approved the design of the huge stone effect fireplace I'd sketched.

'I agree,' I said, siding with him. 'We just need a couple. I only drew them all so you could decide which shape you thought would work best.'

May, seeing the sense in what we said, opted for the ones which looked the most like trees a child might draw.

'These will be perfect for hiding behind,' she said, pointing at them.

There was a pivotal point in the production where a couple of the actors were eavesdropping and the trees she'd picked would hide them perfectly.

'I agree,' I said, setting the other images aside.

'And they're probably going to be the simplest to make,' added Bear, sounding relieved. 'I can give them a really sturdy base so they're less likely to topple over when they're turned around mid-performance.'

'How about making them impossible to topple over?' I asked, grimacing at the thought of them crashing down at a crucial point and potentially crushing one of the cast.

'I'll do my best,' he laughed, 'but The Chapel has public liability insurance, right?'

With a hint of mischief and amusement lighting up his eyes, he held my gaze for a second and I looked quickly back at the drawings. I had assumed discussing the performance wouldn't allow for any deviation from the straight and narrow, but if he looked at me like that again I'd be in danger of jumping off that path and I had no idea what lay waiting for me in the unexplored places which ran either side of it.

'I love that you've made these trees double-sided, too,' said

May, thankfully not noticing how red I'd turned. 'Sort of a seasonal two for the price of one piece of kit.'

Some were going to be painted in full green leaf on one side and in autumnal shades on the other.

'Exactly,' I said. 'I'm making the most of every opportunity to ensure as much of it as possible is adaptable for every performance.'

'I can't tell you how relieved I am that there's going to be a set now,' she carried on. 'It wouldn't have looked anywhere near as good with a completely empty stage.'

'I only hope I can pull it off,' I admitted. 'I've never created anything like this before.'

'You'll do it,' said Bear, reaching for my hand and making me feel hot again.

'You both will,' said May. 'You have to. We're counting on you.'

'So, no pressure then.' Bear smiled, giving my fingers a squeeze before taking his hand away again. 'Is there any more of that trifle going begging?'

It was dark by the time Bear and I set off for the square and I made the most of admiring the Christmas decorations I could see already set up in some of the houses which still had their curtains open. The cosy domestic scenes being played out by the people inside made the tableaus even lovelier.

As a child, I had studied the intricate illustrations in the collection of Brambly Hedge books I regularly borrowed from the library, loving the depth of detail Jill Barklem had achieved, and the walk reminded me very much of that, only in this instance, human subjects had replaced the mice.

'Here we are then,' said Bear, stating the obvious when we reached the entrance to the square.

From there he could cross the road to Prosperous Place, while I could take the pavement just a couple of metres further to Mark and Neil's front door.

'I'll see you at The Chapel then,' I said. 'I'll double check with Eli and the others that they're happy with the set ideas and then we can start making the pieces and planning the backdrop.'

'Yes,' he said, 'the sooner, the better. But I'm not leaving you here. I'll walk you right to your door.'

'There's really no need,' I told him. 'I can see the gate from here and all the Christmas lights are on, so . . .'

My words trailed off when he didn't budge, and as it was chilly, I took the few further paces to the gate. He followed me through it and all the way to the door.

'Oh,' he said, as I fumbled in my bag for the key. 'Where did this come from? It wasn't here earlier, was it?'

I looked up to where he was staring and found a perfectly placed ball of mistletoe, secured with gold ribbon, hanging above our heads in the little covered porch.

'The fairies must have put it there,' I said, wishing they hadn't. 'Because I certainly didn't.'

This was no doubt one of the bunches Lisa had been referring to when she told Beth her mistletoe was always placed exactly where she wanted it.

'The fairies?' Bear grinned, looking amused.

'In this instance,' I said, refusing to allow myself to admire the way the light caught the laughter lines around his eyes, 'a WhatsApp toting one.'

'Oh,' said Bear, as understanding dawned. 'That one.'

'Um,' I said, having finally located the key. 'That one.'

'Shame to waste it as it's up there though,' he said, sounding hopeful. 'Isn't it?'

'Not when the fairy's probably watching our every move,' I pointed out. 'Not that I would have made the most of it if I didn't think she wasn't watching – that's not what I meant. I don't want you to think that I meant I would kiss you if she wasn't lurking somewhere . . .'

I shut up then, having made a total hash of what I was trying to say.

'The lady doth protest too much, methinks,' Bear teased. 'Clearly, I'm not the only one capable of getting tongue-tied.'

'Oh, shut up,' I said, feeling unexpectedly giggly, rather than grumpy.

I could hardly object to him teasing me about tripping over my words when I'd done the exact same thing to him and on more than one occasion.

'I'll leave you then.' He grinned.

Before he could take another step away, I reached for the front of his jacket, stood on tiptoe and went to plant a kiss on his cheek. He turned his face just at the crucial moment and my lips landed right at the very edge of his. They were every bit as soft as I had so often imagined they would be.

His eyes looked into mine for the merest, but most intense moment and my heart thumped hard, fast and loud as his mouth then caught mine. He kissed me properly and I kissed him back. The embrace was passionate and intense and I willed it not to end. But it did, abruptly, when Bear stepped back and raked a hand through his hair. I could see his chest was heaving, but couldn't fathom the expression on his face because he had stepped so far away, he was now out of the light.

'If she is watching,' I breathlessly said, 'Lisa will consider that a definite win.'

I put my hand to my mouth to stop myself laughing, but Bear didn't join in. He just turned around and walked away, leaving me feeling confused and more intoxicated than when I'd drunk all the wine at lunch.

# Chapter 16

It had been literally years – *years and years* in fact – since I'd kissed a man who wasn't Piers. For the whole of that Sunday evening and for most of the night, I couldn't help thinking how I had *never* kissed *anyone* and felt the way I felt after I'd kissed Bear.

I wasn't sure if it was the festive romance of the mistletoe moment, which really had been Hallmark perfection, or the fact that my body had responded to him in a way that suggested I was attracted to him even more deeply than I had previously realised. As I tossed and turned, and tangled my legs up in the duvet, it felt both exciting and absurd to be fidgeting about in bed like a lovestruck teenager.

I had, for the moment, conveniently forgotten my concerns about Bear being May's son *and* that his reaction to our embrace had been decidedly different to mine. Instead, I focused on the thrilling feeling that came with my libido leaping properly back into life.

I was woken by a knock on the door early the next morning. Assuming it was Bear, I rushed downstairs wearing my cutest, and rather revealing, loungewear and rocking a messy bun, but I stopped in my tracks when I reached the bottom step. In the cold light of day and with the wine and sherry out of my system, I suddenly remembered my love for May as well as Bear's reaction to our kiss and consequently changed tack.

'Just a sec!' I yelled as I reached for the biggest coat on the stand and wrapped myself up in it. 'I'm coming.'

I yanked open the door and found not Bear, but a delivery guy, holding an impressive stack of boxes.

'Oh,' I said, taken aback. 'Hi. Can I help you?'

I hadn't ordered anything other than my bright socks online and Neil and Mark hadn't mentioned any deliveries arriving while they were away.

'Are you Holly?' the guy asked hopefully.

'I am,' I said. The second I'd confirmed my name, he handed the boxes over to me, and I juggled to keep the uneven stack from falling. 'What is all this?'

'A delivery from May Madison,' he said, sounding perplexed as I carefully put the pile down just inside the door.

As the box on top was a large one with the name Prada emblazoned on it, I could guess what was inside.

'I only called around to pick up the containers I delivered her lunch in yesterday,' the chap said, sounding dazed as he walked back down the path for the final parcel and a couple of bags, 'and the next thing I knew she'd got me agreeing to act as a courier for her.'

'That sounds very like May,' I laughed and then he laughed too, while shaking his head.

'Gotta love that woman,' he said, handing the last things over.

'Oh, I do,' I told him, feeling excited about what she'd done, rather than frustrated. May had taken matters into her own hands where my dithering over her kindness was concerned, but I didn't mind. Not one bit. I daresay she'd worked out that I felt awkward about accepting the clothes, which were obviously expensive, as opposed to not wanting them. 'I really do.'

May, of course, was the main reason why I'd covered up and donned the huge coat before answering the door. Even though I was starting to feel that I was falling head-over-heels for Bear, I knew deep down that I couldn't date him. I wouldn't do that to my friend, not knowing the heartache and estrangement she'd suffered as a result of his previous break-up and the emotional baggage she carried as a result.

I waved the guy off and almost immediately there was another knock on the door. I opened it, fully expecting the bamboozled driver to be standing there with another box, but this time it was Bear. He'd already pulled off his boots, so dumped them at the side of the mat, then squeezed around me and the boxes and bags, strode along the hall and straight into the sitting room.

I would have much preferred it if he'd made a beeline for the kitchen, because that room didn't have my sketches and stories about Monty and Queenie spread out all over the place. Both the sofa and the coffee table were covered.

'What's all this?' he asked croakily, when I hastily joined him, still wearing the coat.

His voice was gravelly, deep and seriously seductive and I guessed he'd had about as much sleep as I'd had.

'Nothing,' I said, nudging around him and quickly gathering everything together in one huge and haphazard pile which would later take ages to sort. 'It's nothing.'

'Is that Queenie?' He frowned, stooping to pick up one of the sketches which had slipped off the table. 'In a spacesuit?'

'It's nothing,' I snapped again, snatching it from him and feeling my former lovestruck feelings completely melting away. 'What can I do for you, Bear?'

'Just give me two minutes of your time,' he requested, tearing his eyes away from the drawings. 'And a coffee, if there's one going?'

I pointed towards the kitchen, making sure he left the room before I did and I firmly closed the door on my way out. I knew he wasn't going to be able to forget the sight of his pooch in a silver suit destined for a galaxy far, far away, but I did hope he wasn't going to make a thing about it.

'Those sketches really don't mean anything,' I said, thinking it would be better to further fob them off rather than have him drawing his own conclusions. 'They're just doodles.'

'Very accomplished doodles,' he said, slipping off his jacket and sitting on a stool.

'Well.' I swallowed, feeling foolish to still be wearing the huge overcoat, but not wanting to remove it given the scanty outfit I had on underneath. 'I'm an illustrator by trade, remember? So, my scribbles are bound to be a bit above average, aren't they?'

I cringed at how immodest that sounded.

'I thought I saw Monty in a lifejacket too,' he said, sounding puzzled.

Realising Bear had noticed more than I first thought, I then endeavoured to drop the doodle topic. 'Cappuccino or flat white?' I offered, as I held up two pods for Mark's fancy machine.

'Flat white, please.'

'So,' I asked, as I made myself busy with the drinks, 'what did you want two minutes of my time for?'

When I thought it was him who had arrived first, there had

been a full-on fizzy feeling buzzing through me as I rushed down the stairs, hopeful that he'd turned up to pick up where we'd left off the evening before, but since coming to my senses and pulling on the coat, I'd completely changed my mind.

Not only had I remembered how the mistletoe moment had ended – with him walking off without saying a word – but I was also soberly mindful of all the reasons why I had been so keen not to get involved with him in the first place. My lips meeting his in such spectacular style might have bent my rules and blurred the lines for a few hours, but I needed to forget all of that.

'To talk about yesterday,' he said, taking the mug I handed him.

'The meal at your mum's,' I asked innocently while mentally grinding through the gears in my heart to make them fall further in sync with what was now going on in my head, 'or the time we all spent together looking at the ideas I'd had for the set?'

I was super keen to put May front and centre in both our minds. My friendship with her, and the way she now made me feel like I was in the presence of family whenever we were together, coupled with the determination not to break her heart if Bear and I ended up breaking each other's, were the motivating factors for keeping my relationship with him on a friendly footing. Hence my desire to bring her into the conversation.

But it wasn't all about May. I had to think of myself too. Bear was going be heading off as soon as spring had sprung. The thought of him not being around was already upsetting, but it would be a million times worse if we'd embarked on something more serious than friendship and then decided to let it go. Even if things ended in a friendly fashion, it would still be a wrench. One that I would be better off avoiding.

I took a deep breath and reminded myself that I had arrived

in Nightingale Square with the intention of clearing my head, then making plans and moving on. I had become completely distracted since meeting the Madison family and now time was running away with me. I needed to get back on the right path in order to have any hope of achieving what I'd originally set out to do.

'For pity's sake, Holly,' Bear said, sounding frustrated. 'You know full well that it's neither the lunch nor your ideas that I'm referring to.'

I sat on the stool opposite him and chewed my lip to stop myself replying.

'Why are you wearing a coat?' He frowned, only then noticing my unusual indoor apparel. 'Were you going out?'

'No,' I said, knowing I couldn't possibly explain. 'I'm not going anywhere, but your two minutes really are up now, so you'd better get on with telling me whatever it is you've turned up here to talk about. I've got a bath cooling upstairs,' I added, because I knew I'd sounded rather mean.

'It's our kiss, of course,' he said, sounding embarrassed that I'd made him spell it out.

'What about it?' I shrugged, feigning indifference.

'Well, the thing is.' He swallowed, sounding morose. 'I feel bad about the way it happened. I was messing about when I pointed out that bloody mistletoe Lisa had hung up.' And which, I now realised, must still be there. 'I should never have kissed you like that. That's not how I wanted . . .'

His words trailed off and as convenient as it would have been for me to play along with his take on the situation, I knew it would also have been wrong.

'Oh, Bear,' I said with a sigh. 'You need to cast your mind

back. You didn't do anything wrong. I was the one who kissed you first, remember?'

Bear's brow furrowed and I imagined him mentally scrolling through the time leading up to the moment where we had forgotten ourselves for a few seconds.

'Oh,' he said, as his eyes widened. 'It was you who started it, wasn't it?'

'It was,' I confirmed. 'Although you were the one who moved your head at the crucial moment,' I added, just to clarify that it hadn't all been me. 'I had been going to give you a chaste peck on the cheek.'

'I couldn't not move,' he said steamily, locking his eyes on mine. He was directing us immediately into dangerous territory. 'If you knew how many times—'

'Well.' I swallowed, dragging my eyes away from his hugely dilated pupils. 'That's all right then, isn't it? Enough said. I think we can both take the blame for what happened, can't we? And in the spirit of working together over the next few weeks, I'm pleased we've cleared the air because the most important thing for us now is to get this Christmas performance looking the best we possibly can and with no—'

'You're right,' he said, jumping up and cutting me off in just the same way as I'd done to him.

I was so relieved to hear him agreeing with me that I didn't mind being interrupted. I was curious to know if he was as mindful of his mum's feelings as I was, but didn't ask. I didn't want him to think that May had given me a potted history of his past relationships, because that wasn't how the topic had come up.

'Of course,' he cheerfully added, downing the contents of his mug in one. 'We really need to focus on the performance first, before we think about further kisses. Let's get the play under our belts and then we'll be free to concentrate more on us, after.'

No, no, no! That wasn't what I'd meant. Clearly my friendship with his mum wasn't on his mind at all. I'd said what I'd said on the assumption that he was thinking he'd taken advantage of the mistletoe situation but I now realised that wasn't what he had been getting at all. He was saying that an impromptu snog on the doorstep was not how he had wanted our first kiss to happen.

'We mustn't let anything distract us when this play needs to be as much of a success for Mum as it does for everyone else at The Chapel,' he further said.

'Yes,' I said emphatically. 'We really must think of your mum, and—'

'I don't know about you though, Holly,' he then admitted devastatingly, 'but I'm not sure how easy it's going to be for me to resist pulling you back under the mistletoe at every opportunity I get now.'

So, he had been blagging at the switch-on when he'd made out he wanted to spend time with me to convince me not to tie myself to a mortgage after I hadn't responded to his declaration. And now my kissing him had no doubt convinced him that my former reservation was just me being shy or coy or something and that I did actually want to start something up.

'But we must try,' I said, doing my best to sound sincere, even though his words, combined with the thought of yet more of those kisses, were melting my reservations faster than the summer sun could reduce Olaf to a puddle. 'We must try really, really hard.'

I crossed my fingers and sent up a silent prayer that Lisa hadn't been out decking any more halls during the last couple of days. We were going to be in real trouble if she had.

'Right,' said Bear, 'I better get back to work.'

'And I'll get to The Chapel,' I said, standing up and foolishly letting the best opportunity I was likely to get to properly set him straight pass me by, 'and hopefully get the go-ahead for us to start making the set.'

'Excellent,' he said, striding back along the hall, grabbing his boots and throwing the front door open. 'I'll see you later then.'

After his hasty exit, I hung the coat back on the stand and took a moment to catch my breath. I'd let him leave thinking that we could get together once the curtain fell on the Christmas performance and, even though I was flattered to have his feelings for me clarified, I was frustrated with myself for allowing that. Our unsatisfactory exchange might have left me feeling like I'd been hit by a bus but I still should have found a way to dig deep enough to explain and set him straight.

To assuage my guilt, I phoned May to thank her for the unexpected delivery. She refused to let me thank her properly, or offer her a penny towards recouping the cost. I did eventually relent about that though because I'd come up with a novel idea as to how I could pay her back. Although my side of the bargain wouldn't be anywhere near as financially valuable as hers, I was certain she would appreciate it.

'But you were supposed to give me time to think about taking these beautiful clothes off your hands, May,' I reminded her, before finally letting it drop.

'Sometimes we can spend too long thinking about things,' she said wisely, 'and end up missing out on some of the very best opportunities which are right under our noses. That's how

I missed out on a theatre tour of New Zealand. Besides,' she added gently, 'knowing you'd already decided to brighten up your wardrobe, I knew the clothes would be heading your way at some point. I just made it sooner rather than later.'

'Well, thank you,' I said again. 'Now, tell me about this missed theatre trip.'

I tried to listen to her highly entertaining tale, but all the while I was wondering if Bear was going to turn out to be one of those wonderful missed opportunities which was right under my nose. Quite possibly, was the conclusion I came to, but I was willing to sacrifice something more serious than friendship with him if it meant a long-lasting relationship with his wonderful mum. No more messing about. The decision was made and I was going to stick to it. I only hoped that when I did eventually come clean, he would still want to be my friend.

'So, Cally Carson went in my place and that was the end of that.' May tutted. 'But never mind, her career needed it more than mine.'

'How very generous of you,' I laughed, hoping I was saying the right thing because I'd only tuned into the tail end of it.

'Are you coming to The Chapel today?'

'I am,' I told her. 'Are you and Monty going to the lake?'

'No,' she said. 'Bear messaged to say it's slippery underfoot so I'm giving it a miss. I'll book an Uber to take me to The Chapel, too.'

When the pair of us had agreed, right back when we first met, that we would walk together at the lake until the worst of the winter weather arrived, neither of us had known how many other distractions and preoccupations we'd soon have filling our time. It might have been the weather which impacted the decision not to head out that day, but I was still constantly amazed by how my time in Norwich was being spent and I knew May was astonished by the changes to her life too.

'I'll happily come and collect you if that's easier?' I offered.

'No,' she insisted. 'You don't need to do that, but thank you. I'll see you later. I can't wait to see what the others make of your ideas.'

I was looking forward to that too. After finally getting dressed, I reorganised the dog sketches and pages of narrative I'd bundled together after Bear's untimely barge into the sitting room. The time flew by as I again became immersed in what I'd written and drawn, and I ended up rushing out of the door to get to The Chapel on time as I had decided to walk rather than drive now the frost had gone.

It rather took me by surprise when I realised that I had been so drawn in that I hadn't given Bear's visit another thought. If the project which had started out as playful was capable of achieving that, then there definitely was something in it.

'This is all wonderful,' said Eli as he flicked through my pages of ideas for the set. 'Show me again which pieces you and Bear have settled on.'

'And May,' I pointed out. 'She agreed too. It's these.'

I separated the pages out and put the others to one side so they didn't get muddled.

'Perfect,' he agreed. 'And you can make them all with what Luke's donated?'

'I think so,' I told him. 'We might need a few extra things, but not much and I'm hoping I'll be able to use the floor space in here to paint the backdrop. The dustsheets are huge, so I'll need to spread them out completely to get the perspective right.'

It was the thing I was most nervous about.

'Pete said he'd give you a hand with those, as a thank you for sorting the posters and flyers,' Eli then said and I felt a weight lift. If two of us had our artistic eyes on the sheets, they were bound to turn out okay.

'I'm seeing the posters everywhere,' said May who then came in carrying a tray of drinks and with Monty hot on her heels.

'Me too,' I agreed. 'There were at least half a dozen on display in shop windows as I made my way here.'

'That's down to Tamsin,' Eli told us. 'She and a couple of mates did the rounds at the weekend and the tickets are selling like hotcakes now.'

'We best make sure there's a performance worthy of the price then, hadn't we?' said May. 'When are you and Bear starting on the set pieces, Holly?'

'Now Eli has given me the nod, there's no reason why we can't get on with them from today.'

'You'd best drink this and get off to Prosperous Place then.' May winked. 'I'm very much looking forward to seeing what the pair of you do.'

Her words sounded rather loaded but in the spirit of what she'd said earlier, I tried not to overthink what she might have meant.

I headed straight to Prosperous Place, checking the workshop door for mistletoe carefully before I went in. I started drawing out the shapes on the MDF and plywood that Bear would then cut out with Luke's industrial size jigsaw. I wouldn't have minded having a go at cutting them myself, but with limited time and resources, there was no margin for error or time to acquire new skills.

Rather than go and find Bear to tell him the shapes were ready to cut out, I instead left notes attached to each of the pieces and messaged him via the WhatsApp group. Not only would that method of communication keep everyone else in the loop about our progress, it would also keep the two of us on an even keel and our conversation public rather than private.

The second I sent the message, I ducked back over to the square, just in case he came to have a look while I was still there.

I managed to cleverly keep that back and forth going for the next few days, avoiding setting eyes on him completely. I went over to do the painting when I was absolutely sure he was with Freya or even better, off-site with Luke, and only when I'd completely finished my part in getting the pieces ready did I let him know there was more for him to do.

It felt like a rather foolish game of cat and mouse, but given Bear's confession that not pulling me under the mistletoe again so soon – an action I knew I still would have been hard pushed to resist – was going to be tough, I felt it was the best one to play, for all our sakes.

# Chapter 17

By the following Thursday evening all of the pieces for the set were cut and fixed together and most were painted. Finn had kindly transported all of them to The Chapel in his van where Bear had arranged them on the stage that morning in my absence.

The trees which would be repositioned midway through the performance had turned out much sturdier than I hoped and it was extremely unlikely that any of the actors were going to be squished under an avalanche of plywood apples. I knew the others had thought I was joking when I'd mentioned it, but I'd been genuinely worried about the possibility.

There were only a few things left for me to do now. Some final flourishes, such as battery-operated lights in the realistic looking fireplace and a padlock for the treasure chest, would complete the look on stage and once Pete and I had created the backdrop, a job we'd scheduled for the following Monday, the scene would quite literally be set and with just enough time for the actors to get used to it.

Bear still had to hang the bamboo pole, but Eli had assured me that job was in hand too. My crafty plan to avoid Bear had been a total success and even though I didn't feel all that proud of my cunning actions, I knew that needs must. It was for the greater good.

May and I had got back into the habit of taking our early walk together and, much to her delight, I had worn one of the colourful jumpers she had gifted me – red and pink stripes which made me look rather like a candy cane – more than once. Seasonal. And I can't deny I revelled in her praise. Even though her kindness wasn't exactly a mother's love it felt as close to it as I'd ever got and it was a sensation I cherished.

'Okay, folks,' said Lisa, just after six that Thursday evening once we'd all congregated inside The Chapel, 'the tree isn't going to be delivered tonight after all.'

This piece of news elicited a collective groan and some frustrated muttering.

'I know, I know,' Lisa agreed. 'I'm disappointed too, but it can't be helped. I'll deal with it tomorrow. The main thing is not to let it spoil tonight. If anyone asks, tell them we're eking out the festive excitement.'

That seemed to placate the volunteer helpers, so hopefully it would work on everyone waiting to get inside, too.

'Now,' she instructed, 'brace yourselves. I'm about to open the doors!'

Rather than putting the decorations up without involving the attendees, she and Eli had come up with the idea of taking a night off from rehearsals and inviting everyone to come and play a part in making the place look festive. It was a shame the tree hadn't arrived yet, but there was still plenty else we could decorate and do.

I had agreed to help when May mentioned that Bear was

spending the night in Cambridgeshire, sussing out a potential future job. As well as being one of the team on drink and Christmas cookie distribution duty, I had also been assigned as joint leader at the craft and painting tables. As the 'arty ones' among the group of adult volunteers, Pete was going to be helping out, too, but he was running a little late so I would be flying solo to start with, but in the presence of one of the other official volunteers as I didn't have a DBS.

'Hats on!' Lisa shouted, as she headed over to the door.

We'd each been allocated a festive themed hat or headband. I'd got the elf and May was looking fetching in antlers, while Eli was Santa and for some reason, Sara had an old-fashioned nightcap.

'Scrooge,' she told me as she pointed at her head. 'Lisa and I are running a creepy Christmas creative writing workshop session.'

'That'll explain the crutch,' I laughed, guessing Lisa was Tiny Tim and not, in fact, suffering from a previously unmentioned ailment.

She opened the door and there was a sudden influx of people. A few of the parents lingered until their younger kids were settled and then headed off. I'd never seen the place so busy, but then I'd never been there when the full team and all the kids who took part in the classes were in attendance. I guessed it didn't happen all that often.

Eli fired up a playlist of festive tunes and collared some of the taller lot to help hang the gaudy ceiling garlands and lanterns, the likes of which I hadn't seen for years. I gave a quick run through to my keen crafters and the other volunteer about how to make the decorations which would be hung on the tree as soon as it arrived and stay there until The Chapel closed for the holidays. Quite a few eager faces stared up at me, all desperate to get started.

We were also supposed to be painting a couple of the smaller set pieces together, including the hinged treasure chest, but that was all set out on another table and could wait until Pete arrived. I didn't want to spread my limited child corralling skills too thinly.

'You can take your decorations with you when we close for Christmas and hang them on your trees at home.' I smiled, getting into the swing of things as I handed round the tubs of glitter along with the gingerbread and tree-shaped templates.

'Can I do two?' one of the girls asked.

'I don't see why not,' I told her. 'There should be more than enough to go around.'

'I stay at Mum's one half of the week,' she then explained, 'and Dad's the rest, so I've got two trees.'

'Lucky you,' said one of the others.

The girl looked thrilled to be considered so fortunate.

'I'm the same,' said one of the younger boys. 'So, can I do two, too?'

'Of course, you can,' I told them both, thinking that was only fair. 'Make a start on your first ones and I'll get going cutting out some more. Go steady with that glitter though,' I added as the tub of red was almost upended. 'That's all we've got and Lisa will tell Santa to put me on his naughty list if it ends up all over the floor.'

That elicited a few giggles.

'That she will,' said Pete, who rushed up looking hot and flustered. 'Sorry I'm late.'

'No worries,' I told him. 'Catch your breath for a minute, then you can take over here while I help check everyone's got enough to drink.'

'And enough cookies,' one of the keen crafters piped up. 'We need more cookies!'

By eight o'clock, The Chapel was thoroughly festooned and the set pieces were finally all painted. The application of colour was a little haphazard on some of the apples and leaves, but that was part of the charm. It looked like a real team effort and the kids had loved being involved.

'I want to be a painter when I grow up,' one of the younger brush-toting crew members told me. 'And make things like that treasure chest.'

'That would be a great job,' I said encouragingly. 'You should go for it.'

Had there been more time, I would have told them what I did for a living.

'You've got a splodge of red paint,' they then confidentially whispered, 'right across your forehead.'

'Occupational hazard,' I said as I shrugged and laughed, and they laughed too.

'Great job everyone,' said Luke. 'There's no way Santa will miss this place when he comes looking for us now!'

A collective cheer went up and I looked around.

There wasn't a surface that wasn't adorned in some way. The ceiling was barely visible and the tree, when it turned up, wouldn't have a single empty branch. Along with the tinsel and flashing lights to cover it in, I now had a whole box full of decorations to add to it. The plates of cookies had been reduced to crumbs and there was a Mexican wave of yawns, mostly from the adults, as everyone settled to listen to a couple of the creepy Christmas tales.

'This is for you,' said a boy called Ben when it was time to go, handing me a still-sticky gingerbread decoration. 'You didn't get time to make one for yourself, so I made an extra one for you.'

'Oh, thank you, Ben,' I said, feeling touched. 'It's absolutely beautiful.'

He seemed thrilled that I thought so. He ran off to where his dad was waiting and gave me a cheery wave. I wondered if he could see the paint on my head from that distance. Lisa stood at the door with a list of names and checked everyone out, making them all promise to go straight to sleep when they got home because tomorrow was a school day.

'You'll have to hang that on your tree,' said May, who came over to admire my gift from Ben.

I was trying to encourage the last of the glitter back into a jar I'd relabelled as 'mixed'.

Most of it had ended up blended, but it was still beautiful. I'd always been a big fan of glitter. My mum hated it though. She considered its ability to get everywhere and defy the hefty power of her vacuum a total nuisance which far outweighed its aesthetic. Glitter had been banned in our home after one spill too many.

'I would if I had one,' I said to May, looking at the weighty gingerbread figure. It would take forever to dry out given the amount of glue it was covered in. 'I didn't have the heart to tell him that I won't be having any decorations this year.'

May looked appalled.

'It's not my house,' I reminded her. 'So, no decs.'

'Rubbish,' she said, handing me a tissue and indicating I still needed to scrub my head. 'Your friends will no doubt have some that you could find if you look for them and I'm sure they wouldn't mind if you put them up. In fact, they'd probably be devastated to think you'd seen the season out without so much as a fairy light to lift your spirits. How are you supposed to get that festive feeling with no decs?'

'My spirits are fine,' I said with a laugh, thinking devastated was too strong an emotion, but then, knowing Mark's love of a theatrical reaction, she was probably right. Just as well he'd never know. 'And after tonight I'm feeling even more festive,' I continued. 'And I've got the lights up out the front of the house. I don't need more than that.'

May didn't look convinced, but let the topic drop.

'Can you be at mine at eight in the morning?' she asked.

'I think rain is forecast,' I responded, looking at the still pristine tissue. It hadn't wiped off so much as a drop of the streak of red, which must now have dried into questionable face paint.

'I wasn't planning on going for a walk.'

'Oh,' I said. 'So, just a social call then?'

'I have a favour to ask,' she admitted.

'Can't you ask me now?'

'Not really,' she said, sounding shifty, which made me suspicious. 'It's for Monty,' she then added, knowing that would be a clincher if I had been about to turn her down.

'In that case, yes, I can be at yours at eight,' I said, falling for her ploy.


Unfortunately, I wasn't the only early morning caller that May had. It was Bear who opened the door to let me inside the bungalow, completely scuppering my plan to avoid him, which was frustrating given how well it had been going.

'I thought you were in Cambridgeshire,' I said with a sigh as I hung up my coat on the obliging arm of the faun statue in the hall.

'Well, hello to you too,' Bear laughed. 'I got a warmer welcome from the dogs.'

I bent to fuss both Monty and Queenie who had loyally left the warmth of Monty's cosy nest bed to come and say hello to me.

'I was away,' Bear carried on, when I didn't say anything, 'but only briefly. The job turned out to be a no-go, so I headed back last night. I didn't need to look at the site again so there was no point hanging on until this morning.'

'I see,' I said. I stood back up, but refused to look at him.

'Is everything all right?' he asked.

I could tell from his tone that he was frowning and he would be, wouldn't he? As far as he was concerned, we were just biding our time until the Christmas performance had received its last ovation and then we'd be back exchanging kisses under the mistletoe, or wherever. I still hadn't worked out how I could quash that idea without hurting his feelings.

'Fine,' I therefore said airily. 'I've just got a busy day lined up and I'm curious to know what this favour is that your mum wants to ask.'

'Favour?' he repeated.

'There you are, Holly,' said May, popping her head around the kitchen door. 'Come and have some coffee. I've got gifts for you both.'

'More gifts?' I frowned as we entered the kitchen.

'Only a little one this time,' she said, handing first me and then Bear identically wrapped packages. She looked up at my face. 'I'm relieved to see that paint has come off.'

'Me too.' I smiled, touching my forehead.

There was no weight to my package and I had no idea what could possibly be inside.

'Can we open them now?' asked Bear, clearly itching to get inside his as he shook it to see if it rattled. It did a bit.

'Of course,' said May. 'Given the date, you must.'

We ripped into them together and the penny dropped.

'An advent calendar.' I smiled.

'For December the first,' said Bear. 'Thanks, Mum.'

'Yes,' I said. 'Thank you, May. I haven't had one of these for years.'

'Well,' she said, taking the wrapping paper from us and depositing it in her recycling box by the back door, 'as you seem to be behaving like kids, I thought it felt fitting.'

'And Divine chocolate, too,' said Bear before I had a chance to ask what she meant. 'Delicious and ethically sourced. You know how much I love this stuff.'

He gave her a kiss on the cheek, while I read more of the details on the box. As I took in the words and looked at the picture on the front, I began to feel rather ... not unwell, more unsettled, perhaps? Whether I was still getting my head around Bear's unexpected presence or if the feeling was something to do with the calendar reminding me of the formal and functional Christmases of my childhood, I couldn't tell.

'Monty and Queenie both have calendars too,' said May, pointing at the matching pair the pooches had. 'Though not chocolate ones, obviously.'

'Obviously,' said Bear, who had already devoured his day one.

'Which reminds me of why I'm here, May,' I said, pulling the conversation around to finding out what she was going to ask of me that involved her canine companion. I hoped the change of topic would help me shrug off my unfathomable discomfiture. 'What was the favour you wanted to ask me, related to Monty?'

Cue tail thumping from the dog bed in the corner. I had to smile when Queenie joined in, too, even though her name hadn't been mentioned. Synchronised tail swishing could well end up featuring in one of their stories. The thought of that soon set me back on the path to feeling better.

'Ah, yes,' said May, beckoning me over to the table and the aforementioned coffee. 'I was wondering if you could possibly help me out with him on Sunday?'

'This Sunday?'

'Yes.' She nodded. 'Now Finn has delivered your perfect set, Holly, and it's painted and all in place, we've called the cast in to rehearse all day Saturday and Sunday, so they can get the hang of working around it.'

'That sounds like a good idea to me,' said Bear. 'It's bound to be different, acting with a fuller stage.'

'Exactly,' May agreed.

'I'll help with Monty if I can,' I told her, 'but won't I be needed to make drinks and hand out the biscuits?'

'Ordinarily, yes,' agreed May, 'and if you could do that tomorrow, it would be hugely appreciated but my dear boy has an appointment on Sunday. One it's taken me a great deal of trouble to secure at such short notice and I really don't want him to miss it.'

'In that case,' I said, concerned by the frown on May's face and feeling worried in case Monty was unwell and it was a medical appointment, 'count me in.'

Although, I then realised the second I'd promised, vets didn't generally work on Sundays and there didn't appear to be anything wrong with him. And more to the point, why hadn't she asked Bear?

'So, you'll definitely take him, in my place?' May asked, sounding hopeful and wanting me to clarify.

'I'll definitely take him in your place,' I clearly and concisely confirmed because it would have been unfair to back out.

'Oh, that's a weight off my mind,' she said, already looking happier as she put a hand to her chest and let out a long breath. 'I hate to miss it myself, but needs must and with the performance only a couple of weeks away . . .'

'It's fine,' I told her. 'Whatever it is, I'll sort it.'

'Good,' she said, clapping her hands. 'That's settled then.'

'But what is it, Mum?' Bear asked. 'You haven't said.'

I noticed he didn't offer to step in or ask why she had picked me over him while May looked over fondly at her pampered and much-loved hound.

'A festive photo shoot.' She beamed and I choked on my coffee.

Bear burst out laughing at both his mum's words and my reaction to them.

'A festive what?' I spluttered, wiping my mouth on a tissue I had up my sleeve.

'Photo shoot,' May repeated. 'I couldn't get him a spot to see Santa and this place was fully booked when I first enquired, but then a slot became unexpectedly available after my hundredth phone call and I nabbed it. I just knew it was meant to be.'

I doubted that. I daresay the slot became available in the hope that she'd stop repeatedly ringing.

'You should see the collections of clothes they've got for him to try on,' she continued dreamily. 'I've been browsing through the outfits online.'

I really didn't think I should.

'Oh, May,' I wheedled, 'surely, you don't want to miss out on that?'

'Of course, I don't,' she said, 'but The Chapel crew have put a lot of faith in me and I can't let them down. They're counting on me and because of the age of the attendees, weekends are the only time when we get a lengthy clear run at working through things because they're at school during the week, so ...'

'All right,' I relented, understanding why she couldn't budge. 'It's fine.'

At least Monty would be a willing participant. He loved nothing more than dressing up and showing off. I daresay he'd have a whale of a time and all I'd really have to do was act as his chaperone.

'The platinum package is all paid for,' May then explained. 'You'll come away with snow globes, bookmarks and cards to send to all our friends. I'm relying on you to pick which outfit works the best, Holly.'

'No pressure then.' I swallowed, feeling the full weight of responsibility descend on my shoulders. 'And I don't know what you're looking so happy about,' I snapped at Bear, who was clearly revelling in the prospect of my Sunday spent playing assistant to Monty.

'But he has every reason to smile,' said May, patting his hand, 'because I've booked the session to include Queenie, too.'

That soon wiped the smile off his face!

# Chapter 18

Bear tried every trick in the book to get him and Queenie out of having to attend the photo shoot. He even went so far as to bring up her horrid start in life and how she was likely to find the experience traumatic.

'It's bound to be triggering for her,' he said to May. 'It could set her back months.'

'You do that dog a disservice,' May shot back, sounding disappointed in him as Queenie happily sat wearing one of Monty's many hats as a trial run. 'She'll be fine, especially with Monty taking part. If she doesn't go, how do you think she'll feel when he starts doling out personalised gifts for Christmas and she hasn't got any to share?'

I bit my lip as May winked at me. She knew full well that Bear hated any talk like that associated with the dogs and she only did it to wind him up. At least, I think she did.

'Anyone would think you don't want to spend Sunday with Holly,' she then said, which reined my good humour in.

Bear looked at me and swallowed. 'Of course, I do,' he said.

'Good,' said May. I wished that he had succeeded in convincing his mum that he and Queenie didn't have to attend, but

May had drawn a line under the conversation. 'You all need to be at the studio at eleven sharp and there'll be no diva behaviour from any of you.'

I certainly wouldn't be acting up. I'd be keeping my head down and just getting through it because, as amusing as I had found it to observe the many looks on Bear's face as he had tried to talk May out of making him and Queenie attend, I knew it wasn't going to be easy to spend time with him and not fall further under his spell, the strength of which I hoped he had no real understanding of.

Neither Bear nor I were looking our best on the Sunday morning and I guessed he was looking forward to the Pooch Shoot – as the timed tickets informed us it was called – with as much enthusiasm as I was.

Monty had spent the night in Bear's horsebox, so May could make an extra early start at The Chapel, and the trio walked over to the square to meet me as I was going to be driving us to the venue.

'Hey,' said Bear, sounding gruff.

'Morning,' I said. I tried to smile.

'I hope you got more sleep last night than I did,' he commented as Queenie happily hopped up onto the back seat of my car with Monty in hot pursuit.

Bear's voice was all gravelly again and he sounded super-sexy, but I refused to respond. Outwardly, at least.

'This pair were fidgeting all night.' He sighed. 'Queenie's usually fine on her own, but put them together and they turn into total terrors.'

I looked at Queenie and she cocked her head. I couldn't

imagine she was anywhere near as bad as Bear was suggesting. Monty, on the other hand . . .

'Perhaps they're just excited for the Pooch Shoot,' I said, trying to cheer Bear up.

I didn't tell him that I had also laid awake for much of the night and that the reason for that had been the advent calendar his mum had gifted me. I had finally got to the bottom of why I found it so unnerving, but I didn't feel in the mood to share. The imminent photo session was enough to contend with and I would be better off focusing on that rather than my reason for feeling so stirred up by twenty-four chunks of chocolate.

'Don't you start,' he tutted. 'You sound like Mum. And Queenie wouldn't be excited if she knew what was coming. She'd be a bag of nerves.'

'If you keep talking her nerves up and sounding so negative, she will be,' I shot back, beginning to lose patience. 'You'll transfer your feelings on to her.'

He didn't respond to that, but climbed into the passenger seat, sliding it all the way back to accommodate his long, jean-clad legs.

'Do feel free to adjust the seat,' I commented sardonically, as I read the address on the ticket and keyed our destination into my satnav. 'And make yourself at home.'

That did get a smile out of him, but not a particularly convincing one. Annoyingly, however, his continued grumpy mood only served to make me feel fonder of him because I knew it was born out of concern for his beloved companion.

A short while later Bear frowned as he peered out of the passenger side window at a nondescript-looking unit on the out-of-town industrial estate. 'Are you sure this is it?'

I didn't know what either of us had been expecting, but the unassuming location before us certainly wasn't it. I was relieved May hadn't been able to come, because I was beginning to think she'd fallen foul of some scheme or scam. The tickets hadn't been cheap and the place looked deserted. I had resisted checking out the website the previous evening, but now I wished I had.

'According to the satnav we're in the right place.' I shrugged. 'But I'll drive around again, just in case there's somewhere we've missed that's done up like the proverbial dog's dinner.'

Monty happily yapped in the back, while Bear rolled his eyes. I had just engaged first gear when the unit door opened and a family came out with three Dalmatians, one of which was wearing a set of cow horns.

'Forget that,' said Bear, sounding resigned. 'We're in the right place.'

I parked up properly and Bear gave the two stars of the shoot a quick once around the block before we pressed the intercom, gave our names and were buzzed inside. The exterior might have looked boring and bland, but inside it was doggy heaven. Or doggy heaven for a dog like Monty.

'Well, hello, you beautiful pair,' said the guy who let us in and gifted the dogs with a treat apiece. 'Aren't you looking fabulous? And the pooches aren't bad either!'

I laughed at that and Bear looked so surprised, I laughed all the harder.

'Okay,' said the guy, taking the leads from us. 'My name is Simon and I can already tell that one of us got out of the bed on the wrong side this morning and it wasn't me.'

'He did,' I said, making matters worse by pointing at Bear and

then flushing scarlet in case Simon assumed the two of us had
been in the same bed.

'Okay then.' He smiled. 'In that case, we'll get to work on
your sense of humour in a bit, Teddy.'

'Great,' Bear said sarcastically, looking entirely unhappy at the
prospect of that. 'But before you disappear with my dog, there
are a few things you need to know about Queenie.'

'Don't worry,' said Simon, trotting through to the main
dressing area which had racks and racks of outfits in a huge array
of sizes, shapes, patterns and colours. 'Your mum, the fabulous
May Madison, so I've been told, has already filled us in. Queenie
couldn't possibly be in better hands.'

I was sure Bear was pleased on the inside, but as Queenie
cosied up with Simon and looked completely unfazed by the
hustle and bustle happening around her, he appeared to be a bit
miffed on the outside.

'Just go with it.' I nudged him. 'The sooner you submit, the
sooner it'll be over.'

I was sure he growled in response. He certainly sounded more
bear-like than usual.

After a few attempts at finding the perfect outfits, Queenie
settled on being transformed into the fairy on top of the tree,
complete with sparkly tiara, and Monty became a gingerbread
man. His suit was hilarious – it was the sort which had the legs
on the front so, face on, he looked like he was standing up. They
were both impossibly cute and I knew May would adore them.
I wished then that she was with us.

'And now for Mum for the day and Dad,' said Simon, making
me feel suddenly less fond of my new friend.

'What?' I stammered.

'Who?' Bear added.

'You two, of course,' said Simon, pointing to each of us in turn. 'This has been booked as a family session. We need outfits for you two, too.'

Bear and I looked at one another.

'No way,' said Bear as Simon walked over to another rack.

That explained the size of some of the other costumes. I had been looking at them and wondering if they were too large even for a wolfhound or Great Dane.

'This is perfect for you, Teddy,' said Simon, pulling a huge Olaf outfit off the rail. 'Queenie looks like she could have stepped straight out of *Frozen*, so this will complement her perfectly.'

'Oh yes, Teddy,' I teased, unable to resist. 'Go on. I dare you.'

He glared at me as Simon handed him the costume, poking him in the face with the carrot nose in the process. The outfit was a sort of thickly padded all-in-one, complete with stick arms and coal effect buttons.

'And now for you, Holly,' Simon said, diving back into the rack again.

Initially, I wasn't sure what would go with a gingerbread outfit, but then inspiration struck. I decided to follow the advice I'd given Bear and just go with the flow.

'What about something from *Shrek*?' I suggested. 'Have you got a Princess Fiona tucked away in there? Or even a Donkey? I don't mind making a fool of myself,' I added with a smile at Bear, 'as it's for such a good cause.'

I was rather enjoying playing along now I'd got more into the swing of it.

'No Fiona and no Donkey,' said Simon, his fingers flying along the rails, 'but this'll work.'

He handed me an outfit that didn't appear to have a lot to it, along with a hat which had a huge feather attached and a pair of thigh-high black boots.

'You're a size five, yes?'

'What's this?' I asked, holding both the hanger and the boots up.

'Puss in Boots,' grinned Simon. 'A slightly racy version, I grant you, but it'll still work. There are cat ears here somewhere,' he added, starting to rummage in a box. 'To go over the top of the hat.'

'What about a cat onesie instead?' I asked, rather desperately. 'That would work better than this minuscule dress if I'm replicating the character from Shrek.'

'We couldn't have a proper cat costume in here, could we?' Simon laughed, pointing at the dogs. 'No, it's what you've got in your hand or nothing.'

'Go on.' Bear nudged me, laughing at my shocked expression. 'I dare you.'

It took the two of us longer to get dressed than it had the dogs and I hoped the nose and whiskers I'd had drawn on my face would come off so I wouldn't be rocking a Rachel and Ross in Vegas look for the festive season. Bear was in the same boat with bright pink rosy cheeks either side of his stuck-on carrot nose, although, on closer inspection, I realised they might well have been real.

I wished that phones had been allowed on the Pooch Shoot, because the sight of him shuffling along in the snowman-shaped costume with his arms trapped inside to take his spot on the snowy set with Queenie was one I would have loved to record and share with May. I committed it to memory to amuse myself with in any future low moments.

'Nice,' he said huskily as he looked at my legs, or the bit of them he could see above the tops of the boots and below the hem of the shockingly short buckle-belted dress. I stuck my tongue out in response. Given what he was currently wearing, his seductive tone had absolutely no impact on me at all.

It took Monty a few seconds to be convinced that it was Bear inside the costume and for a moment, I thought we were going to have to abandon the whole thing, but we got there in the end and the person behind the camera, who looked extraordinarily bored given the hilarious spectacle in front of them, snapped away.

'Come back anytime between two and four,' said Simon, checking the images to make sure the photographer had got just the shot he'd been hoping for, 'and your platinum package will be ready for collection.'

He then handed us over to another assistant who helped us out of the costumes and gave the dogs, who were beginning to exude pent-up energy, a couple more treats. I could hear high-pitched yapping in the welcome area by the time we were ready to leave and guessed the next attendees weren't quite as placid as our pair had been.

'Do not,' said Bear, as we stepped back out into the chilly winter air with the dogs skittering around our ankles, 'say a word.'

I really, really wanted to say so much, but I bit it all back.

'I was only going to suggest we go and find somewhere to have lunch while we wait to pick the photos up,' I said innocently.

'And the snow globes,' he groaned. 'Don't forget the snow globes.'

'You should be happy about those, Olaf.' I beamed. 'It will be wonderful to see you in your natural habitat.'

'Just get the car warmed up,' he said, rolling his eyes, 'and I'll take this pair for a jog around the block.'

Queenie and Monty were panting by the time he came back so I guessed Bear had walked off some of his feelings as he strode around the estate.

'I've found a dog-friendly pub that's not too far away,' I told him, showing him my phone as he settled the exhausted dogs in the back. 'Shall we aim for there?'

'Why not?' He shrugged.

'Or I could just drop you back at Prosperous Place and come back later on my own?' I offered as an alternative, realising that would be a more sensible suggestion, given that I was trying to spend as little time with him as possible and we did have quite a bit of time to kill. 'I don't mind. We should do what best suits the dogs. They do look pretty tired.'

He looked over the seat to where the pair had already curled up together and closed their eyes.

'Let's head to the pub,' said Bear. 'They can nap on the way.'

'Queenie surprised you, didn't she?' I said softly.

'She really did.' Bear swallowed, making my heart melt. 'I honestly didn't think she'd tolerate any of that fuss, but she was amazing.'

'Maybe seeing Monty always dressed for every occasion has rubbed off on her.' I smiled. 'And she was happy enough wearing one of his hats when May set up the trial run, wasn't she? Perhaps you'd better order her a couple of outfits for Christmas.'

As he turned back around, he gave me a look best described as withering.

'Perhaps I should get you a pair of those thigh-high boots for Christmas instead, Holly,' he teasingly said back.

At least I think he was teasing.

'Touché,' I said, turning my attention to carefully pulling out of the parking space.

There were more cars parked up than when we'd arrived and another family was already waiting outside the Pooch Shoot door. I wondered if people were turning up early or if something had happened with the appointment after ours which had thrown the schedule into disarray. The yapping while we had got changed had been pretty persistent. I was pleased we'd avoided that. Tangled leads and squabbles over costumes would not a happy doggy duo make.

'Did the session give you some more ideas for your doggy doodles?' Bear asked, making my foot slip a little on the clutch and the car lurch as a result.

I stamped on the brake.

'A few,' I confessed. I waved a huge guy carrying a tutu toting chihuahua across the space in front of the car. 'I thought I might add an Olaf to the growing collection.'

'Touché back,' Bear sighed, rolling his eyes.

When we arrived at the pub, we found it was open at lunch only to those who had reservations, so Bear ended up buying a bag of snacks from a mini supermarket, while I stayed with the dogs and prepared to eat a scratch picnic in the car. I had offered to take us back to the square again, but he vetoed that suggestion.

'I've got a better idea than this,' he announced, soon after we had parked up again and started eating. 'How do you fancy going on a bit of a magical mystery tour?' He didn't appear to be enjoying sitting in the steamed-up vehicle with the pair in the back. They had woken the second a packet rustled and were watching out for any dropped crumb with an intensity that made me twitch.

'Yes, why not?' I shrugged, glancing over my shoulder.

'Give me a minute,' he said, climbing out of the car again.

I watched him pace up and down, chatting to someone on his phone and wondered what he was up to. Queenie was watching him, too, and started to whine until I fussed her.

'Right,' said Bear, when he'd finished the call and climbed back into the car. 'We're off to Downham Market.'

'Where's that?' I frowned.

'Right on the edge of the Fens.' He grinned, turning to stroke Queenie and as a result putting himself in much closer proximity to me. 'And a much nicer venue for eating a makeshift lunch than in a car with the dogs breathing down our necks.'

'Sounds good to me,' I laughed. 'Is it a long drive?'

'About an hour,' he told me, then quickly added, 'A bit of a trek, but I promise it'll be worth it.'

I knew there were nice places to eat a picnic much closer than that, but he did sound keen, and I was curious about where he wanted to show me.

'All right,' I said, repacking the picnic. 'You'd better tell me which way to go.'

I knew spending longer with him was going to do nothing to quell my feelings. In fact, watching him dress up as a giant Disney character had already strengthened rather than weakened them but for the time being I decided to throw caution to the wind and go along with whatever it was he had in mind.

# Chapter 19

When we finally arrived at our destination, I instantly knew that Bear did, in fact, have much more in mind than a picturesque picnic and given the unsettled feelings the advent calendar from his mum had aroused, I felt very grateful for what he'd come up with.

'This is it,' he said. He directed me to pull off the road and into a makeshift car park which bordered a stretch of creek where I could see a narrowboat moored up. I shook my head. 'What?' he said, shrugging.

'I know what you're up to, Teddy Madison,' I happily responded, my heart pounding in my chest.

'Do you now?' He grinned.

A guy wearing a holey jumper not all that dissimilar to the ones Bear favoured climbed off the boat and waved. Bear put up a hand in reply and climbed out of the car.

I watched the two men embrace and clap each other on the back. Clearly, they were firm friends. I guessed this was the guy Bear had mentioned when we'd previously talked about life on the water and his clever way of introducing me to it couldn't have been better timed.

My mind tracked back to May's calendar again. I knew now that the emotion I had experienced when I unwrapped it was anxiety. As I had popped that first chocolate into my mouth, I had become mindful of the date. That innocuous looking door with number one written on it, had made me suddenly aware that I had been staying in Nightingale Square for almost a month which meant that my allotted head clearing time was up and I needed to turn my attention to making some proper plans.

The passion project featuring the dogs was helping on the work front, but I was still no closer to deciding where I wanted to move to or what I would live in when I got there. That said, I was undoubtedly feeling more open to Bear's ideas about alternative living now and that was why I felt more than a prickle of excitement at the prospect of seeing inside the narrowboat currently moored next to me. The trip really was perfectly timed, though Bear couldn't have known that.

He rushed back to the car again, opened the passenger door and grabbed our makeshift picnic.

'Come on,' he said, handing it to me, 'you take the food and I'll grab the dogs.'

My legs felt a bit wobbly as I climbed out of the car and followed him.

'Holly, this is my friend, James.' Bear smiled, introducing me. 'James, this is my friend, Holly.'

'Hi,' said James. He shook my hand, which felt a bit formal. 'So, you're the friend Bear can't stop talking about.'

I knew my cheeks were flaming, but Bear's were too.

'Thanks for that, mate,' he said, slapping James on the back. 'Yes, this is who I'm trying to convince that an alternative home is the way forward.'

I wondered if that was all he had talked about when he'd mentioned me to James. Given the way James's eyebrows shot up, I guessed perhaps not.

'It's lucky I happened to be moored here then, so you could come and say hello, wasn't it?' he laughed.

'Are you staying for a while or just passing through?' I asked.

He paused, giving the question some thought. 'I'm not sure,' he said. 'I haven't really got a plan for the next couple of months. Would you like to have a look inside?'

'Yes, please,' I said, because by then I was itching to see the set up.

'Come on, then,' he said. 'Come and see what you make of it and I'll try to talk you out of living on a boat.'

'You'll try to talk me out of it?' I repeated, assuming I'd misheard.

'Yep.' He grinned, holding out his hand to welcome me aboard. 'It's not all sunshine and sunflowers, my friend.'

'That's not helpful, James,' said Bear, following on with the dogs. 'That's not helpful at all.'

'It is,' I contradicted him. 'I want to know the good, the bad and the ugly.'

'Kicking off with the ugly then,' said James, as I stepped inside. 'Have you considered the joys of dealing with the loo on a boat?'

'Er, no,' I admitted. 'I can't say that I have.'

Before settling down to eat lunch, we had an in-depth tour of the space inside. That surprisingly took longer than I might have expected, mostly because I wanted to stop and admire everything, in spite of the freshly landed reservations about the facilities and their maintenance.

'It's so warm,' was the first thing I said.

I had expected to need to keep my coat on, but once we'd let out a tabby cat, who wasn't impressed to see the dogs, and closed the doors behind us, the inside was toasty.

'Diesel fired central heating,' said James. 'It's been a game changer. I had just the stove before and it wasn't quite enough to keep the place comfortable and condensation free.'

'And so many cubby holes,' I commented as we ventured further in.

'You need those.' James smiled. 'And you need to be prepared to dramatically downsize your possessions, too, assuming you have a lot. Bear did say that you've been living in a house up until now.'

'That's right,' I said, my eyes darting around to take more of the details in. 'And I do have quite a lot of stuff.'

'But nothing you'd want to hang on to if you could be mortgage free as a result of parting with it, right?' said Bear, reminding me of the financial freedom that shedding my storage boxes could potentially gift me.

'Well,' I admitted, having thought it through and realised that most of the things I'd packed didn't fit in with the fresh and colourful aesthetic I was now looking forward to embracing, 'there's actually not much I've missed during the last few weeks.' Bear looked thrilled. 'This place is wonderful, James.'

'I'm delighted you think so,' he said. 'Especially as you're seeing it at the toughest time of year. It's even lovelier in the summer with the windows open and the outside space full of plants and boat-grown veg.'

Having admired the narrowboat's compact bathroom, and not voiced my opinion about sacrificing my Saturday night bath – a simple indulgence I hadn't considered having to part with – we settled at the table to share our picnic. James served up a fruit-cake and made us tea while I quizzed him about doing laundry onboard and asked how the loo situation did actually work. The reality of that wasn't anything like as unsavoury as I'd imagined.

'I know Bear's keen for me to embrace this sort of life or one similar to it,' I told James, once Bear had taken the dogs for a walk to stretch their legs, 'but there's so much to consider. Owning something outright and being debt free is the biggest temptation, but I'm still not sure if it's for me.'

'But you do like the boat, don't you?' James asked. 'I can tell by the look on your face.'

'I do,' I confirmed, again picturing the colourful patchwork interior of the boat called Hope that I'd painted for Monty and Queenie to travel about on and imagining myself living among it. 'I really do.'

'Well,' he said, pouring me more tea. 'That's a step in the right direction.'

'I suppose it is,' I happily agreed, but then my thoughts turned to whether I'd find life on a boat too isolating. 'What do you do for a living, James?'

'I'm a garden designer,' he told me. 'That's how Bear and I met.'

'A garden designer, with no garden,' I pointed out.

'A garden designer with no garden at the moment,' he corrected. 'Who knows what I'll have or where I'll end up in the future.'

'Does the thought of not knowing stress you out?'

'Never,' he laughed. 'It's exciting. I haven't got anyone who depends on me, so I don't have to worry about factoring them into my plans.'

That was something we had in common.

'And you don't get lonely, living alone on the boat?'

'Because of the nature of my work, I'm off it as much as on,' he told me. 'But if that's something that concerns you, then why not consider a permanent mooring in a marina? Lots of those have a great community spirit and all the services you could possibly need available on site.'

'Oh, yes,' I mused. 'I hadn't thought of that.'

'What's your line of work, Holly?' he then asked. 'Bear has never mentioned it.'

I wondered if that was because I had told him I was currently struggling with it.

'I'm an illustrator,' I explained. 'I create images to complement other people's wonderful words. I mostly work on children's books.'

'Oh, wow.' James smiled. 'That must be an amazing job.'

'It has its moments.' I nodded. 'But I work from home,' I added, looking around.

'Ah,' said James, understanding the implications. 'There's not much room in here for an entire artist's studio.'

'No,' I agreed, biting my lip, 'though I often draw on a tablet now, so it might not be too much of a squeeze to make it work. How do you manage it?'

'I work exclusively on a screen,' he explained. 'And I can set this whole area up as a home office in just a few minutes, so you could do the same, but that said, if you did want more space, you could look out for a wide beam.'

'A wide beam?'

'Yes,' he said. 'They're more expensive because they're bigger, but you'd have a few more feet to play with if you did want to put up an easel on a permanent basis.'

I wondered if there'd be room for a bath.

'Or, you could go for something like Bear's created,' he further said. 'You can go where you want at the drop of a hat then, though you might not have more space to spread out in than you've got here. His place is amazing, isn't it?'

'I haven't seen it yet,' I admitted.

James almost dropped the mug he was holding.

'I can't believe it!' he gasped, sounding shocked. 'He's so proud of that place and given that he's trying to get you to join his crusade, I'm astonished that he hasn't shown you or taken you out in it already.' We heard footsteps and shuffling on deck as Bear and the dogs returned from their walk. 'Hey, mate,' said James as Monty and Queenie nudged their way back inside the boat ahead of Bear, 'what's all this Holly's telling me about you not having treated her to a tour of your place?'

'We've both been so busy,' I said before Bear had a chance. 'We just haven't got around to it.'

'Well,' said James, looking between us, 'you better get a move on before he fires her up and moves on again.'

I didn't like to consider that and felt the bubble of happiness I'd been floating about the boat in deflate a little.

'I'm not going anywhere for a while yet,' Bear said placidly.

'Set a date for a viewing then,' said James, 'before Holly buys herself a boat and you've missed your chance to cajole her into joining you on the road.'

'Are you seriously considering it?' Bear gasped, looking at me.

'You know what,' I said, laughing at his shocked expression. 'I think I might be.'

'Well, I never,' said Bear, sounding every bit as flabbergasted as James had when I told him I hadn't seen inside the horsebox.

'But I'm going to consider the four-wheel option too,' I said, getting completely carried away.

'What about a double decker bus?' suggested James. 'You'd have loads of room in one of those. Let's have a look online, shall we?'

After that, we completely lost track of time. It wasn't until May phoned Bear to say that the Pooch Shoot team had been in touch because we hadn't collected the platinum package, that we realised how late it was.

'I'm so sorry, Mum,' Bear apologised and I looked at my watch. 'Yes, we're absolutely fine. All four of us and yes, we're still together. We drove out of the city for a picnic and completely forgot we had to be back.'

I don't know what May's response to that was, but Bear looked a little flushed and seemed to press the phone closer to his ear.

'Yep,' he said, turning slightly away. 'I'll go and get them first thing. And no, I'm not going to tell you what the dogs picked out to wear.'

James raised his eyebrows at me and I shook my head.

'Don't ask,' I mouthed.

'Gotta love May Madison.' He beamed.

It wasn't the first time someone had said that since I'd met her and given her influence at The Chapel and commitment to making the Christmas performance shine, I knew it most likely wouldn't be the last.

'Where do you put your Christmas tree?' I whispered to James.

'I never have one,' he said, which I thought was a little sad, until he added, 'It's not the lack of space, it's the cat. I got sick of picking the damn thing up every time she launched her-self into it.'

I stifled a laugh just as Bear promised to collect a takeaway and there was still a smile on my lips when he caught my eye and gave me the widest one in response. I quickly looked away, knowing that all of my efforts to steer clear of him during the last week in the hope of suppressing my feelings had been a total waste of time. Perhaps going with the flow today hadn't been the wisest move on my part, after all.

'Mum's demanding a takeaway large enough to feed ten, so you're more than welcome to eat with us later, Holly,' he said as soon as he'd ended the call. 'And you too, James, if you don't mind the drive.'

'I would have loved to,' he said, 'but I've got plans.'

'Me too,' I said, even though I hadn't got anything organised beyond another bowl of soup and part-baked baguette. I ignored the flash of disappointment that crossed Bear's face as I turned him down. 'Was your mum cross that we've missed picking up the photos?'

He fidgeted in his seat and looked a bit shifty. 'No,' he said, rubbing a hand around the back of his neck. 'She was fine. I told her I'd pick them up tomorrow.'

'I'll pick them up,' I told him as a sop to turning the takeaway down, and as I wondered at the reason behind his fidgeting. 'It's too far to walk and you'll struggle to manoeuvre the horsebox in that car park. I'm going to The Chapel tomorrow, so I can pick them up ahead of that and then give them straight to your mum then.'

'I'm intrigued,' said James. 'What are these photos?'

Bear stood up again and stretched out his back. 'If you're on Santa's nice list,' he told his friend, 'you'll probably get one.'

'In which case,' I said, also standing up and reaching for my coat, 'we won't spoil the surprise.'

'Good plan.' Bear beamed at me, making my heart race and not for the first time that day.

# Chapter 20

'Are you sure you won't come in?' Bear offered, when I pulled on to the bungalow drive. 'You can see from this lot that Mum has completely over ordered.'

The smell wafting out of the three takeaway bags in the passenger footwell was weakening my resolve to head home but I shrugged it off and cracked a window instead.

'Best not,' I said, drawing in a lungful of the sharp, crisp evening air. 'I've got stuff to do and, as a result of our impromptu picnic location and conversation on the drive back, lots to think about too.'

Bear looked thrilled about that and I wondered if he'd be even happier if he knew I was going to be mulling over much more than just my potential next home.

The hours spent with him that day had been so easy, comfortable and relaxed that I was finding it impossible not to imagine what our time in Norwich might look and feel like if I gave into temptation and pulled him back under the mistletoe.

I daresay his assumption would have been that I had found him irresistible, given that I was letting him live with the illusion that, like him, I was simply trying to bide my time and waiting

until The Chapel performances had played out before we shared
kisses again. Under those circumstances, he most likely wouldn't
have been surprised to feel my lips on his at all.

'Could you please tell your mum that I'll give our walk a miss
tomorrow?' I requested, trying to shrug off the thought of what
those lips felt like. 'I'll pick the photos up and then see her at
The Chapel.'

'No problem.' He nodded, opening the door, unaware of my
pulse-racing thoughts.

'And thanks again for today,' I further said, finally getting a
grip. 'This afternoon, especially. It really has given me a whole
new perspective on where I want to live.'

'My pleasure.' He smiled, before climbing out, then, reaching
into the back, he somehow managed to manhandle the dogs and
the takeaway bags to the bungalow door.

I pulled away before May let him in because it would have
been impossible to resist joining them if she spotted me and
asked me to stay.

'Soup here we come,' I murmured as I pulled back on to the
road. I had closed the window again to banish the winter cold
but the tempting smell of takeaway lingered.

As, predictably, did my thoughts about Bear. Once I'd filled
up on my virtuous soup, and the not-so-virtuous butter-covered
warm baguette I had heated to go with it, I reached for my phone
and typed out a message to send him. I read it, reread it, then
amended its tone, subtly making it a little more than friendly
before going upstairs to get changed.

It was the sight of May's colourful clothes, now my clothes,
hanging in the wardrobe that made me rush back downstairs to
delete it. I'd already thanked Bear for the trip when I dropped

him off, so a message repeating the sentiment and suggesting we could do it again and check out other potential abode options really wasn't necessary. It could too easily be misconstrued as encouragement.

And yes, I admit, that had been my intention when I typed it, but not at the potential risk of costing me May's friendship if things didn't work out. I stuffed my phone away out of sight and reached for my sketch pad instead. My mind and my hands needed another occupation to stave off further temptation to text.

I drew some rough sketches of Monty and Queenie playing dress up and not just wearing the outfits they'd tried on at the Pooch Shoot. I put Monty in a skirt and Queenie in a formal suit and tie and wove a story around both with the emphasis being on the garments they had picked out being just clothes.

Not clothes for girls or clothes for boys or colours for girls or colours for boys. The message was only lightly expressed, but there was no missing it. By bedtime, I was thinking that it was my favourite creation of the lot. I'd become so immersed in it, I hadn't given a single further thought to the pros and cons of living life on a narrowboat, but that was okay because I hadn't been lusting after Bear either.

The new week dawned dull, damp and surprisingly mild. It didn't feel festive at all, but I had an inkling that the contents of the platinum package box that I handed over to May when I arrived at The Chapel would soon ramp up the seasonal feels again.

'I'm itching to open this and take a look.' She beamed. 'Bear said you looked amazing in the outfit the assistant picked out for you, Holly.'

'Did he?' I blushed. 'I daresay it was the boots—'

'Don't say another word,' she said, putting up her hands. 'He didn't tell me what you'd both ended up wearing and I want it to be a surprise.'

Oh, she was going to be surprised all right.

'Come on then,' I said, passing her some scissors. 'Pete's not here yet, so I can't start drawing out the backdrop. Why don't you open it now?'

She didn't need asking twice. She quickly slid the blade through the tape and ripped open the box.

'I can't believe it!' she laughed, just seconds later. 'How on earth did you get my Teddy to agree to wear that?'

I laughed too. I was secretly pleased with the way I had almost managed to pull off playing a sultry Puss in Boots, and both of the dogs looked great, but it was Bear who stole the show as the six foot plus Olaf.

'No wonder Monty went nuts when he saw Bear waddle out of the changing area!' I giggled, holding the photo closer for a better look.

'Did he?' May tittered.

'Yes,' I said, 'he didn't recognise him at all. For obvious reasons.'

'I would have loved to have seen my little gingerbread man acting up,' laughed May. 'That must have been hilarious.'

'It was,' I said, thinking back. 'The whole morning was a hoot, really.'

'These are going in the post as soon as I've written out the cards.' She then beamed, giving one of the snow globes a good shake. 'And Teddy was right, Holly. You do look good. Your legs look as though they go on forever.'

'Well.' I shrugged self-deprecatingly. 'I daresay that was down to the boots.'

'No wonder Bear sounded so smitten,' she then added thoughtfully, making my temperature rocket.

'Won't some of the people you send them to think it's a bit weird' – I frowned, again voicing my concern – 'that you're sending them a card with a stranger on?'

May looked aghast.

'You're not a stranger to me,' she tutted. 'And besides, I'm going to include a little round-up, telling everyone how I'm settling in and making new friends. And finding new family,' she added, putting the globe down and giving me a hug. 'You've turned my life here around, Holly, and I want everyone to know that. You're not going to be a stranger to the old gang I've left behind for long.'

'You're making quite an impact on my life, too, you know,' I told her, feeling emotional as I squeezed her back. I pulled away a little and looked down at her. 'Friends forever?'

'Family for life,' she firmly said back, pulling me closer again and making me feel relieved that I hadn't acted on my desire to take things with Bear further or sent the over-friendly text.

The Chapel door suddenly banged open and Pete charged inside, looking out of puff. The man was always rushing and most often, a few minutes late.

'What's all this?' he wheezed, striding over. 'Props for the play?'

'No,' said May, quickly putting the cards and globe away. 'Nothing for the play, but you'll find out what they are soon enough.'

She winked at me and I smiled. Once she had delivered these

to my Nightingale Square neighbours, they would think of me in a completely different light. Hopefully not one that encouraged Lisa to try to get me up on the stage! I felt my temperature spike again, just at the thought of it.

'You catch your breath, Pete,' I told him. 'And I'll stick the kettle on.'

The moment of calm would settle my heart rate as well as his.

'Good idea.' He nodded, his face gradually returning to a healthier colour. 'Something tells me we're going to be drinking a lot of tea today.'

Once we'd spread out the dustsheet backdrop, which Sara had already managed to sew a channel along the top of, we climbed up on to the stage and looked down at the vast expanse of fabric.

'If we keep coming up here to check the perspective,' said Pete, 'I don't think we'll go far wrong.'

I wished I had his confidence. There was a lot of fabric to fill.

'And you've kept the designs simple enough,' he said, squinting at the sketch I'd given him.

Rather than overcomplicate the background with a design showing some sort of interior, I'd opted for us to paint a landscape, which could be simply – I hoped – scaled up from the sketch Pete was looking at.

'I've been watching Bob Ross for years,' Pete proudly told me, hopping down again. 'How hard can it be?'

'I'm not going to answer that,' I said, letting out a breath.

'Let's draw it out first,' Pete then suggested.

'That's not very Bob Ross,' I pointed out.

'No,' he agreed, 'but on this occasion, I'm going with the old adage, measure twice, cut once.'

'Good plan.' I nodded, tossing him a pencil.

It wasn't easy drawing directly on to the fabric, which had a tendency to move especially when we had to walk on it, but it did give us a chance to rectify any mistakes and scale things up and down before we reached for a paintbrush. We were just peering down at the marked-up sheets for the hundredth time, when Lisa arrived with a couple of bags from Blossoms and we sat down to more tea and a communal lunch.

May had been sorting through the props that Eli had been begging and borrowing and Lisa had plans, now that she'd hit her word count for the day, to run through the costumes with Sara.

'She's coming straight here after her shift at the care home,' Pete told us. 'She started early, so she might look a bit bleary-eyed. Best not let her near the sewing machine.'

'I think she's finished the sewing now,' Lisa said, shaking her head. 'How she's done so much while working all hours, I have no idea.'

'She's enjoyed it too,' said Pete, also sounding incredulous.

'We're all enjoying it,' said May. 'I didn't realise how much I was missing the footlights until I walked back on to that stage.'

'Are you sure you don't want a cameo role, May?' Lisa asked. 'We could easily write you into the script.'

'No,' said May, 'the Christmas performance is all about the kids and there are more than enough stars who come here to make it shine. You don't need me. Although, it would be lovely to see a tree up to enhance the festive feeling.'

Lisa's smile vanished. 'I am working on it,' she said, sounding furious, though not with May. 'The one we've already paid for should be here any time now.'

'Have you thought more about my spring fundraising idea?'

Eli asked May, neatly changing the subject which was obviously a sore one.

'What's this?' I frowned.

'Yes,' said May, 'I have and I will.'

'Really?' Lisa gasped.

'Really.' May nodded.

'Oh, thank you, May,' said Eli. 'We're going to sell tickets for an evening with May Madison,' he told me. 'Lisa is going to interview May—'

'And I'm going to supply some music,' said Freddie, who had just arrived. He tipped his battered old hat to the assembled group. 'Assuming I haven't fallen off the twig by then.'

'You've still got plenty of years left in you, Freddie Fanshawe,' said Lisa, standing up and adding another seat to the group.

'I certainly hope so,' he said, squeezing her hand as she kissed him on the cheek. 'Oh, Lisa,' he flirted, 'if I were just a decade younger . . .'

'Or three,' she teased.

'We'll make a fortune with these two on the bill,' said Eli, nodding his head towards May and Freddie.

I knew he was right. The pair both exuded star quality and were bound to be a draw.

'You'll have to save me a ticket,' I told May. 'Goodness knows where I'll be living by then, but I'll come back for your evening of entertainment.'

May's face fell. 'I don't like the thought of you moving miles away, Holly,' she said sadly.

In that moment, I didn't much like the thought of that either. I looked around the group remembering how I'd initially been so resistant to Lisa's efforts to get me involved with anything that meant moving out of reach of Mark and Neil's sofa. Now, just a few weeks on, here I was, completely immersed and surrounded by new friends. And family. When I thought back to the plan I'd originally had for my stint of house-sitting, I realised that this was all as far from it as it was humanly possible to get. And yet, I was loving it.

'Well,' I said cheerfully, 'there's nothing to say I have to go all that far, is there?'

'Oh,' said Lisa, sounding intrigued. 'Have you found somewhere?'

'Not yet,' I told her, winking at May, 'but I am considering a few more different options now.'

Catching on, May winked back. 'I think I know what that means,' she laughed.

'Tell us then,' Lisa urged.

'All in good time,' I said, refusing to elaborate.

I wondered if it would take as long to go through the motions of buying and setting up something a bit different as it would to purchase a regular house. That was another thing I needed to take into account. I was going to have to find somewhere else to live during my search, because it was highly unlikely that I was going to find and settle on something between now and when Neil and Mark arrived back.

In the past, I might have panicked at the thought of that, but this different person I was morphing into remembered James's laidback attitude and approach to life. May's advent calendar might have pulled me up short, but I was acting on the realisation it had sparked and I knew the best thing for me to do was take my time. The most sensible, and thrilling, course of action would be to seek out some unusual places to visit and stay in for a few days before making any big decisions about where I spent the money I had sitting in the bank.

As tempting as it was, I knew it would be foolish to get caught up in the romance of the decision I'd made to look for somewhere unusual and rashly commit to spending my cash on some boat or vehicle when I had no real understanding of how life living in them would actually work. I would be far better off speculating with some of the funds to accumulate some knowledge and hands-on experience before finally settling on what would work best. In my quest to find a new home, that, I decided, should be my next step.

'And I daresay Bear will have moved on by the time you've set the date for the event, won't he?' Pete then put in, bringing me back down to earth with a bump. 'He'll be off on one of his adventures.'

'He is working when he's traveling about in that horsebox, you know, Pete,' said Lisa, rolling her eyes.

'I am aware of that.' Pete pouted, turning red and I knew I'd guessed right about him being in awe of Bear and his lifestyle when they'd first met.

'But I'm sure he'll come back for the event,' May said, looking intently at me. 'It's going to be a proper family reunion.'

I realised that if I stayed reasonably local to Norfolk, that would mean being hundreds of miles away from Bear when he went to Cornwall, but then of course, he was only going to be working in the south-west for a while. Given the nature of his job and his nomadic lifestyle, it would be both impossible and impractical to base my property plans on where he happened to be at the time, especially if they didn't have four wheels and an engine. Not that I needed to be near him, but his future proximity had been playing on my mind.

'I can already picture the after-party,' Freddie said wistfully, imagining the event coming to a rousing end as he helped himself to a cake from the plate. 'It's going to be epic.'

'Totally,' May agreed. 'There's no point in doing things by halves, is there?'

'A woman after my own heart,' Freddie said, turning the full force of his charm on her. 'Now, who fancies a little musical accompaniment while they work this afternoon? I haven't got to be back at the Cavell until teatime.'

While Freddie took us through his entire repertoire, thankfully not bashing any of it out too loudly, Pete and I set to with the paintbrushes. By the end of the afternoon, we had a more than passable backdrop, complete with mountains, trees, rolling hills and even an unplanned Bob Ross style building in the distance but which was more castle than cabin. That was purely from Pete's imagination and was the cherry on the cake.

'You guys,' gushed Sara, who was now looking more than ready for her bed. 'This is amazing!'

Her praise drew the attention of the others and they all joined us on the stage to look down at what we'd done.

'It will look even better when it's hung,' said Pete.

'It looks fantastic already,' said Eli, turning to consider where it was going to be displayed. 'Bear reckons suspending the bamboo pole from the ceiling right at the back of the stage will be the best option. He's going to fix it so it's secure for performances but can be taken down when we don't need it.'

I wouldn't be watching him wobble about on a ladder when the time came to put it up.

'He's a clever so and so,' said Freddie.

'He is,' Lisa agreed, looking a little too closely at me. 'His idea is going to save us quite a bit of money, too, which is always appreciated.'

'When's it going up?' I asked, doing my best to look completely unaffected by her attention and most likely failing.

'Tomorrow or Wednesday,' she told me.

'I don't think I'll be able to be around for that,' I said. 'I've got a project I need to finish working on.'

'No worries,' she said, looking back at the embellished dustsheets. 'I think the bulk of your work here is pretty much done, Holly.'

'And we're extremely grateful that you've helped out,' said Eli. 'And you, May. The Chapel is in for a much merrier Christmas thanks to you two.'

'And Bear,' added Lisa, as I began to blush.

'Yes.' Eli nodded. 'And thanks to Bear, too.'

# Chapter 21

Having told The Chapel team that I had a project to complete, during the following week I turned my attention to polishing and perfecting my growing collection of Monty and Queenie sketches and accompanying stories.

I had also started an online search of quirky places I could stay in for a few days while I further puzzled out the exact sort of property I wanted to live in. There was a diverse and dazzling array to choose from and the more I investigated, the more excited I became. My life after my marriage was morphing into a completely different shape to the one I had previously imagined and that was all thanks to Bear. Bear . . .

I tried not to let my thoughts linger on him for too long, but after the transformative trip to see James, I had begun to feel increasingly guilty for not setting him straight since he'd latched on to the idea of us getting together after the Christmas performance.

It didn't help that ever since that conversation, where he had admitted that he was going to be hard pushed not to kiss me at every subsequent mistletoe moment, he had behaved like a perfect gent. The cheeky thigh-high boots comment aside, he had

treated me with nothing but courtesy and respect and, knowing
he was finding it hard not to flirt, only served to raise him higher
in my estimation. If only he would do something terrible then I
would have been able to dismiss him and move on, but I could
tell that wasn't his style.

When I woke on Thursday, having slept better than I had in
a long time, I discovered the weather had returned to bracing
and bright. It felt entirely fitting as it matched my mood, which
had lifted with every image I had enhanced and every word I
had added to my pooch files during the previous few days. I
might have still been feeling guilty about leading Bear up the
wrong path, but at least my passion project was heading in the
right direction, and my spirits lifted further when I turned on
my laptop.

I hadn't logged on with the expectation of finding anything
interesting in my inbox. I had simply wanted to again read
through the speculative proposal email I had typed out to my
favourite editor and check the scanned drawing and story files
I had attached to it. I found it, still sitting snug in my drafts
folder, addressed to Natasha and I knew it would stay there
while I further pondered over whether I was brave enough to
press send. However, I did find something else waiting for me,
something intriguing from the very editor my draft mail was
addressed to.

Natasha had sent me a new commission to consider. One,
she wrote, which was completely different to the projects I had
worked on with her before, but which she thought I might like
to think about. She apologised for the imposition at a time when
I had said I wouldn't be working, but the author involved had

expressly asked her to get in touch. I can't deny I found that flattering and eagerly read on.

The required artwork was going to bear little resemblance to anything I had worked on since my student days, and it was work from those times that the author remembered. They had, in a strange twist of fate, visited an exhibition I was a part of during my final year and been most taken with my Arthur Rackham inspired pen and ink fantasy collection. They now thought that style would be the perfect fit for the gothic young adult series they had just secured a deal for and having given my name to Natasha as their preferred illustrator, hoped I would consider creating the artwork to go along with them.

I quickly scanned the pages of the story Natasha had attached and my mind immediately began to imagine the creatures and settings I could draw to accompany them. None of it was anything like the Baby Bee books I had spent so long working on, but the contrast made it all the more appealing and I felt the familiar fizz of excitement I had once so often enjoyed, but in this instance for something wholly different.

Determined not to overthink my response, but rather go with my gut reaction, I quickly typed out a reply saying that I would most definitely be interested in considering the commission and in the new year I would love to meet the author as Natasha suggested. I pressed send before I had a second to dither and then, feeling buoyed up and brave, I threw caution completely to the wind and also sent the email with the Monty and Queenie words and pictures attached.

My hands shook as I sat back and considered what I had done. Not only in recent days had I decided I wanted to live somewhere unconventional, I had now potentially found a different professional path to walk down. It was impossible to stop the laugh which had bubbled up escaping, and I was still giggling when my phone pinged with a notification from The Chapel WhatsApp group.

'Oh, wow,' I gasped.

There was a photo attached to the message. Mine and Pete's painted backdrop was now hanging at the back of the stage and held in place by the bamboo pole Bear had so cleverly designed and installed. Between us we had made a great job of our first attempt at creating something so substantial.

It looked absolutely perfect, especially with the rest of the set pieces arranged in front of it. My work there really was done, drink-making and biscuit-offering duties aside, of course. I responded with a line of love heart emojis and was poised to put my phone down when the screen lit up with an incoming call from May.

'Hey, May,' I answered, my smile still very much in place.

'Hey yourself,' she responded. 'You sound happy.'

'I am,' I told her. 'I've just seen the photo of the stage and it looks magnificent.'

I could have told her about the exciting email, and even the dog project, but decided to keep it all to myself for the time being. Given that I had told her weeks ago that I was feeling disillusioned with my work and that having nothing pending meant I could join her in helping out at The Chapel, she had naturally been curious when I mentioned a project the day Pete and I painted the backdrop.

She'd asked me more than once since then what it entailed, but I hadn't told her. My slowly developing confidence would only carry me so far and I wanted to find out what Natasha thought of my efforts before I further considered sharing this new venture with my new friend.

'Doesn't it?' she agreed. 'The place is quite transformed, thanks to you, Holly.'

'And Pete and Bear,' I hastily added, still smiling. 'And you.'

'Well,' she carried on, 'it is, as you say, quite magnificent. Although there's still no Christmas tree.'

'But there's plenty of time for Lisa to rectify that,' I said, 'and I'm sure she will.'

'I hope so,' said May. 'Are you working today, my dear? How's the mystery project coming along?'

'I'm not working,' I said, shutting my laptop down so I wasn't tempted to keep checking my inbox for a response to the emails I had just sent and which I realistically knew I wouldn't have a reaction to for ages. 'But it's coming along rather well.'

'Well, that's wonderful,' said May. 'I'm still bursting to know what you're up to, but I know you'll tell me when you're ready.'

I couldn't help but laugh at that. Her assumption that it would be a case of *when* I filled her in as opposed to *if* was completely accurate.

'So, what are your plans for today?' she asked.

'Sitting by the fire,' I informed her.

'That sounds perfect,' she purred. 'Do you think you could be as comfortable cosied up next to my hearth as you would be in front of your friends' fire in Nightingale Square?'

'I don't see why not,' I confirmed cautiously, hoping that Bear was ensconced in the knot garden with Freya, rather than lounging in front of his mum's glowing embers.

'Good,' she said, 'because I really need your help with something again, Holly. If that's not too much of an imposition. I thought I could manage it on my own, but I can't and with rehearsals ramping up, today's the only day I've really got to do it.'

'Well,' I said, thinking it didn't sound like I was going to get the opportunity to cosy up to her fire, after all, because she was going to put me to work, 'if I can help, I will.'

'You've always been the greatest help,' she said kindly. 'Right from the very first moment we properly met when you rescued Monty.' That had definitely been one of my finer act of kindness moments and thinking of the subsequent inspiration which had led to my artistic change of direction, it had helped me too. 'Now, tell me, my dear, are you happy on top of a stepladder?'

'It's not my preferred place to be,' I told her, feeling suddenly less inclined to be kind. 'But then, I'd far rather it was me at the top of a stepladder than you.'

'Fab,' she said briskly. 'In that case, I'll go and get the kettle on and I'll see you in a bit.'

When I arrived at the bungalow, my face already flushed from the walk and further thrilling thoughts about the possible new commission along with the prospects of my pooch project, I soon discovered that I had been wrong about the Thursday morning whereabouts of Bear and my cheeks coloured brighter.

'Holly.' May beamed, as she let me in and the sound of swearing further along the hallway met my ears. 'Come in. Let me take your coat. I knew that red jumper would look good with your beautiful blonde hair because it went so well with the hoodie you wore before.'

'I do love it,' I told her, smoothing down the soft, long sleeves before I was bombarded by the dogs.

It was a very bold shade of red, but as I was growing in

confidence about so many things, including wearing all the colours of the rainbow, I had barely batted an eye when I caught my reflection in the bathroom mirror as I got dressed.

'Did Queenie sleep over?' I asked, as I fussed her and Monty and even though, courtesy of the bad language, I already knew Bear was in residence.

'Nope,' said the man himself, who suddenly loomed large in the kitchen doorway. 'Mum summoned me here at an ungodly hour this morning.'

'I see.' I nodded, feeling my heart thump at the sight of him. 'I got the call, too, but obviously a bit later than you. I didn't know you were going to be here.'

He looked at May and narrowed his eyes and I wondered if she was up to something.

'I take it the bamboo pole met with your approval?' he then said, looking back at me. 'Assuming I've not misinterpreted the love heart emojis. They don't mean something edgy and ironic these days, do they?'

'Not as far as I know,' I laughed. 'In my book, they're still all about love.'

'Well, that's perfect.' He smiled, making my stomach flip.

'So, May,' I said, as I quickly looked away. 'What's with the summons? You don't need me if Bear's here, surely?'

'I need you both,' she insisted. 'Come into the kitchen and you'll see why.'

'I think you mean, come into the kitchen and you'll see *some* of the reason why,' Bear corrected her.

I followed them into the room, which didn't resemble a kitchen anymore because it was packed full of boxes. It looked more like a house moving holding area.

'What's all this?' I asked.

'The sitting room's the same,' said Bear, running a hand through his hair which already looked as though it needed another cut. 'But I think we've got the lot now.'

'Are you moving, May?' I frowned, knowing she couldn't really be but unable to account for the vast number of boxes otherwise.

'Of course not,' she laughed, squeezing her way through the tiniest gap between the stacks to flick the kettle on. 'These are usually all in the box room.'

'No pun intended,' huffed Bear.

'So why are they in here and the sitting room?' I asked.

'Because they're full of Christmas decorations, of course,' said May, as if it was obvious. 'I want you to help me get my decs up. I'm going all out this year, because I thought I could host The Chapel performance after-party, but only if the bungalow looks the part.'

Bear gave me a long-suffering smile and, as much as I would have loved to suddenly remember an urgent appointment I couldn't possibly miss, I knew I couldn't abandon him to suffer death by May's decs alone.

'We'd best get on then,' I said stoically, pushing up my sleeves. 'Where do you want us to start?'

It took the two of us over three hours just to get the three fake trees up for May to then embellish in her own inimitable style.

'The kitsch as Christmas one can go in the hall,' directed May as Bear carried the six-foot-tall bright pink tree to where she directed him. 'I'll cover that one with decs from the brights boxes, so he matches the friendly faun.'

I had seen quite a few boxes bearing that title and the faun was already colourfully adorned with a tinsel crown and baubles attached to his ears. The poor love bore it with an expression which suggested he had been similarly decorated before. I wondered if there would be a mention of him or his kind in the new manuscript I was considering illustrating. The thought of that got me all fired up again and I had to resist the urge to grab my phone and check my inbox.

'And the seven-foot pre-lit Lapland fir can go in the sitting room,' May carried on, rushing energetically between rooms. 'I think a winter wonderland theme will work well in there.'

'So, that leaves the five-foot white tree for the kitchen?' I assumed because it was the only place left for it to go.

'Um,' said May, tapping a finger against her lips. 'I suppose so. I'm not really sure what to do with that one this year.'

'How about a snow-family theme?' I suggested and Bear groaned.

'Oh, yes,' said May, clapping her hands. 'Maybe I could make the party fancy-dress and Bear could give a repeat performance as Olaf. I'd love to see that in person.'

'No way,' Bear refused. 'Poor Monty would be traumatised.'

On hearing his name, the little dog skittered into the hall and gave the trees an exploratory sniff.

'He doesn't look to be suffering from PTSD to me, so you should get away with it,' I said innocently.

Bear childishly stuck out his tongue in response, making me laugh.

'Let's have something to eat,' said May. 'I'll get the oven going.'

'Don't panic.' Bear grinned, setting my mind to rest. 'She's only warming Blossom's festive sausage rolls and mince pies.'

'Oh, thank god,' I sighed.

'I heard that!' May shouted from the kitchen and the two of us exchanged a look.

I felt my face start to flush again as our eyes met and I knew I was still in trouble. Bear was as irresistible as ever.

'Come and retune this radio, would you please, Bear?' May called. 'And Holly, you can whip up the hot chocolate, while I set out the chutney and clotted cream.'

'What a combo,' Bear cringed.

Once we had eaten our fill of seasonal carbs – the sausage rolls enhanced by the chutney made by Poppy, who lived in the square, and the pies by a dollop of cream – we then finished it all off with thick, marshmallow-topped hot chocolate before setting to unpacking May's vast and eclectic array of decorations.

Every piece told a story and I was willing to listen to them all. Bear often chipped in with his own take on the tale or happy memory and by the end of the day, the entire bungalow was bedecked. Ceilings, floors and all. I'd never experienced anything like it but I adored it all and had fallen further in love with May's home as a result.

'I'll carry on filling the trees,' said May. They were already groaning under the weight and with barely a spare inch on any of their branches to hold anything else. 'Why don't you two treat yourselves to a trip to the pub?'

I rather liked the idea of spending the evening in The Dragon with Bear. In fact, I liked it too much. Listening to him and May reminisce and watching the pair of them together had, rather than make me more cautious about risking our friendships, made me yearn even more to be the one to pull him back under the mistletoe.

'Will you come with us, May?' I suggested, thinking her presence would help keep me in check if the desire lingered.

'I can't,' she said, mysteriously. 'I'm expecting company, but it's lovely of you to suggest it.'

She was handing us our coats before I had a chance to ask who her mystery caller was and I was out of the door when I realised I wasn't the only one carrying a secret or two.

'Pub then?' Bear asked, as we set off with Queenie trotting slightly ahead.

It was already starting to freeze and I wished I'd driven, rather than walked, but then that would have ruled out a pint in the pub.

'Why not?' I smiled up at him. 'May would be disappointed if we didn't. Not that it's any of my business, but I wonder who her visitor is.'

'I don't know either,' Bear said thoughtfully.

The Dragon was quieter than the first time I'd visited and we easily found a table before Bear went to order drinks and a beef and ale pie apiece. Warmed from the fire, I was starting to feel drowsy by the time he came back.

'The pies won't be long,' he said, taking the seat next to mine, rather than the one opposite and waking me back up again. 'Do you mind if I sit here?' he asked. 'It keeps me out of the way a bit as it's bound to get busier in here before long.'

'No,' I said, a delicious pulse beating through me as he took off his jacket and brushed my arm in the process. 'I don't mind.'

While we waited for the pies, we fell to chatting about May's love of Christmas and her extraordinarily large decoration collection.

'I didn't say anything back at the bungalow for obvious

reasons,' Bear said, looking bright eyed, 'but I couldn't help remembering that Mum didn't put anything up the year Dad died. Not so much as a card.'

'Oh, Bear.'

'She didn't have the heart for it and after losing Dad, seeing the house without anything up further broke mine, because as you can probably tell, she absolutely adores the festive season.'

'I'm so sorry.' I swallowed.

My last Christmas had been pretty grim, but I could tell it hadn't been anywhere near as hard as the one May and Bear had been through.

'It's okay,' he said with a sigh. 'I should have been expecting it really. Given how long my parents had loved each other, his loss was bound to knock Mum for six.'

Even so, it must have been excruciating for Bear to see his ebullient and beautiful Mum so affected.

'I suppose so,' I agreed. 'But given the excitement of what I've witnessed today, it must have felt like a further blow.'

'Yes,' he confirmed. 'It was.'

Compared to Bear's experience of it, Christmas when I was growing up really had been a mean-spirited affair. There had been no parties, not even a neighbour dropping in, or decorative abandon in our house. It had all been very reserved and the celebrations, if you could call them that, had only lasted as long as Christmas Day.

It struck me then that my parents were living their lives solely reliant on the company of each other and I wondered if I had inadvertently been doing the same with Piers. Not that I really wanted to be thinking about him, while I was sitting in the pub with Bear, but it was food for thought. I could see now that there were aspects of my life which been extremely limited during my marriage and it felt good to stretch my formerly clipped wings and allow them to spread.

'But now she's turned a corner.' Bear nodded, shifting in his seat to properly face me. 'I don't mind telling you that when I was away, I was really beginning to worry about her. I could tell she was putting a spin on how well she was settling in, but since she's met you, Holly, her entire life has been turned around and I love you for that.'

'I'm not sure I deserve to take the credit.' I swallowed, colouring at his choice of words.

'Yes, you do,' he said, reaching for my hand and holding it. 'One hundred per cent.'

Any verbal response I might have formed, dried and died in my throat and I couldn't stop staring at his hand holding mine.

'Two pies,' announced the server with our food. 'Both beef and ale?'

'That's us,' said Bear, letting go of my hand and moving ever so slightly away.

The tiny gap between us felt cold by comparison to the warmth his pressing proximity had given off and I shivered.

'This'll warm you up.' Bear beamed.

'No extra chips?' I croaked, harking back to our lunch in the café.

'Not today,' he said, prising off the crisp pie lid. 'This is a meal in itself.'

He was right about that and it was a delicious one, too, though I struggled to finish mine, and not because I didn't want it.

'Bear,' I said, once he'd set his cutlery down on the empty plate and wiped his mouth with the serviette. 'We need to talk.'

'We do?' he asked, a frown forming as he took in my expression.

'We really do.' I nodded.

'Given the look on your face, I'm guessing it's not about narrowboat interior design, is it?'

'Afraid not,' I confessed.

'I think I'm going to need another drink, aren't I?' he said, reaching for the empty glasses. 'Same again for you?'

'No, I'll have something else, but thanks,' I said, jumping up. 'And I'll get these.'

I ordered another pint for him and a lemonade for me. The pint of Winter Warmer had hit the spot, but I wanted to keep a clear head for what I was going to attempt to say next. Bear took a pull at his drink the moment I handed it over.

'Come on then,' he said heavily. 'Put me out of my misery.'

'The thing is,' I started, then stopped.

'The thing is?' he prompted.

'The thing is,' I said again, 'I'm really sorry, but I think I've been stringing you along a bit. I haven't meant to, it just sort of happened after that kiss under the mistletoe and I truly am so sorry.'

'You don't fancy me, do you?' he groaned. 'I thought the kiss was amazing, but you obviously didn't feel the same way. Or was it that bloody Olaf outfit? I did wonder if that might have scuppered my chances.'

'No,' I said quickly, before he rambled further on, 'it wasn't the Olaf outfit.'

He dropped his head into his hands.

'It was the kiss then,' he groaned through his fingers. 'That makes me feel worse because I really gave it my all.'

'It wasn't the kiss,' I told him, smiling at his choice of words and remembering that *his all* had been utterly wonderful. 'Believe me, there was absolutely nothing wrong with that kiss. The kiss was ... perfect.'

I forced myself to stop remembering it as he lifted his head back up.

'In that case, I don't understand.' He frowned, his eyes fixed on mine. 'If the kiss was perfect, then what's the problem?'

'The thing is, I just can't be with you, Bear,' I said quietly, 'and I should never have kept quiet when you said we'd get together after the Christmas performance, because we can't.'

'But if you do like me and I more than obviously like you,' he pointed out, 'then I can't see what the problem is. Unless,' he carried on before I could tell him, 'you think there was no reason for us to wait and my hesitation has meant that you've gone off me in the meantime.'

'Of course, I haven't,' I interjected.

I felt a little offended that he could think I would be capable of flicking my feelings for him on and off like a switch.

'Are you worried about it being too soon after your divorce?' he then suggested.

'I admit I was surprised to have such intense feelings given that my marriage hadn't ended all that long ago, but that's not why I'm pulling back.'

'Is it because I'm leaving in the spring?' he then asked, still not working it out for himself or giving me the opportunity to spell it out for him. 'Because the project in the south-west isn't going to be all that long and I thought we could easily do the long-distance thing while I'm down there.'

'Given that I still haven't decided where I'm moving to,' I pointed out, 'it might not be long distance.'

'I suppose not,' he said, biting his lip. 'So, what is it then? From what I've heard, you haven't come up with a single plausible reason to justify us not being together, Holly. You say it's not a rebound dilemma or a distance thing, so what is it? I know now that I don't physically repulse you, so what else could there possibly be that could balls this up for us, Holly?'

I took a deep breath.

'You really are being dense, Bear,' I admonished.

He shrugged, still none the wiser.

'It's your mum, of course,' I said on the out breath.

'Mum,' he said, shaking his head. 'She won't mind. In fact, I'm certain she'll be thrilled. She absolutely adores you.'

'Exactly,' I shot back. 'And I adore her too.'

'So, what's the issue?'

'The issue is that since I met her, she's become my very best friend,' I succinctly told him, 'and along with that, she's showered me with a love that's bordering on parental. Given that I've never received that from either of my own parents, I really want to hang on to it. I felt the sting of being abandoned when I was dropped by Piers's parents and it was devastating. It hurt so much. I won't risk that happening again, Bear. I can't.'

'Oh.' He swallowed. 'But I'm sure—'

'And,' I carried on, cutting him off, 'I also know that May has lost a lifelong friendship herself as a result of one of your own relationships ending badly.'

Bear's face flushed at the mention of that.

'She only told me what happened because I had told her how Piers's family had abandoned me for his new partner,' I quickly clarified. 'We were sharing experiences, not gossiping.'

'Of course,' he said, his voice thick in his throat.

'As much as I want to be with you, Bear, I know it would break more than just our hearts if we broke up and your mum felt obliged to pick a side.'

I knew she'd pick Bear's. That was inevitable.

'I can't believe you're assuming that we would break up,' he said, sounding hurt.

'I haven't assumed anything,' I told him. 'I'm just trying to be practical and keep us all safe. I'm simply telling you why I can't be with you. Please keep in mind that it wasn't all that long ago that I thought I was going to be married forever and look how that turned out. I'm not saying that what we have is in any way related to that, I'm simply trying to demonstrate the point that things change, and not always for the better, even when we can't possibly imagine that they will.'

Bear took a few moments to take in what I'd said and I tried to imagine how it was going to feel to carry on being May's friend when I found out that he had started up a relationship with someone else. That was bound to happen at some point, but I supposed I would just have to face it when the time came.

'Shit,' he muttered, raking a hand through this hair. 'This is totally shit.'

'I know it is,' I said, swallowing over the lump which had formed in my throat.

Queenie, sensing that something was amiss, hauled herself to her feet and pushed her way between Bear's knees. He let out a breath and stroked her ears.

'The really, really shitty thing is,' he further said, 'you're right. I completely get what you're saying and why you're saying it. I do understand.'

That was something, I supposed. The situation would have

been a million times worse if he'd jumped up and stormed out. But he was right, it was shitty.

'I really appreciate that,' I whispered. 'I was hoping you'd get it.'

'I do,' he reiterated. 'I'm desperate to be with you, Holly, but you are right. We can't risk Mum being hurt again. Or you.'

'Oh, Bear.' I swallowed.

'I'll back away from the mistletoe,' he heroically carried on, 'but I'm not going to stop being your friend.'

'You'll still help me find my new home?'

'Of course, I will,' he told me, just about managing to smile. 'Whether it's got four wheels or no wheels, I'm going to see that through.'

I reached for his hand and gave it a squeeze. I'd never wanted to kiss him more than I did in that moment.

# Chapter 22

I knew it was completely contradictory and went against everything I had said I wanted from my relationship with Bear, but his admirable insistence that he would file himself in the friend drawer felt like quite a blow.

I had thoroughly enjoyed our flirtations, I had definitely enjoyed our kiss, and I realised once the prospect of more had been taken away that it had felt rather wonderful to have someone on my romantic relationship radar, even though he had initially been a total surprise.

It was one of those classic you don't know what you've got till it's gone moments. However, I stoically endeavoured to be thankful for Bear's understanding and determination not to potentially hurt either myself or May along with his commitment to keep things on the straight and narrow now we were all above board and had no more secrets.

'Bear.' I therefore smiled welcomingly, as I opened the door to him and Queenie, early the next morning. 'What can I do for you? I thought you'd be working.'

'Hello, neighbour.' He smiled back. 'I'm practically finished across the road now,' he told me. 'I fell to thinking about Mum's decs again last night and wondered when my friend in the square was going to put hers up.'

I couldn't help but admire the fact that he hadn't let any time pass between the conversation which clarified the boundaries of our relationship and turning up to firmly establish himself as my friend. Had a longer time elapsed between our seeing one another, things could have been stifled or awkward and I appreciated that he hadn't let that happen.

'We did that already. You helped, remember?' I said, pointing at the hedge.

'I meant the indoor decorations,' he persisted. 'Not the ones lighting up the front garden.'

'Oh,' I said, taking the familiar bag from Blossoms he handed me and which now felt like a prerequisite for turning up anywhere. 'I'm not bothering, but not because I'm miserable. It hardly seems worth it, just for me.'

Bear eyed me narrowly and shook his head, then unclipped Queenie's lead. She wandered past me, down to the kitchen and made herself at home under the radiator.

'What?' I laughed at her owner's unimpressed reaction to my attitude to decorating. 'I bet your horsebox hasn't been seasonally adorned, has it?'

'That's where you're wrong,' Bear corrected. 'I haven't got room to put a tree up, but there's a fine amount of greenery decorating the ceiling and ledges and plenty of battery-operated tea lights dotted about the place.'

'Well.' I shrugged, walking ahead of him to where Queenie had parked herself. 'The few decs I've got are all in storage.'

'That's as may be,' said Bear, refusing to let it drop, 'but I would imagine the friends you're house-sitting for must have their own decorations around here somewhere. How about we start by searching in the loft?'

I knew Mark and Neil's decorations were outside in the uber-organised shed. I'd spotted them in a large, lidded plastic crate when I'd found the lights for the hedge ahead of the switch-on in the square.

'No need,' I said, knowing it would just be easier to give in. 'They're outside. I'll go and get them.'

By the time I had selected the boxes I wanted and come back in, Bear was in the sitting room. He leapt away from the coffee table as I silently entered the room and his face flushed crimson. I would imagine mine had turned rather pink too.

'Sorry.' He swallowed, with a nod towards the sketchbook. 'I know I shouldn't have, but it was just open on the table. These are so much more than just doodles, Holly.'

'They are now,' I agreed, trying not to feel cross that he'd seen them. 'I've been working on them a bit.'

'A lot by the looks of it.' Bear hesitantly smiled, perhaps sensing that I had half a mind to snap at him for snooping. 'The narrowboat has the loveliest details and you've captured Monty and Queenie perfectly.'

'They're such a unique pairing,' I heard myself say, 'they tell their own stories, really.'

'I didn't know you were a writer as well as an illustrator.'

'I'm not,' I said self-deprecatingly. 'This is all very much an early effort.'

'Well, for what it's worth, I really think you're on to something,' Bear said seriously. 'A dog who loves wearing dresses and a companion with a gift for breaking down barriers and replacing them with tolerance and empathy—'

'Exactly how much did you read?' I cut in, feeling rankled.

I knew he'd had a pretty deep dive if he'd got as far as that.

'I'm a fast reader,' he said, grinning. 'And these are just the sorts of stories the world needs right now, Holly. They'll appeal to adults as much as kids and I'm honoured you've picked Queenie as one of the subjects. I hope you're going to do something with them. Given your profession, you must have contacts.'

I hoped Natasha was going to share his enthusiastic opinion. She hadn't got back to me yet, but that was hardly surprising given the number of emails she received by the hour. However, her lack of response did ensure that just like the decision I'd made to not tell May about them, I didn't tell Bear that I already had done something with them.

Given the way Piers's dismissal of my initial attempt had chipped away at my confidence, it was a miracle I'd managed to garner the courage to send them at all and now I wanted the opinion of a professional before I considered sharing them with my friends and making more of them. For most people, that probably wouldn't have been the way they chose to go about it, but it was how I wanted this potential new venture to work.

'Perhaps I will,' I therefore said vaguely. 'I do know someone who might consider taking a look. I wonder what your mum would say if she knew that I'd been sketching and writing about Monty?' I added, thinking again of May's curiosity about my project. 'Not that I'm planning to tell her.'

'She'd be thrilled,' Bear laughed. 'As long as there's no chance that he'll upstage her, of course.'

'Impossible,' I said back, starting to relax again. 'Monty might have some swagger, but May definitely has the edge.'

Bear agreed with that. 'These could well be your next work project, Holly,' he further said. 'I'm sure there'd be a market for them and looking at the detail you've gone into, I can tell you've enjoyed creating them.'

He wasn't wrong about that.

'Shrug off the old and embrace the new,' he said rousingly. 'Stop beautifying other people's work and create your own.'

'Or do both,' I ventured, thinking of the fantasy commission request.

'Well,' he said, 'whatever you do, don't end up settling. Don't forget how disillusioned you were with it all just a few weeks ago.'

'I haven't forgotten,' I said, starting to feel tense again. 'Now, let's put up some of these decs, shall we?'

The morning flew by and once we'd put up enough of Mark and Neil's decorations to satisfy his festive spirit, along with the sticky gingerbread man decoration Ben from The Chapel had gifted me, I felt much more at ease and Bear made me promise that I would go over to Prosperous Place and have lunch with him in his horsebox home the following day.

'It's high time you saw it,' he said.

'I agree,' I happily capitulated. 'Although I can't help wondering if you're just worried James has convinced me to go for the boat option rather than four wheels. The pair of you did come across as rather competitive.'

Bear laughed at that and shook his head. 'It's not that,' he confessed, declaring the real motive behind his invitation and I had to admire his ability to turn the conversation full circle. 'What I'm really hoping is that you'll set one of Monty and Queenie's adventures in a converted horsebox.'

'But who would drive when they hit the road?' I smiled, willing to play along.

'Queenie, of course,' Bear instantly replied. 'Can you seriously imagine Monty behind the wheel?'

'What I can't believe is that we're taking the question seriously,' I giggled.

'Well.' He shrugged, reattaching Queenie's lead as they were set to walk to May's. 'You have to get these things right. Right?'

'Right,' I agreed. 'I'll see you tomorrow. And remember, not a word to anyone about my doggy doodles and stories, not even your mum.'

Even though Bear's response to them had been enthusiastic, I still wished I'd tidied them away before answering the door. I knew I was a competent artist but finding my way with words had proved to be a completely different matter. I *thought* I'd done a pretty decent job so far, but it was Natasha's professional opinion that would hopefully give me the confidence to completely dispel the power Piers's scathing words had had once and for all.

'Promise,' Bear said, making a right hash of trying to give a Scout's honour salute.

I closed the door behind him and leant back against it. I was pleased he'd nudged me to decorate for Christmas, but it had been tough to be around him for so long. If I had a Christmas wish for every time I'd surreptitiously checked him out while he was up the ladder, I'd be set for life.

# Chapter 23

I thought I'd try to have a lay in on Saturday, to stop me obsessing over my lunch with Bear, but May had other ideas, calling bright and early to cancel our plan for a mid-morning walk.

'I'm hardly seeing anything of you these days, Holly,' she wailed theatrically, even though she was the one cancelling the arrangement.

'It's only until the performances are finished,' I said soothingly, snuggling deeper into the duvet in the hope that I wouldn't fully wake up. 'By this time next week, there'll only be one more to go and we can get back to our old routine.'

I didn't remind her that Mark and Neil would be back not all that long afterwards and, if I had plans to move miles away by then, I'd have to forgo the old routine forever.

'I suppose you're right,' she sniffed. 'But you are going to come back to The Chapel ahead of the performances, aren't you?'

'Of course,' I told her, knowing that I no longer had any reason to keep running away from wherever I thought I was likely to bump into Bear.

Now we had set a new course, after our heart to heart in the pub, I just had to get on with keeping him strapped into the platonic place he'd managed to shift me to. I hoped having lunch with him so soon after putting the decorations up would help rather than hinder that plan. I was considering our intense time together as some sort of drastic over-exposure therapy.

'Well, that's good,' said May, sounding happier. 'We miss your tea, Holly. And Lisa's planning something extra to happen during the day next Saturday now, too, so you'll want to be around for that.'

'Oh,' I said, feeling slightly more alert as I wondered what I was destined to get roped into helping with next. 'What sort of something extra?'

With the performance happening in the evening, it would certainly make for a busy weekend.

'She hasn't said yet,' May told me, 'but I'm sure the WhatsApp thingy will soon be flooded with messages. Anyway – oh my goodness, look at the time! I better fly. We've got an entire weekend of rehearsals lined up. Pop along, if you can, won't you?'

'If I can,' I commented, not committing either way. 'Break a leg!'

I hadn't expected to fall back to sleep, but I did and when I woke later in the morning and found it was almost midday, I rather wished I hadn't. My head was pounding and the painkillers had only just started to kick in as I rushed to get ready to head to Bear's and the house phone rang.

I picked it up quickly. 'Mark and Neil's residence,' I announced.

'Oh my god,' guffawed Mark. 'Have you answered the phone to everyone like that?'

'No,' I told him, feeling thrilled to hear his voice and happy to wind him up. 'Actually, you're the first person who's called. Not exactly popular, are you?'

'Cheeky mare,' he tutted. 'I was only ringing to make sure you weren't still all sad and lonely.'

'Cheeky mare yourself!' I laughed. 'I've never been sad and lonely.'

'How's your hair?' he teased. 'Have you had the *Fleabag* chop yet?'

'No,' I laughed, which made my head thump harder, 'but my wardrobe is looking considerably brighter than when you left, because I've started to embrace every colour in the rainbow.'

'And according to gossip in the square,' he then shocked me by saying, 'your love life's looking brighter, too, so I should have known you weren't still sad and lonely, shouldn't I?'

'What?' I spluttered. 'Who have you been talking to?'

'Never you mind,' he said primly, refusing to declare his source. 'But you better stop dithering and just get on with making the most of it otherwise you won't have had any passion in the sack before we get back, will you?'

'I have no idea what you're talking about,' I shot back, equally as primly. 'I've made a couple of new friends is all. Neither of which I have any intention of forming a romantic attachment to.'

'Romantic attachment,' he scoffed. 'I was suggesting you should get your leg . . . no, Neil,' he then yelped, his voice drifting away a little. 'She won't want to talk to you. I'm the one giving the advice and yes, the house is absolutely fine.'

How he knew that I had no idea because he hadn't asked. He was clearly more interested in gossip than anything that was potentially happening with his house.

'I have to go,' he then said. I could imagine him and Neil tussling over the phone somewhere sunny and laughed again. 'See you next year!'

The line went dead before I had a chance to reply and I was left wondering who had been observing me more closely than I had realised. I'd bet it was Lisa. I hoped she was at The Chapel now it was time for me to head over to Prosperous Place to meet Bear. If she was at home or in the Grow-Well, she'd be bound to spot me and that would further fuel her speculations about my love life.

The horsebox door was already open when I arrived and Queenie stood on the threshold, her tail wagging and ears pricked.

'Holly.' Bear smiled, appearing in the doorway behind her. 'Welcome, at long last, to our home.'

He offered his hand and I gratefully accepted the assistance climbing up the steep step into his cosy abode. Cosy in the sense that it was warm, not cramped. In fact, I was amazed by how much room there seemed to be, especially headroom.

'This is for you,' I said, handing over a bottle of wine that I'd pinched from Mark and Neil's pantry. My eyes tracked around, taking everything in. 'Geez, Bear, this is amazing.'

Just like on his friend James's narrowboat, there were lots of smooth untreated wooden surfaces with cleverly curved edges that I wanted to run my hands along, but resisted.

The seasonal additions of red gingham curtains, red-berried holly and trailing strands of ivy made me feel like I had stepped into a wooden cabin in Norway or even a hobbit hole, though I would never have believed Bear could stand up in one of those.

'Thank you,' he said. 'For the wine and the kind words. I was hoping to give you the full tour before lunch, but there's been a change of plan, which I hope you'll be happy to go along with.'

'Oh,' I said. 'What's going on? Is everything okay?'

'Lisa rang a little while ago in a right old tizz,' he told me. 'Apparently, the person she was supposed to be getting The Chapel Christmas tree from has disappeared without trace and without delivering the tree either.'

'Oh no,' I winced. 'I bet that hasn't gone down well. I know she'd been getting increasingly stressed about it not turning up in time for the performances.'

'She has,' Bear agreed. 'And to make matters worse, she'd paid in advance for it too.'

'That's awful.'

'It is.' He nodded. 'But all is not lost, because someone else has donated a tree and I've offered to go and collect it on behalf of everyone else who is busy at The Chapel.'

'That's a great idea.' I smiled. 'And a really kind offer. I'll go with you if you like.'

'I was hoping you'd say that.' He grinned back. 'Have you got a few hours to spare?'

'I'd set aside the whole afternoon for our lunch,' I told him. 'But where on earth is this tree? Norwich market must be awash with them at this time of year and that's only just up the road.'

'I daresay you're right.' Bear nodded. 'But this one is at the seaside. Wynter's Trees in Wynmouth to be precise. It's the place where Luke orders all his potted trees from.'

'I've heard the name,' I remembered.

'So,' Bear carried on, sounding excited, 'as they can't deliver, I thought I'd drive us there in the horsebox to pick it up. It could really do with another run and it will give you the chance to experience life on the open road. How does that sound?'

'Great,' I said, feeling excited too.

'We could take a quick detour if we set off now and drive along by the coast for a bit. That way I'll really be able to show off the advantages of the elevated driving position. You'll be able to see for miles.'

I hadn't seen the sea in a very long time and loved the thought of the spectacular winter view.

'I better pop back for a thicker coat,' I said, thinking of the practicalities of heading off to the seaside in December.

'Good idea,' said Bear. 'And grab a hat and gloves, too. I'll finish making sure everything's secure in here and you can have a proper look around when we get back tonight. You could even help me set everything back up again if you like? That way you'll be able to see how easy it is to handle and how adaptable the space is.'

'More adaptable than inside a narrowboat?' I teased.

'Infinitely,' he laughed, but I wasn't sure if I believed him. 'You can't rearrange much in there.'

When I thought back properly to the inside of James's boat and then looked around the horsebox, I had to concur that perhaps Bear did have a point and possibly the edge when it came to adaptability.

'I'll see you at the end of the square in ten minutes,' he said and I quickly headed back to grab the extra layers.

When he picked me up I discovered he was right about the position being much higher up than in a car. Queenie was already comfortably perched on the seat next to Bear when I scrambled up the step into the cab and secured my seatbelt.

'All set?' Bear asked.

'I think so.' I swallowed, looking out of the windows.

I'd never travelled in anything the size of Bear's home that wasn't public transport and he laughed every time I breathed in as he negotiated the route out of the city.

'Feeling better?' he asked as we left the busy ring road behind and headed north on a much wider carriageway.

'I'm fine,' I told him, my shoulders finally dropping from where they'd been stuck around my ears. 'Just pleased that you're the one in the driving seat. If I do decide to buy something like this, I'm going to need to sort out my driving licence, aren't I? I've only got a car one.'

'You will.' Bear nodded. 'And I can give you the name of the company I used to learn to handle this beast, if you like,' he added, fondly patting the dashboard. 'They've got centres all over the country.'

'I'll give it some thought,' I said, wondering if I had the nerve to get behind the wheel. There would be little point buying something mobile if I was too scared to move it.

The miles flashed by and we didn't talk all that much, but it was a companionable silence we fell into as opposed to an uncomfortable one. The cloud cover ensured there was no frustrating winter glare to spoil the view and we pulled on to the drive which led down to Wynter's Trees a little after two in the afternoon. I had enjoyed some distant glimpses of the sea along the way, but it was even more thrilling to arrive and take in the festive scene immediately in front of us.

'Oh, wow,' I said, leaning forward in my seat. 'What do you suppose those beach huts are used for?'

There was a whole row of cute, pastel painted huts set up and covered in fairy lights and with an old fashioned red truck with a tree lashed to the top of it, parked to one side.

'According to the website I had a quick look at before we set off, they're shops,' Bear informed me. 'Local artists, crafters and small businesses hire and sell from them a few times throughout the year, but for longer in the run up to Christmas.'

'In that case,' I said, pulling on my gloves, in anticipation of jumping out, 'I'm going to have a look and see if I can find something lovely for your mum to put under one of her many trees.'

A lad in a high-vis jacket who was directing cars as the place was heaving, rushed over and asked Bear if he would mind pulling up on the side furthest away from the main parking area.

'Ned's got your tree all ready,' he shouted up into the cab once Bear had explained who he was picking up for. 'He probably won't be back until after you've gone, but he said to say hello and he hopes the tree is okay.'

'It's generous of him to donate one,' said Bear. 'We really appreciate it.'

'That's him and Liza all over.' The lad grinned. 'Ask anyone wearing a Wynter's fleece to pull the tree out for you. Everyone knows you're expected, so you shouldn't have a problem.'

With a queue of cars forming behind us, Bear swung the horsebox over to where he had been asked to park and I opened the window and took in more of the seasonal scene around us. The day was turning out to be completely different to the one I had been expecting.

'Are you hungry?' Bear asked. 'We can have lunch now if you like and look around after as it's getting late.'

I sniffed the air which was filled with wintery spices and my tummy rumbled.

'I could go for something to eat,' I told him, 'and if there's nothing of yours which will spoil, I wouldn't mind finding out what they're selling here if that's okay?'

'It does smell good, doesn't it?' he said, also sniffing appreciatively and rapturously closing his eyes.

I had to look away.

'Come on then,' he said, when he opened them again. 'Let's give Queenie a quick walk around the car park, then go over.'

The food tasted every bit as delicious as it smelt and once we'd filled up on local crab curry and cinnamon churros dipped in ginger enhanced pots of chocolate, Bear headed off to find the tree and I made a beeline for the beach huts.

I found a unique pair of drop earrings for May, created using an ancient Korean technique called Keum Boo and a stunning scarf dyed using Norfolk grown woad to replace the one she had so kindly gifted me.

'Back again,' said the woman who had made May's scarf and who I hadn't been able to resist heading back to.

'I am.' I smiled, thinking how wonderful it had been to walk around the huts asking questions and making connections with the people who had made the wonderful things on sale. 'I know I'll regret it if I don't buy a scarf for myself too.'

She laughed at that.

'Funnily enough,' she said, stepping aside, so I could look through the rapidly dwindling selection she had left, 'I've heard that before.'

'I'm not surprised,' I told her, pulling out another scarf in a slightly lighter shade of blue than the one I'd picked out for May.

'If you don't mind me saying,' the maker then said tentatively, 'if this one's for you, then with your lovely blonde hair, I'd go for the most vibrant blue.'

I looked back at the rack.

'That one?' I asked, pointing.

'Yes,' she said, reaching for the brightest one of the lot and holding it up. 'It really brings out the colour of your eyes.'

My fresh desire to embrace colour left me in no doubt that was the one I should take and I practically bounced back across the car park, thrilled with my few purchases.

'Did you get the tree?' I asked Bear, who was standing outside the horsebox with Queenie.

'I've seen it,' he said, 'and it's a beauty. It's netted now, ready for us to take away. What have you picked up? Is there anything for me in either of those bags?'

'No,' I said, snatching the bags away as he leant over to look inside. 'There's something for me and presents for your mum. You can see them at Christmas.'

'Tease,' he said and I felt a rush of heat fly to my face.

'So, are you going to get the tree then?' I asked, wondering why it wasn't already in the horsebox.

'I could,' he said, sounding mischievous, 'but I wondered if you fancied staying the night here to really get a feel for living in the box?'

I did fancy it, but I didn't think it was a sensible idea. I was managing to keep a check on myself, but wasn't sure if my resolve would last if we were stuck together for an entire night in such a confined space.

'I can sleep on the pull out,' Bear suggested, as if he wasn't affected at all by the thought of us sleeping just feet apart.

'Ordinarily, I'd jump at the chance,' I said cleverly, 'but my friend Mark called earlier and it turns out there are already rumours circulating about my love life in the square and I'd rather not add further fuel to them. And,' I hastily added, 'I am supposed to be house-sitting.'

'Well, now,' said Bear, tapping his head to suggest he was thinking. 'I wonder where those rumours could have sprung from?'

'Um,' I said, imitating his response. 'I wonder, too.'

'With that in mind,' he said, looking as impish as he sounded, 'how about a little white lie to make staying here easier and potentially not further fan Lisa's romance rumour flames. Assuming, that is, that it is me she's paired you with.'

I was amused by his choice of the word *potentially*.

'Of course, it's you,' I tutted. 'What sort of little white lie?'

'Oh, I don't know.' He shrugged. 'How about something along the lines of the horsebox having a flat battery and we've got to wait here until a replacement arrives tomorrow? And we've arranged for you to stay in the village rather than going top to toe in the horsebox with me?'

Now there was an image!

'Not that you've given it any thought,' I laughed, thinking it was a very competent white lie to have come up with so quickly. 'Had you planned this all along?'

'Absolutely not,' he said. 'I've just been thinking that we should make the most of the opportunity to let you experience life on the road and I'm sure Lisa won't mind checking everything looks okay with the house.'

It was a shame it had to be her, but as she was the nearest neighbour and Mark and Neil had told me in their lengthy list of instructions and info that she did have a spare key, she was the obvious person to call on.

'I'm certain she'd jump at the chance if it facilitated us having a night away, especially if it really is her who started the rumours,' I agreed, biting my lip.

'Of course, it's her!' Bear laughed.

His certainty about that put me off the plan for a moment, but then I thought, why not? Why should I care what Lisa made of it?

I had already made up my mind to try some overnight stays in a few unusual places, so why shouldn't the horsebox be my first? It felt fitting, given that it was Bear who had inspired my desire to live somewhere different. As long as Lisa could go and check on the house, I didn't think much harm could come from having a few more hours away. The place was securely locked and the heating was on, so she wouldn't even need to go inside. A quick look at the door would do.

'I could ask Luke to talk to Lisa,' Bear suggested, 'or just message in the group chat?'

'No,' I hastily said. 'Don't post in the chat. I wouldn't want your mum getting the wrong idea about us staying away.'

'So, you're up for it then?' He grinned.

'I am,' I said. 'Message Luke and we'll make plans on how we want to spend our evening away.'

# Chapter 24

With Luke acting as a go-between willing to talk to Lisa, Bear headed off to ask the staff if we could stay parked up on-site rather than having to find somewhere else. If we didn't have to move, that would immediately free up the rest of the day, and the night, to spend as we wished.

'Feel free to have a poke about,' Bear had said, before he went off. 'Get a feel for the space. I'll leave Queenie with you. She should be able to answer any questions you might have.'

'Idiot,' I laughed.

I didn't like to 'poke about' as he'd suggested, so I had done nothing more than make a broad sweep of the space, missing out the elevated sleeping area, by the time he returned.

'How did you get on?' I asked.

'We're all set to stay here.' He grinned. 'And Lisa messaged to say she'll go over later to check the house and then pop back again in the morning. Didn't she message you?'

'I haven't checked my phone,' I admitted.

'Excellent avoidance tactic,' he laughed. 'And we're sorted for this evening's entertainment too, if you fancy heading out.'

'We are?'

'There's an event happening in the village pub, apparently, and Liza, the owner of Wynter's Trees, said she'd give us a lift each way if we fancied it as she's going.'

'That was kind of her,' I said. 'What sort of event is it?'

'An evening of spooky sea-themed storytelling, with a local called George,' Bear told me. 'Apparently it's enough to curdle the blood, no matter how many times you've heard the terrifying tales.'

'Sounds good to me,' I laughed.

'And there'll be food available, too, so there's no need for us to worry about cooking tonight. If we get peckish, we can snack on what I'd got in for lunch between now and then. What do you make of the kitchen, by the way?'

I looked over to where the cooker and sink were neatly set into the beautiful, bespoke wooden units.

'Compact.' I nodded. 'But more than adequate.'

'High praise indeed,' tutted Bear. 'And the rest of the space?'

'I didn't like to look at too much,' I said, biting my lip. 'It might be an out of the ordinary place to live but it's still your home.'

That made him tut all the harder.

'I'd given you the nod to nose,' he said. 'Come on. We'll have a proper look now.'

By the time he had finished showing me around, I was agog. The kitchen had a good-sized sink, oven and hob as well as a fridge freezer, the bathroom had a surprisingly roomy shower, and the wood-burning stove was more than adequate to keep the place warm, even in the depths of winter.

Even more impressive than the quality of the finishing, were the ingenious storage solutions. Bear hadn't yet shown me the area above the cab that formed his bedroom, but he had lifted the lid on a couple of the treads of the stairs which led up to it to reveal space beneath for all sorts of odds and ends and there was a table and two fold-out chairs which could be tucked away, attached to the wall or set up outside as required. The sofa-style seating which sat on the opposite side to the kitchen had lift up lids under the comfy cushions for storage, too. They looked to hold a roll-up mattress and bedding among other things.

'So,' said Bear, as he filled the kettle at the sink. 'What do you think now you have seen more of it?'

'It's beautiful,' I said willingly. 'A total triumph. You must be so proud of it.'

'I am,' he confirmed. 'And I'm more than thrilled that you like it. Can you imagine yourself living somewhere similar? And, more importantly, do you think there's a place for it in one of your tall tales from small dogs?'

'*Tall Tales from Small Dogs*,' I repeated, honing in on his lovely description.

'You can have that.' He winked. 'Assuming you haven't already got a title for the collection.'

'I haven't,' I said, feeling quite smitten by his suggestion and wishing I'd been able to include it in the email I'd sent Natasha, 'so I might take you up on that.'

It really did fit the dynamic duo to a T. I wondered if it would be pushy to email Natasha again before I'd heard back from her? I didn't want to pester her, but the name was too lovely for her not to know it.

'And yes,' I said, looking around again, 'I'm certain the horse-box could feature at some point. The pair could perhaps travel by narrowboat in the spring and summer and on the road through the autumn and winter.'

Bear looked delighted about that and I thought how lovely it would be to make the seasonal point of difference.

'And you?' he then asked again. 'Do you think you could live in something like this, Holly?'

'Well,' I said, taking my time to pick the words I meant, rather than feeding him the ones I thought he'd want to hear. 'I'm one hundred per cent committed to finding somewhere alternative to live now.' Bear nodded enthusiastically at that, but he didn't interrupt. 'But I'm not entirely sure, as wonderful as yours is, if a horsebox is the answer for me. And if it's any consolation, I'm not completely sold on a narrowboat either.'

'Phew,' said Bear, wiping his brow. 'You had me worried there for a minute. I thought James had won.'

I shook my head.

'So, what's the plan?' he asked. 'Do you have one? Your friends will be back soon after Christmas, won't they?'

'They will,' I said, biting my lip. 'I need to have somewhere temporary to stay sorted by then, because buying anything will most likely take time and getting it set up will take even longer, so I won't be settled anywhere permanent ahead of their return. Finding a place to tide me over in the interim and that won't cost me the earth needs to be my current priority really.'

'It's a good idea to find somewhere temporary,' Bear whole-heartedly agreed. 'Because the last thing you want to do is to rush into anything.'

'Exactly,' I said. 'I'm planning to stay in a few unusual places while I make up my mind and decide what sort of space will work best for me. There is a sense of urgency for me to find somewhere, but I'm not going to force myself into something I'm not entirely happy with. I'm sure I'll find somewhere to stay in the meantime. Something will turn up. I'm learning to let go a bit and trust that the universe has got me.'

That sounded so unlike me. The old me, that is. The new me genuinely was more open to fretting less and seeing what came along. The spark I had felt over the arrival of the new commission request from Natasha, and the challenge and possibilities it carried with it and which I had been savouring, were proof enough of that. There was a time when I would have dismissed it and stuck to what I was familiar with, but not now.

'Yes!' Bear suddenly shouted, then pulled me into his arms and spun me around.

I had thought his initial reaction to me telling him I was taking his preferred path had been reserved but clearly, he had been biding his time and waiting to hear what else I had to say before making the most of the moment. Queenie enthusiastically leapt out of her bed and starting chasing her tail, not wanting to miss out on whatever it was that was afoot.

'Put me down, Bear!' I laughed, feeling giddy and not just from being swept off my feet.

'All right,' he laughed along with me, before setting me down and holding my hands until the world and Queenie stopped spinning. 'I'm so happy for you, Holly. You're about to embark on the biggest adventure.'

'I know,' I giggled, feeling further excited about it now I realised just how far along the path I'd come even if, so far, most of the steps I'd taken had been in my head. 'I know!'

Whereas during the divorce process I had felt rather daunted by the prospect of living a life without Piers and entirely on my own terms, I now felt nothing but elation. A sensation which increased tenfold when I imagined the freedom it could afford me *and* the thrill I would feel when I told my parents that I was living in a shipping container, on a barge or wherever I ended up.

That would be a conversation to relish. I would remember to wear my brightest possible clothes for the visit and then my mind went completely overboard as I imagined turning up at their house with a copy of *Tall Tales from Small Dogs* tucked under one arm and my own dog under the other!

'Do you think you'll live like this, or in somewhere like it, forever?' I asked Bear as he let my hands go. I then added before he could answer, 'Or are you living in the moment, embracing the here and now and not assuming that what makes you happy today will be the same in five years' time?'

'That's exactly it,' he said, clearly impressed by the depth of my understanding.

'Yeah.' I swallowed. 'Me too. That's going to be my ethos from now on.'

There was one moment I wanted to embrace which I knew would make me happier than any other, but as much as I wanted to, I didn't grab it. We'd finally set our boundaries and got ourselves properly on a friendly footing and I couldn't jeopardise that.

'Come on, then,' I therefore said. 'Show me how you make tea in a horsebox.'

'Twit,' Bear chuckled. 'You make it in exactly the same way as in a regular kitchen, but you can make the first pot, just to prove the point.'

He was right, of course, and while we waited for the tea to brew, he set up the table and chairs and I couldn't help but further admire the million cubby holes and clever space saving compartments he had at his disposal.

While we drank our tea and made short work of depleting the contents of the biscuit barrel, Bear took me through the details of how he came by his unusual home along with the intricacies of its transformative refurbishment.

'Dad could turn his hand to anything,' he said affectionately as he explained the role his father had played in the work. 'Acting was his real passion, but he was a practical man, too. He and Mum were the perfect fit,' he added, sounding wistful.

'They were lucky to have each other,' I said, again remembering my promise to remain friends with Bear for May's sake. 'There don't seem to be many relationships which stay the course these days. Not in my experience, anyway.'

'I'm sorry yours didn't,' he said kindly.

'I was sorry, too,' I told him. 'But I'm not now. It would have been a terrible thing if Piers denied himself the chance to become a parent once he'd decided that was what he wanted.'

'I do admire you for being able to accept that, Holly,' Bear said gently.

'It was hard in the beginning,' I admitted, 'but now I'm so excited to be living my new life, the old one coming to an end feels like a blessing, really. If Piers and I had stayed married, I would never have picked up my pen again or even taken a holiday on a boat, let alone considered living in one.'

'You most likely wouldn't have met Monty or Queenie either,' he pointed out.

'Or you.' I shuddered at the thought of that. 'Or your mum,' I hastily added.

'And all our lives would have been the poorer, wouldn't they?'

'They really would.' I swallowed. 'Shall we have another cup? I think there's more in the pot.'

The tea was a timely distraction and I made sure we stuck to chatting about the horsebox, The Chapel and the forthcoming performance until Queenie started to bark and someone knocked on the door.

'I know it's a bit early,' said the woman who Bear introduced as Liza, the owner of Wynter's Trees, 'but The Smuggler's has a tendency to sell out of food fast on these event nights, so I thought we could head into Wynmouth now, if that suits you?'

I was more than happy to go early, having found it harder to stay home alone with Bear than I had expected.

'It suits me,' I said, reaching for my coat. 'And I know Bear will have already said it, Liza, but thank you and Ned so much for donating the tree. It's such a kind gesture.'

'We were both so upset when Luke told us what had happened,' she said, sounding cross about it. 'Cheating somewhere like The Chapel and at Christmas of all times. It's more than criminal. Luke was set to buy the tree himself, but we wouldn't hear of that.'

'Well,' I reiterated, 'everyone back in the city will love you for it.'

'It feels good to spread some festive cheer.' She smiled prettily. 'Although tonight is definitely more Hallowe'en than anything else. Be prepared to be scared.'

'Eek,' I said. 'Is it really that blood curdling?'

'It is if George is on form,' she told me. 'And George is always on form.'

The pub was already busy by the time we arrived and with its dark interior and smoky fire, it felt like the seaside equivalent of The Dragon back in Norwich. Liza introduced us to George, and we watched with interest and bated breath as Queenie and his Jack Russell terrier, Skipper, sized each other up. Skipper looked frighteningly affronted to have had his territory invaded by a newcomer, but Queenie was so affable, it wasn't long before he was putty in her paws.

'Well, I never,' laughed George, looking amazed, and I guessed Skipper didn't usually relent quite so readily.

'Let's grab a table and a menu,' Bear suggested, pulling Queenie away in case the canine dynamics changed.

We picked the hearty sausage, mash and red cabbage combo and, as neither of us were driving that evening, a pint of local bitter apiece. Throughout the evening, as George's tales of lost ships, slighted mermaids and seafaring tragedies ramped up the terror, we downed a few more and I was feeling on the edge of tipsy when I remembered that I hadn't emailed Natasha with Bear's clever book title. Of course, it could have quite easily waited until the next day, but once I'd thought of it again, in my slightly inebriated state, I couldn't wait to act.

'Back in a minute,' I said to Bear, who was talking to the landlord at the bar during the story interval.

'Where are you going?' he called after me. 'Shall I come with you?'

'No need,' I said, waving his words away. 'I just want to send a quick message. I'm only going outside the door here.'

I stepped out into the bracing December air and my breath caught in my chest when I looked up and saw the constellations in all their glory. There was no light pollution or light from the moon to dim the spectacle and it was spectacular. I stood gazing upwards until my phone pinged in my hand and I remembered what it was that I'd braved the cold to do.

However, when I opened the message which had landed, I forgot all about the planned email to Natasha. My eyes filled with tears that I wouldn't in a million years have expected to form as I stared at the image of my ex-husband cradling the tiniest bundle of a baby and looking smilingly into the camera.

He looked like the happiest man on the planet which, I was certain, in that moment he was. The succinct message he'd typed out and sent to, I guessed, everyone in his contacts list, informed me that he now had a daughter who weighed seven and a half pounds and who had been born a little after eight that evening.

I stared at the photo for so long, I still hadn't emailed Natasha when Bear came to tell me the next round of storytelling was about to begin.

'Are you all right?' he asked, looking at me intently when we went back inside.

'Yes.' I swallowed. 'I had some unexpected news is all, but I'm fine. Really.'

I wasn't sure if I was trying to convince him or myself, but he looked as sceptical about how I said I was feeling as I actually felt.

'How about a nightcap?' I suggested, when Liza had dropped us back at the horsebox once George had finished scaring us all witless. 'And some music?'

Bear didn't seem too sure. 'I better not have another drink,' he said. 'Not if I'm driving in the morning.'

'There's no rush, is there?' I shrugged. 'We don't have to whizz straight back.'

'We do really,' he pointed out reasonably, 'because Lisa will want to get the tree up.'

I started to laugh as I scrolled through Spotify on my phone, amazed that I'd got a signal in such an out of the way area.

'Can you imagine if we forgot to take the tree?' I tittered.

'Exactly how much have you had to drink?' Bear asked, sounding amused.

'Not much.' I shrugged as the distinctive voice of Norah Jones filled the horsebox. 'Oh, I love this song. Dance with me, Bear.'

He didn't look sure about fulfilling my request, but I reached for his hand and pulled him close. I clearly wasn't quite as drunk as I had assumed, because his sudden proximity, his body pressed to mine, made my heart pound and plonked me very much in the moment.

'You know,' he said, as we gently swayed in time to the music and I felt my body further meld to his, 'there's a line in this about going away on a bus.'

'I do know.' I smiled into his chest and the warmth of his jumper. 'But I don't think Norah is referring to a converted double decker.'

'She might be.' Bear grinned and I snuggled closer, throwing caution to the wind and wrapping my arms around his broad back.

There was something unfailingly right about the way I fitted into his embrace. We stayed like that and swayed through three more songs, edging closer and closer until it was impossible to work out where he ended and I began. I wanted to stay in his arms forever, but did I feel that way because I was trying to block out my unexpected reaction to the arrival of Piers's photograph, because I had had a bit too much to drink, or because it was Bear who was holding me?

I looked up at him and he looked down at me.

'How about a coffee?' he asked.

It wasn't quite what I had been hoping to hear, whatever my motives for wrapping myself around him.

'I'd much rather go straight to bed,' I softly said and he quickly let me go.

'You're right,' he said, running a hand through his hair. 'It is late. This seating actually pulls out into a bed that's much bigger than a single and, as you're not used to negotiating the stairs, how about you sleep down here, with Queenie, just in case you need the bathroom?'

'Are you admitting there's something not quite perfect in here, Bear?' I teased.

'No,' he said, a small smile appearing. 'I'm just saying there's a knack to walking down the stairs in the dark.'

'Fair enough.' I shrugged. 'In that case, I will sleep down here, but I would like to have a look at your bedroom at some point. I still haven't seen it.'

'There'll be plenty of time before we set off,' he said, pulling the cushions about and rearranging the seating to accommodate the mattress in record time.

As hard as I tried and as comfortable as the makeshift bed was, I couldn't tip into oblivion, and kidding myself that I was doing the right thing by not overthinking the moment, which was completely in line with my new ethos, I padded quietly up the stairs to where Bear was sleeping.

'What are you doing?' he asked drowsily as I laid down next to him, wearing nothing more than my T-shirt and underwear.

'Following my intuition,' I whispered. 'And besides, it's chilly down there.'

As we hadn't been in the horsebox all evening, Bear hadn't lit the wood burner which would usually have kept the space warm.

'And you have lovely lights up here.' There were battery operated warm white fairy lights threaded around the top of the roof space, which gave the area a soft, almost candle-like glow. 'Can I sleep up here, with you?'

'All right,' he eventually relented. 'But only because you're cold. I'd be a rubbish host if I let you freeze, wouldn't I?'

Finally feeling relaxed and warm, I felt as though I was going to sleep for a week. However, when I woke in the early hours, I found Bear was awake, too. He was laying on his side and had obviously been watching me sleep.

Without a word I moved further across the bed and kissed him and he kissed me back. The feel of his lips on mine lit me up, even more powerfully than when we had kissed under the mistletoe.

This time, the kisses had an ever deeper intent and purpose and my breath came in short gasps as we hungrily pulled off the few clothes we were wearing. Bear groaned as he laid back and I lightly ran my hands over his strong, firm body and I arched into him as he did the same to me. The closeness of him drove me wild with desire and his touch elicited both excitement and pleasure, the levels of which I had never experienced before.

'Hurry,' I gasped as he moved over me, but he refused to be rushed.

I might have nodded off in Bear's bed thinking I was going to sleep for a week but it turned out he had all manner of skills and techniques to keep me pleasurably awake right until dawn.

# Chapter 25

I slipped silently out of the bed before it was light and, using the torch on my phone, carefully negotiated my way back down the stairs, which were nowhere near as tricky as Bear had suggested. I sat on the bed I should have slept in with my head in my hands for a few moments, then quickly dressed and, willing Queenie not to give me away, stepped outside.

The air was so cold it almost felt like a slap in the face and I blinked hard as my eyes filled with tears, but whether from the bite of the wind or with regret for what I'd done, I couldn't be sure. Whatever I was feeling, I couldn't deny that I had just spent the most passionate and sexually satisfying few hours of my life in that horsebox bed.

I had never felt so intimately connected to someone and I swallowed over the lump in my throat as I hoped that Bear hadn't felt the same way. It was going to be nigh on impossible to step away knowing him as I did now, but it would be hopeless if he had experienced the same depth of emotion as I'd dived into and wanted to hang on to it too.

Mindful that the battery on my phone was getting low, I took a deep breath and quickly composed and sent the email to

Natasha that I had stepped out of the pub to sort. I experienced none of the excitement the thought of doing it had previously aroused. And then I opened the photo Piers had sent again.

It was a beautiful image, but it in no way had the intense impact it had hit me with the evening before. When my system had been topped up with pints of the area's best bitter it had floored me, but now I didn't feel anything other than pleased that our lives were both turning out how we wanted them to.

'Hey,' said Bear, making me jump. 'Here you are. What are you doing? It's freezing out here.'

I hadn't heard him open the horsebox door and jumped. My cheeks flushed and I went hot, in spite of the temperature and even though I had nothing to feel guilty about.

'I didn't have a signal in the village last night,' I bluffed, waving my phone about. 'So, I've just sent the email I needed to get off.'

His brow furrowed and his eyes flicked to my phone so I quickly turned it off.

'I'm almost out of battery now, too,' I muttered, wondering why he looked the way he did.

I wasn't sure if he was annoyed, confused or a combination of both. It was certainly not the post-sex expression I had been expecting him to wear, but then perhaps he hadn't anticipated he would wake up alone.

'There's tea if you fancy it,' he told me and I followed him back inside.

He didn't make any attempt to reach for me and I didn't approach him either. It was in that moment that I could see and feel just how deeply everything had changed. Everything between us had shifted and not in a good way.

And it was all my fault. I had spent all those weeks denying my feelings and refusing to reciprocate Bear's and then, just when we had reached some level ground as friends and come to a mutual understanding as to why we couldn't be together, I'd gone to him in the night, and . . .

'Do you think we should talk about last night?' he suddenly asked, making me jump again.

'I suppose we have to really, don't we?' I said, after a beat had passed, the words catching.

He looked at me for a moment. His expression was unfathomable again and I wondered if he could glean anything from mine. If I couldn't be certain in my own mind as to what had prompted me to seduce him, then surely, he wouldn't be able to work it out, would he? None of my reasons for going to him had been the purest and I didn't like myself much for that. Bear deserved so much better.

'We don't have to do anything,' he said, sounding surprisingly blasé.

'Oh,' I said, taken aback.

His tone upset me, even though I knew I had no right to feel that way.

'We're consenting adults,' he carried on. 'Free agents. And last night we were just friends with benefits.' The term made me flinch. 'It doesn't have to mean anything.'

Given the honeyed words he'd showered me with in the past, this was not the response I had been expecting, but I knew I should have been grateful for it. Unlike me, he obviously hadn't been as emotionally moved by our hours together or rocked to his very core by the experience of exploring every inch of each other's bodies and that should have been a blessing. But it wasn't.

His words stung and more than that, they didn't in any way match the man I thought I knew. Which in turn suggested that perhaps I didn't know him that well after all. And if that was the case, then maybe I didn't need to feel quite so guilty about what had occurred.

'Okay,' I said, following his lead and feeling determined not to further blur the lines. 'Let's just leave it at that then, shall we? I had a great time and I hope you did too, but it's done. What happens in Wynmouth, stays in Wynmouth.'

I held out my hand to him and he took it.

'Fine by me.' He shrugged, barely touching my fingers before letting them go again. 'Help yourself to tea. I need to take Queenie out.'

He was gone for ages and came back with the lad who had told us where to park the day before. He was pulling a little trolley which had been cleverly painted to look like a miniature sleigh and there was a huge netted tree balanced on top.

'Hi,' he said to me, when I joined them as he and Bear lifted the tree out.

'Hey,' I said. 'You're here early this morning.'

'Well.' He grinned. ''Tis the season, and Liza and Ned need all the help they can get at this time of year.'

'I guess it is,' I acknowledged. 'Can I pour you a mug of tea?'

'No, thanks,' he said, whipping the trolley around. 'I best crack on. Happy Christmas.'

'Happy Christmas to you, too,' I reciprocated.

He gave Queenie a quick fuss and then strode off back to where the Christmas tree plantation barn was already lit up.

'I've just found out there's a car park big enough to accommo-date the horsebox at the top of the cliffs just outside the village,' said Bear as he hauled the tree up the step and inside. 'I thought we could stop there before we head back to Norwich and take Queenie on to the beach. I can't imagine she's ever seen the sea before.'

'Oh, yes,' I said, latching on to the idea and feeling grateful that we had something other than each other to focus on. 'Let's do that.'

With the tree secure and everything repacked into travel mode, we set off. The roads leading to the car park were more like tracks and I felt even more on edge than I had during the drive out of the city, but Bear didn't seem amused this time around. In fact, he didn't seem aware of me at all, but that was probably because he was so focused on the drive.

'Come on then,' he said, once he'd parked, thankfully across the empty spaces furthest away from the cliff edge. 'The tide's out so we've got a bit of a trek.'

It was even colder on the beach than it had been at Wynter's Trees and I pulled the jacket Bear had lent me to go over my coat tighter around me. It smelt deliciously of him, but I tried not to lose myself in that.

When we eventually arrived at the shore, for the first few seconds, when faced with the lapping waves, Queenie stood stock still with her head cocked to one side and her ears blown back by the wind, but then something seemed to snap inside her. She started to yip and prance about. She dashed in and out of the surf, chasing into it and then racing away again before it caught her.

'Have you ever seen her like this?' I asked Bear, my sides aching because I had laughed so much.

'No,' he shouted, over the noise of the wind. 'Never.'

Her behaviour was more akin to a young puppy than a dog

of advancing years and by the time the cold had really started to bite, she was panting hard and looked ready to find a comfy spot in which to sleep her excitement off.

Her reaction had not only been a joy to watch, but Bear and I had been so absorbed in laughing at her skittishness that we had momentarily forgotten the shift in our relationship and when we finally remembered it again, it didn't feel quite so raw. Not for me, anyway. I couldn't be sure how Bear was feeling. Quite possibly less affected than me, if his earlier manner was any indicator.

'Come on,' he said, catching hold of Queenie and attaching her lead. 'We'd better get back otherwise Lisa will be sending out a search party for this tree.'

The journey back was even quieter than the one out and I couldn't shrug off the feeling that it felt like the end of something, too. I hoped that wasn't the case as the horsebox ate up the miles and I tried not to keep thinking back to what had happened in its surprisingly comfortable bed which was positioned right above our heads. Thank goodness mattresses couldn't talk . . .

'At last!' said Lisa, rushing out to meet us once Bear had squeezed the horsebox into The Chapel car park. 'We'd all but given up on you two. Did you have fun?'

'I strapped the tree in really well,' said Bear, ignoring her question as he jumped out. 'So, hopefully it should have survived the journey.'

May had walked around to the passenger door to greet me.

'So,' she said. 'How was your night in the horsebox? Did you enjoy it?'

'Very much,' I said truthfully, focusing my gaze on the step down, rather than looking her in the eye.

I had hoped she wasn't going to find out that we'd stayed away but, given what Bear and I had gone to Wynmouth to do, I knew that was an unrealistic wish.

'Bear has just said he stayed in the village to give you the full experience,' said Lisa, also coming to find me now that Bear had proved himself a useless source of saucy gossip.

'That's right,' I fibbed.

'Weren't you scared?' she asked me. 'I don't think I would have fancied being stuck in the middle of nowhere all on my lonesome.'

She shuddered at the thought. Having not been alone, it wasn't something I had actually considered, but perhaps I should factor the prospect of isolation into my thoughts about life on the road. I remembered then that James had recommended an established marina if I wanted neighbours on a narrowboat. I wondered if any other alternative ways of living offered a community vibe.

'Do you want this tree then?' Bear shouted impatiently.

Having watched him single-handedly load the tree into the horsebox, I was fairly certain he could get it out again, but I was grateful for his timely intervention. I had succumbed to the white lie which had enabled us to spend the night in Wynmouth, but I had no desire to get drawn into embellishing it.

'All right,' said Lisa, rolling her eyes. 'Keep your hair on.'

'Help is at hand,' added May as a man I didn't recognise stepped out of The Chapel.

'Charlie!' Bear shouted, abandoning the tree and jumping down. 'My goodness. How are you?'

'I'm good,' said the man who appeared to be just a little older than May and, for a moment, had looked a smidgen apprehensive, as if he was unsure of his welcome.

'It's good to see you,' said Bear, pulling him in for a hug while May smiled at the pair of them. 'What are you doing here?'

'He came to see me again,' said May. 'And take me out for a spin in Humbug.'

'How did I not spot her?' Bear laughed.

'Humbug?' I frowned, deciding not to comment on the fact that her words suggested this wasn't Charlie's first visit. I did remember her mentioning someone coming to the bungalow before. However, given the size of the secret I was carrying, it wasn't my place to ask her if she had one of her own. 'Who's Humbug?'

'My car,' she said, pointing at a pristine green and white Triumph Herald on the road a little way up from the car park. 'Charlie is the friend who has been looking after her for me. He has a classic car business over near Cambridge.'

'I see,' I said, noticing her flushed cheeks and the sparkle in her eye.

'Charlie and I have known each other for decades,' she further confided. 'The four of us, me and Jonny and him and his wife, used to go out all the time, until she passed.'

'Well,' I said, 'I think it's wonderful when old friends reconnect. It's a shame to lose touch with people who have been in your life for such a long time.'

The words made me remember Piers's photo and I felt frustrated that it had barged its way into my thoughts again. On the journey back, as well as the horsebox bedroom business, I had also imagined the scene where Piers's parents, brother and sister-in-law were introduced to the newest family member. The feelings the fantasy moment had elicited hadn't been the best.

'Unless there's a good reason for losing touch,' Bear said

pointedly. I hadn't realised he had been listening. 'Then I think you're perfectly justified in letting people go.'

May looked between us. She no doubt, like me, was wondering what he was getting at.

'So, are we going to set this tree up or leave it in its net?' asked Charlie, with perfect timing.

I felt quite moved when I stepped inside The Chapel and saw for myself, rather than on my phone screen, the backdrop properly in its place. It might have been our first attempt at creating something like it, but between us, Bear, Pete and I had made a pretty decent job of it. The whole set looked wonderful.

'It looks good, doesn't it?' said Lisa, giving me a nudge.

'I'm amazed at how well it turned out,' I told her.

'You should have more faith,' said May. 'I bet you'd be blown away by what you could achieve if you set your heart on it.'

'I second that,' Bear added as he and Charlie carried in the tree.

I knew what he was referring to that time, but gave no hint of recognition. It was the *Tall Tales from Small Dogs*.

'Me too,' Lisa chimed in, no doubt not wanting to miss out.

'I think I might head back to the square,' I said, wanting to put some distance between myself and Bear and use the walk to further gather my thoughts and clear my head.

'The house is fine,' Lisa told me. 'I went in last night and this morning. There's nothing amiss.'

'Even so,' I said. 'I do feel a bit bad about bunking off house-sitting duty and should get back really.'

'But we miss you, Holly,' May wheedled. 'You will come back and give us a hand ahead of the performances and during the week, won't you?'

With both emails I had sent to Natasha still unacknowledged

and with no further work currently ready to get on with, I had no reason to stay away.

'And I've got something planned for Saturday that I'd really appreciate your help with,' said Lisa, adding her own inimitable layer of pressure, which I was convinced she saw more as temptation.

'Yes,' I told them both. 'I'll be back.'

'And so will I,' said Bear. 'The work at Prosperous Place is all but finished, so I can lend a hand, too.'

As I set off with my bag from the horsebox on the chilly walk back to Nightingale Square, I felt grateful that the trek was a long one. Knowing that I wasn't going to be able to avoid Bear anytime soon meant that I had even more thoughts to gather and set free and an even bigger jumbled up space in my head than the one I arrived with that I needed to clear.

# Chapter 26

During the days leading up to the first festive performance, I really didn't need to worry about how I was going to clear my head and compartmentalise what had happened with Bear, because there was no time to stress over it, or even think about it either.

May had insisted that we take a few of our early morning walks again and initially I had been worried that alone together, these might have been the times when I found myself revealing too much, but I soon discovered, as we paced around the lake, that for much of the time it was impossible to get a word in edgeways.

If she wasn't talking about the joy her rekindled friendship with Charlie had gifted her, it was the details of the finishing touches and final flourishes she had planned for The Chapel and the play. Her nurturing and experience had taken the show to the next level and everyone was extremely grateful for that. And I was more than happy to listen to her wax lyrical about it all, too.

By late Friday afternoon, everything was as ready as it could be for the imminent performance and May was a floral scented vision in a striking linen trouser suit, long floaty jacket and silk scarf. She looked just luvvie enough, in the theatrical sense, without being over the top and I couldn't help but again admire her effortlessly chic style. Once we had set out the rows of chairs to accommodate as large an audience as the room could hold, there was nothing more to be done.

I found Lisa in the kitchen looking more than a little peaky. 'Are you all right?' I asked her.

'No,' she said, taking a shallow breath and clenching and unclenching her fists. 'I'm not. I'm freaking out. I reckon that smoke machine is one effect too far, don't you?'

'No,' I said calmly, filling the kettle for what must have been the fiftieth time that day. 'It's the icing on the cake. Now Pete's got the hang of it, it's going to add wonderfully to the ambience.'

When he'd first tried it out, we'd had to open every window and door in the place and evacuate for a while, but he'd toned it down a lot since then and the addition of the extra sensory element really gave a depth to the scenes in which it featured.

My attempt to calm Lisa down obviously failed by a mile, though. 'And the dress rehearsal last night was a total disaster!' she wailed.

'But that's a good thing,' said May, who bustled in, carrying one of the costumes. 'Sara's just fixed the hem on this.'

During the disastrous rehearsal, Jodie, the main player in the performance, had caught her foot in the bottom of the dress and ripped right through the hem. It had been just one fiasco in a catalogue of many.

'How do you work that out?' Lisa frowned at May.

'A dreadful dress rehearsal guarantees a word-perfect performance,' May said with authority. 'You mark my words, they'll be spot-on tonight, and tomorrow they'll be so buoyed up by their success, they'll breeze through the whole thing again.'

'I hope you're right,' said Lisa, biting her lip.

'There's a queue forming,' said Eli, who suddenly appeared just outside the door.

'A really long one,' added the dame, who was called Daniel and had arrived looking resplendent in a flamboyant glittery gown and mile-high beehive wig.

'Well, they'll have to wait,' said May, checking her watch. 'They're not getting in yet, but it's great they're so keen.'

Eli rushed off again, straightening his bow tie. He looked as flustered as Lisa but Daniel swept out behind him, looking altogether far more composed.

'How are things coming on for the after-party on Sunday, May?' I asked, hoping to distract Lisa from further thoughts of smoke triggered calamities.

May had decided to throw the party during the Sunday afternoon rather than straight after the final curtain the evening before. Given it was all youngsters who were involved in the performance, she thought it only fair they had time to rally and she was keen to keep the excitement going for as long as possible.

Everyone involved with The Chapel in any capacity had been invited. I might have miraculously ended up managing to avoid being in close proximity to Bear all week, but I knew I'd have to get on with it when Sunday dawned because I wouldn't be able to distance myself from him in the bungalow. I then wondered if perhaps he had been going as far out of his way to not see me as I had travelled to miss seeing him. Given that previously our paths had so often crossed, I wouldn't have been surprised that our recent avoidance of one another had been a successful joint effort.

'The scene is set,' May told me, with a dazzling smile. 'It's going to be fully catered and fabulous.'

'Sounds good to me,' said Freddie, who had a habit of popping up whenever food was mentioned.

He was looking very dapper in a smart shirt and paisley-patterned cravat. His nose had been pushed a little out of joint by Charlie's popping in during the week, but after a spin in Humbug, he seemed to have made his peace with his presence.

'And what about the plans you've got for the fun day here tomorrow, Lisa?' I asked, now more aware of what it was she had been planning. She was so organised that I was sure discussing it would help her feel more confident in how it was all going to go, but I was unwittingly undoing my good work even before she'd absorbed the benefit of it.

'Don't ask,' she huffed. 'I don't know why I thought it would be a good idea to do it. It's too much. It's all too much.'

'Now, Lisa,' May said sternly. 'Am I going to have to give you one of those soap opera slaps I was once famous for and tell you to get a grip?'

Freddie looked at me and winked and we all burst out laughing.

'No.' Lisa grinned, finally sounding more like her usual ebullient self. 'I'm not quite that far gone.'

'Good,' said May, tossing the repaired dress to me. 'So, come on, my loves. It's almost time.'

Just as May predicted, the performance was a roaring success. The audience were in thrall of what played out on the stage and there was barely a dry eye in the house during the songs which were solo performances. If anyone had been wondering if the mix of kids who turned up at The Chapel had any talent, they were left in no doubt that evening.

It was a shame that a mainstream school curriculum didn't cater for their needs, but I wasn't going to get bogged down thinking about the politics. I just wanted to enjoy the moment I had, in a small way, helped to enhance and feel grateful that The Chapel existed.

Eli and Daniel gave wonderful speeches at the end, reminding everyone that everything they had witnessed had been created by the attendees. The script, the music, the choreography was all their own work. I was on tenterhooks in case either of them mentioned the set creation and pointed me out, but thankfully they didn't and I applauded and stamped along with everyone else as May said a few words too and congratulated the stars of the show.

We were still all buzzing when the audience and performers had gone home and while we helped to pack away the chairs, ready for Lisa's fun day. But when I arrived early to help set up the next morning I felt nowhere near as hyped.

'No!' I heard Lisa shout, the moment I opened the door. 'The tombola needs to go over there next to the stage.'

Clearly, the pre-show jitters she had succumbed to the evening before had been banished and she was back in charge again.

'So, where's the photo booth going to be?' came John's terse response.

'In the room next to the kitchen. The dressing up boxes are already in there. We went through all this back at the house, John.'

He gritted his teeth and I caught his arm as he walked by carrying a huge box covered in wrapping paper.

'Is this Lisa's usual level of bossiness?' I asked quietly, having experienced for myself nothing quite like it before.

'Nope,' she responded, having caught my question. 'I'm in overdrive today and with good reason. We've got a crisis on our hands.'

She rushed to the door, a clipboard full of papers in her grasp and grabbed Bear who had just walked in. She then shoved us together and looked us up and down in a way that made me feel most uncomfortable. I didn't particularly want to be standing so close to him and I certainly didn't want to be scrutinised while it was happening.

'What do you think?' she asked John, once she'd finished sizing us up.

'They're a bit young,' he said, screwing his face up, 'but he's certainly got the size. They might be the only hope we have, assuming we can spare someone to spend the day with them to fulfil the safeguarding requirements.'

I didn't like the sound of that and a quick look at Bear's face suggested he wasn't all that keen either.

'A bit young for what?' He frowned.

Given the eager look written across Lisa's face I found myself wishing I hadn't made my promise to May to help out again.

'The thing is,' Lisa said, putting the clipboard in John's box before stepping between us and linking one arm through mine and the other through Bear's, I presumed, so we couldn't escape, 'we've got a bit of a disaster on our hands. One which could potentially ruin the entire day.'

'Well, that doesn't sound good,' said Bear.

'It doesn't, does it?' said Lisa, squeezing us both tighter. 'However, I do believe that the two of you, if you're willing, could completely turn the situation around.'

'How?' I sighed.

'Yes, how?' asked Bear. 'What can we do?'

'Well, the couple we had booked to be Father and Mrs Christmas have both gone down with food poisoning, so—'

'Oh, no,' said Bear, but it was too late now.

'The kids are expecting Mr and Mrs Claus,' Lisa wheedled. 'And there'll be tears and tantrums if they're not here. Not to mention dozens of disappointed parents who can't afford the expense of a package deal to sit with Santa in one of the upmarket department stores.'

I had noticed how much those packages cost during my trip into the city and I knew May had shelled out a ridiculous amount for the Pooch Shoot, so Lisa was making a valid point, even if I didn't want to consider the consequences attached to it.

'Why can't you and John do it?' Bear asked reasonably.

'John's got to work and I'm crowd control.' Lisa shrugged. 'And before you ask, everyone else has already been assigned jobs, too. I did have you lined up for something else, Holly, but this is far more important.'

'I get why you need a replacement Santa,' I piped up, trying to save myself and cling to the craft table role I guessed I'd previously been assigned, 'but Mrs Claus. Is she really necessary?'

Bear shot me a look, but I didn't relent.

'She is,' Lisa said firmly, crushing my selfish suggestion. 'Not every child who visits the grotto wants to be greeted by a big bloke. Not every little one has had the benefit of a positive male role model in their life.'

I realised the implication behind her words and a lump formed in my throat.

'Of course,' I said, as I tried to swallow it away.

'I will, if you will, Holly,' Bear then said, sounding resigned to his fate.

I caved, thinking of the kids rather than my dignity. 'Oh, go on then, but I'm not wearing anything trimmed in sleigh bells.'

It turned out there wasn't a sleigh bell in sight. In fact, the costumes were stunning.

'I'm gifting this and the Santa outfit to The Chapel,' said May as she helped me into the dress. It was a full-length red velvet creation with white fur trim around the collar, wrists and hem. 'The rentals were so expensive that these will have paid for themselves in just a few outings.'

'That's so kind, May,' I told her.

'It's just a small thing, really.' She shrugged, but I knew it was going to mean the world to the kids who turned up.

'Well,' I said, biting my lip as I looked in the mirror which had been set up in the photo booth room and had a wobble about whether I was going to be able to pull it off. 'I look the part, even if I don't feel it. You would have been far better at this than me.'

'There's a hat, too,' said May, ignoring what I'd said as she handed it over. I supposed it would have looked a little odd if Mrs Claus was so much older than her husband. 'And don't worry, my darling, you'll soon get into the swing of it.'

I had taken my nephews to the grotto enough times to know what was expected so I hoped I would get into the swing of it, as May had put it.

'Oh.' I gulped, taken aback by the sight of Bear when he appeared in the doorway. He was a spectacular Santa. 'You look amazing.' I faltered. 'I love your buckle. It's very ... shiny.'

I felt my face flush with embarrassment. What a stupid thing to comment on.

'I've just polished it,' he said, looking down at it and thankfully sounding every bit as ridiculous as I did. 'You look good, too,' he added, taking another look at what I was wearing.

'That's enough flirting, you two,' Lisa butted in, making my cheeks flame brighter.

'We weren't,' said Bear.

Had I not ruined the relationship we'd had by seducing him at the seaside, we might have succumbed to some friendly flirtation. I turned away, not liking the sharp tang of regret which I could feel building in my gut. Or perhaps that was just nerves.

'Right,' said Eli, clapping his hands. 'It's time to let everyone in. You two,' he added, pointing at Bear and me, 'better head for the grotto.'

As I left the photo booth room, I couldn't help but admire what Lisa and the team had achieved. Along with the dressing up, crafting, tombola and raffle tables, there was also a cookie decorating station, card making area and face painting. Seasonal snacks and drinks were on offer, too. And then there was the tree, of course. Packed full of decorations, including those the attendees had previously made, it looked spectacular, so at least some good had come from the night away in Wynmouth.

'Isn't it all amazing?' I said to Bear and he nodded in agreement.

One of the side rooms had been decorated magically overnight by a couple of elves who couldn't have had more than a few hours' sleep between them and now housed two large comfy chairs, each with their own huge sacks of presents and with an electric wood burner stove set between them. The walls had been draped in red fabric and there was a trio of light up deer that I recognised from Lisa and John's own front garden arranged on a large patch of cotton wool snow.

'What are the presents?' I asked, peering into the sack by my side.

'Books, card games and simple festive craft kits,' said Beth, who was setting up a speaker to play a soundtrack that was supposed to emulate Lapland.

She turned it on and the sound of sleigh bells filled the room. My hunch had been right: I'd known bells were going to be involved somewhere, but I didn't really mind because they added to the ambience and enhanced the experience.

'Nothing gender specific then.' I smiled. 'That's great.'

'Exactly,' she said. 'And I'd better take a photo of you two for the website.'

Bear groaned at that, but I didn't bother. I had accepted my fate now.

'Shame you couldn't bring the dogs in today,' Beth further said, once she was happy with the photos. 'Where are they?'

'Asleep in Mum's kitchen,' said Bear, as he readjusted his beard. 'Right where I'd like to be.'

'It's too late to back out now,' I said with a nod to the door where I could see families streaming in.

'And I don't want to,' he said, rolling his eyes. 'Not really.'

'I do,' sighed Pete, who then plodded in, dressed as an elf.

'Oh, Pete,' I stammered, trying not to laugh.

'Damn,' said Bear, also smiling. 'All of a sudden, I'm feeling like I got off lightly.'

'Don't say another word.' Pete grimaced through gritted teeth, as he readjusted his red and green felt hat. 'I have to be here on safeguarding duty.'

'I was just going to say, I like your ears,' I said, biting the inside of my cheek to stop a giggle escaping.

'Yeah, right,' said Pete. He sounded as little like a cheerful Christmas elf as it was humanly possible to be.

Throughout the day, the grotto had a steady stream of visitors and there were only a couple of screamers amongst them. It didn't matter who the parents tried to get them to stand next to, they bawled relentlessly and had to be taken out and soothed with promises of gingerbread and hot chocolate.

Predictably, Bear had far more visitors than I did, but it was a real pleasure and privilege to be there for the kids who wanted to pick Mrs Claus over him.

'She's never been able to do this before,' one of the mums confided as her daughter tore into the present I'd picked out of the sack for her. 'Because I've never found somewhere with a Mrs Claus. You've made our Christmas.'

I felt rather bright eyed at hearing that.

'Oh, wow!' said the little girl. 'I love these stories! We have all of the books at school.'

She'd picked out one of the titles Beth and Pete had contributed and I turned to make sure Pete had noticed. The tears in his eyes told me he had.

I wondered what it would feel like if I could come back next year and add a few of my own dog tales to the piles of presents. That would really be quite something, but I'd have to get them published first.

'I happen to know,' Pete said gently, 'that the lady who wrote that book is here today. Would you like her to sign it for you?'

The girl's eyes widened. 'Oh yes, please!'

'Is she really?' asked her mum, sounding as if she couldn't believe their luck.

'Yes,' said May, who happened to be doing the rounds and had just looked in. 'I can introduce you, if you like.'

The girl was off like a shot and Bear gave me a smile. He was looking a bit emotional too.

'That could be you next year,' he said, while Pete was distracted with the next visitor, then switched seamlessly back into character. 'Now, who do we have here?' Pete mouthed the name behind the boy's back. 'It's Joe, isn't it? Come and tell Santa what you're hoping to find under your tree this year.'

Joe's face was a picture and I daresay mine was, too, as I carried on imagining myself arriving with armfuls of my own books.

As well as the wonderful activities Lisa had organised and everyone attending had enjoyed, there was also an impromptu carol singing session at the end of the day. Freddie and Eli supplied the music and everyone joined in with the words. Lisa needn't have worried that the day wasn't going to be a success because if the amount of glitter on the carpet and the number of empty tubes of icing were indicators, it had been a total festive triumph.

It was gone four o'clock when the last of the families left and then it was all hands to the pumps in an extremely fast and furious turnaround to get everything ready for that evening's performance. Pete and Beth dashed off to buy fish and chips for the troops and we all collapsed until the actors started to arrive, ready to put on the final show.

'You were right,' Lisa said to May, above the noise of the stamping and clapping at the end as the actors all bowed and beamed. It had gone off without a hitch again and with only a little more smoke than the night before. 'They were word perfect.'

'With all my years of experience in the industry,' May told her, 'you do genuinely get a feel for these things.'

Whereas the evening before a couple of us had got off lightly, there was no escape that night. Eli called everyone on to the stage, including me and Bear, and thanked us all in turn after explaining the parts we'd played.

I hadn't expected to enjoy the exposure at all, but, as I stood there and took in the smiling faces of the new friends I was surrounded by, I felt both happy and proud. I might not have had a role in the actual performance, but I knew I was lucky to have been press-ganged into turning up and then making the decision to get more involved. As modest as I was, even I could tell that the set myself, Bear and Pete had created had enabled the show to really shine and, added to that, I had made the day even better for some in the guise of Mrs Claus, too.

I wasn't always sure who this person I was turning into was. My behaviour with Bear aside, I was proud of her though. I had embraced so much and changed in so many ways since arriving in Nightingale Square and everything I had done was in stark contrast to what I had arrived intending to do.

As I recalled, I hadn't planned to do anything more than have a proper rest and a good think. I hadn't rested for a second yet, but I had thought and more than that, I had acted on those thoughts. I definitely liked this new version of me. I liked her very much and I was excited to see what the thrilling new future she now faced had in store for her.

# Chapter 27

I would have loved to have had a lazy start the next day and the opportunity to process what I'd achieved at The Chapel, but there was no chance of that.

For a start, I hadn't slept well. Bear had slunk off long before the rest of us the evening before, on the pretence of checking on the dogs, but I was worried that there was more to it than that and my concern was enough to stop me properly nodding off. I had come to the conclusion that he had been going as far out of his way to avoid me as I had him and, given that I was the one responsible for ripping up the rulebook when it came to our relationship, that was far from fair.

His time in Norwich and with May had an expiration date and, given that they didn't see all that much of each other throughout the rest of the year, I didn't want to monopolise what time they did have by hanging around like the proverbial spare wheel.

I had promised May that I would go to the bungalow well ahead of the time the guests were due, to help with any last-minute setting up and, assuming Bear would be there too, I decided I should attempt to further clear the air with him and,

if that failed, resolve to make myself scarce now the curtain had
come down on the two performances.

'This feels like the old days!' May announced, throwing the
front door open and beckoning me inside hospitably. 'Doesn't it,
Bear?' she called along the hall. 'Doesn't it feel like the old days?'

She was dressed in her characteristic kaftan and turban combo
and her face, which was entirely without make up, glowed with
excitement as she took the handful of helium balloons that I had
made a detour to collect from somewhere that didn't usually
open so early on a Sunday, but which May had somehow bent
to her will.

'It does,' Bear agreed, as he stepped out of the kitchen.
'Exactly like the old days. Morning, Holly.'

'Hi,' I said, feeling absurdly shy.

'I've been mixing up some Christmas cocktails,' May confided, thankfully not noticing my blushes. 'All non-alcoholic,
of course.'

I was amazed that her exuberance hadn't been helped along
even the tiniest bit by a morning Buck's Fizz or breakfast Bellini.

'As we've so many under-agers coming and after what
happened with your friend Harry that year, Teds, I thought
we'd better stick to the alcohol-free drinks, until later in the
evening, anyway.'

'How long are you expecting this party to last, Mum?'
Bear laughed.

He didn't appear awkward at all. Perhaps I needed to rethink
my plan to corner him. Maybe it would be more prudent to let
sleeping dogs lie and power through.

'Never mind that,' I therefore said, suiting my words to the
thought. 'I want to know what happened to your friend, Harry.'

Bear rolled his eyes and May laughed.

'Let's just say,' she confided, rearranging the balloon strings, 'the year that boy turned fifteen, the Christmas gift he remembered most vividly was the self-inflicted hangover he had after helping himself repeatedly to our Christmas Eve punch.'

'Oh dear.' I grimaced.

'Oh dear, doesn't even cover it,' said Bear, unable now to resist joining in the retelling. 'His father never got over the cost of having the inside of his car valeted after he refused to stop when Harry asked him to on the drive home.'

'Eek,' I squeaked, trying not to picture the scene.

'Our parties were legendary,' May sighed wistfully, 'but I realised after that one, that teenagers couldn't be trusted unchaperoned around the punch bowl.'

'That's hardly fair,' said Bear. 'I bet they're not all as foolhardy as Harry. I certainly never was.'

'No, darling,' said May, patting his face, which he tolerated with good humour, 'but that was most likely because your father and I always let you have a taste of what we were drinking and you grew up respecting alcohol as a result.'

'Thank goodness,' said Bear, wrinkling his nose. 'Because Harry said the smell of his dad's car was—'

'Let's talk about something else,' I said, waving my hands about. 'I swear I just got a whiff of it. Come on, May, let's organise these balloons and you can tell us what needs doing next.'

By the time the first revellers arrived, the bungalow was further bedecked with more fairy lights draped around doorways and a tiny tree added to the cloakroom windowsill and we had opened a couple of windows, too. It was already feeling warm inside, but that could have been because four of us were feeling

the heat wearing fancy dress. Monty was fabulously adorned
for the occasion as a hot dog, complete with roll, ketchup and
mustard. Queenie, by contrast, had taken herself off to May's
dressing room where the door was left slightly ajar so she could
make an appearance when she wanted to. My money was on her
staying out of sight.

'No thigh-high boots,' commented Bear, when he saw what
I was wearing.

'Not today,' I said, looking down at the Christmas tree costume May had picked out for me, complete with angel headband.
'And no carrot for you either.' I smiled, remembering him as Olaf.

Bear awkwardly shuffled around to show off the full effect of
his Christmas pudding ensemble.

'It's very rotund,' I laughed, 'and you're going to boil, just
like the real thing.'

'I haven't got much on underneath it,' he confessed.

'Well, let's hope no one tries to light the sprig of holly on
your head.' I swallowed, refusing to allow myself to imagine him
standing there without the speckled pud covering his modesty.

'Come along, come along,' said May, who had elegantly transformed herself into a pink glittering fairy godmother, complete
with wand. 'I can hear feet on the drive!'

That afternoon she made more than one dream come true
as she played hostess perfectly and kept plates and glasses filled
as well as the youngsters entertained. She was entirely in her
element and I found myself wishing I'd met her years ago. I
would have loved to have been privy to more of these legendary
Madison parties.

'This place is amazing,' I heard more than one person say. 'I
don't know what I had been expecting, but it wasn't this.'

I supposed I had got used to the eclectic and colourful bunga-low, but to the party guests visiting for the first time, there was a sense of awe and wonder that was only enhanced by the extra addition of the dazzling decorations, not to mention the fact that everyone in attendance was wearing fancy dress. I'd seen cracker costumes, the Grinch and even a turkey among the throng and they were all having the best time.

'If I still had even the slightest concern about Mum's move to Norwich and whether she was settling in,' Bear told me as the afternoon progressed, 'watching her do her thing here today would have squashed it flat.'

I thought back to when I had first met May and Monty, just a few short weeks ago. Her life had changed beyond measure thanks to the timely introduction to The Chapel. And indeed, so had mine. It had been fate in action for all of us.

'I'd say she's more than settled now,' I agreed, wondering if it might be a good time to say a little more about what happened between us, or whether it really was all water under the bridge.

'Hey, you two,' said Lisa, stealing the moment before I had decided what to do with it. 'I just wanted to say thank you again for stepping in when we needed you. Yesterday was a triumph thanks to you, and that set and backdrop really gave the perfor-mance some depth, too. We'll definitely be using it all again.'

I knew the success of the day wasn't all down to Bear and I donning the red outfits, but it was wonderful to know our time in the grotto had helped.

'I'm so pleased,' I said. 'And if I happen to ever be visiting when there's another show in the offing, I'll help again if you'd like me to.' Lisa looked thrilled about that. 'And I love your costumes, by the way.'

Lisa and John and their children were all dressed up as Christmas presents. They were each wearing a different sized box to match their age and all topped off with huge ribbon bows atop their heads.

'Thanks,' said Lisa, looking down at herself. 'They're a bugger to get on, but they make quite an impact, don't they?'

'Come on,' said Tamsin, trying to drag her mum off as I wondered how they would manage if they needed the loo. 'Dad's got the photo booth set up for us to use and the others are getting antsy.'

She didn't seem at all fazed that she was in public dressed up as a giant box. In fact, her bow looked to be the biggest of the lot.

'You look great, Tamsin,' said Bear and she blushed.

'Christmas, isn't it?' She shrugged. 'You can't worry about making a tit of yourself when the tinsel's up.'

'Er, right,' said Lisa, steering her away. 'That's enough out of you, I think.'

'Peas in a pod, aren't they?' I laughed as I watched them try to walk away without bashing into each other.

'More like presents out of the same stocking,' said Bear, attempting to be clever, and I groaned.

'Do you think you'll help out at The Chapel again?' I asked him.

'If I'm visiting and they need a hand,' he told me, 'for sure.'

'Hey, guys,' said Pete, who wandered up. He was dressed to look like a giant carrot, complete with a green frond top. I wondered if it was Sara's handiwork with a needle and thread. 'Great party!'

His cheeks were flushed and I looked over to where May was ladling punch. Had she added a little something extra now the time was drawing on?

'There you are, Pete,' said Sara, rushing up in a reindeer outfit that complemented Pete's get up perfectly. 'I thought I'd lost you.'

'Are you in need of a nibble, my little reindeer?' he asked, reaching for her waist and making her laugh.

'Not right now,' she said, pretending to fend him off with her hooves, 'but I wouldn't mind a photo to remember the occasion.'

'That photo booth is proving as popular as it was at the family fun day,' I said to Bear as Sara and Pete headed off in the same direction Lisa and Tamsin had taken. 'And I hope you won't mind having some pics taken because I think I'm going to want to record this party memory for posterity.'

'Fair enough,' said Bear, with a smile which didn't quite reach his eyes. 'I don't mind, because as a wise teen once said, you can't worry about making a tit of yourself when the tinsel's out. We've all proved that today, but especially Charlie.' He pointed to where someone in a penguin costume was fanning themselves with a paper plate and pulling at the neck of their costume.

'Is that Charlie?' I laughed. 'I had no idea. I didn't see him arrive.'

The room fell silent then as May tapped her glass with her glittery wand and gave the most wonderful speech.

'I can't deny I was feeling a little forlorn as the days began to grow short and the darkness descended,' she said bravely, 'but a chance meeting with Holly has changed my life. Not only has she become the daughter I never had, but she has introduced me to all of you.'

I was totally taken aback by her choice of words, but thrilled she felt as strongly for me as I did for her. I wondered if she would feel the same way if she knew what I had got up to at the seaside.

'We love you, May!' shouted one of The Chapel attendees from the back of the room.

'And I love all of you,' she said, sounding emotional. 'Especially you, Travis. I told you that you had it in you to take on that role, didn't I?'

The lad in question gave her a thumbs up and blew her a kiss. Eli had told me that Travis had been even more of a handful than Vincent when he first came to The Chapel, but he'd started to find acting, rather than acting out, cathartic. He certainly had the talent to go further, which he no doubt would under May's guidance and encouragement. They all would.

'Here's to many more stand out performances to come!' May finished up, raising her glass. 'To The Chapel and everyone involved in making it such a special place to be!'

'The Chapel,' we all chorused, toasting future successes of which I was certain that with Eli, Lisa and May at the helm, and backed up by the rest of the team, there would be many.

Before everyone emptied their glasses and began chatting again, Eli quickly added, 'And to you too, May!'

'To May,' we all wholeheartedly joined in.

The party ended up going far longer than I had expected it to and no one was in a rush to leave. May, however, had planned for the long haul and had made sure the catering more than covered the hours her guests wanted to enjoy her hospitality. When the music was cranked up and the dancing began, Bear had disappeared for a while to walk the dogs and I was disappointed to note that he had changed out of his costume to do it.

'You couldn't expect me to pick up poop dressed as a Christmas pudding,' he said, defending his disrobing when I expressed my upset. 'I couldn't bend down for a start.'

I supposed he had a point.

At the very end of the evening, after the last guests had left and she had waved off Charlie, who had to get back to Cambridge, May kicked off her sparkly trainers. 'Well, my dears,' she said, 'I think that went rather well, don't you?'

'More than well,' I said, noticing the many empty plates, glasses and platters. 'There's not so much as a single mince pie gone to waste.'

'And more importantly,' chuckled May, 'not a single one of those teens has gone home wasted.'

'They're a good bunch,' said Bear, who was sitting on the sofa with Queenie melded to his side.

She hadn't attended much of the party and looked relieved it was all over. Monty, on the other hand, was still happily trotting about in full costume, hoovering up any stray crumbs. I had changed out of my tree costume and back into my civvies, so it was just him and May in fancy dress.

'The best.' May yawned. 'And don't worry about the clearing up,' she then said to me as I began stacking plates. 'I'll deal with all of this tomorrow.'

'That's hardly fair,' I told her. 'I'll come back and help.'

'And so will I,' Bear offered. 'But not first thing because I have a groaning inbox to deal with before everyone starts to sign off for Christmas and then I'm off to visit a reclamation yard with Finn and Freya.'

'As you wish,' May said, 'but I honestly don't mind. I rather enjoy the post-party clear up as it gives me the opportunity to think about the celebrations again. But there is just one more thing we have to do tonight.'

May disappeared into the kitchen and came back with a

perfectly chilled bottle of champagne, one she had set aside especially for the three of us, which she opened with a pop.

'I do love a glass of bubbly,' she said, as she filled the glasses right to the top.

'Me too,' I agreed.

'Me three,' chimed in Bear.

It felt like the perfect end to what had been another wonderful day and I was pleased I hadn't stirred up what had happened between me and Bear again. The expression *don't poke the bear* came into my mind and I smiled at the image it created in my head.

'And we have so much to celebrate.' May beamed at us both. 'Even more than I realised before today.'

'Oh?' I said, taking my first taste of the deliciously crisp champagne.

'As I understand it, Holly,' she elaborated, her eyes twinkling, 'you've got the bit between your teeth with a new project featuring our perfect pooches.'

I choked as the bubbles caught in my throat and I threw Bear an accusatory look.

'Have I?' I asked sharply, after swallowing down another mouthful to clear the cough.

May looked concerned. 'Well, that's what I heard,' she told me, but in the face of my reaction, she didn't sound quite so certain of her facts.

'I wouldn't listen to gossip,' I said, feeling deeply upset. 'People so often get the wrong end of the stick.'

I stood up and handed May my glass. For once she was lost for words.

'I better go,' I said. 'I'll see you tomorrow.'

'I'll walk with you,' said Bear, also standing up.

'No need.' I scowled. 'I'd rather go alone. Thank you for a wonderful party, May,' I added, remembering my manners as I rushed out, grabbed my coat from the obliging faun and left.

I had barely reached the end of the road before I heard Bear jogging to catch me up.

'Holly, wait!' he called, but I marched on.

Head down, I didn't want to be anywhere near him.

'Wait,' he said, when he reached me. He stepped right in front of me so I had no choice but to stop. 'If you'll just let me—'

'No,' I said, pushing around him. 'I'm not going to let you do anything.'

His stride easily matched mine and I was out of breath before he was.

'I have to say I find it amusing that you've gone out of your way to avoid me,' I puffed, when I had to wait for a break in the traffic before I could cross the road, 'but have still been talking about me. So much for out of sight, out of mind.'

He shook his head at that.

'Is it any wonder I've avoided you after what happened in Wynmouth?' he shot back.

He sounded every bit as angry as I did, but I had no idea why. Surely, on this occasion, I had the right to harbour the worst bad mood.

'I thought you were fine with that,' I volleyed. 'Consenting adults, friends with benefits, blah, blah, blah.'

'Bullshit,' he said, raking a hand through his hair. 'All bullshit and you know it, but what was I supposed to say once I'd worked out why you'd come to me that night? I thought I'd had the best sex of my life with someone who genuinely wanted me, but that bubble burst when I realised you'd just used me.'

'Used you?' I practically shrieked, not in that moment taking in that what he'd said about us being together meant he had been every bit as connected as I had. 'What are you talking about?'

A car beeped to let us cross and we marched over the road and began the row again.

'When you came back into the pub after going out to send that email,' Bear ranted, 'you said your change in mood was down to some unexpected news.'

I tried not to flush as I thought about how I had reacted to the photo Piers had sent me of him holding his newborn daughter.

'So?' I shrugged, sounding like a petulant teen.

'But the next morning you seemed to have forgotten all about it and said you were back on your phone again because outside the pub you hadn't been able to get a signal.'

I took a moment to digest that. Having had so much to drink I hadn't been able to piece together exactly what I'd said with any clarity.

'What I probably meant was . . .' My words trailed off as Bear shook his head again.

'Fuck the phone signal,' he said. 'It's not relevant. The point is, when I came to find you that morning, I saw what you were looking at on your phone. I saw a photo of a man holding a newborn baby and I knew it had to be him. Your ex. I also' – he swallowed – 'knew that was the news you'd received at the pub and then I realised that you'd come looking for me, not because you wanted to be with me, but because you . . . I dunno . . . maybe wanted to feel better or get over the shock or forget what you'd seen. None of it had actually been about me, or you and me. It was all you.'

I opened my mouth to respond, but couldn't find the words to defend what I'd done.

'Well, whatever your reason for seeking me out,' Bear carried on, sounding increasingly deflated when I didn't offer either an explanation or an excuse, 'it wasn't the one I had hoped it had been and that was why I launched into the blasé *friends with benefits* speech.'

He gave the term the sarcastic air quotes that, in this instance, it deserved and strode off, this time with me following on behind him. I tried to mentally compose a sentence that could prove he was wrong, but part of me knew he was right.

'Would you believe me,' I said, willing myself not to succumb to tears of frustration, 'if I said that the reaction I had to that photo was down to all the beer I'd drunk?'

The look Bear stopped to give me suggested he didn't.

'And I know that,' I carried on, further trying to make him believe me, 'because when I looked at it the next morning, it hit completely differently.'

It was true, but it sounded feeble even to my ears. I tried to imagine how he had felt when he saw me looking at the photo. Sick to his stomach was my own gut reaction.

'Was it really the best sex of your life?' I asked, the words little louder than a whisper as my brain finally acknowledged what he'd said.

He carried on walking and I had to practically jog to keep up.

'Will you please just stop?' I begged, grabbing his arm, after we'd covered some distance.

He yanked it out of my grasp.

'Why don't *you* just stop?' he said, coming to such a sudden halt that I overtook him. 'Do you have any idea how hard it was for me to agree to be your friend, Holly? Even though I was doing it with Mum's best interests at heart. Have you any idea of the torment I've tried to pretend I'm not feeling since that night when you instigated stamping all over everything we'd previously agreed on?'

'I'm sorry,' I told him, meaning every word. 'I'm so, so sorry and if it means anything to you, I've been in torment too.'

He ground his jaw. A hard look crept into his eyes and in that moment, I remembered why I had left May's in such a rush.

'But none of that gave you the right to tell your mum about what I've been working on,' I said, in a small voice.

I watched as the aggression drained out of him and his shoulders sagged.

'What?' he said croakily.

'I specifically asked you not to talk to anyone about any of it,' I reminded him, making what was already happening a million times worse. It wasn't the time to bring it up, but I couldn't stop myself. 'And just because I'd upset you—'

'Upset me,' he echoed and I stopped talking, suddenly aware that I really had gone too far. 'I'm going to walk away now, Holly, and you're going to let me.'

As I watched him stride off, I knew I'd made even more of a mess of the situation and sobbed as I wondered if I had just sacrificed the very relationships I had spent the last few weeks trying to protect and save.

# Chapter 28

With The Chapel winding down for the festive break and as long as the weather didn't turn too inclement, there was no excuse for May and me to miss any more of our early morning walks around the lake and that was what she rang and suggested ahead of me arriving to help clear up the morning after the party.

I had been in two minds about turning up at the bungalow, in case Bear had filled her in about what had happened once we'd left the evening before, or worse still, before that, but then I figured if he had, it was only fair that I got to share my take on the situation, too.

The last thing I wanted was for there to be any unnecessary bad feeling between us. It was the one thing I had been striving to avoid from practically the moment we had joined the dots between our connections when we were first all together under The Chapel roof and I would continue to try to keep things as clear cut as possible.

'Oh,' I said, when May opened the door and both Monty and Queenie rushed out to greet me. 'You've got Queenie, too.'

I'd been in such a state when Bear and I had argued, that I'd completely forgotten he hadn't had time to bring her with him when he'd rushed to catch me up.

'Bear didn't come back for her last night,' May told me. 'He sent a text asking if I'd look after her while he went to the reclamation yard with Freya and Finn today. Apparently, it's not suitable for dogs and he didn't want to pick her up and then have to leave her on her own in the horsebox.'

'I see,' I said, bending to give the dogs a fuss.

I felt quite choked as they smothered me in affection, completely unaware of the rampaging range of emotions and actions that their introduction to my life had unleashed.

'I'm so sorry about last night,' said May, her eyes filling with tears to match my own. 'I didn't mean to put my foot in it. I had no idea your work featuring this pair was a secret.'

'It's fine,' I said, standing straight again and trying to sound as cool as Bear had done the morning after our night of passion. 'And I'm sorry, too,' I then sincerely added. 'I hope what happened after it didn't spoil the party for you?'

'Absolutely not,' she insisted. 'Though I do wonder why you hadn't—'

'Do you mind if we don't talk about the project,' I cut in, making it a statement rather than a question.

'Of course.' She nodded. 'Did you and Bear have a big row?' she then asked, her brow furrowed. 'I wasn't sure what happened and he hasn't told me anything.'

'Quite big,' I admitted. 'And if it's all right with you, I'd rather not talk about that, either.'

Now I knew that Bear hadn't shared the details with May about any of what had occurred, there was no reason for me to say anything about it either.

May put up her hands. 'Of course.' She smiled. 'Mum's the word. I'll just grab the leads and we'll get off.'

With the most recent events vetoed, our conversation around the lake was a little stilted. I was pleased that Bear hadn't gone further blabbing to his mum, but his silence did leave me wondering how we were all going to move forward with the inevitable elephant taking up so much space in the room. May was no fool and she was bound to realise there was more to the situation than an argument over some sketches.

I might have still been feeling angry with Bear, but he was cross with me, too, and I knew we were both justified in feeling upset. One of us would have to be the first to offer the olive branch, if we were going to resolve the stand-off, but who was it going to be? The oppressive weight of the guilt I carried told me I should just seize the day, but I wasn't sure I could. Not yet, anyway.

'Are you seeing Charlie today?' I asked, once we'd exhausted the topic of the changeable winter weather and I had admired Monty's new sou'wester which May had ordered to replace the one which had been roughed up.

'Not today,' she said, with a sigh. 'Not for a few days actually. He's winding the business down to close up for a few weeks over the Christmas period and into the New Year.'

'But you'll see him over Christmas at some point, won't you?'

'I think so,' she said, sounding unsure.

I looked at her and found she was frowning again.

'What is it, May?'

'Oh, I don't know,' she sighed heavily. 'Do you approve of my rekindled friendship with Charlie, Holly?'

'What?' Had she not sounded so serious, I would have laughed. 'Of course I do. Not that it's any of my business.'

'It isn't anyone else's business really, is it?'

'No,' I said seriously, 'it's not. You told me you've been friends for years, so what's the issue?'

Clearly, there was one.

'It's Charlie's daughter,' May huffed.

'What about her?'

'Well, she seems to think that it isn't quite seemly that the pair of us are seeing so much of each other when we used to be a very happy foursome.'

I couldn't believe what I was hearing.

'I would have thought,' I blurted out, angry on her and Charlie's behalf, 'that your shared history and happy memories would make your rekindled relationship even more special. Bugger the daughter,' I said forthrightly. 'You go for it, May.'

She caught my arm and linked hers through it.

'How angry you sound,' she laughed.

'Well,' I said, grinning. 'I am.'

'And I appreciate your passion,' she further said, 'but you have to remember I've already lost one lifelong friendship over a failed relationship. I'm not sure I've got it in me to cope with losing another.'

She didn't know it, but her words pierced my heart.

'You need to take a lesson out of my book,' I told her, pulling her closer and myself together. 'Stop overthinking things and just go for it.'

'If that's the ethos you've really adopted,' she then cleverly said, 'then perhaps you might consider doing something with the drawings you've made of the dogs. From what I've heard, they're totally unique—'

'I was talking about with a view to relationships,' I interrupted.

'Oh, well, in that case.' She shrugged. 'I could say the same to you, couldn't I?'

In the next second, Monty and Queenie's leads became impossibly tangled and by the time we'd unwound the skittish pair, I'd completely lost the nerve to either ask her to explain what she had meant or blag my way through a response.

'Right,' I said, as I pulled back on to the bungalow drive a little while later. 'Let's get the Marigolds out, shall we?'

'No need,' she said, opening the car door. 'I did all the clearing up last night.'

'You didn't?' I gasped. 'There was loads.'

'It took my mind off you and Bear rushing off,' she told me, neatly bringing the conversation right back to where we'd started before we set off. 'Would you like to come in for a coffee in lieu of taking out the recycling and filling the dishwasher?'

'No,' I said, 'but thanks. I'll head off as I know you don't need me.' *And ahead of Bear returning to collect Queenie*, I thought but didn't say. 'I've got things to do.'

'Just before you go,' she said, as she climbed out and released the dogs, 'I've been meaning to ask you about Christmas.'

'What about it?'

'It's only a week away now,' she exclaimed. 'Can you believe it?'

'Not really,' I said, puffing out my cheeks and thinking how my time in Nightingale Square had flown by. 'I really must get my presents in the post, mustn't I?'

'If you want them to arrive before the twenty-fifth then I'd strongly advise it,' she said. 'I've sent off the Pooch Shoot packages.'

I wondered what the recipients would make of those when they arrived on the doormat.

'And I'm hoping you'll come here for Christmas Day, Holly,' she further said. 'That's what I wanted to ask you.'

'Oh, May,' I said. 'That's so kind. I haven't actually given any thought as to how I would like to spend the day just yet.'

'Well,' she said, 'I'd love you to come here and if it makes any difference to what you decide, Bear will be in charge of the dinner.'

Depending on the state of things between us in a week's time, it could make all the difference in the world.

'Let me know when you can,' she said, unlocking the front door. 'Perhaps you could use Christmas as the excuse to settle whatever it was the pair of you were really arguing about last night.'

Back at the house, I tried not to think too deeply about what May had observed and consequently said. I parcelled up Sara and Pete's books that I'd picked out for Daisy and my nephews. I lingered over whether to include a note for Maddie, my ex-sister-in-law, but, in the end, decided not to. Had she wanted to maintain contact, she could have easily called my mobile but I guessed she, and the rest of Piers's family, were now too preoccupied with the new arrival to give me a second thought.

And actually, that was no bad thing. During the last few weeks, I'd properly moved on and even though I had been briefly floored – albeit thanks to a few pints of best bitter – when the photo of Piers and his daughter popped up on my phone, I hadn't sent a return message. I picked up my phone, clicked on the image again and then, without a moment's hesitation, deleted it.

'First class recorded delivery please,' I later asked at the post office before handing the parcel over without any hint of emotion at all, which further proved that I had properly let my ex, and his family, go.

Once I was back in the square and with a coffee to hand, I toyed with the idea of tracking Bear down and forcing him to hear me out and properly take on board what I had tried to explain when we'd rowed. However, by the time I'd emptied the mug, I'd talked myself out of it. If he was still seething, he wouldn't be any more inclined to listen than he had been the night before. And besides, he would most likely still be out with Freya and Finn or collecting Queenie from May's.

Instead, I set my laptop up in the lounge and reread the email from Natasha, outlining the exciting new commission proposal. Having been preoccupied for a few days with events at The Chapel and now the issue I had with Bear, I hadn't given it a great deal of focused thought, but in my experience, distractions were often a blessing. Giving ideas time to ruminate and settle often proved more productive than sitting at my drawing board, or with my tablet in my hand, willing inspiration to land.

I opened two new documents and, some time later, having exhausted one creative well by writing down all the ideas I now had about how I could embellish the fantasy stories, I turned my attention to the other.

The sight of Monty at May's party, along with Queenie's absence from it, had made quite an impression on me and I had a whole new story idea as a result. I was still adding notes to the party plot and looking through some of the paper sketches I'd previously made when someone knocked on the door.

I quickly closed my laptop, wondering if it might be Bear. My heart rate quickened at the thought, and I checked my reflection in the hall mirror before answering, but it was Lisa, and she wasn't alone.

'Hey,' she said, looking tense. 'I'm sorry to drop by unannounced.'

Had she not looked so stressed, I would have quipped that it hadn't bothered her before, but reading the situation, I let the opportunity pass.

'It's fine,' I said instead. 'Come in and tell me what's up.'

She led the way down to the kitchen with her son, Archie, following on. The set of his shoulders and his hands shoved deep in his trouser pockets suggested he wasn't any happier than his mum.

'Coffee?' I offered.

'No time,' Lisa sighed, 'but thanks. I shouldn't have come in really.'

'What's going on?' I frowned.

'There's been an incident at school,' she said, cutting to the chase. 'And I wondered if you might be able to watch the culprit while I pop up there to sort things out with the head?'

'Oh, I'm the culprit, am I?' Archie huffed, sounding both belligerent and defensive.

'Are you the culprit, Archie?' Lisa demanded.

'Yes,' he confessed, deflating and slouching further.

'Tamsin has got Molly next door,' Lisa carried on as if she and Archie hadn't just snapped at each other, 'but she's adamant she can't manage Archie as well and Carole's not home.'

Archie smirked and I thought he was pushing his luck, but Lisa ignored him even though she'd seen.

'It's fine,' I said. 'Archie can stay with me while you go. As long as he doesn't mind me sticking him in front of the television.'

'Do you mind if Holly sticks you in front of the television?' Lisa asked him.

'Have you got Sky?' He frowned at me.

'Yep,' I said. 'The full package. Make yourself at home.'

He loped off and by the time Lisa had thanked me we could hear him flicking though the channels.

'I shouldn't be long,' she assured me. 'It's not his first offence, so I know the drill. Ordinarily, he gets dragged along too, but the head asked me not to take him in this time.'

'Oh dear,' I sympathised, wondering if that was a good or a bad thing. 'Well, don't worry. We'll both be here whenever you make it back.'

'If John finishes work before I'm here, Tamsin will send him round to pick the boy up.'

'Fair enough,' I said. 'I'll see one of you later, then.'

'Thank you,' she said, giving me a hug. 'You're an absolute star.'

Archie turned down the offer of a drink, but soon depleted my stock of biscuits. He stretched out along the length of the whole sofa, thankfully having taken his shoes off first and was so immersed in whatever it was he was watching, he remained uncommunicative for practically the entire duration of his stay.

I took the opportunity to make sure I'd properly saved the documents I'd previously made and shut my laptop down again. I tried not to count how many days had passed since I'd sent the emails to Natasha. I had fallen into the habit of regularly checking my inbox, spam and junk folders and it was really beginning to play on my mind that I hadn't heard back from her.

I knew the countdown to Christmas would have started ages ago in her office, but I would have hoped to have had some response by now. It would have been lovely to be heading into the new year with either a confirmed work plan or a completely clean slate.

'John.' I smiled, opening the door to let him in about an hour later. 'Lisa did wonder if you might make it back before her.'

'She's been up there a while, hasn't she?' He frowned.

'I honestly couldn't say,' I told him. 'Because I don't know how long it would have taken her to get there after she left here.'

'Not long,' he sighed. 'Where's the boy then?'

'Watching telly,' I said. 'Come in.'

John pulled his work boots off and followed me into the sitting room where Archie was already tying his laces and the television had been turned off.

'Thanks for letting me crash,' he said, looking up at me from under his long floppy fringe. 'And these are really cool, by the way,' he added, pointing at the sketches I'd tucked under the coffee table, but not quite out of sight, I now noticed. 'I love the dog in the spacesuit one.'

That wasn't the sketch that he could see. It was one of the narrowboat images which was on the top.

'I wasn't snooping,' he quickly carried on as my eyebrows shot up. 'That one was out on the table when I came over with Mum to check on the house the night you were away. She loved it, too.'

'A dog in a spacesuit?' John laughed as the implication of Archie's words sank in for both him and me.

'It's Bear's dog, isn't it?' Archie further said, nodding at the table. 'And the dachshund in the spacesuit belongs to May.'

'That's right,' I croaked. 'They're Bear and May's dogs.'

'I'm surprised Mum hasn't asked you about them.' He smiled. 'She was really taken with them.'

I had completely forgotten that Lisa would have seen them the night she was house-sitting on my behalf.

'She hasn't mentioned them to me,' I said, beginning to feel hot all over, 'but I think she might have described them to May.'

'You should put them in a book or something,' suggested Archie as John's phone buzzed.

'That's a great idea.' I nodded, feeling not quite there.

'That's your mum,' said John, squinting at the screen and giving Archie a nudge. 'She's on her way so we better get back. It might be nice if I had some dinner on the go for her for a change.'

'I'm sure she'd appreciate that,' I said, my own appetite taking flight. 'I'll see you out.'

Once they'd gone, I walked back down to the kitchen and sat at the breakfast bar with my head in my hands and then, as a headache began to build, I rhythmically rubbed my temples and thought about this second disservice I'd done Bear.

Not content with having messed up the best sex we'd both ever had because he had sussed out my confused motives for instigating it, I'd now also wrongly jumped to the conclusion that he had been the one to tell May about the dog sketches and outright accused him of doing it, too. No wonder he had walked away from me without a backwards glance.

I had spent so long refusing to start anything romantic up with him for fear of hurting May and losing her love if it all went belly up, that I had completely overlooked my ability to completely screw up our friendship and risk losing May anyway. Given the horrible situation I now faced, I might just have well spent the last few weeks making the most of Bear's beautiful body, searing kisses and inimitable technique, because I was now up to my neck in the mire I'd been tiptoeing around the edges of all along.

I was perfectly poised to slide deeper into the murky pool of self-pity when my mobile started to ring and I told myself to get a grip.

'Hello,' I said, still rubbing my thumping head with one hand.

'Holly?' came Neil's concerned tone. 'Are you okay?'

'Neil,' I said, sitting up a little straighter. 'Hey. Yes, I'm good.'

'You don't sound it,' he said. His voice was so quiet I could barely hear him. 'Are you sure you're all right?'

'Yes,' I said, clearing my throat. 'Why are you whispering?'

'Mark's in the shower,' he confided. 'But you know he's got ears like a bat.'

That made me smile, even though I wasn't in the mood.

'I just wanted to check in with you, without him in earshot,' he carried on.

His voice was a little louder now, so I guessed he'd either moved away from the bathroom or closed a door or something.

'Why the cloak and dagger?' I frowned. 'Are you okay?'

He didn't answer for a second.

'Neil?'

'I, that is, we,' he eventually said, 'wanted to ask if by any chance you'd seen . . .'

His words trailed off and I imagined him pulling a face as he tried to find the least uncomfortable way to frame what it was he wanted to say. I decided to put him out of his misery.

'The photo of Piers holding his daughter?' I said in a matter-of-fact tone. 'Yes, he sent it to me the night she was born. She's cute, isn't she?'

I heard Neil let out the longest breath and imagined him wilting with relief.

'Well, yes,' he conceded. 'She looks beautiful.'

I knew that he and Mark had previously been considering adoption and wondered what their reaction to seeing yet another friend holding a baby had been. Or someone who had once been a friend, in this instance.

'So, you haven't gone into a decline then?' Neil now felt able to forthrightly ask.

'Yes,' I sighed. 'I have, but it's got nothing to do with Piers. I've screwed something up and now I've got to figure out a way to fix it or I won't be getting Christmas dinner cooked for me.'

'It wouldn't have anything to do with that new hot neighbour everyone in the group chat was taking bets on you hooking up with, would it?'

'Well, I never,' I gasped, feeling the whiplash of Neil's sudden change of tack.

'What?'

'It's true what they say.'

'What do they say?'

'That the longer a couple is together, the more they start to sound like each other.'

'I don't bloody think so,' Neil groaned. 'Anyway, it's look like each other, isn't it?'

'Dunno,' I laughed. 'But you're out of luck either way.'

'Hey,' Neil yelped. 'Don't be mean.'

'Well, don't be making bets on my love life, or lack of love life, then.'

'You know,' he said, 'you're much feistier since the divorce.'

'I do know,' I agreed.

'Damn,' he swore. 'Mark has turned the shower off. I better go. Have a lovely Christmas. We won't be able to call on the day as we're going to be somewhere with no signal.' Given the way the pair always teased me, that was the best present ever. 'And don't worry, you're not going to starve because we've ordered you a Fortnum's hamper, so you'll be able to live off that for a while.'

'Oh goodie.' I smiled, feeling a little bit bad for revelling in the thought of missing our usual Christmas Day chat. 'Thank you.'

At least if I did find myself flying solo for Christmas now, my snack game would be high-end.

# Chapter 29

Rather than rushing off to find out if Bear was back and blurt out my apology, I decided it would be wiser to make sure I had a complete understanding of all the facts before I made contact.

Archie had unwittingly brought to my attention how wrong the conclusion I had jumped to about Bear spilling the book beans had been, but I wanted to hear it from Lisa's own lips, that she had been the one to mention to May what she'd seen set out on Neil and Mark's coffee table. It wasn't that I still doubted Bear, rather that I wanted to do everything in my power to avoid any further muddles and mess.

I grabbed my house keys and went to rush next door, but then remembered the family were already having quite a day and were most likely still thrashing out the details of whatever it was that Archie had got up to at school. I put the keys back down and decided to wait until after the school run the following morning to seek Lisa out.

It did occur to me, as I spent the rest of the day fussing and faffing with laundry and housework as a distraction, to pick up the phone and ask May to clarify exactly who had told her about the sketches, but then I realised that might lead to explanations having to be made and as she was still none the wiser as to any of the details of what had occurred between me and her son, I decided to bide my time and talk to Lisa instead.

I was waiting to see her car arrive back from the school run the next morning when a van pulled up bearing my Fortnum's hamper from Neil and Mark. The postman was hot on the courier's heels and he delivered a parcel I was expecting and a card from my parents, along with the present I had ordered for Bear a couple of weeks ago.

The card from Mum and Dad was as far from the *to our delightful daughter* kind as it was possible to get and there was no loving message inside. When I put it on the mantelpiece next to the one May had given me, it paled in comparison. I tried not to let the difference niggle and reminded myself that I was lucky I'd received a card from Mum and Dad at all, even if it didn't bear any resemblance to the specific daughter and son-in-law ones Piers and I used to be sent.

'The one you sent them wasn't all that much better,' I scolded myself, rushing to the window as Lisa pulled back on to her drive.

I grabbed my keys again and dashed out, keen to catch her before she became ensconced at her keyboard.

'Holly.' She smiled, when she found me on her doorstep. 'Hello, love.'

She hadn't even got her coat off by the time I'd knocked.

'Hey,' I said, my heart hammering now my plan to put things right was finally about to launch. It had been a long night mulling it all over. 'Have you got a sec or do you need to crack on upping the word count?'

'I've actually finished for Christmas now.' She winked. 'But don't tell my editor. Come in.'

The house was a warm and welcoming chaotic jumble of family life with an abundance of festive flourishes thrown in for good measure.

'Coffee?'

'Yes, please,' I said, smiling as I spotted that the fridge was covered in sugar paper glitter and cotton wool seasonal scenes.

'The kids made those when they were little,' Lisa laughed, following my gaze as she went to get the milk. 'They moan about me putting them up every year, but I can't resist.'

'I can well imagine their response,' I laughed along with her. 'I'm guessing they think keeping them on display doesn't do much for their street cred.'

'You've hit the nail on the head.' She nodded. 'Tasmin doesn't bother so much, but the other two are always trying to hide them when they've got mates round.'

My parents had never displayed anything I'd created. I wondered if that would change if I managed to get the *Tall Tales from Small Dogs* into production. Which reminded me again of the reason behind my visit.

'Thank you for taking Archie in at such short notice yesterday,' Lisa said, sliding the sugar bowl in my direction, before I had the chance to bring up the purpose of my calling in.

'Don't mention it.' I smiled, adding a sweet spoonful to the reindeer head shaped mug she handed me. 'I hope everything was okay.'

She perched on a stool on the opposite side of the island to where I was sitting.

'More than okay,' she said, pushing aside a pile of ironing and a stack of books. 'It turns out Archie was in trouble, but there was a twist in the tale.'

'Oh,' I said, intrigued to hear more.

'I know I shouldn't condone what he did,' she said with a wry smile, 'but even the headteacher was willing to show some leniency which isn't something I can usually say where his dealings with Archie are concerned.'

'What on earth had he done?'

'Well,' she told me, 'there's a lad in Archie's form who has cerebral palsy. He joined the school in September and it was recently discovered that he's come in for some pretty underhanded bullying during the last few months. When Archie found out, he decided to join forces with the lad, Ross, and they took matters into their own hands and shut the bullies up once and for all.'

'What did they do?' I asked, agog.

'Let's just say,' she said, biting her bottom lip to stave off a laugh, 'that if the headteacher had been considering making Archie write lines as punishment the sentence would have read, "I must not use a wheelchair as a weapon".'

My mouth fell open and she did laugh then.

'Yesterday was a very proud day,' she said, wiping her eyes.

'I had no idea what it was you were going to tell me,' I laughed along with her, 'but it certainly wasn't anything like that.'

'I've told Archie he's got to lay off the vigilante stuff,' she added. 'He's going to Ross's after school today, so I hope they're not going to egg each other on to get into even more mischief.'

'It's probably just as well it's the end of term,' I said. 'The holidays will give the dust time to settle.'

'And the bully's ankle opportunity to heal,' she sniggered. 'Not that I'm in favour of violent action, but the little sod really did have it coming.'

I decided not to comment on that.

'Top up?' she offered.

'No, thanks,' I said. 'I really can't stay long.'

'I know why you're here,' she then said, looking a little sheep-ish. 'I would have come and apologised last night, but it was a bit hectic after I got back. I had planned to come and see you this morning.'

'What exactly were you going to apologise for?' I asked, just to make sure we were on the same wavelength.

'Mentioning to May about those pictures of the dogs that you've drawn,' she confirmed. 'Archie said you looked absolutely gutted when he commented on them.'

'So, it definitely was you,' I whispered, even though I had known it couldn't have been anyone else.

'I really am sorry if I've put my foot in it.' She grimaced. 'I just assumed you would have shown her as they're so good and I didn't go looking for them. I went in the room to shut the curtains and they were there on the coffee table.'

'I know,' I said. 'It's okay.'

'It doesn't sound okay,' she said, picking up on my mood. 'What's wrong?'

'It's not your fault' – I swallowed – 'but the only person who I thought had seen them was Bear and I'd asked him not to tell anyone, so when May mentioned them . . .'

'You assumed that he'd told her.'

'Exactly.' I nodded, feeling another wave of upset as I remembered our row again. 'And I outright accused him of doing it, too.'

'Ah,' she said.

'We haven't spoken since.'

'Oh, bloody hell, Holly.' Lisa frowned. 'I feel terrible. Let me

go and find him and tell him that it was my fault you jumped to
the wrong conclusion.'

As tempting as that was, I knew it was the cowardly option
and given that our argument had turned out to be about so much
more than just my drawings, the problem wouldn't have been
properly resolved anyway.

'It's kind of you to offer,' I therefore said, 'but there was some
other stuff said too.' Which was putting it mildly. 'So, I really
need to sort it all out myself.'

'As long as you're sure?' she said seriously.

'I am,' I responded stoically. 'I shouldn't have assumed and
now I need to make up for it.'

'Well, however you decide to make it up to him,' she urged,
her tone loaded with innuendo, 'you'd better get a move on
because by this time next week it'll be Boxing Day and you'll
have had hardly any time under the mistletoe at all.'

I didn't mention that it had been her mischievous mistletoe
which had been the instigator for shifting mine and Bear's relationship into an entirely different stratosphere.

Having finished my coffee, I decided I would go back to the
house and take a few minutes to think about what I was going
to say to Bear rather than rushing straight to Prosperous Place
and making a hash of it.

'Hello, Holly,' said Kate, who was walking back down the
path which led to Neil and Mark's front door. 'I was just looking for you.'

'Hey, Kate. Would you like to come in?'

'No, no,' she said, 'it was just a quick visit. I'm in the depths
of gift wrapping across the road. I'm trying to get it all finished
before the end of term.'

'That sounds like a good idea,' I commented, thinking that I really needed to get what I'd picked up for May, Bear and the dogs wrapped up, too. 'What can I do for you?'

'Well, I'm not actually sure you'll be able to help, but I've had a bit of a lightbulb moment about what to get Luke for his birthday next year and it involves Bear. You don't happen to know where he is, do you?'

'No,' I said. 'Afraid not. I'm guessing you've tried the horsebox?'

'It's not there,' she said, as her phone began to belt out what sounded like a Michael Bublé ringtone. 'Sorry,' she apologised. 'It's Freya. Two secs.'

It felt like a lead weight had landed in the pit of my stomach as I tried not to listen to her side of the conversation or wonder where the horsebox had gone.

'Sorry about that,' she said, once the call was done. 'My plan will have to wait a bit longer because according to Freya, Bear has left the city for a few days. No idea where he's gone, but I'm guessing he'll be back in time for Christmas, won't he? He wouldn't want to miss out on seeing May over the holidays, would he?'

'I wouldn't have thought so,' I agreed croakily, the weight in my gut slipping down to my feet.

He couldn't have properly gone, could he? He couldn't have left for good? Not before I'd had the chance to say how sorry I was. It wasn't a conversation I wanted to have via a stilted video call.

Kate's phone buzzed again. It was a message this time and she groaned as she read it.

'Right,' she said. 'I better get back. Luke's supposed to be taking the cats to the vets but he can't find Violet. Dash, her brother, is as good as gold, but she's part minx, part invisible cat, I reckon.'

I said goodbye and let myself into the house. As preoccupied as I was about where Bear had disappeared to, I did fleetingly fall to wondering if the cats might make a guest appearance in a future telling of the *Tall Tales from Small Dogs* . . .

The whole of that day was torturous. I'd gone to call Bear's mobile at least a hundred times, but never once hit the icon which would connect my phone to his. In my heart, I knew the best way, the only way really, to make things right between us, was in person, but with him off goodness knows where, that was impossible. I found myself experiencing every bit of the same level of torment he had told me during our row that he had endured after our night in Wynmouth.

'Do I need to remind you both,' tutted May, during our early walk around the lake the following day, 'that we're practically knocking on the door of Christmas now and that your excitement should know no bounds?'

She was addressing both Monty and me. He was down in the dumps because he was missing Queenie and my smile was absent because I'd buggered things up with Bear. The only difference between us was that I had been trying – though obviously failing – to disguise my upset so May didn't work out just how devastated I was that I still hadn't had a chance to make things right, while Monty was making no attempt to wag his little tail.

I had asked May the day before if she knew where Bear had gone. She said she didn't, but she wasn't impressed that he'd done a bunk and wasn't answering her calls. Consequently, I had changed the subject and briefly touched on the dog drawings. She confirmed that it was Lisa who had told her about them and further said that she couldn't wait to see them, whenever I was in the mood to share.

'I am excited about Christmas,' I said, dredging up a smile. 'I was just trying to work out if I'm going to need more wrapping paper.'

I wasn't going to need more because everything was all now wrapped and labelled. I'd killed a little time getting it all sorted the day before, but I had to offer some excuse for the pensive mood which suggested my festive feeling had fled.

'I have plenty to spare,' May said briskly. 'So, you needn't worry about that. I daresay it's not that at all though, is it? You're doubtless still fretting over where Bear's got to, aren't you?'

'Not fretting exactly,' I said, not wanting to lie by suggesting that his absence was having no impact at all.

'You know, I'm certain that if the pair of you had stopped fannying about and got your act together sooner,' she then said, her own mood seeming to dip a bit in the face of mine, 'then you could have gone off together, couldn't you?'

I took a moment to digest that.

'But I could hardly disappear when I'm house-sitting, could I?' I said, feeling my emotions threatening to get the better of me. 'I've already had one night away and I don't see why you would think that we would have wanted to go off together anyway.'

She stopped walking and looked me full in the face.

'Oh, Holly,' she huffed, her tone implying she wasn't impressed with my response. 'I thought you would want to go off together because it has been as plain as the nose on both your faces that you've fancied the pants off each other, right from the moment you met!'

'May!' I gasped.

I knew I couldn't dispute her observation, but it came as something of a surprise that she had picked up on our feelings right from the off. There had been me, assuming, naively as it turned out, that between us, Bear and I hadn't done or said anything to give the game away when all the time May had seen right through both of us.

'Holly!' she shot back, sounding frustrated, and I looked away. 'I've done my share of trying to push you together and I know something more than either of you have let on happened the night you were in Wynmouth.'

I swallowed hard and angled myself towards the lake so I could blame any tears that thought they might put in an appearance on the chilly breeze.

'I'm right, aren't I?' she said, plucking at my sleeve.

This was exactly the sort of situation and conversation I had wanted to avoid. I hadn't wanted there to be any upset or drama that might make May feel anything other than delighted to be my friend. All these weeks I had been protecting our relationship and yet here we were anyway and all because I hadn't been able to resist going to bed with her son or stop myself jumping to conclusions about him sharing my secret passion project.

I tried hard not to cry, but no matter how many times I blinked, no matter how hard I swallowed, the tears fell anyway. If I didn't sort things soon, I was going to start regretting leaving Mark and Neil's sofa and getting involved with anything to do with the square, The Chapel or indeed, moving on with my life.

'Yes,' I sobbed. 'You're right. And for the record, I'm the one to blame for the entire mess that's followed it. Bear isn't responsible for any of it.'

May looked rather taken aback by my sudden and forthright confession.

'Come on,' she said, reaching for my hand and tugging Monty's lead. 'We're going home.'

Back at the bungalow she insisted on lacing my coffee with a good measure of brandy.

'I'll call you an Uber,' she said, when I pointed out that I wouldn't be able to drive after I'd drunk it. 'And I'm turning the heating up. It's chilly in here today.'

Wrapped in a fleecy blanket, I curled up on the sofa with Monty on my lap and took occasional sips of the heavily laced, but warming and fortifying, coffee.

'Now,' said May, sounding all business. 'I know the ins and outs are none of my business, but I would like to know a little of the reason why two beautiful people, who clearly have quite intense feelings for each other, and are both free to be together, aren't.'

I let out a long breath.

'Unless,' she then thoughtfully added, 'if what I think happened in Wynmouth did happen in Wynmouth and you turned out to be a bad fit. If it was a bedroom thing—'

'It wasn't a bedroom thing,' I blurted out, keen to cut her off. 'Well,' I then conceded, 'not a physical thing in the bedroom sort of thing, anyway.'

It was all a bit TMI for my liking, given that we were discussing her son, but I didn't want her thinking he was a lacking lover.

'Well,' she said, sitting back in her chair, 'I'm more than pleased to hear that. So, what was it then? I know for a fact that

Bear isn't a one-night stand kind of guy and I don't imagine for one second that you'd be looking for a quick fix on those terms either, Holly.'

What a way with words my wise friend had.

'Definitely not,' I confirmed. 'But you are right in that I don't want to go into the ins and outs as to what went wrong after, because I need to talk to Bear first.'

'Of course.'

'But the reason we didn't get together before, was . . .'

'Yes?'

'Well,' I said, gulping down a larger slug of the coffee, 'it was because of you actually, May.'

'Me?' she gasped, sounding horrified. 'But what on earth did I do to put you off?'

'Oh, I dunno.' I smiled wryly. 'Loved me like a daughter and treated me with far more affection than my own mother.'

'And that put you off dating my son?'

'Totally,' I said and she looked completely confused. 'Before I knew you were Bear's mum,' I therefore reminded her, 'you had told me how heartbroken you'd been to lose a close friend, your closest ever friend, in fact, when Bear's relationship with the woman's daughter came to an end.'

'But I don't see—'

'I'd been completely smitten with Bear from practically the moment I'd met him,' I carried on, wanting her to hear the whole of it as she'd already guessed some of the details, 'but when I found out the connection between you, I knew I had to back off. I couldn't cope with the thought of losing your love and friendship if I started seeing Bear and then we broke up. I didn't want to have to live my life without you in it, May, and given that you'd already experienced a tragedy like that once, I couldn't risk doing anything that might mean you had to endure something like it again. And don't tell me that what happened before is easier to cope with now because you brought it up again when we were talking about Charlie's daughter, only the other day.'

'But what if you and Bear didn't break up?' she was quick to say.

'That's exactly what Bear said when I told him my reason for not wanting to be with him.'

'Great minds think alike,' May sighed, and then added, sounding hurt, 'but why would you think I'd cast you aside if your relationship did end?'

'He said that, too.' I swallowed. 'But don't forget I've very recently lost an entire family who I thought loved me. They set me adrift even before my divorce was finalised.'

May shook her head. 'Please,' she said, 'do not tar me with the same brush as those people.'

'I'm sorry,' I apologised. 'I really didn't mean it to come across like that, but I just couldn't run the risk of—'

She immediately put a hand up to cut me off.

'I know,' she said. 'And I do understand, but please, please don't think for another moment, Holly, that I would do that. You really do feel like a daughter to me and no matter what happens between you and Bear, you will *always* have my friendship.'

I felt a tear slide down my cheek as she said that.

'I know what I'm about to say is a bit of a cliché,' I said, trying to smile, 'but hearing you say that really does mean the world to me.'

'Good.' She beamed. 'Because I mean every word.'

I could only hope that talking things through with Bear would go as well.

'And I hope with the whole of my heart,' she said, making me cry all the harder, 'that you do end up together, because nothing would make me happier than seeing two of my favourite people in the world falling in love.'

# Chapter 30

Having drunk more than one of May's laced coffees throughout the day, she later poured me into an Uber and I told her I would go back and collect my car the next day.

'Never mind the car,' she said, checking my seatbelt as if I was a child she was sending off on a trip, 'I just want you to focus on what you're going to say to Bear when he gets back.'

I took comfort in the fact that she felt certain he was coming back and, as instructed, spent the rest of the day and much of the night rehearsing what I intended to say when I did eventually get to see him again.

Having talked through with May the reason why I had been putting off a relationship with Bear – until I slipped tipsily into his bed – made me feel a whole lot better. And knowing that what-ever happened between me and her son going forward, she would still be my friend, made me feel braver about facing it all, too.

It was a late start the following morning, and it would have been much later, had May not rung my mobile and roused me from the restless sleep I'd finally fallen into.

'May,' I mumbled, squinting at the screen as I answered. 'Have I missed our walk? Am I late?'

'No and no,' she shot back. 'Are you still in bed?'

'Yes,' I said, sitting up and slowly feeling less confused. 'I didn't sleep well.'

'I'm not surprised,' she tutted. 'Anyway, never mind that. I'm ringing to let you know Bear's back. He phoned a few minutes ago. I asked him to call round here, but he said he's too tired to head out anywhere today.'

I was suddenly wide awake.

'I'd get over there if I were you,' she carried on.

'But if he's tired,' I interrupted, 'he won't want to be disturbed . . .'

'Holly,' she said firmly. 'Seize the day or I'll have to come over there and bang your heads together. He sounded utterly miserable and I know you're the one person who can cheer him up.'

'I wish I had your confidence.' I swallowed, my former determination heading for the hills now I had the opportunity to act.

'Just get on with it,' she said. 'You know you want to, really.'

Deep down, I knew she was right, of course. This was the moment I had been waiting for. I threw off the duvet and jumped out of bed, willing my mental state to catch up with the physical action.

'Yes,' I said, rolling my shoulders. 'I do.'

'Go on then!' She hung up without another word and I headed straight to the bathroom.

I had showered, brushed my teeth and dressed in the newest addition to my wardrobe within the next hour, but I hadn't bothered trying to eat or drink anything. My tummy felt empty, but I didn't think I'd be able to keep anything down. Not even a cup of tea.

I checked my reflection in the hall mirror, picked up my

keys and stepped outside. I hadn't got around to opening the curtains, so was surprised to find it was snowing. It was only falling lightly, but it had started to settle and the green looked picture perfect. I locked the door and headed off along the pavement, running through what I had spent hours planning I would say as I crossed the road and reached the Prosperous Place gate.

I was just keying in the code to unlock it, when it was pulled open from the other side and I came face to face with Bear, with Queenie standing at his side. My pre-planned speech took flight and for a moment I was speechless.

'Holly,' he gasped.

I knew I had jumped as high as he had and we both looked as shocked as each other.

'Bear.' I swallowed.

'I was just coming to find you,' we then both said together.

'I wasn't expecting to see you just yet,' I rambled on. 'I haven't finished . . .'

'Going over what it was that you were planning to say,' he suggested, neatly finishing the tailed off sentence on my behalf.

'Yes,' I said.

'Snap.' He smiled.

Queenie looked between us, her head cocked first one way and then the other. I would have loved to know what she was thinking. Stupid humans, most likely.

'Would you like to—' we again struck up in unison.

'You go,' Bear said gallantly.

'No, you,' I insisted.

Given that I was the one in the wrong, I felt it only fair to let him say his piece first.

'I was just going to ask if you wanted to come back to mine as we're closer to the horsebox than the house,' he said, looking over his shoulder, along the snow covered path.

I thought we were equidistant, but wasn't about to split hairs, especially as it was the horsebox I had been heading to and had been imagining myself standing in when I apologised.

'I've got the wood burner going,' he further said. 'And I popped to Blossoms earlier.'

'Well,' I said, stepping through the gate, 'in that case.'

'Great,' he said, letting out a long breath, which streamed ahead of him.

I wondered if he was feeling uneasy. If he was, he certainly didn't need to be. I was the one who had been in the wrong about everything and I would go out of my way to remind him of that as soon as I got the chance.

He closed the gate and we set off, the snow still settling prettily around us.

'Your mum said you were too tired to go out today,' I told him.

'Did she?' he laughed. 'She didn't waste any time telling you I was back then.'

'Oh dear,' I said. 'Have I dropped her in it?'

'No.' He shrugged. 'I knew she wouldn't be able to resist calling you. And I told her I wasn't going out, rather than that I already had plans for today, because I didn't feel inclined to explain them. I will later though,' he added, 'if they work out.'

A wave of warm air rushed out to meet us as Bear opened the door and I climbed the step up into the horsebox.

'This feels much cosier than it did in Wynmouth,' I said.

My cheeks flamed when I remembered that I had used the temperature as an excuse for slipping into his bed.

'Let me take your coat,' he offered. 'Wow,' he said, when I handed it to him. 'That's quite a colour.'

'Flamingo pink,' I said, looking down at my new dungarees. 'These are brand new. I've just snipped the label off. I thought I'd wear them in case we ran out of things to say and I could fall back on them as a talking point.'

'I like your thinking.' Bear nodded. 'And there's always the seasonal weather we could resort to now it's snowing. That said, I don't think we're in danger of any awkward silences today.'

The moment he said that, of course, one descended.

'So,' I said, turning around on the spot. 'These have got really roomy pockets.'

'Stop.' He smiled. 'Sit down and I'll put the kettle on.'

Queenie jumped up on to the seat next to me and after I'd fussed her, she snuggled close with her head resting on my lap.

'I missed you, Queenie,' I told her, stroking the length of her smooth back. 'And so did Monty.'

'And what about me?' Bear asked, turning to look at me.

'Yes,' I said. 'I reckon he missed you, too.'

Bear rolled his eyes at that.

'Sorry,' I said. 'I think I'm using humour as a diversion tactic. Or trying to.'

'Do you think it's working?'

'No idea.' I shrugged. 'But I'm not really about to forget what it is that I want to say.'

'Which is?' he asked, reaching for one of the chairs which went with the table.

He spun it around and sat astride it, his arms, encased in one of his most holey, knitted sweaters, resting along the back. I couldn't recall a time when I'd fancied him more, which was no help at all when I was trying to keep focused, with a clear head.

'Well,' I began, having licked my lips. 'The first thing I want to say is that I'm sorry I accused you of telling your mum about my dog sketches. I know now that it was Lisa who spilled the beans after she'd seen them in the house when she looked after the place while we were away.'

'Hadn't you packed them away?' Bear frowned.

'No,' I told him. 'I had no reason to. Initially, we had only planned to be away for the day so it didn't cross my mind that anyone other than me would go into the house.'

'Oh yeah,' he said, remembering.

'Lisa had gone in the sitting room in the evening,' I elaborated, 'to close the curtains and as she'd opened them again the next morning, it didn't occur to me that she'd even been in the room because it was exactly as I'd left it.'

'That makes sense,' he sighed.

'Didn't your mum tell you it was Lisa?'

'No,' he said. 'She didn't mention the sketches to me before she talked about them in front of you and I haven't spoken to her about any of it since.'

'Well,' I said as the kettle came to the boil, 'that's one thing off my chest. I really am sorry about it.'

'It's okay,' he said, accepting my apology with good grace as he went to make the tea and plate up the pastries. 'I would have eaten these already,' he confessed, 'only I wasn't sure I'd keep them down.'

'Funnily enough,' I shared with him, 'that's exactly why I didn't eat breakfast back in the square.'

He moved the table over to where I was sitting and set the plate and mugs down. Queenie sat up in anticipation of crumbs.

'So,' he said, 'what else was it that you wanted to say?'

'Most of it I've already been through once,' I bravely told him, feeling a little less exposed now we had the table between us. 'Or at least tried to go through.'

'Oh,' he said, sitting back down again. 'Right. You mean what you said about our night together that I wouldn't listen to, don't you?'

I nodded. Suddenly, the words weren't as easy to get out second time around.

'You know what,' I said, my voice nowhere near as steady as it had been before. 'I think I might just start telling you about the size of these pockets after all.'

'No, don't,' said Bear. 'In fact, you don't have to tell me anything because I'd quite like to pick up the thread from here, if that's all right with you?'

'Okay,' I said, drawing the word out as I pondered what might be coming.

'I went to see James yesterday,' he then surprisingly said and I momentarily wondered if he was using his friend in the same way as I had embraced the dungaree pocket topic. 'And I told him everything that had happened between us. I hope you don't mind that I did that. I needed someone to confide in and he's a good mate.'

'We all need a friend,' I said, thinking how much good knowing and talking to May had done me.

'When I got to the part about accusing you of sleeping with me because you were upset about your ex,' he said, sounding sheepish, 'James reiterated what I had already started to think for myself.'

'Which was?'

'That I was a knob about it,' he tutted. 'Had I been in my right mind, I would have remembered the night James did a lot of drunken texting to an ex on the back of a message which actually meant nothing when he read it again in the cold light of day.'

I was shocked by that. James hadn't struck me as the drunken texting type, but then we were all capable of doing and saying things under the influence, weren't we?

'I see,' I said.

'Had I thought about what he'd done, in relation to what you said, I would have got everything into perspective about us far sooner,' he sighed. 'I'm so sorry,' Holly.'

'It's okay,' I said. 'It was my fault and I can understand how it must have looked.'

I was grateful that he did now understand that some of what had occurred had been alcohol fuelled, but I still wanted to be sure that he knew the sex we'd had was about so much more than just lowered inhibitions.

'That's not all of it,' he said, picking up and handing me a mug.

'It's not?'

'No,' he said, as I started to drink my tea. 'I've also remembered that after you came and got in bed with me, you fell asleep pretty quickly.'

'Well,' I said, 'it was warmer up there with you.'

I nodded in the direction of where the bed was and felt my face colour again.

'And I daresay,' Bear continued, running a hand through his hair, 'that if, when you woke up in the night, you hadn't found me looking at you, you most likely would have just turned over and gone back to sleep, wouldn't you?'

I wondered if I would have done that. I couldn't in all honesty say.

'I appreciate you offering me a get out of jail free card for jumping on you, Bear, but I don't think I can accept it,' I said, putting the mug down again. 'I've questioned my motives multiple times since that night and still not settled one hundred per cent on the final answer. But one thing I do know is that the result of my rash action was spectacular. You told me it was the best sex you'd ever had, well, it was the best for me, too. It surpassed each and every one of the expectations I'd been carrying around in my head.'

He grinned at that. 'I never make connections to people in the way I've forged a link with you, Holly,' he said huskily. 'And there's no denying that my unusual lifestyle and being away from you some of the time will make going on regular dates tricky, but I can't not get involved with you. No matter how hard I try to distance myself from you, whether that's physically, mentally or both, all of my paths now lead back to you.'

It was the most romantic thing anyone had ever said to me.

'I know you're worried about my mum—'

'I'm not anymore,' I cut in. 'I've talked to May. She knows we've had the hots for each other from the off and says she'd like nothing more than for us to be a couple. In fact, she's been trying to push us together this whole time and if we don't sort things out, she's all set to turn up here and bang our heads together!'

'She said that?' he gasped, then shook his head. 'Of course, she did. I should have known she would. If I'd seen her today, I bet she would have told me that herself.'

'She's told me she'll love me no matter what happens between us,' I said, feeling my breath catch. 'Not that I think anything bad will happen.'

'Of course, it won't.'

'And I've deleted that photo, you know. I didn't give it a second thought, so please don't be thinking—'

'I won't think anything,' Bear said, reaching for my hand. 'I don't think anything.'

'So.' I swallowed as he stood up and I scrambled to my feet to join him.

'So,' he said, pulling me into his arms. 'You're not worried about losing my mum and you're not harbouring any regrets about your ex . . .'

'And you've forgiven me for accusing you of doing something you didn't,' I added, looking up at him. 'And you know from past and present experience that things said and done under the influence of a few pints of best bitter aren't always the most reliable.'

'Absolutely,' he said, lowering his lips tantalisingly close to mine. 'So, there's only one thing left to worry about.'

My heart had been beating a tattoo in my chest but I swear in that moment it stopped completely.

'Which is?' I squeaked.

'The quickest way of getting you out of these dungarees, of course!'

Bear made short work of releasing me from the confines of all my clothes and while we were otherwise engaged, Queenie made short work of the pastries. It wasn't the sort of bad behaviour she usually indulged in, but it was hours before we paid her any attention and Bear did admit that in his muddled state that morning, he'd completely forgotten to give her any breakfast.

'In that case,' I called down from where I was wrapped up in the duvet in his bed, 'you can hardly tell her off, can you?'

He had ventured down the stairs, naked as the day he was born, to feed more logs into the wood burner.

'You won't be saying that when I offer you her kibble in lieu of the apple and cinnamon muffins, will you?' he called back.

'No,' I groaned. 'I didn't know there were muffins! Please tell me you have something other than dog biscuits in your cupboard.'

'As luck would have it,' he said, climbing the stairs again and joining me on the bed. 'I have a pack of bacon and some fresh rolls. How does that sound?'

I kicked off the duvet and straddled him, pinning him to the bed.

'Delicious,' I purred, kissing him again.

It was late in the afternoon by the time I got to taste that bacon, but that was fine because I'd had a thoroughly pleasurable time.

'I never would have believed two people could fit in that shower,' I giggled as we tucked into the meal that, according to the clock, was neither lunch nor dinner.

Bear raised his eyebrows at the towel mopping up the patch of water on the floor.

'Well,' I conceded, 'almost fit. So, where else did you go when you were off on your travels, trying to put some distance between us?' I asked.

He had explained that had been his reason for disappearing – to get me out of his head – and confessed that it hadn't worked. If anything, it had made him want me all the more. I could have quite happily listened to him talk like that all day. Especially knowing that the words could be enjoyed with the full knowledge of May's blessing.

Bear's brow furrowed. 'I went to see Charlie,' he said. 'I called in at the business as I was in the horsebox and knew I wouldn't be able to get it through the gates at his house.'

'A gated entrance,' I commented. 'That sounds swanky. Did you find him?'

'I did,' he said, 'and he wasn't alone. His daughter was there, bending his ear about the amount of time he's been spending with Mum.'

'He has become something of a regular visitor, hasn't he?'

'He has.' Bear nodded. 'And I'm all for it. When Dad and Charlie's wife were alive, the four of them were always together and I don't see why that should change now it's just Mum and Charlie. Even if . . .'

'Even if, what?'

'Even if Mum and Charlie might consider a more than friendly relationship some time in the future.'

'Do you think they might?' I asked.

'Maybe,' Bear said thoughtfully. 'That was the impression I got from Charlie anyway. And why not? Why shouldn't they if it would make them happy?'

'I couldn't agree more,' I told him. 'Your mum did mention to me that Charlie's daughter had been sticking her oar in about all the time they were spending together.'

'Well.' Bear grinned, pinching the last rasher of bacon. 'She won't be from now on.'

'Hey,' I said, 'I think we should split that bacon. We nearly fell out over a chip before, remember?'

He laughed at that, then took a medium sized bite and gave me the rest.

'So go on,' I encouraged, popping the rest of the rasher into my mouth. 'What happened that's shut Charlie's daughter up?'

'Charlie,' Bear laughed. 'He completely lost it and told her in no uncertain terms to keep her nose out of his private life.'

'Good for him,' I said, punching the air.

'And he told her she could stick her Christmas, too,' Bear carried on. 'He reckoned the grandkids were only ever interested in the thickness of the envelopes he gave them, so they could do without them this year and then they'd be all the happier next December. He's joining us at Mum's on Monday now.'

'Monday?' I frowned, licking my fingers.

'Christmas Day, you loon.'

'But it's Thursday today,' I gasped.

'I know,' he said, jumping up and scooping me into his arms. 'So, it's about time we put a few more hours in to making the most of the mistletoe, isn't it?'

I didn't point out that there wasn't any hung up in the horse-box. Or that all people usually did under it was kiss.

# Chapter 31

The square looked like a perfect winter wonderland when Bear and Queenie walked me home that evening. The temperature had dropped like a stone so I knew the snow would still be there the next day. With the school term now ended I would imagine there'd be a snowman on the green by lunchtime if Lisa's brood had anything to do with it.

'It's the solstice tomorrow,' said Bear, lingering at the door to make the most of the mistletoe Lisa had hung up weeks ago and I had never got around to taking down. 'Shall we go somewhere to celebrate it?'

'As lovely as that sounds,' I said, between kisses, 'I think our next port of call should be to see your mum. She'll be bursting to know what's happened today.'

'Well, I'm not filling her in on *all* the details.' He grinned, before kissing my neck and making my knees cave.

'You know what I mean,' I said, breathlessly.

'Yes,' he said, 'I know what you mean.'

'I have something I need to do in the morning,' I told him. 'So why don't you ring and ask her if we can go to the bungalow for lunch? We could pick up something to eat on the way.'

'All right,' he said, releasing me from his tantalising kisses. 'That sounds like a plan. I hope the thing you have to do is submit your *Tall Tales from Small Dogs* to your favourite editor. Although' – he frowned – 'I suppose she's most likely finished for the holidays now, hasn't she?'

'Oh, that,' I said coquettishly as I unlocked the door and stepped inside. 'I did that weeks ago.'

'What?' Bear gasped, his eyes as round as saucers.

'And before you ask,' I said, the thrill of telling him diminishing a little as I said the words, 'I haven't heard anything from her and yes, she will have definitely finished for Christmas now.'

'Hang on,' he said, trying to follow me in.

'That's your lot, Bear Madison,' I squealed, closing the door a little. 'You've tired me out today. I'll see you tomorrow.'

'Not fair.' He pouted, laughing, as I closed the door properly.

Not surprisingly, I slept like a log that night which went some way to make up for all the sleepless and disturbed nights I'd had since I'd arrived in the square.

'Bear.' I smiled as I answered the video call he was making from his bed to mine early the next morning.

Seeing him topless and flushed with sleep, I was hard pushed not to run back across the square and join him, but there was something I really needed to get on with, so resisted the urge. Just.

'I'm surprised you're awake already,' I said, stretching out.

My muscles ached, but in a way that made me smile rather than wince because I had the pleasure of remembering why and how they had been put through their paces.

'I only am because you were right about Mum,' he told me, stifling a yawn. 'She rang hours ago. I don't think I gave anything away about us, but she woke me up and caught me off guard, so I can't be sure. I'm surprised she hasn't called you, too, actually.'

'I've only just turned my phone on,' I told him. 'So, there are probably unanswered calls stacked up I haven't seen yet.'

'Well, anyway,' he said as Queenie jumped on the bed and her face momentarily filled the screen which made me laugh. 'I'm going to call round for you at eleven and then we'll go to the bungalow. That is, if the timing works for you?'

'Can we make it half eleven?' I asked, wrinkling my nose.

'What is this?' he tutted. 'I know absence is supposed to make the heart grow fonder, but—'

'It's thirty minutes.' I smiled. 'You can survive an extra thirty minutes.'

'I know I can,' he said, waggling his eyebrows, 'but can you?'

He ended the call before I could think up a witty response and I practically skipped down the stairs thinking what a wonderful way it was to start the day.

It didn't take me as long as I had expected it would to put the finishing touches on the sketch of Monty and Queenie that I had decided I would give to May as one of her Christmas presents. There was no time to get it mounted or framed, but I was quite keen for her to see it in its raw state, straight from my sketchpad. Once she'd seen it, I would take it back again and then make the arrangements for it to be finished somewhere local in the new year. I was sure Pete would be able to point me in the right direction.

While I was perfecting May's gift, I had considered taking the plunge and showing her all of my drawings over our lunch, along with print outs of the stories, but ultimately decided not to. Not because I was chickening out, but because if I shared them with her ahead of giving her her own sketch, then the gift wouldn't be as much of a surprise. And it wasn't as if the visit wasn't going to be thrilling enough, what with being able to tell her that Bear and I were finally, officially, an item! Yes, that would be enough to focus on for one day.

Having finished ahead of time, while I waited for Bear to arrive, I had a quick look at the websites and chatrooms he'd recommended I should keep an eye on in my quest to find my new home. With it being so close to Christmas, I wasn't really expecting to find anything new had been uploaded, but I was wrong.

'Come and look at this,' I said, pulling open the door and practically dragging Bear and Queenie into the hall.

'Well, hello to you, too,' he laughed.

'Sorry,' I said, planting a quick kiss on his luscious, full lips and then lingering to do the job properly. 'Now come and look at this and tell me I'm not mad to be so excited.'

He pulled off his boots and pouted at my words.

'I'm supposed to be the one providing the excitement around here,' he reminded me. 'Don't tell me the honeymoon phase is over already? Are you bored with me, Holly?'

'Bored with you not getting a move on,' I grumbled, yanking at his arm. 'Come on!'

Bear had barely glanced at my laptop screen before becoming as entranced by what he could see and read about as I had done, just minutes before.

'They're not far from here,' he said, looking from the screen to me and back again.

'I know,' I said, tugging at his sleeve.

'And they've already had the bulk of the conversion work carried out,' he read on.

'I know that too.' I nodded enthusiastically. 'I think it's just the aesthetics that need addressing and with my colourful new mindset,' I added, looking down, 'I know I can handle that, no problem.'

I had spent so long out of the dungarees the day before, that I had decided to wear them again and wondered what May would make of them.

'But it sounds like a rental situation, rather than owning outright.' Bear frowned. 'I thought—'

'I know, I know,' I said, cutting him off. 'It's a bit of a turnaround ...'

'A bit,' he laughed. 'Just a few weeks ago you were all set to tie yourself to a twenty-five-year debt and now you're considering this. What's changed?'

'Well,' I said, taking a big breath. 'I've been hanging out with this guy who has a really refreshing attitude to life and believes you can get the most out of it, if you live it on your own terms. He's really against the whole blundering along, just conforming to societal norms and expectations because everyone else is.'

'Oh, really,' said Bear, a twinkle in his eye. 'I like the sound of this guy.'

'He's really cool,' I laughed. 'He's made me completely rethink the whole huge mortgage thing. I'm thinking I could rent these and keep the bulk of my settlement money safely invested if I start earning again soon.'

'I hope I haven't got competition for your attention already,' he laughed. 'This guy sounds like he knows what he's talking about.'

'He does,' I said, looking at the screen again. 'And he's made me take a fresh look at everything. Thanks to him, I know now that with my career feeling precarious and my marriage coming to an unexpected end, I'd latched on to the one thing that I thought would make me feel secure and safe.'

'A whopping great mortgage.'

'Exactly. I got bogged down thinking that I had to carry on following the same built of bricks and mortar path that I'd always been walking along. I hadn't taken the opportunity to step off the edges to see what else was on offer. That is, until you came along. Before we met, I was too preoccupied with doing what was expected. Even though I had come to the square with the intention of working out my next steps, and even though I haven't got anyone relying on me to make the conventional decisions, I still wasn't looking far enough around me to work out what might be right for me.'

It was quite a declaration, but one that I meant with my whole heart.

'Thank goodness I came along when I did,' said Bear, putting an arm around my shoulders. 'I really could see you living somewhere like this, you know.'

We both stared at the screen and the converted railway carriages, set up in a field in the Fens awaiting the arrival of whoever was going to finish kitting them out and live in them. They still needed a fair bit of finessing but we could see and read that the right things had been done.

Planning and conversion permission had been properly granted, so there were no concerns about moving in and then getting kicked out when the council came looking for the relevant paperwork. And they'd been set in the location which took best advantage of the stunning landscape and dramatic skies. And they were situated somewhere with access to amenities, such as a laundry room and farm shop, too. They were perfect!

'I'm surprised the owner isn't going to use them as more holiday lets,' Bear commented. 'They'd earn far more by doing that than renting them out.'

'Well,' I said, giving him a squeeze. 'When we go to view them, I request that you don't suggest that, but given that they're part of a business that already lets out vintage caravans, I would imagine that must have been an option they've already considered and dismissed.'

'That's a valid point.' Bear nodded.

I leant into him and rested my head on his shoulder.

'I feel a road trip coming on,' I told him. 'And the sooner, the better because they won't be around for long.'

'If they're meant for you,' Bear said, kissing the top of my head, 'you won't miss out. But maybe you could make a call to express your interest and book a viewing. The name of the nearest town I can see on the map here sounds familiar for some reason.'

'Yes,' I said. 'Wynbridge rang a bell with me, too.'

By the time I'd got off the phone, Bear had remembered why Wynbridge struck a chord.

'That's the town where that artist that Mum's so enamoured with lives,' he reminded me.

'Of course,' I said, 'the one with the funny vintage car who delivers her canvases with the top down.'

'That's the one,' he said, clicking his fingers. 'So, did you get through?'

I was too jittery to make the call in front of him and had gone into the sitting room.

'No,' I said. 'I had to leave an answerphone message for a woman called Lottie. I hope she doesn't take too long to call back, otherwise I'll be a nervous wreck.'

'Yes,' said Bear. 'What with that and waiting for a response to the *Tall Tales from Small Dogs*, you'll be on tenterhooks all Christmas.'

'I hope you don't mind that I didn't tell you I'd sent them off.' I frowned. 'I've been trying not to get my hopes up and thought it would be easier if no one else knew. And I wanted to gauge the editor's reaction to them first, too.'

'I do understand,' he said. 'You were under no obligation to tell me, but there's no way she'll turn them down.' I gave him a look and he shook his head. 'Sorry,' he apologised. 'I promise I'll try not to go on.'

'Please stick to that,' I said, 'and I don't want you to say anything further to your mum just yet, either.'

'Crikey,' he then said, looking at the clock on the wall. 'Mum. Come on, we're going to be late.'

It was still snowy underfoot, so we took my car rather than walked and stopped at a deli on the way to pick up some extra bits for lunch which would complement the huge, herby sausage rolls from Blossoms which May had told Bear she already had.

'Well?' May demanded, dispensing with the niceties right from the off.

Bear was barely out of the car and I hadn't even undone my seatbelt, when she wrenched open the bungalow door and rushed out. Monty, as always, was fussing around her feet in pursuit of finding Queenie. It occurred to me then, that a lot of our conversations had happened on this drive.

'Sorry we're late,' Bear apologised, handing her the bags so he could let Queenie out.

'I don't mind that you're late,' May tutted, eyeing me

shrewdly. 'If anything, I was hoping you would be. My goodness! Look at those dungarees.' She gasped, catching sight of what I was wearing. 'How stunning are they?'

'Thank you, May.' I laughed, thinking how cruel Bear and I had been to prolong her agony even if she had been hoping we wouldn't be on time. 'But why were you hoping we'd be late?' I then asked.

'Because,' she said, 'that would suggest that you were doing something which meant you lost all track of time.'

'Well,' I said, 'actually, we were.' Her eyes widened at that. 'We were looking online for my next home. Weren't we, Bear?'

'We were,' he laughed.

May's shoulders dropped. 'And did you find anything?' she asked, her tone suggesting that she didn't care either way.

'Time will tell,' Bear said mysteriously.

'But we needed to look today' – I winked at him – 'because having spent the whole of yesterday in bed together, I was worried we might have missed a new listing.'

Poor May. The sudden confession was too much. She dropped the bags she was holding, burst into tears and threw her arms around me. Bear stooped to recover our lunch and smiled at me over the top of his mother's head.

'Oh, you two,' she said, leaning back and taking my face in her hands, before kissing me on both cheeks. 'About time.'

'And absolutely no head banging required,' Bear laughed.

'When I video called you this morning, Teddy,' May said, releasing me and treating her son to the same embrace and kisses, 'and found no Holly in the bed, I was convinced the pair of you still hadn't got your act together.'

'Is that why you called so early?' I guessed.

'Of course,' she said, scooping Monty up. 'Now come inside, before the whole street hears our business.'

We ate a very jolly, if slightly squished, lunch. Thanks to the continued cloud cover and sporadic snowfall, the shortest day certainly lived up to its name. It was barely three o'clock before May was lighting up the bungalow with her many festive lights.

'There have been times these last few months,' she said thoughtfully, sitting back down to admire the effect, 'that I thought this year was never going to end.'

'Oh, Mum,' said Bear, sounding choked.

'But since meeting you, Holly,' she continued, with a warm smile. 'And you coming home, Teddy and spending time at The Chapel, the months have picked up apace and now the year is racing to its end. I can't believe it.'

'And don't forget Charlie,' I said. 'He seems to be properly in your life now, too.'

'That he is,' she said. 'He's going to come and deliver my car on Christmas Day morning now my ban's come to an end. And if you don't mind, I think he's going to stay for the night, too. I'll drive him back the next day. It will be good to have a passenger while I get a feel for being behind the wheel again.'

'Of course, we don't mind him coming,' Bear immediately said. 'It will be lovely to have him here. But what about his daughter?'

'I think they've had words,' May confided. 'I didn't ask for details.'

Clearly, Charlie hadn't mentioned that Bear had been present when the words were said.

'So,' I said, stroking Monty's silky ears as he yawned and stretched out on the sofa between Bear and me. 'It will be the four of us on the day, six with the dogs, and after that, I'm really going to have to get my head in gear about finding somewhere to stay while I properly look for a new home.'

'Your friends won't turf you out the moment they return, will they?' Bear frowned.

'No,' I said, knowing they wouldn't. 'But I won't want to outstay my welcome.'

'You've been doing them a favour.' May smiled. 'I'm sure they'll let you stay as long as you like, but what I'm really hoping is that you'll agree to move into my spare room while you're house, bus or boat hunting.'

Bear and I looked at each other and then at her.

'Do you mean that, Mum?' he asked.

'Of course, I do,' she laughed. 'I wouldn't have said it otherwise, would I? We don't want Holly paying extortionate rent when she has no need to and besides, if she's living here, there's every likelihood that she'll take me with her when she's off doing viewings or whatever the drill is and I'll love that.'

I didn't know what to say.

'There's plenty of room for your drawing board or whatever it is you'll need to set up when you start working again,' she added for good measure.

I was almost tempted to tell her about my submission then, but thought I would fill her in about the railway carriages near Wynbridge instead. As it turned out, Bear had remembered right; it was where her new favourite artist lived and if that wasn't fate in action again, I would never know what was!

# Chapter 32

Just a few short months ago, had anyone said to me that I would be enjoying a very merry Christmas that year, I never would have believed them. However, with a thrilling new relationship to enjoy settling into, an appointment made to view a potential – and extremely unusual – new home thanks to Lottie calling back, and a prospective new commission on the horizon, I was ending the year on cloud nine and my festive feeling had reached unprecedented new heights.

The only disappointment was that I hadn't heard back from Natasha, but not even that was enough to dull my sense of enchantment on Christmas Eve. I told myself that all that really mattered was that I was in love with the *Tall Tales from Small Dogs* and that if Natasha turned them down (something Bear had said a hundred times wouldn't happen in spite of his promise not to keep mentioning them), then I would consider where to send them next or even whether to publish them myself in the new year.

Bear and I spent almost the whole of Christmas Eve at the bungalow with May. We were keen to get ahead with the preparations for the next day so Bear wouldn't be too chained to the kitchen, and I had headed out to do a last minute shop in the city so I had something to put under the tree for Charlie.

The snow had all but gone, but there was no mistaking the sensation that only the hours before the clock struck midnight and the calendar turned to December the twenty-fifth could elicit. Everyone out of doors was willing to generously pass the time and wish each other a merry Christmas, and the expectation for the celebration to come made for a delicious cocktail with a flavour all of its own.

After listening to *Carols from King's* with May and Monty, Bear, Queenie and I headed back to the square.

'And don't worry about your presents,' May called after us. 'I had a word with the big man and he knows to drop your things here.'

'Assuming we're on the nice list,' Bear called back to her.

'Oh, yes,' she giggled. 'I didn't think of that!'

I hadn't bothered to check the forecast, but I could tell the temperature was glacial the moment I opened my eyes the next morning and when I drew back the curtains and looked out, I was proved right. Everything was covered in the thickest frost and it magically sparkled as the day slowly began to dawn.

'Merry Christmas, Holly,' said Bear, as he rolled over in the bed and opened his eyes.

'Merry Christmas.' I smiled, turning away from admiring the view outside the window to take in the one in front of me. 'How did you sleep?'

We hadn't planned to spend the night together, but by the time we'd finished the festive movie marathon and put out a mince pie and glass of milk for Santa, it was so late I convinced

Bear that he should stay. There was nothing at the horsebox requiring his attention because he already had Queenie with him after the day at May's so he didn't take much persuading.

'Better than I expected to, given the size of the bed,' he said, pulling himself further up in it and treating me to a glimpse of his broad, toned chest. 'In fact,' he said, 'I'm feeling full of festive beans this morning.'

'Good.' I grinned, mindful of the time and willing myself not to succumb to taking advantage of those beans. 'Because your mum has a turkey big enough to feed a dozen awaiting your attention in her fridge, so you better get up and tend to its needs if you want to eat before midnight.'

'I'd rather tend to yours first,' he said, reaching for me and pulling me back into the bed as quick as a flash. 'I've never been a fan of eating lunch too early on Christmas Day.'

That turned out to be just as well because it took ages to eventually load up the presents and extra treats and defrost my car.

'Merry Christmas, merry Christmas!' May beamed when we finally arrived. 'Oh Holly, you look absolutely divine.'

'Thank you,' I said, accepting her praise. 'I thought I'd push the boat out.'

I'd found a wraparound dress online which had a black background but was covered in sprigs of holly and I hadn't been able to resist surprising May by buying it. I had teamed it with red tights and black Mary Janes. The shoes only lasted two minutes though, as May had purchased Christmas slippers for all four of us. Mine were elf style, hers looked like wrapped presents, Bear's were enormous turkeys and Charlie had reindeer heads, complete with antlers which I was certain would be a trip hazard. It was classic May and a fun alternative to the usual Christmas jumper tradition.

'Happy Christmas, Mum,' laughed Bear, as he wriggled his toes then, echoing my thoughts, added, 'These make a change from Christmas jumpers.'

'That's exactly what I thought,' she laughed back. 'And I'll tell you what else I thought, shall I?'

'Go on,' Bear said cautiously.

'I had a feeling you two would be distracted this morning, so I put the turkey in myself.'

'Oh, May!' I laughed along with her as we took in Bear's expression.

'Don't look so worried,' she quickly said to her son, who was no longer smiling. 'I didn't slip a disk lifting it and I remembered to get it out of the fridge for a good while before it went in *and* I covered it with that bacon you picked up, too, so it won't burn.'

It sounded as though she'd gone through the right motions but Bear rushed off to investigate anyway. Once he was happy that the turkey wasn't in any jeopardy, we arranged the rest of the presents under the tree and set to with the last of the foodie preparation. May kept our glasses topped up with Buck's Fizz as we prepped and with her radio tuned to a dedicated Christmas channel which belted out all the old favourites.

'That'll be Charlie.' She beamed when the doorbell rang late in the morning and she rushed to let him in. 'I hope he likes reindeer.'

It was a few minutes before he joined us in the kitchen.

'Merry Christmas!' he said, carefully coming in and keeping an eye on his feet which were now encased in the reindeer slippers.

'Merry Christmas!' Bear and I chorused and feeling relaxed after the Buck's Fizz, I gave him a hug.

'I love your jumper,' I told him, admiring the snowman and Santa decorated sweater. 'Very festive.'

'Thank you,' he said. 'And you look lovely, too.'

'I was beginning to think you weren't coming,' said May, pouring him a glass.

'I just thought I'd better pop in and see the family on the way,' he explained. 'My daughter wasn't very happy that I hadn't changed my mind about staying, but she'll get over it. You know what they say, you can't pick your family. Not your biological one, anyway.'

'Tell me about it,' I said, rolling my eyes and clinking my glass against the one May handed him.

I had sent my parents a message and they'd sent one back. Neither they nor I had suggested an actual conversation or video call, so having exchanged warm wishes with everyone in The Chapel WhatsApp chat, I'd turned my phone off again. I already knew I wouldn't be hearing from Mark and Neil, and everyone I wanted to spend the day communicating with was right here.

'Well,' said May, refilling her and Bear's glasses and smiling kindly. 'At least you've both got us. Your non-biological family.'

'And who could want for more than that?' I sighed, happily.

We all thoroughly enjoyed the traditional lunch, which Bear had cooked to perfection. I loved the pigs in blankets and roast potatoes swamped in proper gravy and after the last crackers had been pulled and we were all wearing paper hats, there was an abundance of presents to hand out.

I was amused to note that there were as many for the dogs as us humans. Charlie was thrilled with his bottle of single malt which May had suggested I pick up from The Whisky Shop in the city and I also knew I'd picked the right things for her and Bear because I felt every bit as excited about watching them open their parcels as I felt about receiving my own.

'Oh, Holly,' May gasped, as she tore into the tissue and lifted up the pretty scarf which she immediately wrapped around her shoulders. 'This is stunning. Thank you so much, my darling.'

She loved her earrings too and I felt my breath catch as she opened the sketch.

'It isn't finished yet,' I said, my nerves gabbling over her reaction. 'Well, the sketch is,' I added, as Bear laid a hand on my arm and gave it a squeeze. It didn't help with the jitters, but I appreciated the gesture nonetheless. 'But it needs a frame and a mount. I'll sort that in the new year.'

'My goodness, Holly,' she said, when I eventually shut up. 'This is exquisite. No wonder Lisa was so impressed. You've captured the essence of the pair of them perfectly. Look at my babies, Charlie? Isn't Holly clever?'

'You never drew this?' Charlie gasped and I laughed.

'She did,' said Bear, sounding proud.

'Well, I never,' Charlie said, looking at me. 'I had no idea we had an artist in the family.'

'Now you,' I said, turning to Bear.

'Well,' he said approvingly. 'I like the size of the box.'

It was a smallish rectangle.

'I was hoping you'd say that,' I told him. 'What's in it will take up no space at all in the horsebox.'

He and May had told me that they didn't buy gifts to exchange. As a rule, their present to each other was the time they spent together because it was always a few months since the last time they had been in each other's company. I thought that was rather wonderful but I was still thrilled with what I had picked out for them.

'Open it then,' May encouraged. 'Let's see what's inside, Bear.'

He ripped off the paper and I was delighted to see his eyes widen as he took in the embossed name on the box.

'Oh, Holly,' he gasped, when he pulled off the lid. 'It's beautiful.'

'And practical,' I pointed out.

'And that too.' He smiled.

He picked up the handmade pocket knife I had ordered from a Sheffield company and turned it over in his hands. I couldn't think of anyone else in the world I'd buy something like that for but then, there was no one else in the world like Bear.

'This is stunning,' he said, his eyes fixed on the smooth and deeply grained wooden handle. 'The craftsmanship is exquisite and it's so light, too.'

'I hoped you'd like it,' I said.

'I love it,' he told me, balancing it on two fingers and then passing it to Charlie who was equally as impressed.

It was my turn next.

'These are all exchangeable,' May told me, 'but I'm hoping you'll like them.'

'I wouldn't want anyone other than you picking out clothes for me, May.' I beamed as I stroked the three colourful outfits she had gifted me, complete with accessories. 'Thank you so much. I love them all.'

'I've only gone for staples.' She smiled back, clearly pleased with my reaction and words. 'Because until you're settled, I have no idea what wardrobe space you'll have.'

'That's a good point, Mum.' Bear nodded.

'Once I know that,' she then added gleefully and he rolled his eyes, 'we'll have a splurge.'

We all helped Monty and Queenie tear into their gifts then. Monty, like me, also loved the new additions to his array of outfits and strutted about the sitting room showing off a crown and cape, while Queenie sedately settled down to devour her doggy treat filled Christmas stocking. She didn't look at all impressed by Monty's showing off, but that didn't temper his desire to be the belle of the ball.

'There's just one left,' said Bear, picking up the final gift under the tree.

'I wasn't expecting you to buy me anything,' I said, as he handed me the slender box.

'I know you weren't,' he said, 'but I couldn't resist.'

Given the shape, anyone else might have thought it was jewellery, but I knew Bear better than that.

'Oh, my goodness.' I swallowed as I eased off the lid. 'It's a Conway Stewart.'

'Oh my,' added May, leaning over for a closer look.

Nestled inside was a stunning cherry red Conway Stewart fountain pen, complete with gold nib.

'I was pretty certain you had all the kit to illustrate your stories,' Bear whispered in my ear, 'but nothing particularly special to use to write them.'

I swallowed over the lump in my throat.

'I love it,' was all I could manage to say, before putting the box down and throwing my arms around him. 'Thank you.'

I kissed him hard on the lips and then revelled in the feel of his strong arms wrapped around me. By the time I could bear to ease myself away, May had picked the box up and was looking from it to me and back again.

'So, what exactly is this beautiful pen going to be used for?' she asked, her eyes shining with excitement.

'Why don't we open another bottle of champagne?' I suggested, jumping up. 'And then I'll tell you.'

I knew there'd never be a better opportunity.

# Chapter 33

Just as I had known they would, the days after Christmas all became a blur and I couldn't have told you what day of the week it was for all the publishing deals in the world. Boxing Day had been memorable though as May had opted for a last-minute open house.

I had assumed that no one would come because they'd have other places to be, but I hadn't taken into account May's star appeal. Guests had turned out in droves and even the traffic officers who had asked if the cars parked along the road could be moved had left wearing paper crowns and wide smiles.

The day I invited May and Charlie to the square to read the *Tall Tales from Small Dogs* was one I wouldn't forget either. They had been enthralled when I described the words I had woven around the sketches on Christmas Day and they sat enraptured on Mark and Neil's sofa as they read the stories and looked at the drawings for themselves later in the week.

'I can't get over the quality of these sketches,' May gushed, making me feel about ten feet tall. 'I mean, I know this is what you do and everything, Holly, but the expressions and details are so extraordinarily well captured. It's like you've literally brought them to life on the page.'

Not surprisingly, I was scarlet by the time she'd finished saying that.

'I know the stories are a little rough around the edges,' I said, wrinkling my nose and thinking of the lack of reaction they'd received from Natasha. 'But then I've never written anything like them before. Aside from one brief failed effort, these are very much a first attempt.'

'They don't come across as rough to me,' Charlie said kindly. 'But if the editor you've submitted to thinks they are, she'll help you polish them. That's her job after all.'

'The pair of you make it sound like a done deal.' I swallowed.

I hadn't been sure how I was going to feel after I'd decided to tell them on Christmas Day about what I'd done, but they and Bear had been so kind and enthusiastic that I felt buoyed up, rather than embarrassed, which was how I would have felt discussing it in Piers's presence. Not that I ever would have shared the details with him given what had occurred the first time around.

When I'd voiced my concern to the three of them about having taken the direct submission route, as opposed to looking for an agent first, Bear disagreed that that might make the situation tricky. Instead, he vociferously reminded me that I'd recently started jumping off the expected path and that I should keep the faith and embrace that professionally, too. Given that I had already worked independently with Natasha for so long, I don't suppose, if she was interested, my lack of agent would necessarily be an issue.

'That's because we think it will be a done deal,' May had said. 'When the *Tall Tales from Small Dogs* reaches the top of that editor's inbox, she's going to snatch your hand off.'

I wished with my whole heart that she was going to be right.

*

'Do you know what day it is?' I asked Bear, once I'd finished kissing him hello in the hallway on another of those Twixmas mornings.

'Um,' he said, looking skyward in the effort to concentrate. 'The day before New Year's Eve, I think ... don't quote me on that though. Why?'

'I just wondered.' I smiled, fussing Queenie and then leading the pair of them down to the kitchen where we were having lunch. 'Have you spoken to your mum today?'

'Briefly,' he told me. 'She's still talking about your stories. Any minute now she and Charlie are heading off to the coast for the afternoon.'

'He still hasn't gone home?' I laughed.

'He still hasn't gone home,' Bear laughed back.

Charlie was currently occupying the spare room, so it was just as well I didn't need it yet.

'I reckon he'll see in the New Year with us now, don't you?'

'I would imagine so,' said Bear. 'I bet his daughter's fizzing.'

'Serves her right,' I said, feeling minxy.

'Yeah,' agreed Bear. 'Serves her right. At least I know Dad would be happy about the situation, even if she isn't.'

'Would he?'

'Yeah.' Bear nodded. 'He used to tease Mum all the time saying that Charlie fancied her. All in good humour, though, you know.'

'What did May say about that?' I asked.

'Something along the lines of, "he isn't the first and he won't be the last", as I recall.'

I was still laughing about that when my mobile rang and I answered it without checking the caller ID.

'Hello,' I said.

'Holly?'

'Yes.'

'Hey, it's Tash. Natasha Chandler.'

'Oh, hey.' I swallowed, suddenly feeling hot. 'Hi. Merry Christmas.'

Bear looked at me and frowned and I grimaced, knowing it was a little late for seasonal salutations.

'Merry Christmas to you, too,' she said back and I let out a long breath in the hope that it would help me get some sort of handle on the words falling out of my mouth.

'I wasn't expecting to hear from you,' I told her, as I waved at Bear and backed out of the room then closed the door. 'Not yet anyway. I mean, you're not at your desk this week, are you?'

I obviously still had no control over the words, but if I stopped gabbing relentlessly on, she'd have the chance to say no and that was the last word I wanted to hear her say.

'No,' she said, saying the word anyway. 'I'm not back in the office until after the new year, but I am slowly going through my inbox. It got a bit frantic before we officially signed off and I had fallen way behind which is why I'm doing some work through the holidays. My partner is thrilled.'

'Oh dear.' I swallowed.

'Anyway,' she said. 'I just wanted to say how delighted I am that you're going to take that commission on. It will be quite a departure for you and a challenge, too, but what's life without a little striving?'

'Well, exactly,' I said, juggling the phone and rubbing my sweaty palms down my PJ bottoms.

'But of course, that's not the only reason I'm ringing, is it?'

'Isn't it?' I squeaked, flopping down on the sofa.

'Of course, it isn't,' she laughed. 'And you needn't sound quite so terrified because I absolutely loved your submission.'

I felt the breath leave my body and it took all of my focus to take in more oxygen.

'Holly?'

'Yes,' I gulped, my lungs finally reinflating. 'Sorry. You've rather taken me by surprise.'

'Likewise,' she laughed again. 'After you turned those last projects down, I did wonder if you were going to come back to us at all.'

'I just needed a bit of a break,' I told her. 'What with the divorce and everything. I've been on a sort of sabbatical.'

'And finding a different direction as a result,' she said. I could hear the smile in her voice.

'It appears so,' I responded, biting my lip.

I heard her rifling through sheets of paper and wondered if she'd actually printed out what I'd sent or if she was looking at something else.

'I can't imagine it's been much of a retreat as you've managed to come up with so much material in such a short space of time,' she said eventually. 'Or had you started working on all this before the break?'

'No, no,' I said. 'This is all completely new and the break has been somewhat busier than I expected, too.' I laughed, thinking about Bear, May, the dogs, The Chapel and my involvement with them all.

'I see,' she said, sounding amused. 'Holly, I'm wondering if you've shown these to anyone else?'

I recognised that change in her tone and it made me sit up.

When Natasha really liked an idea, she could become quite proprietorial about it. I'd seen her in action on more than one occasion.

'Not yet,' I said, trying to match her professionalism and most likely failing. 'Given the timing, I thought I'd wait until the New Year before sending them out.'

'Well, that's good,' she said. 'I'm thrilled to be in on this ahead of anyone else.'

'Oh,' I said, unable to stop a smile forming. 'It's wonderful to hear you say that.'

'Monty and Queenie are fantastic,' she said, rustling paper again. 'And the fact that they're real makes them even better.'

She'd clearly read the submission very thoroughly, which was another good sign, because I had explained in the email that they were dogs I knew in real life and not just in my imagination.

'Monty is quite the show off,' I told her. 'His wardrobe is far larger than mine.'

'The publicity opportunities are going to be amazing,' she then gushed, making me feel even more excited. 'I'm thinking AA Milne and Winnie the Pooh. The bear and his chums were real too, weren't they? Well, sort of.' She laughed.

I'd never heard her quite this animated before. I knew Monty wouldn't hold back at any public engagement, if May agreed to letting him put in an appearance, that is, but having seen her at the party, Queenie wouldn't feature. I hoped that wouldn't be an issue, but then perhaps I was getting ahead of myself in imagining pet themed signings and more doggy photo shoots.

'Look,' said Natasha, making me realise I wasn't getting carried away after all. 'I'm not going to beat about the bush, Holly. The stories do need some refining and finessing, but I want these

*Tall Tales from Small Dogs* and as soon as the wheels start turning again, I'm going to show them to the team and then take them to acquisitions. How does that sound to you?'

'Amazing,' I breathed, trying not to succumb to a dead faint.

It sounded surreal, too. In my experience, this wasn't how publishing worked. This was a Hallmark movie moment, rather than real life.

'And I'm going to put you in touch with an agent friend of mine,' Natasha carried on, keeping the dream alive. 'You're just the sort of client she'd love to represent. Does that work for you, too?'

'It all works for me, Natasha,' I told her, thinking I might as well just play along until I woke up because surely, I had to be dreaming.

'Great,' she said. 'I'll be in touch properly in a couple of weeks, but I'll send you a quick email summing up our conversation by the end of today. Speak soon. Oh, and happy new year!'

'Happy new year to you, too,' I told her just before she hung up and I started doing a very happy dance around the sitting room.

I clumsily stubbed my big toe on the coffee table and realised I was awake. I was definitely awake.

'Bear!' I screeched and he came thundering along the hall.

'What's happened?' he gasped, spotting me hopping about and clutching my foot.

'I think I'm about to be offered a publishing deal!' I beamed up at him as I fell in a heap on the sofa. 'The editor I submitted to wants to take the stories and illustrations to an acquisitions meeting!'

'Oh my god, Holly!' he shouted. 'That's amazing!'

'I know!' I shouted back.

Queenie, caught up in the excitement, began to bark and do laps of the sofa. I felt every bit as dizzy as she must have done.

'What a way to start the new year,' said Bear, plonking down next to me.

'It's not a bad effort, is it?' I grinned, forgetting all about my throbbing toe.

'I can't wait to tell Mum,' he added, pulling me into his arms and kissing me firmly on the lips.

'Do you think we should?' I asked, between kisses. 'Wouldn't it be better to wait, in case it doesn't happen?'

'It will happen,' he said forthrightly. 'I can already imagine exactly what the books are going to look like.'

I was about to tell him that I could picture them too, but he covered my mouth with his and by the time we'd finished celebrating, I was too worn out to find the words.

It felt fitting that Bear and I should celebrate the arrival of the new year in the place where we'd met and as The Dragon was going to be even busier than usual because they were holding a party, we decided not to take Queenie in case someone heavier than me stood on her.

When we dropped her at May's to spend the night with Monty, I made a huge and grateful fuss of them both and then took the opportunity to tell May and Charlie that I'd had a call from the editor and that she was as keen to share my passion for the pooches as I was.

'They're just the sort of stories we all need right now,' May said warmly, as she wrapped me in one of her all-encompassing hugs and Charlie gave me a thumbs up over her shoulder. 'And you're an incredibly talented woman, Holly.'

I was delighted that she thought so.

'Why don't you and Charlie come with us to the pub, Mum? That way we can all carry on celebrating,' Bear suggested and the four of us set off together.

I felt as light as air as we walked along. Given Natasha's enthusiasm for my work, I felt hopeful that even if she didn't end up acquiring the stories, her agent friend, hopefully soon to be my agent, would be able to place them with someone else.

'What a thrilling end to the year,' I sighed, my arm linked through Bear's as we walked along. 'I can't believe so much has happened in such a short space of time.'

'Me neither,' he agreed. 'I didn't even arrive in Norwich expecting to work, let alone fall in love.'

I stopped walking and looked up at him and he stared down at me, his eyes wide.

'I just said that out loud, didn't I?' he croaked, his Adam's apple bobbing as he swallowed.

'You did,' said May, who had also stopped. 'I definitely heard it. Didn't you, Charlie?'

'Leave the poor lad alone,' Charlie admonished mildly, but he didn't encourage her to keep walking.

'I didn't expect to work or fall in love either,' I said back breathlessly, looking deep into Bear's beautiful eyes, 'but I've done both.'

Without another word he lifted me up and swung me around.

'Now that,' said May, sounding impressed, 'is how you sweep someone off their feet.'

She and Charlie did carry on walking then and Bear took the opportunity to kiss me until I was even more out of breath than before.

'Come on,' he then said. 'Let's get inside, in the warm.'

He'd already heated me up very nicely, but as there were a few soft snowflakes starting to fall I was happy to follow his lead into the pub.

Charlie had already been served and was just returning from the bar with a tray of drinks. 'May has found us some seats near the fire,' he said.

The place was heaving and I was thrilled to recognise so many people. Sara and Pete were at a table with Beth and Eli and I made a mental note to thank them later for guiding me in a new professional direction. Had I not met them, I might never have given a thought to finding the words to sit alongside my illustrations. Lisa and John were also there and their whole family had in one way or another played a part in transforming my life, so I needed to thank them, too.

'Cheers,' said Charlie, once he'd distributed the drinks. 'Here's to a happy new year.'

We all clinked glasses.

'And to me finding a new roof to go over my head,' I added.

It was the only thing I hadn't managed to tidily tie up with a bow, but I wasn't feeling worried about that because thanks to Bear, I now had more options to consider than I had ever thought possible when I'd bundled my boxes into the back of a van and waved them off to storage.

I was still surprised to think that I would consider living somewhere unconventional, but why shouldn't I? If the last few weeks had proved anything, it was that anything was possible. I was still looking forward to seeking out some different places to visit and stay in for a few days, but I did have a really good feeling about those converted railway carriages in Wynbridge.

'And living with me while you look for it,' May reminded me.

'Unless,' said Bear, taking my hand in his, 'you fancy coming on a road trip with me in the spring. Depending on how the Wynbridge viewing goes, of course.'

I looked between them both and burst out laughing.

'Perhaps I'll find a way to make all the options work,' I said confidently. 'I'll rent the carriages, stay with May the odd weekend *and* come on the road trip. As long as I've got the room to work and Wi-Fi, the world's my oyster now.'

'I bet you didn't think you'd be saying that even just a few weeks ago,' May laughed, tapping her glass against mine. 'Good for you, Holly.'

'It is good for me,' I agreed, toasting them all. 'And so are you three. Thank you all so much.'

'Here's to the future,' said Bear.

'The future,' I echoed, looking deep into his eyes.

There had been a time when I had no idea what mine was going to look like, but since arriving in Nightingale Square, I'd found friends who had become family and I had fallen in love with the man sitting next to me. I had also fallen back in love with my work and I was extremely happy to toast it all.

I took a sip of my drink, then set my glass down and considered just how fabulous my future now looked. As Bear's lips met mine, I felt a heady mix of excitement and confidence welcoming in my thrilling new life. I couldn't wait to embrace it.

# Acknowledgements

2023, where have you gone? It genuinely feels like no time at all since I was settling down to write *The Book-Lovers' Retreat* acknowledgements and yet here I am again. Already! Right at the end of the trip to Lakeside, I promised you a Christmas book 'packed full of festive frolics' and I hope *That Festive Feeling* has given you all the seasonal feels I set out to deliver. It has been an absolute treat to take another trip back to Nightingale Square. With five titles in the series now, the characters feel like the closest of friends and I always have the best time hanging out with them.

Huge thanks to my agent, Amanda Preston, editor Clare Hey, Judith Long, Pip Watkins and the entire Books and The City team, for another fabulous year. Kicking it off by winning the RNA Popular Romantic Fiction Award practically guaranteed that it was going to be a good 'un!

Thanks also to the Famous Five, Sue Baker, Fiona Jenkins, the incredible blogging community, (Lucy and Sheree, you've gone above and beyond), the library staff and volunteers and every single event organiser, for your wonderful support. It is always appreciated.

The hugest of hugs for my dear friend Claire Howard. This book is dedicated to you, Claire, as a thank you for being a part of my life for the last thirty-eight years. And yes, that is right, I checked! Nearly four whole decades of keeping an eye on me. You're a star!

And last, but never least, huge thanks to every reader who picks this book up. It's a pleasure to welcome you into my fictional world. Wishing you all a very merry Christmas and a content and healthy new year.

Until next time, may your bookshelves – be they virtual or real – always be filled with fabulous fiction!

H x

# About the Author

Heidi Swain lives in Norfolk. She is passionate about gardening and the countryside, and collects vintage paraphernalia. *That Festive Feeling* is her seventeenth novel. You can follow Heidi on Twitter @Heidi_Swain or visit her website: heidiswain.co.uk

Turn the page to read an extract from

# The Book-Lovers' Retreat

# Prologue

It was utterly impossible for the three of us to get our heads around the fact that we'd been living in the cottage by the lake for three whole months now or to believe that in just a few hours we'd be handing back the keys and setting off for opposite ends of the country.

We had been serendipitously thrown together, three strangers leaving reality behind for one whole summer but now we'd got our lives working exactly how we wanted them to and we were ready to face the future, armed with our fresh starts. The three of us had become a unit, a solid one. Our shared trauma and soul-searching had pulled us together during our three-month journey and consequently we had formed a bond which we all knew would last for life.

'Unshakeable and unbreakable,' carefree Rose had said the night before as we sipped chilled champagne by the campfire next to the lake.

When she'd arrived, Rose had maintained she was just 'along for the ride' but between us we had scratched off the surface of the veneer she had coated her life in and discovered someone sweet, vulnerable and lost, floundering beneath. Now she had a life goal and a plan as to how she would achieve it. She was still the most outgoing and laidback one out of all of us, but she no longer used her up-for-anything attitude as a smokescreen.

'Unshakeable and unbreakable, for life!' Laurie had beamed, slurring the toast slightly and then snorting with laughter because she still couldn't drink more than one glass of anything without getting the giggles.

Even though she had been reluctant to admit it, Laurie had been the one out of all of us who had been properly running away. In the early days, when we were first getting to know each other, she had insisted that she was looking forward to her fast-approaching trip down the aisle with her Mr Right (Mr Not So Right as it turned out), but it took until our visit to Hope Falls for her to crack.

We'd each of us made a secret wish at the waterfall. Rose and I had been happy with ours, but Laurie had burst into tears and confessed between sobs that she had wished for something to happen which would enable her to break off her engagement without upsetting anyone.

It had been a big ask, but between the three of us we had managed it and Laurie had promised she'd never run away from a situation again and would stop trying to be a people pleaser, which was the thing that generally made her want to run away.

And what about me? Well, I'd arrived with my head in every bit as much of a muddle as the other two, but I was sorted now. Feeling brave and set to follow my heart, I had let go of the ifs, buts and maybes. I had decided that I should stop dithering and blindly following the path already set out for me in the family business and embrace my creativity while the spark was still ignited and I had allowed myself to fall in love again, too. It turns out you couldn't – and really shouldn't – tar all relationships with the same brush ...

'Heather!' Laurie screeched, pulling my thoughts away from the new man in my life. 'Please, hurry up!'

'Are you chickening out?' pouted Rose, standing naked as the day she was born and with a hand on one hip as she looked me up and down.

Laurie by contrast was mostly covered by the huge hoodie she'd just pulled over her head. I was sure she'd chosen to wear it with the purpose of covering her modesty until the last possible moment.

'No!' I shouted back, unzipping my jeans and wriggling out of them. 'Of course not. I'm coming now.'

Laurie peeped over the edge of the jetty and into the dark water beneath.

'I can't believe you've talked me into this,' she muttered to Rose as I quickly stripped and joined them.

'It will properly seal our bond,' Rose insistently said.

'Skinny dipping in the lake and developing pneumonia will seal our friendship?' Laurie frowned.

'Either that or the shock of the cold will kill us,' I shot back, grabbing both their hands which made Laurie drop her hoodie. 'Think of the headlines!'

Rose threw back her head and laughed and Laurie joined in too.

'Come on then,' she said, pulling us further back so we could have a decent run up. 'We'll do it on three.'

We looked at each other again and I felt a lump begin to form in my throat. No matter where our lives took us next, I would never forget the summer I'd spent beside the lake with these two incredible women.

'Let's go then!' Rose smiled, her eyes full of tears as Laurie sniffed.

We squeezed hands and ran.

'One, two, three!' we shouted together, not caring who could hear as our voices reached a crescendo and we jumped with complete abandon as far and as high as we could into the lake beneath us.

# Chapter 1

Friday night drinks with my two best friends, Rachel and Tori, had been a solid tradition for almost a decade. Nothing was supposed to get in the way of our end of the week regular night out, but Rachel's increasingly clingy boyfriend, Jeremy, Tori's Thursday night hangover and my, at times, obsessive work ethic, had meant the ritual had taken a bit of a hit of late.

Not that my work ethic was much in demand now that I'd been made redundant from what I had once assumed was a data analyst job for life with a defined career path, but you get the idea. Friday night drinks had always been a big deal, even when cashflow was tight – for me and Rachel at least – at the end of the month. The trip out had been a priority since our student days so why Tori hadn't showed up after she'd picked The Flamingo, of all places, as the venue for our extremely important get together on that first Friday in July, was a mystery.

'She said this place was beyond tacky when I chose it three months ago,' Rachel reminded me as we made our way to a table as far away from the marabou bedecked bar as it was possible to get. 'And not in a *good way*,' she added, putting down her glass and embellishing her comment with air quotes. 'I am remembering that right, aren't I?' She frowned.

'You are,' I confirmed, twirling my glass to shift the paper umbrella and flamingo topped twizzler before taking a sip of the over-sweetened cocktail. 'But,' I added, wincing at the syrupy taste as I took another look around, 'I don't care about any of that. Not tonight.' I felt my insides fizz again and with more than the alcoholic hit. 'Nothing can spoil tonight.'

Rachel shook her head but didn't crack a smile as I had hoped she would. She'd been preoccupied all week, but then given the high school she worked in, trying to coax and coerce students into digesting and dissecting an English literature curriculum which they had no interest in, along with books that bore no resemblance to their lives, it was no surprise that she was looking stony-faced.

I opened my mouth to remind her that it was almost the end of term but then snapped it shut when I realised that reminding her of *that* would remind her that she still had three gruelling weeks to go until the summer break and our long-anticipated dream come true.

'Here,' she then said, and her face did finally break into a smile as she held out a long paper straw for me to take. 'I pinched this from the bar. We'll need it later, won't we?'

I took it from her and danced about on the spot, almost spilling my drink. 'You are excited then?' I ventured, once I'd done a few twirls.

'Of course, I'm excited,' she giggled as she watched me. 'I'm not going to let the prospect of end of term burn-out ruin anything.'

I was relieved to hear it.

'We should have gone to Glitter to have a celebratory bop,' she beamed, naming a popular local nightclub as I carried on jiggling about completely out of time with the music.

'Or we could have gone to Raunch, for . . .'

'I don't need to go to Raunch,' she cut in with a laugh. 'Not now I've got Jeremy.'

I didn't respond to that but mentally crossed my fingers in the hope that he wouldn't somehow miraculously turn up and spoil our fun. Again. His Friday night gatecrashing was becoming a horrible habit.

'We're not going to be able to hear ourselves think in here,' Rachel pointed out when I didn't say anything. 'Let alone finalise details.'

'I still can't believe it's happening,' I grinned, pitching my voice above the noise of the DJ who had just turned the volume up further. 'We really are doing it, aren't we?'

'We are,' she shouted back, tapping her glass against mine before we downed the contents in one. 'Well, we will be if Tori shows up and we can firm up the final details.'

The three of us had The Best (caps totally justified) summer break on the horizon and, as the countdown on my phone and the circled date on the kitchen calendar reminded me, we now had only twenty days to get through until it would finally be happening.

'Six whole weeks,' I dreamily sighed, mentally recalling the images on the website I must have visited at least a million times. 'Six whole weeks in that cottage.'

I wondered what my grandad would say if he knew we were going to be staying in the very lakeside property which had been used as the main setting for the film adaptation of *Hope Falls*, the most wonderful of all the books he had introduced me to when I was growing up.

The book had helped us through my annual summer stay in the Lakes after Nanna had died and I loved it all the more for that. Not a day went by that year when Grandad didn't read from it and by the end of August, I could have recited great chunks of it almost by heart.

To begin with, it was the descriptions of the dramatic landscape which captured my young imagination, but as I was transformed from a gawky tween to a moody teen, it was the love story and the friendship of the three very different main characters, strangers thrown together in a bid to escape their individual problems and tragedies, that I had fallen for. I still wished Grandad had been around to see the film and I knew that if he'd met my friends, he would definitely have wanted to make the trip with us!

The getaway had been years in the planning and I still couldn't really get my head around the fact that it was so close to happening. I had the book and film obsessed friends I had always dreamed of and we really were moving into *the* cottage next to the lake for almost the entire summer!

'We won't be spending the whole time inside,' Rachel keenly reminded me. 'Not with all the locations to check out.'

'And lakeside picnics to re-enact,' I nodded, getting into the familiar but still thrilling swing of it. 'And the skinny-dipping.'

'Not forgetting the trips to the pub.'

'Absolutely not forgetting those,' I squealed, feeling like I was going to combust.

'I wonder who will get Heather's room?' Rachel asked, nodding at the straw which we would use to finally settle the argument.

'Me, I hope,' I quickly said. 'I'm more Heather than you and Tori put together.'

'Hm,' she said, pulling at one of the many threads we had always good naturedly tussled over. 'We'll see about that.'

Rachel and I had initially bonded over our obsessive love of the book when we spotted it in each other's packing boxes the day we moved into the same flat in university halls and then, having decided to spend a freshers evening giving our respective livers some respite from the endless shots which were still the favoured rite of passage used to initiate eighteen-year-olds into student life, the deal was sealed when we watched the film and sobbed and laughed in all the same places.

I had then wasted no time in recruiting fellow enthusiast Tori, who was on the same course as me, to take up the role of third superfan. I had easily picked her out on the first day of lectures because she was wearing a *Hope Falls* T-shirt.

Unbelievably, the three of us had added our names to the cottage waiting list and stumped up the deposit to stay at the idyllic location almost three years ago, such was the demand of *Hope Falls* obsessives and we'd been saving to have enough in our bank accounts by the time we reached the top of it and had to pay off the balance ever since. Well, Rachel and I had been saving, Tori just had to ask her super wealthy dad to sign a cheque when the time came. Which was going to be very soon!

We had plans to re-read the book, re-watch the film and visit all the locations featured in and around the village of Lakeside. We were going to literally be living the book-lovers' dream and, unbeknown to my friends, I had another hope for the trip too.

I was going to use it to work out what I was going to do with the rest of my life now I had been made redundant, in exactly the same way that Heather had done. Granted, it was an ambitious ask to transfer something so monumental from the pages of a novel into real life, but one I felt the time spent living in the cottage would be equal to.

'I'm going to message Tori,' I said, pulling out my phone as another kaleidoscope of butterflies began to flutter in my tummy. 'I don't want anything screwing up tonight.'

'No need.' Rachel grinned, lightly touching my arm. 'She's here.'

As ever, it took a while for Tori to reach us. Her profusion of dark curly hair, porcelain skin and commanding presence always drew attention and coupled with the sequined cami romper and Suola So Kate Louboutin heels, both of which pulled admirers in like a moth to a flame, it took even longer.

'Oh my,' said Rachel, when Tori eventually arrived at our table.

'I agree,' I joined in, my relief that she'd finally turned up chasing the butterflies away. 'No wonder you're late. You must have been fighting them off ever since you left your flat. You look stunning.'

'She didn't leave her flat,' Rachel said meaningfully with a nudge, as Tori took the empty seat opposite ours and crossed her long legs. 'She was wearing this outfit last night.'

Tori had the grace to blush as I threw her a faux shocked expression. Faux because, in truth, nothing Tori did shocked me anymore.

'Oh my,' I added myself as Rachel showed me the pre-drinks photos Tori had posted online as she had got ready to head out the night before.

'It's not how it looks,' was Tori's opening line, and not for the first time since we'd become friends.

'No?' laughed Rachel, arching an eyebrow.

'No,' said Tori, her usual sparkle and shine looking a little faded in spite of the dazzling outfit. 'But I'm here now, so ...'

Looking back, I probably should have spotted something was amiss, but in the moment, I was too giddy and excited about our up-and-coming adventure to pick up anything other than another cocktail.

'So,' said Rachel, in a teacherly tone. 'Let's get down to business, shall we? First things first, let's find out once and for all who gets to sleep in Heather's room.'

'Me, me, me!' I giggled and Rachel rolled her eyes.

Having torn the straw into three pieces, two short and one longer, she flagged down a stubble enhanced server, who was wearing a pink feathered sheath dress and carrying a tray of garishly coloured drinks, to help.

'Make it quick then,' they said, putting down the tray and taking hold of the lengths of straw, once Rachel had succinctly explained the purpose. 'And good luck,' they added, lining them up in their grasp so they all looked the same length.

I held my breath as Tori took her turn first. She didn't react when she showed us how short her piece was, but my heart thumped. Unlike the others, I didn't just want the room because it was the prettiest. I wanted it because it was where Heather had decided about her future and that was exactly the purpose I had in mind for it. It was going to be my sanctuary and my safe place to explore all of the life-changing possibilities ahead of me.

'You go next, Em,' Rachel said generously.

'Sure?'

'Come on, girls,' said the server. 'I need to deliver these drinks.'

I swallowed hard and pulled at one of the pieces of the straw. It was longer than the one Tori had picked, but I didn't want to count my chickens. Rachel took the third and I finally realised I had been victorious. I had bagged the room!

'I can't believe it,' I said breathlessly, kissing a less than enthusiastic looking Tori on the cheek as I brandished my piece of the straw in her face and the server sashayed away. 'I can't believe it!'

I hoped everything else was going to fall as neatly into place.

'I bloody can,' said Rachel, but with no rancour. 'Looks like we'll be sharing the twin room after all, Tori.'

'Actually,' she croaked, folding her straw in half before dropping it on the table as she cleared her throat. 'We won't.'

Her porcelain skin had turned pale under her custom blend foundation and Rachel and I exchanged a look.

'What do you mean?' I asked, slipping my straw stub into my pocket as a memento.

'I'm really sorry,' sniffed Tori, her eyes suddenly filling with tears, 'but I'm not going.'

My mouth opened and closed, but no sound came out.

'What do you mean, Tori?' Rachel gasped. 'I don't understand.'

'You have to come,' I said, trying to jolly her along. 'We're the three musketeers, remember?'

Tori shook her head. 'I'm not coming,' she said again, her thickly mascara-lashed eyes flicking from one of us to the other. She looked mortified. 'Because I can't.'